Homicide
in
Pacific City

Leonard G. Collins

No portion of this book may be used without the written
consent of the author.
Cover art by the author
leonard.collins@comcast.net

With thanks to my lovely wife, Elizabeth Ann Collins

Chapter 1

He jumped off the high cliff his arms all akimbo. The wind ripped the sunglasses from his face. He tried to scream, but the wind tore his scream from him and threw it away with his sunglasses.

Then he hit the water.

It was a warm summer's day; it was very much like living on a beautiful desert island in the South Seas. Children played in the sand. Surfers plied the sea for that perfect wave. Gulls squawked and squawked lazily overhead. Lovers strolled the beach hand in hand or huddled under blankets behind driftwood logs. The tantalizing aroma of the sea wafted ashore on a warm and gentle breeze.

It was a Cape Cod Day in Oregon. It would remain so… for about ten minutes.

Pacific City is a small beach town in Oregon. On one end of town, the beach lazily stretches out with the curvature of the earth until it finally disappears into a misty and far horizon. North of town, the surf batters up against a steep sandstone cliff and a high sand dune that is nearly always dotted with children frolicking and rolling down the sand dune. Pacific City is families, surfboarders, kites, beach-side fires, and dory boats.

For Rob, this special day felt like like a vacation, which, of course, it was. It is one thing, however, to be on vacation and quite another to *feel* like one is on vacation. Rob felt it.

It was a rare and glorious day. The sun was warm, and the air was crisp with the smell of the sea. The sky was a sparkling Pacific blue to die for. Surfboarders dotted the horizon. Dozens of vacationers waded in the tide pools and shallows inspecting behind every rock, nook, and cranny for starfish or mussels, for sea crabs and for treasures. Dreams and wishes floated on the breeze. Dory boat trailers stood silent and abandoned, while their boats and crews could be seen on the horizon plying the ocean depths for dreams and wishes but finding only cod, and salmon.

Pacific City is a remote coastal town. Merchants and hotel owners say that Pacific City is only two hours from Portland, but it's really three. It is six long hours from Seattle; and Rob's bad leg was stiff from the drive. He gazed at the beach and reminded himself that he was on vacation. The very word conjured up feelings of serenity, and laziness, and bliss. As he turned, his gaze took in the sand dune, and he steeled himself for the difficult and steep climb up the cliff. His uncle would be there on top of the cliff. The climb would be difficult but worth the effort.

He ignored the chronic pain in his leg, dismissed the lazy feeling in the air, and started onward with his face set hard to the cliff north of town. He was determined to enjoy this visit to the beach with his uncle, and he wasn't about to let mere leg pain get in his way, but he knew it would be a difficult climb. He would rather have lingered in the sand or gone back to the bar, but he knew there would be ample time for that later. With his face set in determination, he limped past all the surfers, and the families, and the playing children, and the barking dogs. He smiled at the charred fire-rings left over from last nights adventures. He ignored the girls in bikinis, and the footballs and Frisbees, the colorful kites, and the bumps in the blankets behind sand-blown logs. A parasail passed across the horizon. Fixed on the cliff ahead, he trudged on. He would enjoy this vacation, if it killed him. It nearly did.

At the base of the sand dune, he began the most strenuous part of the climb. The hill was steep, and the sand was loose under his feet. As hard as he tried, it was two steps forward and one step back. He attempted to time his steps so that he slid back on his bad leg and drove for gain with his good; but it was a difficult proposition. When he stopped several times to rest, he turned to gaze at the town and the stretch of beach below. With each yard he gained in height, his view changed. The surfers became smaller and smaller. The vehicles in the parking lot became toy cars.

During one of his brief stops for breath, a young girl in pig-tails and a yellow bikini ran up the hill- running up the hill seemingly without a care. When she saw Rob panting for breath, she stopped at his side. "Is there something wrong, mister?" she asked with big, rolling eyes of wonder.

Rob attempted to answer. His mouth opened and closed, but no sound came out. She was gone before he could catch his breath and answer, but his eyes watched her lightly bounding up the hill. With a mutter, he cursed his life. "I'll bet you, Robert Smith, she was never shot in the leg, and your drill instructor, Gunnery Sergeant Anthony B. McClelland, USMC retired, would not be proud of you today, Rob! Out of breath and whining!" His voice was raspy, and his throat was dry and sore. Rob looked back at the toy cars and longed for another cold beer at the bar in the parking lot.

As he waited for his air to return and his breathing to steady out, Rob picked up a handful of sand and lofted it into the breeze. Rob watched it wisp away. When his breath finally came easier, he stood, turned, and began again. Two up and one back.

Finally, he eased himself over the top of the sand dune. As a victory gesture, he kicked out of his shoes and walked along like a little boy with his head down watching his toes kick up puffs of sand. With great pride in his assent, Rob walked along on the wrong side of the double strand of wire fence that was intended to keep tourists away from the cliff's edge. He, like his uncle, always climbed through the fence to the forbidden side. On the safe side of the wire, his uncle felt hemmed in and not an essential part of the sea spray and cliff edge that he felt were so necessary for his painting moods. Rob laughed aloud thinking about his uncle, bounced his hand on top of the wire fence as he walked along, and hummed a tune about a little girl in a yellow polka dot bikini.

Rob knew he would soon spy his uncle's painting easel standing against the backdrop of the blue Pacific Ocean. It was a familiar scene and a favorite memory. Since he was a boy, Rob could remember finding his uncle on the cliff with his painting easel weighted down against the light wind and ocean spray. It was one of dozens of fond memories of his uncle working joyously away with brushes and paints, and Rob's approach was always a favorite part of the visit.

What new angle, or light, would Uncle May find in the same old scene? It was a constant marvel to Rob how his uncle's paintings would all be so original and stand-alone? Anticipation filled him with wonder.

A photograph of Cape Kiwanda, with the same old tired wave hitting the same old, tired cliff, could be purchased on postcards, and although the photographed wave was a work of art, the rock had changed since the photo was taken. The cave roof had fallen in and had filled in the cave that had produced that marvelous picture perfect postcard. The postcard failed, because it never reflected the changing moods of the sea-battered cliff. The post-card wave remained static. Nothing remains static against the unrelenting battering of the Pacific Ocean.

To the contrary, Uncle May's paintings seemed to change with the minute. He never tired of the cliff and the sea. The cliff remained Uncle May's personal study in infinite diversity. How Uncle May continued to capture such metamorphous through the march of time, and storm after storm, was always a mystery to Rob? Fifty times May painted the cliff, before and after the cave in, and fifty times the scene turned out different. Somehow, Uncle May could always find a new and refreshing look in an old, familiar scene- like a man still finding beauty and a new turn in the face of his wife even though he has looked at that same face for years. Somehow, May could always capture the cave in a new and alluring combination of colors, and light, and shadow.

It was fair turnabout between May and Rob. To his Uncle May, Rob's writing talent was always a mystery? How Rob could invent a novel or a cute little story… out of thin air? May was just not able to understand it? How Rob could twist a sentence, and make a stranger cry or laugh until tears filled the eyes! How was that possible? Theirs was a mutual admiration between the uncle and the nephew. May was fond of addressing Rob as his sister's son, and Rob of calling May his mother's brother.

Rob and May were the last of their kind, the only two living relatives of what was once a large and thriving family. All were gone, now, except these last two. It was up to Rob if the family failed to thrive or ultimately ended- for Rob was the last. Once, he had made a good shot at making a family, but his young wife had died. Since that tragedy, Rob had never developed the inclination. He no longer considered the carrying on of the name a right that needed… well, carrying on. He had given romance and family his best shot, and both had failed him.., or had he failed both? He often told himself that he had no guilt in the matter and cared not for society's expectations of family longevity, but that only gave a lie to the tragedy, and he knew it. Rob lived alone, and perhaps that was his destiny? Once he had been happy, deliriously happy, but that was a time long gone. He looked no longer for enchantment or love. He looked at life as a lottery.., where he never purchased a ticket.

Uncle May held a similar view on life and shared few of the delusions that younger men have about their lives. May was an artist and wore isolation, bachelorhood, and tragedy as proud badges of courage. Lately, he had surprised himself by taking a very young girlfriend. He had no desire for more than a casual companionship and often reminded himself that he had no illusions; that illusions are for the young- or for the paintbrush. He did admit to an occasional tinge of guilt over the girl, but it amounted to no more than an old man's knowledge that he held a young and beautiful girl back from meeting a young man who might take her forward to some kind of future. May felt concern for the girl, but not the slightest concern for the young men. He held the Tiger Woods philosophy of winning; he had not the slightest sympathy for the losers, the men who constantly drooled over Peggy's beauty and winsomeness. He had played the game, and he had won. The others had lost. He flaunted the young girl's beauty, for she really was strikingly beautiful, nearly breathtaking. She was a ten before midnight, when the bar doesn't close until three.

May admitted to himself.., whenever he cared to dwell on the matter, that it bothered him that he had begun to feel more protective, than anything else, toward the girl. Paternal feelings were replacing the passion. May was a simple man; his solution was… not to dwell on the matter. The difference in their ages bothered him more than it bothered her. More and more, he did things for the girl that he thought he should do out of responsibility, rather than love. Instead of being driven by desire, he was feeling more and more like a caretaker. While they were not in love, and both knew it, May was afraid that she wanted more. He often just wanted out. He worked on his paintings, and she worked as a television reporter. She had her own career. He had his. For some time, he had been expecting things to take their natural course- expecting the young girl would find another, and that would settle his dilemma. Then he could find more time for his paintings. It was May's last romance, and he knew it, and he felt too old for it.

Casually, Rob walked along in the warm sun bobbing his hand on the fence wire. He laughed as he strolled in the sand looking far ahead trying to catch the first glimpse of his uncle's painting easel. He had done this very thing many times before. Finally, in the distance Rob spied the easel almost on the edge of the cliff where the cave had fallen in, where few people walked, well past the throng of families and children. It was… a picture postcard scene, he had to admit.

From a distance, Rob noticed that he could not see Uncle May at the easel, but that was not unusual in itself. Rob innocently continued shuffling along kicking up warm puffs of sand like the carefree little boy he wished he still was. He continued to watch his feet and to take pleasure in each gentle puff of sand blowing mindlessly away in the soft, gentle breeze. He yawned. Seaward, he could hear the pleasant, offshore sound of the buoy clanging its warning for errant ships to keep away, keep away. He walked on. In the air, there remained the tang of salt and sea. In his yawn, the sea-tang tickled his tongue and filled his lungs.

The absence of his uncle at his easel did not, at first, alarm Rob. His uncle would often leave his paintings to explore among the rocks or sit and have a cool drink in the shade of one of the pine trees bordering the division between dune and sandstone rock. Perhaps May would stop his painting and toss smooth, round stones into the water with a small tourist child, or he might take a minute and throw a stick for Spark. May's was an ideal and laid back life style; or rather, it had been until three minutes before Rob arrived. Had been. So often, life turns on a verb tense.

Fifty yards from the easel, Rob stopped humming. It was as if something unrealized made him worry. Some premonition began to alarm him, but as yet, Rob had nothing on which to put his finger. He just came to an illogical conclusion that there was something wrong. He couldn't see his uncle, couldn't see any trouble, couldn't tell, for sure, what made him uneasy? Then, finally, Rob realized what it was that was disturbing- May's canvas painting was not on his easel but setting in the sand, and there were tubes of paint scattered about. A lump caught in his throat. He tried to take a breath, but it was as if he could not find any air. He stopped humming and started running. Suddenly, he had become very concerned… very concerned, indeed.

It was as if it took a week to run those last hundred yards, and on finally arriving at the easel, Rob found not his uncle but a young woman. She was on her knees staring steeply down to the fallen rocks and crashing waves far below. Precariously perched on the edge of the cliff, she was peering down over the edge and yelling something that Rob could not hear over the crashing of the surf and that damnably irritating warning buoy. Instantly, and with his heart in his throat, he threw himself down onto his stomach next to the girl. He was afraid of what he might find, and yet he desperately needed to know at what, or to whom, the girl was yelling. With an evil premonition, Rob craned his neck over the edge of the cliff and- even before he saw the body- knew the girl had to be yelling and pointing at his uncle. Rob winced at the sight. His stomach turned. He reminded himself that his loved ones had a strange and terrible habit of ending up in the water at the base of cliffs. How could this be happening, again?

Years of experience as a police officer trained Rob to instantaneously draw conclusions and make lightning-quick decisions. He was trained to perform immediately on those decisions, trained to ignore his personal safety in trade for the well-being of others. He hated that.

Immediately, on taking in the horrible scene below, Rob Smith knew he would jump. He hated that, too. Of course, it also frightened him. But in some weird way, fear for his personal safety did not fit into his assessment of the situation; fear was not part of the equation. Rob loved his uncle. He saw a need, and Rob knew he would jump. It was simple. Even though the fright was nearly over powering, he ignored it. It was a matter of intensive, professional training and personal conviction- a throwback to his military and police training. It was his uncle, his mother's brother, on the rocks below. What choice had he? In spite of his fear, he was the master of his own destiny, and that destiny had always been to intervene against evil and pain. That realization made him angry.

"Why can't someone else ever be the hero?" he said.

The girl heard him, but she thought his words were queer. Her face slowly turned towards his with a quizzical look, as if she heard the words but had not understood their meaning.

He looked off the cliff. He had jumped into frigid waters before. Perhaps some decisive part of his mind figured the experience gave him an edge. But something else nudged his mind too; some small voice told him that he might be wrong this time, that the edge always belonged to the house, and that this house was really really big. It was like going all in with a two and an eight- off suited. That small part of his mind tried to reason with him, told him that heroism does not, in itself, guarantee success. However, that small caution-filled part of his mind also knew that it was running out of time, knew it was losing the battle to years of training and Rob's ill-fated hero complex, knew that Rob was, even then, deciding that it was time for action.., and that small, cautious part of his mind knew that it had lost the argument. The chips began tumbling towards the center of the table.

It was a simple equation, really; whenever there was a need- solve it. It was his police training and his training as a U.S. Marine before that. It was something that had, at some indefinable time, become a deep and unshakable part of Rob Smith. He had become someone who took charge. He fought his country's enemies and wrestled with armed criminals. He righted wrongs. He sometimes wished it was not so. He especially wished, when looking down from high cliffs, that he wasn't the kind of person to take charge and bull right into things. He looked down, then, and he hated the equation.

The girl in the blue blouse turned back towards the water and resumed yelling and crying. Tears were flowing down her cheeks. She was so close to the edge that her knees were pushing sand over the edge to be blown away on the breeze. Rob got up onto his feet and put a hand on the girl's shoulder to steady her. She looked up at Rob with tear stained cheeks as he pulled her away from the precipice.

"Are you a hero?" she asked.

Eighty feet below the girl lay the body of his uncle, small indiscriminate looking remains of what many in the weeks to come would call a great and wonderful man. On the rocks, at the base of the cliff, Uncle May's torso rested peacefully on its back on a low barnacled shelf. His feet and legs bobbed crazily in the waves almost as if even in death he was trying to kick himself further up and out of the surf. But Uncle May wasn't kicking, and Rob knew it at first glance. He knew his uncle was dead. But wait! Was there a movement of his uncle's head, his eyes? Did he grimace? Was there a nearly imperceptible movement, or was that just wishful thinking on a nephew's part? At that moment, the fearful little man inside Rob lost completely to the larger man of compassion.

Suddenly, to Rob's shock, he saw in the waves beyond his uncle's body, Spark, Uncle May's Irish Setter. The dog was trying to swim in the battering surf, trying desperately to reach May and climb out of the water and onto that slippery ledge where May's body lay. But the relentlessly crashing waves kept pushing him back away from the ledge, pushing him farther and farther out to sea. In the few moments that Rob watched, he could tell from his vantage point above that the dog's struggle was a losing battle; for all the dog's effort, Rob realized that the dog would not survive for long. Not a young dog, any longer, Rob could see that Spark was already beginning to tire. Time and again, water crashed over the dog's head and body pushing him down below the surface of the cold Pacific Ocean. Each time the dog resurfaced, Rob saw how each successive wave pushed Spark back farther away from the shelf where Mayfield Commers lay. After each wave, Spark failed to rise as high in the water as he had on the previous wave. Rob could see, as anyone could have, that the ocean would eventually push Spark out and under until he rose no more- the encouraging yells and cheering of the girl, notwithstanding.

The girl was on her knees, rocking back and forth repeating over and over, "Poor dog! Poor dog!"

Rob shot a glance into her mad eyes and wondered if she could be trusted to go for help? His immediate plans, as well as his very survival, might very well depend on her and her alone. There was no one else to help. He knew he could get to May's body. That was the easy part. What he would do after that, he had no idea.

Quickly and finally, Rob took in the total parameters of the tragedy before him and weighed his chances in a matter of seconds. Those chances, he figured, were scant but not entirely hopeless. He was doing what he had always done: analyzed any situation and gone for broke- even if he couldn't see the end-game solution. Somehow, he would just… find a solution when the time came. He always had. He would find a way to survive. Rob's only miscalculation was that history is no guarantee of current success. As he prepared himself to jump, the house odds grew exponentially.

He pulled the girl to her feet and shook her by both shoulders. "Pull yourself together! You need to get help! Run down the hill. Find someone with a cell phone and call Search and Rescue. I'm going into the water. There is just the slightest chance that Uncle May is still alive. Get me some help! Find someone with a boat!" He wasn't sure if she understood and he roughly shook her shoulders, again, trying to rouse her from the shock of the moment. Finally, to his great relief, the girl's eyes began to show recognition. "Can you get help?" he yelled. "I'm going to need it!" She nodded slightly and bit her lip. The girl was obviously in shock, frightened, and confused, but she was Rob's only slim hope. The house dealer smiled.

Without a word, she turned and ran off- flailing her arms all akimbo as she ran.

Without a word, Rob turned and jumped-flailing his arms all akimbo as he fell.

The house dealer smiled.

The roar of the waves became a thunder! That roar, alone, threatened to envelope him, to completely enfold him. His universe shrank with no world outside the roar and the falling. No sounds existed outside the freight train in his ears. There was no color in all the world except the blue of the sky and water. His falling, and the roaring of the wind in his ears and the absence of proper balance, took on the absolute; there was nothing else in all the world other than falling, and the roar of the wind in his ears, and his new blue universe. He tried to scream, but the rushing wind filled his mouth and carried away his voice.

The wind ripped the sunglasses from his face. He tried, again, to scream. The wind tore his scream away and threw it up with his sunglasses.

Then he hit the water.

Chapter Two

Timed slowed. To a crawl.

As Rob fell, the roar of the wind was suddenly replaced by the roar of the surf- for a millisecond- and then the roaring of the surf also ceased. Silence surrounded him as he was totally enveloped by millions of gallons of sea water and white foam. The fall and being completely enveloped by sea water merged; he was not able to tell where one ended and the other began. One terror was replaced by another. Both were cold, and harsh, and frightening. Both were alien and overpowering. He had no control. He was enveloped by a terror, absorbed by a horror, blotted out in a nightmare. His sensations were overloaded.

For just a few seconds, he gave up; he was scared… to death.

It became difficult for Rob to separate time into neat little blocks as we all do in our daily lives. His was in a world totally apart from any previous reality he had known. Falling had been so incredibly fast that it seemed instantaneous; and yet, falling seemed as if it took a year. Time merged? Rushed by? Slowed to a crawl? Stopped? Time simply became irrelevant. At the end of the fall, *everything* became irrelevant except the white swirling foam and the endless bubbles. The burning in his lungs felt special.

It was the burning of his lungs that almost saved him, for the pain became something on which his mind could focus. But even the pain in his lungs lost out to the all-pervading and absolute terror.

Falling, he became aware of a mysterious sound? He could hear some fool yelling. At first he didn't know who it was, and he wondered where the person was who was screaming? How could there be someone else falling? One thing he did know; whoever was yelling was sure making a go of it! Whoever was yelling sounded frightened… to death.

At first, as Rob fell toward the waves below, the roar of the breaking surf grew louder and louder the lower he fell. The strange yelling for help was all but blown away in the crashing of the wind and the surf. Though he tried to turn his head to look for the screamer, Rob found that he had little control.

In one sense, he fell as if in slow motion. Time inched along. Finally, he became aware of who was yelling, but he just could not do a thing to control his own body. He was his own fool. Rob Smith, for the second time in his life, was not in control as he fell from height into cold and dangerous waters. He was small. He saw himself from afar; against the limitless wall of sandstone cliff, he was tiny, infinitesimal. He was a pawn, a helpless and falling peon in an enormously huge world of wind, noise, and sea. His mind raced. He compared the fall to throwing a pea-size pebble into the gaping mouth of a live volcano where, of course, the volcano would not even notice the pebble. Neither would the Pacific Ocean notice him. "*Not even a ripple,*" he told himself. "*When I hit the water, I won't even make a ripple!*"

Time continued at a crawl.

Rob's memory replayed a time when, on a lark, he had rolled a two-foot rock down the side of a steep hill. The rock rolled end over end. Its crashing echoed loudly off the nearby hills. When the rock finally stopped its noisy tumbling, there was no further sound. All that was left was simply utter… silence. A mere one second after the rock stopped rolling, its crashing and cart wheeling against other rocks and trees might as well have been ancient history. It was at that instant that Rob should have learned that there is no yesterday. Yesterday does not exist. All was still and quiet as if no rock had ever rolled, as if the mountain's sleep had not been disturbed at all. There never had been a rolling rock.

That rolling rock was exactly, Rob told himself, like a

man jumping off a cliff into the Pacific Ocean. No noise, no loud plop followed by a splash, no ripple. One single second after the splash there would be no memory of the man at all. He tried to mumble out loud, "Just like my life," but found it difficult to speak while still yelling in terror and fright. He remembered his psychology class in college and compared his fall to the proverbial tree falling in the forest. *"If there is no one to see or hear, and a man falls into the ocean, does the splash make a sound? Had that man ever had a life? Would he be missed?"*

It had not been until he was in the air, and totally committed, that Rob completely understood what he had done by jumping off the cliff. It was simple, he told himself. He had committed suicide. Until he jumped, how could he have realized the totality of his commitment? Except that he had done it before, and he had promised himself to never, ever, jump off another cliff. But just as with the last time, once Rob was in the air there was no going back, no recalling the scene like some mad movie production, no second chance. He had simply jumped, this time, much like the last time, because *somebody* needed to jump into the water; and there was no one else.

As the air whistled through his hair, he wondered why there was never anyone else to be the hero? As his speed increased, he reminded himself how much he hated being that person to always assume responsibility, always the person to affect the rescue? Why couldn't there ever be someone else… just once? But there wasn't. He was airborne… again.

Time became jumbled. Sequences blurred. Did he fall first, or land in the water first? Would he fall out of the water and land on the cliff?

Notwithstanding his promise to never again jump from a cliff, here he was, again… falling. As he was falling, time was going by so slowly that he found a lifetime to rationalize his reasons for jumping. From the top of the cliff, he had been fairly certain that his uncle was already dead, that he had been killed by the fall off the sandstone cliff to the rocks below. Rob *might* have seen a slight movement of his uncle's head? He just couldn't be sure. Then, too, his uncle was not the only reason for jumping into the cold Pacific Ocean. At this realization, Rob, again, laughed madly at himself. He had jumped to save Uncle May's dog, Spark? The red Irish Setter was a lovely and intelligent creature, and Rob was pretty sure that the dog was already very close to drowning in the waves, but to jump off a cliff for a dog? It made no difference, really, decided Rob. Why he jumped was irrelevant. He was already in the air, with the speeding wind in his hair, laughing like some mad hero gone over the edge. The decision could not be recalled, but Rob now decided that he had failed to fully grasp the gravity of the situation into which he was putting himself. *"For a dog!"* he yelled to himself. *"I could die for a dog! In the cold Pacific Ocean with no way out! No one will find my uncle, or the dog, or my body. It will just be a mystery."*

He marveled; for he seemed to have plenty of time since time had slowed, and his mind could not help replaying the other time he had jumped off a cliff into cold sea water. Like a crazy man, his mind forced him back to his previous jump. *"That, also, was for a person already dead,"* he told himself. But he had no choice in that jump, either, and he knew it. He was familiar with living on the edge, familiar with the possibility of dying, and he knew that surviving and going on with life could be much worse than dying in an attempt to save a loved one. Living with the knowledge that you might have saved someone you truly loved would not be living at all. His life had taught him that. It made perfect sense to give your life away in order to save it… if it was for a good cause. Such a realization is where heroes are born. And die.

All that reasoning, and remembering, made no difference to his present situation, for still… he fell. Did anything else matter other than the falling?

He fell.

Time may have slowed to a crawl, but his mind was

reeling with possibilities. Even while jumping off the cliff to save Uncle May, he knew that once he hit the water there was no way out by swimming. It just was not possible. Yet, even as he fell, some part of his mind was analyzing the situation and looking for possible solutions. An Olympic-class swimmer would drown trying to swim around Cape Kiwanda in the frigid ocean waters. Many had drowned trying just that. Then to, there were the sharks. Great White sharks.

Rob was sure that Uncle May's love for Spark would have forced his uncle to jump off the cliff to save the red Irish Setter, sharks or no- so Rob jumped for May, in his stead. Besides, he told himself, the chances were good that uncle May had fallen off the cliff first and that Spark might have jumped off the cliff in an attempt to save May? The red dog loved Uncle May with an undying compassion. Could Rob be less of a hero than a six year old dog?

As the wind ripped Rob's sunglasses off his face, he noticed that the screaming had somehow stopped? He wasn't sure why he had stopped screaming, or when he had stopped screaming. He wasn't any less frightened. He certainly still *felt* like screaming.

As he fell, his thoughts went back to the teenage girl in the blue blouse. Would she get help? Could she be trusted? She was his only hope; a girl he had never met her before. *"Out of control, and trusting your life to a stranger? Good move, Rob."*

For the second time in ten years, his entire life passed before his eyes… or at least the good parts. About half way down to the water (just as his mind was replaying his mother calling to him from the back porch about his lunch being ready) the good parts suddenly faded, and his sins caught up with him. How good his mother had looked: how young and healthy. He wished the vision could have lasted a little longer. He wanted to climb the back porch and give his mother a hug, to feel her hugging him again, to lay his head on his mother's chest and cry into her blouse about all the years since she had passed away. He knew that he was most probably falling to his death, and he simply wanted his mommy.

Strangely, he found the memories of his past sins coming slowly, methodically and precisely. He could remember them all. Since the fall was taking so long, he casually compared how easy it is for a Muslim to have sins forgiven by simply dying in combat for the glory of his god, while with the Christian God, you had to ask politely. To one god it was important how you died; for the other, how you lived. Rob was no fool (well.., he *had* jumped off a cliff... twice.), so he decided to try asking politely for forgiveness. He had, after all, spent many many years on the seedy side of life first as a combat marine and then as a police officer in a large and cruel city. He was no saint, no paragon of virtue. He had spent most of his years protecting saints, not being one. He hadn't been lucky enough to die in combat. He had survived combat, so that he might... jump off cliffs?

As he was falling, Rob was desperately trying to remember his sins one by one. He was trying very hard and fairly burning up the airways. Was there enough time to squeeze in all his individual little repentances? Logically, he only had the time it took to fall between the cliff edge, above, and the cold waters, below. But there was little logic in his life, at the moment. Perhaps, he wondered, if some kind of generic, "Forgive me, Father, for I have sinned- quite a lot!" plea might work? But that sounded catholic, and God knows a good protestant when he hears one a begging.

The speed of the fall began to become more apparent, and the faster he fell the harder he tried with his myriad of individual sins. Then he became frightened. What if he forgot a couple errant sins? And then there were one, or two, of his sins that came to mind that he wasn't, really, all that sorry about. *"In fact, for those two,"* he thought, considering a pair of really good ones, *"if there is any justice in the afterlife, I should get a reward."* The absurdity of that thought made him smile. Only, when he smiled, he opened his mouth. That was a mistake. Never open you mouth when you are falling towards water. God knows the difference between a good repentance and a mere remembering, and God has the ability to get even. When Rob hit the water, his mouth was opened in a silly grin.

All too soon, the falling stopped.

What came after the falling made the falling, in retrospect, look... pretty good.

Suddenly, the sound of the roaring wind and the crashing of the surf stilled. All was quiet, peaceful and sublime. He never remembered hitting the water. There was just that one moment when he was falling, and the next moment he wasn't. The wind ceased. He could no longer hear the crashing and roaring of the waves; he was *in* the crashing and roaring of the waves. But the waves were silent. It was an all green world full of white bubbles in crazy, mute motion. He was like a small pebble thrown- not into a volcano- but a blender. The blender was on Pulverize.

As a penance for his sins, the saltwater rushed in and around his smile. The saltwater in his mouth was nothing, for a millisecond later he felt the cold. Real cold. All around him. Pervading. Like ice on... ice. It was the last of his sensations before they went on overload, and the circuits shorted out.

Deep into the crazy white world he tumbled. It was as if he had lost all size and dimension. No longer was he a large and powerful man but was, now, small and insignificant. More and more, he was becoming detached from himself and his past reality. He was sure there had been no ripple when he hit the water. How could such a small and little thing like his body disturb the mighty Pacific Ocean in all its grandeur? No sooner had he found himself in the water than he began a head over heels spinning and tumbling in the heavy current. He was pulled three ways at the same time and then jumbled up and dashed against underwater rocks. He became entangled with seaweed.

In the midst of this horror, this being killed alive, his life continued on automatic re-wind. He saw himself seated around the dinner table in his boyhood home. All his brothers were there, and his mother was alive, once again. He heard his father explaining about his monthly paychecks from the shipyard. "Now, right here on the back, it says, 'Do not fold, spindle, or mutilate.'"

"Gee!" Robbie blurted out all full of wonder. "Who would fold up a government check?"

Harold's arm poked where it was accustomed. "Nobody! Stupid! Checks from the government are valuable!"

"That must be it, then," surmised Rob in the midst of his tumbling under water. *"I must be invaluable."*

Saltwater filled Rob's nose and mouth. He gagged and involuntarily inhaled. The saltwater burned his throat and lungs. Head over heels he was rolling in the surf. He lost track with *up*. He knew he should try to swim, or float up to get a breath of air, but which direction *was* up? Everything- *everything*- was blue water, white bubbles, and seaweed.

Then, as clear as day, he once again saw his father scowling and shaking his head, only this time, his father was next to him in the water. Rob plead with his father. "Dad? Don't just swim there shaking your head at me like you used to do. Do something to help! Or do you, also, think that I have no value?"

After an enormously long minute of twirling and spinning under the water, Rob thought that he could feel his mind giving up. Some form of resolution was taking place, as if his body was adjusting to the fatality of it all.

"Up is quite a direction," he told his father. "Down is a lot easier. Down must be toward these sharp, jagged rocks." As if to emphasize his point, he bumped his head on the rocks. He had no idea how to end the nightmare and get to the surface, and it, no longer, seemed that important to him. His lungs were burning, burning like a person burns who was not successful in remembering each and every one of his sins, burning like a person not lucky enough to die in battle.

"I told you," his father said rather impatiently and still

holding that infernal green check from the government, "that folding, spindling, and mutilating are wrong! You look like one of these government checks that could never be cashed!"

Rob saw, as from a distance, his own head as it impacted another large yellow and rather pleasant looking rock all covered with mussels and green seaweed. He noted, with some disinterest, that the crash into the rock did not hurt at all. He felt it, but there was no pain. He started to laugh at the ambiguity of it all, at his previous concern and fear, but the water rushed into his mouth, again, and threatened to further gag him. So he stopped laughing. Some part of him knew that being under water, so long, should bother him. On some indistinct level, he knew this drowning, and dying, must be wrong, but it was no longer a distressing thought, at all. He noticed that just as there was no pain involved in banging into the rocks, there was no pain in any other part of his body. The burning in his lungs had ceased, and he looked over to see himself turning comically end over end in the churning water. As the white and blue water began to fade, Rob was only mildly interested, not overly, to realize that everything around him was growing dark. His lungs felt queer and strangely flat. His bad leg ceased hurting.

Rob, casually and almost with a disinterest, looked over to his left, again, at himself rolling in the surf, and he felt sorry for that poor guy. *"Looks like he is really getting beat up. Poor guy! Wish I could do something to help."*

He looked to his right and saw his father smile while doing yet another silly summersault past him. "Folding, spindling, and mutilating are wrong, son. It's OK for me, because I'm already dead. But it's not for you. Find a way to stop yourself from being beat up like this! Find a way! Maybe you could... oh, I don't know.., ask for help?"

"Hey, Dad!" Rob yelled. "Perhaps this is an epiphany! Or maybe I just got a good idea?"

"You think?" came his father's reply.

So Rob, in response to his father's suggestion and his

great epiphany, simply said, "Oh God? Please help me?"
And He did.

The funniest thing happened. Right there, immediately, in front of Rob's face was the bottom of one of Uncle May's feet bobbing in the surf.

It was not rocket science. Rob grabbed the foot.

Rob pulled himself hand over hand up his uncle's leg, hauling himself up and along Uncle May's body as if it were Jacob's ladder to the promised land. Once cleared of the foaming and tossing sea, Rob laid panting and coughing out seawater. His own face was merely inches from May's.

His lungs lost their queerly stinging sensation, and began to just plain hurt. His head was bleeding profusely. A spasm of pain rolled him onto his side, as his stomach and lungs retched seawater onto the rocky ledge. It was very much like a person coming back to life, he thought to himself. Very very much like that. After the retching, he rolled onto his back and folded his arms across his chest. "This hurts more than dying!"

With an incredible effort, he raised his head to look into May's face and then yelled into May's ear. "Thank you for the leg up! My mother, your sister, would have appreciated the help!" He wasn't quite sure why he was yelling, except that everyone knows that it does no good to simply talk conversationally to a dead man. So, he yelled again. "Thank you."

To Rob's great astonishment, May's eyes opened for a briefest second, and his lips formed the faintest of smiles. May blinked once in recognition, and the light went out, and even though his eyes remained open, Rob knew that Uncle May was gone. He yelled again. "I came for you, uncle! I… came for you!" But those eyes would never, again, blink or show any kind of life.

From seaward, Rob heard faint barking and turned to

see the forgotten Spark still struggling in the surf. After some rather intense struggle against his unrelenting exhaustion, Rob managed to sit up on the ledge of the rock next to May.

"Spark," he yelled loudly to the dog, "I just can't do one single thing for you! I'm that exhausted. You are Uncle May's best friend, and I know I jumped in to save you, but I can't help you."

Then he had another great idea! He remembered about the epiphany. "Maybe God can help you, too, for I sure can't."

Then again it happened. In one surprising swish and a swoosh the next wave threw Spark onto the shelf next to Rob and May. Instantly, the dog rolled onto his side and lay still as death on the rock shelf, the laboring of his lungs his only sign of life.

Rob looked around. From up on the cliff, in times past, he had imagined that a good swimmer could possibly make for a small little cove to the north. Once in the cove, there just might be a way to climb out of the water and make one's way up the receding sandstone cliff. He knew, now, that such romantic notions were just so much insanity sparked from a lofty position high above. From the level of the water surface, he knew that there was just no way out of his predicament. Nothing could make him get back into the water again, and the cliff, above, was actually inverted so that the sandstone cliff leaned out towards the sea blocking any escape by climbing.

Rob, once again, remembered the girl in the blue blouse and knew that she remained his only hope, but she had looked to be in such shock and with the queerest insanity in her eyes. Rob knew that she might just simply run home. She could just as easily tell the world, as tell no one. Even if the girl called the police, he knew his time for rescue was short, for although the tide was out- all tides reverse. Soon, the shelf he was on would be covered by the raging surf. Waves would blow twenty feet into the air. Soon, there would be no choice- it was try for the cove or die without trying.

With his remaining strength, Rob turned himself over

onto his hands and knees. He scarcely noticed the thousand small cuts from the barnacles and sharp rocks. Blood from his head wound clouded his vision. His Levis were, literally, torn to shreds. He peered intently, again, into Uncle May's face hoping beyond hope. "I'm so sorry, uncle. I'm so sorry."

As if he understood, Spark righted himself and began to crawl slowly over the wet, rocky shelf and then pulled himself up alongside May. He was too weak to walk, but did succeed by dragging his battered and tired back legs. The dog then began licking May's hair where it was matted and red with blood.

From where Rob mustered the strength to stand he would never know, but he pulled himself to his feet and hauled the dog away from Mayfield Commers' body. "You can't make him better, boy. You are my dog, now, for better or for worse." No sooner had he said that than a large wave staggered him as it crashed onto the shelf and threatened to wash all three of them to sea. "For about ten minutes, anyway, you are my dog. Then we will both follow May, I guess. The tide is... coming in."

Again he tried to force his mind to take rational stock of the situation. He craned his neck to look up the cliff. "No way up from here, boy," he said to Spark. He turned his gaze from one side to the other. "No way out by walking on the rock shelf, either. It ends in twenty feet in both directions." Then he steeled his jaw in determination and thought once again about swimming to safety. He looked out across the rolling and breaking surf. Once again, his heart sank at the sight of the crashing waves.

Then his heart leaped with joy!

Rob's eye caught, to his never ending relief, two distant dory boats that had pulled away from the small fishing flotilla that frequents Cape Kiwanda. Rob watched in wonder as the boats slowly pulled straight for his location. Help was coming! He yelled to the dog. "Maybe," he screamed, "they saw me jump? Or maybe my dad called for them? I don't know?" He looked around again at the small shelf. "I, also, have no idea how they will get an exhausted man and dog off a shelf in such dangerous water?"

He thought of his father's possible help, and it was then that he realized how close to death he must have been while being tossed to and fro under the waves. Death had been close enough for him to believe he was communicating with his long dead father? But still, he reasoned, it was a good thing his father nudged him toward that epiphany. Or was it just a good idea? He started to laugh, but retched again and threw up more sea water and grime, instead.

How, he wondered, they could ever get May's heavy body off the rocks and into a dory boat, he did not have a clue?

Dory boats are heavily constructed, flat-bottomed wooden boats. To the novice eye, they may look simply like junky old wooden boats crafted from heavy, solid, wood planking, but they are made for the harshest conditions the Pacific Ocean can throw at them. They are built to take a beating and come back for more, because one thing the Pacific does not give is a second chance once things start to go wrong. Dory boats are constructed heavy enough that the boats never need a second chance because they either get the job done the first time, or else.

Daily, the dory boat fleet launches directly into the surf from Pacific City. The boat trailers back up into the waves, and the deck hand spins the boat around, so the boat is pointed bow first towards the open ocean. Still, the deck hand is not finished, for if the captain was to turn on the engine, at that point, the engine torque would break the propeller off in the sand. In order to free the prop, the deck hand must wade into chest-deep, cold, ocean water to push the boat further into the surf. Of course, the Pacific Ocean fails to cooperate. The surf attempts to push the boat back onto the beach. The ocean has no compassion. When the boat is deep enough, the captain turns on the powerful engine, and the deck hand scrambles over the stern.

In years past, before powerful outboard motors were available, crews of strong men rowed dory boats out over the surf to fish for salmon, halibut, and cod. They stayed close to shore afraid to leave site of the beach in front of town, afraid of the rolling fog that could easily hide the way home. Still today, the dories stay close in to shore and group up forming small fishing fleets, for they still fear, and very rightly so, the Pacific Ocean with all its charms and dangers.

The sight of two dory boats heading his way brought tears to Rob's eyes. He knew the boat captains were experts, so he and a cold and shivering Spark just scrunched up against the cliff as far from the water as they could get. All they *could* do was scrunch and wait. Against Rob's back, the sandstone felt cool and solid. It felt secure and safe, but it wasn't. The rock shelf they were on was narrow and slippery, and even with his back up against the cliff, Rob's feet were still in the water. Soon, the tide would come in, and without the help from the dory boats, he and Spark would very soon be in the water, again.

As the lead dory boat came nearer, it began to be tossed around more and more by the crashing tumult of surf against the rocks and hidden shoals. When the boat was near enough, Rob could see a stolid fear on the deck hand's face. He stood in the bow intent on the churning water ahead. At the wheel of the boat, the captain's face, in contrast to the deck hand's, was calm and grimly set in concentration. His was a job too complex for fear. His cigar had already been put out by the waves and sea spray, and although ragged-ended, it remained clenched firmly in the captain's teeth. However, as determined and confident as the captain appeared, the dory boat, itself, seemed at the whim of an angry and determined sea.

The boat came straight at Rob, and then, when twenty feet out and in the worst part of the tumult and confusion of sea spray and smut, with massive waves crashing on all sides, the boat paused. "Don't stop!" Rob wanted to yell but couldn't. *"Don't hesitate, now! Do something, anything. But hesitation will get us all killed!"* He would have yelled that very thing, except that he had no strength left, and Rob knew that his yelling would have been futile, since it could not have been heard through the crashing of the waves. He sat and wondered at it all and resigned himself into the captain's hands.

Of course, the captain wasn't hesitating- but timing the waves. At just the correct moment, the captain gunned the engine and ran straight for the shelf holding Rob and Spark. With well practiced skill, he shifted the engine into neutral at just the correct moment, and as he did so, the boat surfed up high on an incoming wave. Then, as the captain shifted into reverse and the boat ceased its forward motion, the boat plopped its flat bottom high and dry on the rock shelf next to Rob and Spark. With the nose of the boat up against the cliff, the next wave lifted the stern into the air and threatened to crash the boat to pieces. The stern fell, with the receding of the water, and slammed onto the shelf. But it held. Rob could see it would hold… for a few waves, at least, but no more than that. In a very short time, the ocean would rip even a battle cruiser to shreds if it remained in such a precarious position. For a few waves, the boat could take the punishment. He hoped.

The captain's voice came loud and surprisingly clear through the roar of the sea, as he took his soggy cigar out of his mouth and yelled, "Throw in the dead guy and jump aboard."

Rob was too stunned to move. When he finally tried, he failed. He tried to stand, but when he leaned on his arms to push himself up they were lead. On all fours, he watched, in horror, as the stern of the boat again lifted to an impossible height by a second wave and then again crashed loudly back onto the shelf. The plop of the thick wooden hull hitting the rock shelf sounded like a high-powered hunting rifle.

Realizing that Rob was done in, the captain yelled to the deck hand in the red hat. "It's not too good right here, son. Over you go, lad. Do your job, now."

The young man was obviously frightened but not daunted by his fear. Immediately, he vaulted over the side of the boat and onto the rock next to Rob who, with great difficulty, managed to shake off his shock and exhaustion long enough for the two of them, Rob and the boy in the red hat, to ingloriously manhandle uncle May off the rock. They simply tumbled him into the boat. May's body slid over the sideboard to flop down and settle onto the floorboards. Uncle May had ceased to exist as the town celebrity, artist, brother of Mary, uncle of Rob; he had been reduced by necessity, and the need of the moment, to "the dead guy." As tired as he was, Spark followed his master into the boat. Rob and the young man tumbled after.

A third wave hit the boat and lifted it high, once again. With the added weight of two adults and the red dog, the boat slammed the shelf even harder than before. Rob thought he heard a crumpled sound like soggy wood when the boat hull crashed back onto the rock shelf. Two feet of water came over the stern. The deck hand's eyes opened wide.

The captain pointed with his big black cigar. "Get back out with you, boy!" the captain roared. "Don't go getting wimpy on me, now. I need you to turn us around just as if we were launching off the beach. We'll swamp trying to back out of here. Just turn the boat around, nice and easy. Go ahead, now, with you! You've done it dozens of times. Do it one more time just like we were starting out from the beach. I'd like to get the boat off this rock, here, and you back safe and sound to my sister."

Rob marveled. The young man never even hesitated. Trained by constant and instant obedience to orders at sea, every command a response to a need, he instantly leaped back onto the rock shelf just as another gigantic wave lifted the boat high up and into the air. This time, however, the boat slanted off the wave and crashed against the boy's legs knocking him to the barnacles and rough rock. As Rob caught his breath, the boat started its decent towards the young deck hand. But the boy didn't stay down. He had the quickness of youth and was helped by pure luck. The same wave that nearly pinned him under the boat, also splashed him out from under the hull and back against the cliff face, like a leaf in a storm. There, he gained his feet faster than Rob thought possible, and, without a word, got back to his duty of turning the boat to face the sea. Even before, the wave had fully withdrawn, he was already pushing the bow around using the outflow of the wave, itself, for a pivot.

Pointing with his stogie, the captain yelled to Rob. "My sister's son. He'll do!" Ordinary beach launches, he would later say, were good practice for emergencies. Halfway through the turn of the next, and last wave, the sea again attempted to hurl the boat over on top of the young man, but by sheer strength of will, he held her firm and managed to push the bow all the way around. As the last wave receded, the sea begrudgedly gave way to the young man's persistence. "Hold us steady, lad! Don't let go, now," yelled the captain. "Take your time. Push the prop away from the rocks, or we'll all be dead bodies in the bottom of some other skipper's dory boat!"

Grunting and groaning with the impossible task, the boy dutifully pushed the boat away from the rock ledge. With an all clear signal, from the young man, the engine roared to life and the boy quickly shimmied aboard. The heavy boat's bow crested the wave and powered cleanly through the rough sea. Soon they were miraculously skidding smoothly along atop the brown, smutty spray and flotsam as the boat powered into open water.

"My sister's son!" yelled the captain, again, to Rob.

Rob looked down into the blood and water pooling in the bottom of the boat around the body of his uncle. "My mother's brother," he returned.

The boat was riding low from the water taken in, and as they passed close to the sounding buoy, the boy in the red hat started bailing water out from the bottom of the boat.

From shear exhaustion, Rob slid to the bottom of the boat next to Uncle May's body. It was grimy and filthy, but he just did not have the energy to lift himself up and onto a seat. It was the first time Rob thought he might be injured rather than just exhausted. He should have been able to rise, should have found a dry seat out of the muck, but the thought came to him that he felt folded, spindled and mutilated. That thought made him smile. Without swallowing water.

Rob turned and watched the cliff receding in the distance. *"Funny,"* he told himself, *"how that cliff looks so small from here? So peaceful it looks! How lovely! How many paintings of that clif had Uncle May painted? How much money had he made off that sandstone heap selling its portrait-all the while painting something that would eventually kill him."*

When they were half way around the sandstone spit heading for the launch, Rob heard the captain yelling into his radio, trying to be heard above the motor and surf. "Viking, here. To Coast Guard."

"Come in Viking. This is Newport Bay Coast Guard. The chopper should be approaching your position, now."

"Coast Guard: This is Viking. Rescue successful. We have them aboard and are heading to the launch."

"10:4: What is your status?"

"Better get an ambulance. You can cancel the chopper. We have one who looks DOA. That artist guy who's always painting around town? He's dead. We also have a dog that doesn't look too bad off; a big Irish Setter. He's some hurt, but he should be OK."

"Coast Guard. Roger, Viking."

"Viking, here. We also have one surviving adult male cut up pretty badly."

It wasn't until then, that Rob looked down and realized that his arms and legs were covered with blood. The barnacles and sharp rocks had, in fact, taken their toll, and blood was flowing onto his shoulder from a nasty head wound.

"Viking, here, Coast Guard?"

"Go ahead, Viking."

"The cut up adult male for the ambulance?"

"Go ahead, Viking."

"He's the man we saw push the other fella off the cliff."

Rob's head shot around at the captain's accusation! It was then he noticed the small revolver resting in the captain's loose hand.

"Pushed! What do you mean pushed! I thought May fell!"

"Well..," was all the captain would say.

Spark hung his head over the boat's sideboard and made little simpering noises.

The only place one can find a fleet of dory boats that launch right off the beach is in Pacific City, Oregon. It is a tradition going back to the early 1900's. Even today, the dory fleet remains a small and quaint, but viable, sport and commercial fishing industry. Up and down the coast, fish caught by the dory fleet are sold to local restaurants. Rides in the boats are $12.50 an hour. Rescues are free.

The Viking captain ran half throttle through the crashing surf directly toward the sandy beach and his awaiting truck and boat trailer. The Viking was also running towards a police car with flashing lights. The last hundred feet before the beach, the boat rode like a surfboard on the crest of a large wave. Just before smashing down onto the sand and scree foam at the water's edge, the captain goosed the motor to give the boat a little extra momentum for its slide across the wet sand. To protect the prop, the young man, who had gone onto the rocks to help lift uncle May, tilted up the motor just as the captain cut all power. It was a well rehearsed ballet. With the motor tilted up, the boat glided smoothly onto the wet sea foam and then plowed over the wet sand some thirty feet onto the dryer sand, where it came to rest with a jerk.

Rob lifted himself up and peered over the sideboard enough to see that a crowd had gathered at the landing site. He was relieved to see that a Lincoln County Sheriff's Deputy started for the boat even before it came to a complete stop. Being a retired police officer, Rob had not the slightest bad will towards the sheriff's deputy. He was relieved to soon be in the hands of one of his own kind.

When the deputy trotted up to the boat, the captain pointed a long, straight arm and finger at Rob who remained sitting on the floorboards amongst his own blood, gore, and about a foot of seawater. "There's your killer!" yelled the captain. "We saw him kill this other fella. Pushed him off the cliff."

Rob did not react.

The deputy looked at Rob, noted all the blood on his head, legs, and hands and hooked his thumbs into his gun belt. "You need some help, fella. The ambulance is just about here." He crooked his neck toward the sound of an oncoming siren.

Rob plopped back into the bottom of the boat oblivious to the gore and did not move. He was too exhausted from his ordeal, and had lost more blood than he cared to know. He thought about trying to climb out over the side of the boat but just felt like the uncashable government check. He simply relaxed into the water next to Uncle May. He knew better than to try to control the situation from here on out. Medics and police all had their jobs to do, and he knew better than to interfere or challenge any one of them.

Rob looked up at the deputy and squinted into the sun. "I surrender."

Nearby, sitting in the sand with her knees tucked tight up against her chin, was a young woman in a blue blouse. In obvious mental distress, her arms were tightly wrapped about her knees. Her tears were falling and staining her blue blouse. Shivers convulsed through her body. She was just one of a hundred onlookers, but what differentiated her from the others was her open and outright distress as if she were somehow involved in the tragedy. Most of the curious simply stood and watched. This girl was near to loosing control. Becky began to rock to and fro.

Through her tears, Becky had an obscured view of the dory boat. She watched, sneaking peaks over her knees and around onlookers, as Rob was lifted from the boat and placed on a stretcher. She saw the heavy, dark blood on his shoulder and all the blood stains on what was left of his tattered jeans.

She watched and cursed a man named Billy. "It's not my fault," she kept saying over and over. "Billy would kill me if he knew I was involved. Billy would kill me. Billy would kill me." The tears flowed freely, and her body continued to shake and shiver from fear of Billy, from fear and compassion for the poor man all covered with blood and from her deep remorse over not helping. She had promised to find help, to phone the police, to find someone with a cell phone. In the end, she had done none of those things. She had simply run down the hill back towards town and collapsed in the sand. It was by sheer chance that she collapsed near where the dory boat would come ashore.

As the minutes went by, her tears began subsiding, and her shaking became less violent. Slowly she began to wonder what she could do to find some kind of absolution for what she thought to be an unforgivable sin; she had simply run off and left a man to die. She hadn't done one thing to save him. So frightened was she of Billy, that she simply threw herself down into the sand and cried like a frightened little girl, which, of course, she was.

Even straining up onto her knees from where she was, Becky could not quite see inside the boat. She was unaware that the body she had spied from the cliff was lying there in a pool of blood and gore. She became concerned when the captain's mate lifted the tired and exhausted Spark from the boat and gently laid him onto the sand. So worn out was Spark, that he just laid still and did not move. Not even a whimper came from Spark. He just laid there panting and pitifully gasping for breath.

Still, the girl in the blue blouse did nothing but watch as one lone deputy sheriff followed the wounded man to an ambulance. Rob's one best and true alibi watched as he was taken away.

Becky continued to watch as people began crowding around the boat to look inside and then reel away in horror. But no one was helping the poor exhausted red dog. As she looked on in shock, Spark raised his head and looked right into her eyes as if he recognized her from up on the cliff. In fact, he did. He stared at the girl. A low whimper escaped from the dog. A low whimper escaped from the girl.

Slowly, and with final resolution, the girl stood to her feet and wiped the tears from her eyes. Carefully, and tediously, like walking on glass, she took the few steps to where the dog helplessly lay near the bow of the boat. She knelt on the sand at the dog's side. Slowly, she began to caress the dog's matted and bloody hair. "You poor dog," she said out loud. "Billy will not understand. But I don't care. You poor dog." She lifted Spark up and slid under his neck and shoulders to cradle his head in her lap. The move was hard on the injured Spark, but it made Becky feel better.

She had failed the man, but by showing care and simple compassion for a helpless animal, she was trying to find some kind of inner strength to fight her fear and self-disappointment. Perhaps, if given the chance again, she would be a stronger woman and summon aid for the man. If the same thing ever happened again, she might just find the strength to do something good, instead of just running away in such abject and unreasonable fear.

She prayed for a second chance to help someone, so that she might make up for her failures. An involuntary sharp intake of breath swelled her chest! She had prayed, before she realized it. She never prayed? "Now, what's with that, I wonder?" she asked the dog. For the first time, in a very long time, she was pulling down prayers and well wishes from on high. It felt good to her but alien. It was the cleanest thing she had done for as long as she could remember.

A very large man approached and dropped to his knees in front of Spark and the girl. He waved his hands to a wide expanse of the beach. "I think Spark may have been forgotten in all this… tragedy." The large man petted Spark and spoke kind words to the dog. Then after a few moments, the man looked up at Becky and smiled. It was a clean smile with none of the dark undertones to which she was accustomed. She saw none of Billy in him. The large man spoke carefully to the girl. "The dog's name is Spark. He is such a fine and loving dog, and you must be a fine and loving young lady to take time out of your day to care for a tired and exhausted animal." He smiled kindly at Becky, but she did not smile back. Men had smiled at her before.

The large man enfolded Spark in his arms, lifted him in one quick swoop of a movement, and stood to his feet. "Thank you for helping Spark," he said to Becky. "It's works of kindness that set us apart."

"My name is Buck, or at least that's what people call me."

From the sand, the girl looked up at Buck. "Set us apart from what?" she asked.

It was then that Buck noticed the look in the girl's eyes. Until then he had been so preoccupied with Spark that he had failed to notice the vacant look of desperation and fear on the girl's face. There was a distance, there, a far-away absence that disturbed him. Long ago, Buck had battled with the priorities of life, and he recognized one now. Always take time for a kindness, was his motto. People are what are important. He wanted to take a few important moments with the girl, but he feared for the nearly lifeless body of the dog.

"It sets us apart from the savages," he answered evenly.

The girl stood and looked into Buck's eyes. It was if she was studying him, trying to open him up to look inside. "Savages?" she asked. Then, she asked a second question. Her eyes never wavered; they kept boring deep into Buck's soul. "Did you ever molest your daughter?"

Buck could sense the importance of the question. He could read behind the inquiry.., behind the injury. He rose to the moment, held her eyes with his and never wavered. "No," was his quiet, and still, answer. He waited.

The girl did not answer. Her eyes softened minutely. They shifted so slightly that he almost failed to notice.

Then the girl turned and started to walk away but stopped. "Savages. I know lots of them. But.., are you a… hero?"

"I want to be. More than anything…I just haven't had my proper chance."

She looked towards the ambulance. "Two heroes in one day!"

Chapter Three

As the paramedics loaded Rob onto a stretcher board and carried him across the soft sand to the waiting ambulance, he was so exhausted that he didn't fight them; he just lay quietly and bore the jostling and bouncing. Curious onlookers, who continued to try to see closely and stare at whoever was on the stretcher, all wanted to be part of the happening, to take a memory home of being special, of being in the know. With considerable difficulty, the medics parted the crowd to make their way to the ambulance.

Half way to the ambulance, Rob recognized Peggy, Uncle May's girlfriend, standing in the sand watching him. She had a dumbstruck look on her face as he was carried past. Her arms were folded tightly against her chest as if holding the world tight lest it fall to pieces at her feet. But the truth was that her world had already fallen apart, and try as she might she could not put it back together. As the stretcher passed by her, Rob and her both took a sharp intake of breath. Their eyes met and locked. Neither could turn away. Her feet were as if rooted in the sand; she stood as if in shock. It took a few seconds for her legs to work, but then she ran as best she could in the shifting sand to catch the stretcher. She begged the medics to stop.

"Rob Smith! May's nephew! How did you get in a dory boat? You've been hurt terribly? How did all this happen?"

"I'm glad you... recognized me," interrupted Rob. He was nearly too exhausted to lift his head. "May is... dead, Peggy!"

Peggy's head shot back as if punched by a left jab, and Rob thought she might lose her footing. But she didn't. Summoning all the strength she had, she spun on a heel and started rapidly for the dory boat. For her, it was the longest hundred feet ever. She was trying to grasp what Rob had just said, but even as she repeated it to herself, she hoped he was wrong, mistaken or delirious from his injuries. "You mean that May is seriously injured," she whispered. "May can't... die!"

Rob tried to yell, but couldn't. His voice came out broken and weak. "Don't go over there, Peggy!"

Thankfully, Rob's half yell attracted the deputy's attention just before Peggy reached the boat, and he tried to turn her from the gruesome sight. "Peggy.., you don't want to...see. It's May!"

She did see... past the deputy' shoulder. The blood in the boat was Rob's, of course, and the sight was so gory and horrible that she was nearly overwhelmed by the picture of such a viable and robust man reduced to a bruised and battered corpse covered with unspeakable gore. She was utterly shocked, more than she thought possible by the death of Mayfield Commers. Hours before, she had kissed him goodbye as he set out to climb the dune. He had been such a comical and lovable character with his easel under one arm and his paints and brushes and endless paraphernalia threatening to fall from his grip at every step. Now, two hours later, she stared into the blood soaked bottom of the dory boat where May's body lay limp and lifeless. "*Is this the same man?*" she asked herself. "How could it be?" she muttered aloud. "May is alive." She looked pleadingly in the deputy's eyes. "May is up... on...the...cliff!"

Peggy and May had met at an art show two years before. She remembered being thrilled by May's paintings, his light touch of the brush, his fame. He was thrilled by her striking beauty and youth. She became a source of pride for him, and he loved being involved with a young, beautiful woman everyone knew from the 6 O'clock News. People said that she was his girlfriend. Now, standing in the sand looking down at the broken shell of the man, she wasn't quite sure what that meant? That was not quite true. She admitted to herself that she knew what it meant to be a girlfriend, but thought it not quite an accurate description of her. "*Or, maybe,*" she thought to herself, "*that is what is so upsetting about all this? After two years, I should have been more than just a girlfriend.*"

The deputy gently turned her away from the boat and pointed to the stretcher. "The man on the stretcher is Rob, May's nephew!"

She followed his gaze. "I know. I recognized him, Mel. He went up on the cliff to meet May. May is not dead."

She was torn. She kept hurrying her glances back and forth between Mayfield and Rob and back. She knew she had loved May to some extent, but there was the queerest feeling deep inside her when she glanced at Rob on the stretcher.

At the ambulance door, the medics were treating Rob's injuries, mopping up the blood, and bandaging his deepest slices and cuts where the barnacles and sharp rocks had done their worst.

Twice she caught Rob's eye. Twice he held her gaze for a moment or two between bandages and swabs. Both times there eyes met, she involuntarily turned away and glanced towards the dory boat. It was as if she was feeling guilty about something with May, but a sticking and creaky door was being forced open with Rob's glances? On one hand, she liked the idea, and on the other she was pushing it back to keep that particular door from opening. She was not willing to let one door open while she felt like the first was not quite closed. But death closes such doors… tightly. And throws the bolt.

Thoughts of last summer's barbecue intruded into her mind, how Rob and she had been so mutually attracted to each other; and how May had recognized that mutual attraction. "*That's why Rob hurried off and went back to Seattle,*" she reminded herself. "*I was his uncle's girlfriend, and Rob did not want to interfere.*"

A troubling idea pushed out the thoughts of the barbecue. The thought crossed her mind (although she immediately tried to put it away) that May and Rob might have fought over *her*. She tried very unsuccessfully to push that particular thought aside. She knew that worrying over what might have been and who might be at fault would always come back to the same illogical conclusion. That was the path to insanity. Why, it's Peggy's fault! The thought nagged! No, she would not dwell on thoughts of that ilk, she warned herself. Besides, Rob idolized his uncle. "Why, he's everything I always wanted to be!" she had heard Rob say several times. "Why, he's everything I always wanted to be!" she had heard May say of Rob. They would not have fought. She settled the idea in her mind and then dismissed it.., almost.

The sight of Peggy Richards forced Rob also to remember the barbecue. He remembered how he and Peggy had sure done a lot more than just meet for the first time. That was, in all actuality, the one and only reason why Rob had stayed away from Pacific City since the barbecue. He knew that she was May's girlfriend, and Rob felt like a heel. But there was simply, and undeniably, instant chemistry between Rob and Peggy. At first, it was just that they couldn't keep their eyes off each other. Then, later into the party, they accidentally met in the hallway and just fell into each other's arms. Rob left the barbecue and Pacific City without explaining to May or saying goodbye to Peggy. No explanation was necessary for May, thought Rob. He was sure that May had a feeling about the two of them, but May never said anything. Rob was pretty sure that May knew about the kiss.

Peggy tried to fixate on the ambulance instead of the dory boat.

Earlier, she had seen Rob when he first pulled into town, before he climbed that fateful cliff, when he first pulled in from his trip down from Seattle all tired, dried out and limping on his bad leg. She thought, then, watching Rob climb out of his truck that her whole world was about to turn upside down. It was. And it did.

She tried to look as if she was just absently watching out the window of the Pelican Pub when Rob Smith just happened to walk in and sit himself at the bar. It had been a long and arduous drive from Seattle to the Oregon coast, and Peggy had been waiting all day. When Rob's truck finally pulled into the sand covered parking lot and boat launch, he looked just like he and the truck were both bone dry and out of gas.

Rob looked at the beach and the cliff in the distance. Then he turned to glance at the pub. He was torn. It was such a warm day at the beach, and if he was going to climb the sandstone cliff to meet his uncle there was a beer or two in his more immediate plans. As much as he cared for his uncle, his uncle could wait. For Rob knew that even after hours on the cliff with brushes and paints and turpentine his uncle would still not be eager to leave, that his uncle would just linger, and paint, and paint, and paint. It made perfect sense for Rob to have a couple beers to delay Rob's time on the sandstone cliff in the hot sun waiting around for his uncle to finish. Not that Rob didn't appreciate his uncle. For appreciate him, Rob did. He would admit to even loving his uncle after a couple beers at the Pelican. After three beers, Rob would confess to a crime.

It's a relaxed atmosphere at a good coastal bar, and the Pelican Pub is the best. Scott simply set a pale ale on the bar and walked away knowing he could settle the bar tab later. He recognized Rob, and although he hadn't been to the barbecue he had sure heard about it. People knew Rob because they knew May. "You're Commer's nephew? Catch you later," was all Scott muttered over his shoulder.

To Rob's surprise, a red headed girl with green eyes set her own ale down on the bar next to his drink. She was attractive and petite and had obviously been drinking a few beers before Rob showed up. She pointed her index finger at him as if she was shooting a gun. "Hey, I know you. You're

May's nephew, or somethin', from Seattle. I… met you a few months ago at the barbecue." She said it with a tease in her voice and a twinkle of light in her eyes. She knew him, all right. How could she forget him? And, she knew that he remembered her. If he hadn't remembered her, he would have come back to visit May some months ago.

Rob's eyes twinkled back all over her for a few long seconds and then, without saying a word, he casually reached over and picked up her beer and took a long, slow pull. She didn't protest or lift a hand to stop him. It was a pick-up trick Rob had… picked up. One had to perform it just right maintaining eye-to-eye contact during the entire theft.

Her eyes followed Rob's theft. She watched him gulp her drink but did nothing to stop him.

"It's always nice when a beautiful woman remembers me," he said.

She had a sweet smile, and he really did remember the barbecue, but she was his uncle's property. He could tease her. He could drink her beer. But he would never, again, be caught with her in a dark hallway.

In return for Rob's theft, undaunted and game, she reached over and took a sip of his beer. She returned his stare deep into his eyes. "You are cute. I remember you all right. And you remember me."

"Sure. How could I forget," Rob answered. "You're May's girlfriend. Or at least you were six months ago." She watched his index finger point back at her like a gun cocked to go off. "Peg… Peggy. That's it. Isn't it?" he feigned. "Are you still May's girlfriend?"

She smiled. "It's Peggy.., and you remember my name." She looked at the hand he pointed at her. "You have large hands.., like your uncle."

"As far as I'm concerned he is sitting right here next to us. Have you seen him today?" Rob asked. "I'm supposed to meet him on the cliff."

"He's up there on the rock. I watched him go up there

a couple hours ago totin' all his paints and stuff. Spark was taggin' along, like always. Are you going up to meet him?"

Rob took a long cool pull... on his beer. "Yep. He's expecting me. Although, he won't remember until he sees me. Right now, in the middle of a seascape or whatever, he won't remember anything other than the painting he's doing. But he invited me to stay for a couple days, so I better go on up and help carry things back. He said he had something incredible to show me. So, here I am."

Peggy's eyes took another turn all over him. Her voice was slow and sultry. "I remember you from the barbecue. You could show *me* something incredible."

"Peggy!" blurted out Rob. "Are you drunk?"

She slid in a little closer to him so that only he could hear. When she was an inch too close, she stopped. "That will be my defense," she whispered.

It had taken a little encouragement for Rob to agree to a few days at the beach. He loved spending time with his uncle and more than enjoyed the sea and the sand. The beach scene was a pleasant diversion from what had become a dismal existence for him. On the bar stool in the pub and under Peggy's spell, his mind was having trouble remembering why he remained living in Seattle instead of moving to the beach. He loved Pacific City. He always had.

"Are you still my uncle's girlfriend?" he asked again.

She pointed her finger back at him again.

"Wonder what it is he wants to show me? Any ideas, Peggy?"

Her eyes cooled, wandered over the room and out the window to the sandstone cliff in the distance. "He never said. He was just excited about something and was happy you could come down for a few days. He's got something up his sleeve. Maybe it's just another painting he has finished, but I don't think so. Usually, he is content to just show his new work with me or his neighbor, the art gallery owner."

She turned back away from the windows and, again,

her body rubbed just a little too close, too close for his uncle's girlfriend. "I was anxious for you to come down from Seattle." Her voice returned to its sultry undertones. "Maybe we should have another barbecue, or perhaps all we need is a dark hallway?"

Rob didn't know what to say, so he didn't say anything. She waited for his reply all the time smiling coyly. He knew what he wanted to say but knew that he didn't really want to say it. Well… at least he wasn't sure that he wanted to say it to his uncle's girlfriend. Rob was very sure that he could carry her away, right now this very minute, but he also knew that he would be throwing away a relationship with his only living relative and a man he admired.

At Rob's prolonged hesitation, Peggy dropped her smile.

He watched her walk away, threw down a five, for his beer, and walked into the sunshine.

With her eyes, Peggy followed Rob as he left the bar. She pointed her finger like a gun.., and let the hammer drop.

Rob worked his way through tourists and dory boats for a mile to the base of the cliff. His legs were like lead from the beer as he started up the steep trail, and he cursed the beers effect on them. He struggled up the sand dune that spilled off the side of the cliff only to find, at the top, his life changed forever.., only to find his uncle in the water below.

A short time later, Peggy was standing in the sand looking at a pathetic Rob Smith on a stretcher. She shook her head as if to clear it of old memories. The affect of the alcohol had been driven from her by the tragedy in which she had become enveloped. Time slowed to a crawl. She felt as if she were falling. She felt a knife wound deep in her chest. In spite of the beer, she had become stone, cold sober.

Robs injuries, from his plunge into the Pacific, bordered on severe, but looked a lot worse than they really were. He had experienced a concussion where he had bounced off a large rock or two, but mostly he just had dozens of small bleeding cuts that looked life threatening but weren't.

Rob winced in pain, and Peggy overheard him ask the medic if he knew the difference between an epiphany and a really good idea? The medics reply was to ask if Rob knew what day of the week it was? In reply, Rob asked if the medic knew how to get his sins forgiven. Rob was asked to name the president.

"Jimmy Carter. Or Obama… What's the difference?" Rob answered.

The medic hesitated.

"With either one of them, you can't get a home refinanced to save your life."

The medic's head nodded, and the look of concern in his eyes softened.

There were so many small cuts and lacerations that the medics eventually gave up treating all of them and just wrapped arms, hands, and feet in gauze. His neck they put in one of those troublesome, foam neck braces. For the coupe de grace, his head was wrapped in a white turban of gauze that tended to make him look like a Muslim who had not succeeded in dying in battle, and, therefore, would be haunted forever by his sins.

Peggy continued standing helplessly in the sand with nothing to do with her emotions as they overflowed. She felt left out and confused by the great and nearly overwhelming loss of her lover and friend and her nearly over-powering compassion for a man who did very strange things to her. She wanted to cry over one man but couldn't quite. She wanted to hug the other but couldn't quite. One she wanted to bring back to life. With the other, she wanted to share her life.

Peggy watched the deputy and medical personnel as they loaded Rob into the back of the ambulance.

When the EMT started to shut the door, the deputy stopped it from closing to speak to Rob. "You realize you are under arrest, don't you?"

Rob craned his neck up as best he could to look over the length of his stretcher to which he was tethered for the jostling ride over the sand. The neck brace made the maneuver nearly impossible but not quite. His voice came out with more of a croak than anything else. "I am a police officer."

The deputy nodded. "I know that. You are Officer Rob Smith, Seattle PD."

Rob's head dropped back onto the stretcher. "How do you know that?"

"I was at the barbecue."

"Was everyone at the barbecue?"

"Everyone who was sure remembers you!" answered the deputy. "You made quite an impression."

The deputy nearly acquiesced to the ambulance medic who again tried to shut the door- but the deputy held the door open, nonetheless. "I'm not putting you in cuffs because you are a police officer. I'll be following the ambulance in, but I'm not going to cuff you."

"I didn't do it," Rob said flatly.

Rob felt as if he was in an old black and white movie or some cheap suspense novel. As he uttered his denial, he was afraid to look at the deputy. He was too afraid that his glance might contain a guilty look, so he continued to stare at the ceiling of the ambulance. "I didn't kill my uncle. Oh, man! I loved that guy! I wouldn't kill him!"

The deputy put the flat of his hand on the door to push it shut but paused once again. "I never figured you did. But the dory boat captain said he saw you fighting with your uncle and then push him off the cliff."

"He doesn't know what he saw," replied Rob. "He must have been a half a mile away."

"That's what I figured. More like a mile."

"One other thing, deputy?"

"Yeah."

Rob's eyes bored into the ceiling. "Make sure they do

a thorough job investigating the crime scene up on the cliff, will you?"

Once again, the deputy dismissed the medic with a glance and continued to steadfastly hold the door.

Finally, in exasperation, the EMT walked away and climbed into the front passenger seat.

"Crime scene? I figured it for an accident," said the deputy very quietly. "That's the reason you're not in cuffs."

Rob waved off the deputy's conclusion. "Something's been bothering me since I first ran up to that cliff edge. Something was wrong, but I didn't get it at first. I couldn't place it until now. The paints and the canvas were thrown all around. They were scattered. If May just fell, the easel might be knocked over, but the paints would not have been scattered like that. He was killed, I tell you! He fought with someone, and he was murdered."

"Who would want to kill Mayfield Commers?" asked the deputy.

"There was a girl on that cliff that might have seen everything."

The deputy's eyes lighted up. "What girl? What girl?"

"Young girl, early twenties, white female in a blue shirt. Find her. She saw me run up after it all happened.., whatever happened. She's the one who phoned the police."

The medics were becoming more frustrated and wanted to be off on the long trip to the hospital. The driver was gunning the engine time and again. The passenger EMT got out to, again, stand impatiently by the back door. "Can we do this later fellas? We have to get to the hospital.., sometime. The longer we wait the more blood this guy is gonna lose."

The deputy continued to ignore the EMT. "Nobody phoned the police, Rob. Nobody called until the dory boat captain called the Coast Guard."

Rob's head shot up in defiance of the neck brace.

Silently, the deputy closed the ambulance door. To Rob it sounded more like the in-take door in a jail clanging shut.

As the ambulance started off through the rough sand and as the ride smoothed out when the ambulance hit the parking lot, Rob pondered it all. The girl didn't call? She just ran off just like he thought she might? But why? Why not call the police? Did she have something to hide? Was she involved in May's death? Had she killed Uncle May or been a witness to his murder? Was she simply frightened and afraid to become involved?

The deputy watched the ambulance bump over the wind-blown sand in the parking lot and then he turned toward the beach. His gaze took in the mile of beach in front of the boat launch and pub. "A girl in a blue shirt? I can take my pick. There has to be ten on the beach right now? Why would a young woman be up on that cliff alone, anyway? Had she been alone? Was whoever with her responsible for May's death? Did the girl and a friend kill May? Was there a girl?"

Peggy stood on the beach and watched the ambulance disappear down the beach road. For several seconds, she did not turn back towards the dory boat. When she again looked at the boat, her eyes filled with horror as several men struggled with May's body. They lifted him over the sideboard and rested his corpse on the sand.

Peggy fled.

Later that evening, the girl in the blue shirt huddled in fear in the dining room corner behind a small table. She scrunched up as far from Billy as she could get. Her back was pressed hard on the window glass behind her. "I didn't go far, Billy. Really! I only went down to look at the water. Nobody saw me. Nobody knows me!"

Some of her story was true. She hadn't gone far- just over the hill to the cliff. At the cliff's edge, something terrible had happened. She had witnessed a murder, and she had seen Rob jump into the water. She had accidentally witnessed the dory boat landing with Rob, Spark, and the body of Mayfield

Commers. She had comforted the red dog, Spark, and she had met a local town leader named Buck Jensen. She had done everything which Billy had warned her against. When she tried to just sit peacefully on the cliff and watch an artist paint on canvas, she had witnessed a murder. When she attempted to run away from the crime scene, she had bumped into the tail end of the rescue effort and met someone who could identify her.

Just now, she was worried about Billy's temper. She had seen it explode before. It was her unfortunate experience that his temper turned on a dime and didn't leave much change- just carnage. She marveled that Billy could be the nicest and sweetest guy one moment, and then the he could be brutal, violent, and twisted- just like he had been at the house they had robbed. He hadn't needed to kill that woman, there was no need. What was the point? It sickened her heart to know that she, herself, had a hand in helping Billy kill an innocent old woman. But how could she have known Billy would kill someone? All he had to do was break in, collect all the loot he could find, and then run out to the car where she was waiting at the wheel. Becky realized, now, that Billy found some perverted pleasure, or turn on, with violence and murder. He needed violence, thrived on it. She also knew that his need for violence was not his only perversion.

"I only sat on the cliff," she said quietly trying her best to calm Billy down. "I sat and looked at the water."

She was telling the truth- to a point. She had just sat and watched the waves crashing in. At least, that was all she had intended. She had been fascinated watching the artist painting a seascape, but she had held back, partially hidden in the shadows of the cliff and had not made her presence known. Then, to her horror, another man had come storming up and started fighting with the artist. She watched in horror as the unfortunate artist was pushed over the cliff to his death.

At first, the second man walked up and just began talking. For a few minutes, the artist continued his painting, and then, all of a sudden, the artist slapped his paint brush down. The artist shoved the man, and the man shoved back. Becky watched in terror as the men fought. She could not hear their voices, but it was more than obvious that something had been spoken between the two men that brought both to instant alarm and violence. The artist was much smaller than his attacker and fell back towards the cliff when the larger man shoved him. Even from Becky's view point, she could see the fear in the artist's eyes when the man shoved him again. Obviously overmatched, the artist attempted to run past the larger man, but the man caught him and spun him around. The two men fought. The smaller man, so obviously out of his league, tried striking his attacker with his fists, but his blows fell with little effect. Finally, the larger man simply pushed the artist backwards over the edge, and the artist fell.

How suddenly final that shove was. It shocked Becky! One minute there were two men, and then there was just one. Seeing what he had done, the large man seemed to throw his arms out towards the cliff as if to bring the artist back. He held his arms aloft for a few seconds before dropping them to his side in silent resolution. From the back, it seemed to Becky that the large man's entire body slumped in regret.

The artist's dog had been alarmed by the fight but had not entered into the fray. Of course, the dog jumped back and forth and ran in circles around the two men. He barked excitedly, but he did not enter into the battle. It was not until the artist had fallen backwards off the cliff that the dog rushed in and grabbed the attacker by the ankle. At first the man struggled with the dog. Then he simply kicked the dog and turned towards town.

Becky watched as the dog's head dropped in a threatening pose that reminded her of a wolf. She heard the dog's growl and watched the man turn back in a defensive posture. Then, surprisingly to Becky, the dog whirled and ran to the cliff and peered over the edge. The dog paused for a few scant seconds, and then Becky watched in horror as the dog hurled itself into the air to follow its master!

So shocked was she, that Becky hadn't even realized that she had jumped to her feet in alarm. Unconsciously, she took a few steps towards the conflict just as the killer turned. When his eyes met Becky's, he stopped abruptly and then ran the opposite direction to where the trail led up and over the sand dune to the north.

Becky warily watched Billy getting closer to her, stalking around the table, getting closer and closer. He was screaming and cursing vehemently.

She remembered how he had come into her life. She recalled how, in one day, he had completely taken over her existence and changed everything for her and her sister. One minute there were two women, and the next instant there was someone new, someone who took control, someone whose personality completely enveloped their lives. It was not a slow assimilation, or a casual assuming of command, but an immediate change. One minute Billy was not: the next he was. And he was in charge.

Six months earlier, her sister, Veronica, took up with the handsome young man who was now before her on a vile rampage. When they first met Billy, he was light on his feet, polite enough, and always had a buck. He was glib of tongue and had a solid, clear gleam in his eye that belied his black and deadly temper when angry. He was the kind of man their mother would have liked, and their father would have avoided. Billy always had cash, and cash always talks. Billy spoke like a gentleman when he was sober. He didn't speak at all when he was drunk. When he was drunk, he talked with his fists... to women. He enjoyed speaking to men with a knife.

Becky had noticed, back then at first, that every time the cash wore down Billy had a mysterious way of coming by more of it. Strangely, though, Becky and her sister, Veronica, never caught Billy working. He had a habit of playing all day, staying out late all night, and coming home with money- when he came home. When she asked about the money, he said he was lucky. What Becky was to learn was that every time Billy got lucky, someone else paid.

That had been in Portland. Becky and her sister were in a nice little apartment overlooking Burlingame, where Becky worked part-time in a grocery store. Veronica worked part-time in the bars. It was a good and quiet life for Becky, and she never told Veronica what to do. Becky brought a paycheck home from the department store every two weeks. Veronica brought money home every morning. Becky never wanted much after escaping from the oppressive home in which the two girls had grown up. Veronica wanted everything. Becky hated men's grasping hands. They filled all of Veronica's dreams.

One night, Veronica brought her work home with her. And he never left. Billy just moved right in and took over their lives like a steam roller on a downhill run with no brakes. He had dreamy hands for Veronica... and sometimes, when Veronica wasn't looking, those hands tried to stray.

At first, when Billy showed up, their lives took a turn for the better... for about two weeks. At first, Veronica stayed out of the bars unless Billy was with her, and Billy was generous with his money, so Veronica had no need for her part-time job in the bars. As time went on, however, he became generous only with his eyes. For Becky, it seemed as if their apartment shrunk in size. Then Billy started drinking more and more. The more he drank, the more his hands seemed to grow, and the more his eyes would wander. More and more, he began to remind Becky... of her father.

A couple weeks after he moved in with the two girls, Billy started using Veronica and Becky to help him on his night jobs. Becky would drive the getaway car, and Veronica would go in with him. Veronica refused to talk much about their "jobs". When they would come out, her eyes would be all aglow, and she would scrunch up next to Billy in the back seat as the three of them made their getaway. On the last few jobs,

Becky noticed that Veronica's eyes began to glow *before* the job, but she usually came out with money or jewelry or something else of value, and she always shared with Becky in the front seat.

Becky never got in the back seat of the car, even though Billy's eyes said she could. She stayed in the front silently brooding for a way out.

One night, they left their Portland apartment for good. They hurriedly grabbed a few things and drove to the Oregon coast. Billy was in such a hurry! It was, Becky teased, as if the Nazis were coming. They grabbed what they needed, left behind more junk than they took with them, and drove off into the night. They loaded up and were driving away in twenty minutes. Billy never said why.

The police rolled up to their Portland apartment scant minutes after the trio departed.

Billy had never liked their apartment in Portland. He had always been upset about its setup. He kept obsessing, anxiously, about the long driveway into their apartment complex. On the day of the hurried move, he was standing at the bottom of the long drive and watching anxiously as far up the street as he could see into the night. "One way in and one way out!" he whispered with power and fright in his voice that Becky had never heard before. "No good. Just one way in and one way out!" The three of them made their getaway with no problems and no close calls with the police... or whoever was chasing Billy. He refused to come up to the house but just stayed at the bottom of the driveway. He jumped into the car when Becky and Veronica finally descended the long drive to the street.

The two girls never knew exactly why they packed up hurriedly and moved off into the night, although Becky asked him twice. The first time she asked was an innocent mistake. The second time left a lump on the side of her head. It was then that she decided to find a knife.

In the robberies and burglaries, she became adjusted to

driving the getaway car. Somewhere in the recesses of her conscience, she could probably find a small voice that would tell her that what she was doing was wrong- if she bothered to listen. Somewhere, she undoubtedly knew that robbing and stealing were wrong, but in a few short weeks, she had become more callous than she would have thought possible. Robbing and stealing might be wrong, but they were just crimes. To hit a woman was immoral! Nice men did not do that, and it would not ever happen again, if she could help it. The trouble was for Becky- that Billy had never been a nice man, and there was very little help for it.

On the first job in Lincoln City, something went wrong, drastically wrong, and an elderly lady had been hurt. Billy and Veronica had gone into a large sprawling house near the beach in Lincoln City. It was a ranch with what Veronica described as having about a thousand windows on the beach side of the house. They simply tried window, after window, until they found one unlocked, and Veronica shimmied in the window. Becky, the ever-faithful little sister, and getaway driver, stayed outside with the motor running. After a few minutes, Billy and Veronica came running out and jumped into the jeep. They were out of breath, but were both laughing and talking faster than Becky could listen.

Later, Becky saw the news on TV about a home invasion and robbery. The homeowner had been killed, needlessly killed, just for the fun of it.

At the unexpected news that a woman had been killed, Becky became distraught, but Veronica remained adamant that it was all exciting- like being in the middle of a movie. Only Becky knew it wasn't a movie; the poor lady who died never got up again after the scene was over, she never held her grandchildren again, she never, again, walked on the beach or smelled the salt in the air. It wasn't like changing the channel on the TV. This was real, and Becky was frightened for her sister. For the first time, Becky suspected that Veronica might not be altogether normal, that she did not completely understand the depth of the situation, that she did not quite grasp life correctly. Becky wondered how long Veronica had been that way, and why she hadn't noticed it until now? Becky wondered, too, how much of the blame could be put on their father, and if it was just coincidental that Billy and their father were so much alike. Sometimes, Veronica called Billy "daddy".

Slowly, Becky came to realize that Veronica was so easily influenced by men that she had become demented by Billy and the evil he perpetrated on those around him. Becky became more fearful, and began trying to figure a way out for Veronica and herself, a way to escape from Billy and the life of crime into which they had been dragged.

Because she knew that she, herself, shared in the blame for the crime spree they were on, Becky was beginning to hate herself nearly as much as she hated Billy. As time went on, she had fewer and fewer illusions about what the three of them were doing. More and more, they were robbing and hurting helpless people who did not need hurting, and she was helping by driving the getaway car! Every time Becky drove Billy and Veronica to a crime, she made it possible for them to hurt again. She realized that even if she stayed in the car she was still taking an active role in murder and mayhem. She knew what was happening even if Veronica did not completely grasp the seriousness of it all. Becky wondered if she and Veronica could ever be normal, again, if the two of them were ever to get away from Billy. She wondered if Billy would ever let them escape.

But even with all the feelings of guilt and worry, with all the money coming in from selling the stolen jewelry, and other items, they were… living the good life… she told herself with a wry and sour smile- in a double wide mobile home. On the last job, they had made such a haul that they could afford to "lay low", as Billy called it, in their rented trailer near the beach, in Pacific City. It was a good hideout down a rhododendron lined street and up a long driveway behind an old, dilapidated beach cottage that only the occasional vacationer visited. Of course, the three of them could not go to town, could not shop in any stores, or buy new clothes. They could not go to movies or bars. They could not go dancing or eat in fancy restaurants. Billy said they were lucky. They could just stay in the mobile home and "wait it out." Becky was not sure what the good life was, exactly, but whatever it was she was pretty sure they were not living it.

With all her troubles, Becky loved the neighborhood at the beach. It was quiet and nearly deserted during the week, and sparsely populated with weekend tourists. In the quiet of the evenings, Becky listened to the crashing of the sea and sometimes could smell the salt air wafting in on the breeze. There were no neighbors to ask questions, and nobody to pry. The weekend vacationers assumed the three of them to be permanent residents and left them alone. Permanent residents assumed they were on a summer-long vacation and left them alone. Billy said it was a great hideout, and that the police were so stupid they would never find them. The three of them did not party and did not go out any more than necessary. Billy always bragged about how they were living in luxury. He bragged that he was so much smarter than the police. Veronica's eyes sparkled whenever Billy talked it up about dumb cops and the three of them living the good life. Becky's eyes shot sparks… and just kept looking for the door.

Through the long hours of lounging around in the good life in a mobile home, Becky's conscience began nagging like a small pebble in her shoe on hot blacktop. It wasn't exactly pain, but the nagging wouldn't exactly go away, either. Becky was confused by the change in both Veronica and herself. Slowly, she realized that she had lost a sister and best friend, when her sister had turned to Billy with all his perversions and devious ways. It was as if Becky's sister had died, and a new Veronica- an uncaring and selfish Veronica- was born in her place. More and more, Veronica's days were filled only with Billy. Becky's days were filled only with loneliness. She was the unwanted third to a happy, if demented, couple. Billy and Veronica had each other. Becky had nothing but a shim.

Becky had never had a boyfriend, never had a hug she cared to remember, never had anyone treat her as if she were special. What she did have wasn't much. She had a shim with a three inch flat blade that she normally carried in her back pocket concealed by her shirt falling down and over its flat wooden handle. But even with only this, Becky smiled every time she thought of it, and found that she had to constantly stifle the urge to put her hand comfortably against its handle underneath her shirt tail. It was a small knife, she knew, but thought it might prove enough length if she pushed it in and then tilted it up toward the bottom of Billy's heart. It just might be enough, she told herself. Of course, its main value came in the fact that Billy didn't know about the knife.

She backed up into the window casing behind her in fear of Billy. She turned just a little to hide the movement of her right hand… and palmed the knife. Of course, Billy did not know about the knife, but Billy also did not know the extent of Becky's fright. The truth was that he frightened her so much that she knew she couldn't just hurt him. She would have to kill him- completely- dead. Hurting him would only make matters worse. She could not afford for there to be retaliation from Billy. She would just have to kill him. She laughed a little as she thought about it. She laughed to herself, because she didn't want Billy to see anything but the fear he expected. She did not want to give him any pause to think that she might have a weapon. She laughed, to herself, because she had come upon the decision to kill Billy so easily without really much deliberation. One moment she worried what to do? What to do? The next moment she had the solution. It was as if she had a really good idea all of a sudden! She almost remembered the name for an instantaneous insight, or solution, to a previously unsolvable problem? But the word failed her. Perhaps, she thought, it was just a good idea.

Billy edged closer around the table, his voice getting louder and louder, his words beginning to slur from the rum and the beer, his body odor growing. His neck muscles corded red and were twitching with pent up anger. "You shouldn't have gone out! I told you to stay inside! I told you!" He slammed his open beer can on the table splashing beer onto the table and the floor. Slowly, he stalked closer and closer, and then just when Becky was sure he was going to hit her, just when she tightened her grip on the knife and tensed her muscles- it was Veronica who came to her rescue... and saved Billy's life.

Becky knew she had been walking a fine edge with Billy since they moved to the beach, and mostly she simply hid out in her bedroom with a carefully placed chair jammed up against the door knob. She rarely came out of her bedroom sanctuary. She could never be sure just when Billy would go completely over the edge. Several times, she watched him get red hot- teetering right on the precipice of violence and then either back off or just explode verbally. But she knew that he could do more than yell. Sooner or later, she was sure that he could, and most probably would, hurt her or Veronica. Becky was confident that he was fully capable of killing her, just like he killed the old lady in the robbery. He had been sorry about the killing, later. Billy *said* that he was sorry. The old lady wasn't saying anything. She was stone cold finalized.

Becky wasn't going to let that happen to herself or to Veronica.

Forgotten in the background, the TV blared. A beautiful red headed reporter was on the television screen. It was Veronica who first noticed it and turned to see the reporter speaking about the home invasion. Veronica animated her voice just as much as possible in an attempt to pull Billy's attention away from her sister. She pointed an outstretched arm to the television at the far end of the room. "Look! They are reporting the robbery!" Veronica was trying to save her sister.

You had to give her that. By just a split second, she may have, unawares, saved Billy.

To Becky's great relief, Billy swiveled his head on his shoulder like an owl in heat, and then he spun on his heel- with Becky completely forgotten. He ran over to kneel, on the floor, in front of the TV like a child on Saturday morning. "Oh, yeah!" he screamed. "Oh yeah!" Filling the screen of their television was the front of the house they had burglarized. The screen showed a shot of the coroner's van pulling away from the house. To anyone else, it would have been a gruesome sight, something to try and forget; to Billy, it was a celebration, a validation. He had made the evening news!

Becky shoved the knife back into her pocket and pulled her shirt down over the handle.

"Good evening. I am Peggy Richards, and this is the Six O'clock News!

"Lincoln City Police, still, have no leads on the horrendous home invasion of a west-side home and the murder of the ninety-two year old resident."

The beautiful reporter kept at the story, but her words became lost in Becky's revulsion. Her sister had participated in killing a ninety-two year old grandmother? "She was ninety-two!" Becky blurted out loud. When she got no answer from either Billy, or her sister, she repeated herself. She raised her voice. She didn't care what the repercussions! This was too much! It was over the line. She could kill Billy, now, with his back turned to her and not feel any remorse. "Ninety-two?"

Billy didn't even hear. He was lost in the story trying to catch every word. He was famous! All the world's attention was on him! He would show them! He would do it again! He would do something calculated to get even more media attention. He would do something big! Like another bank robbery or maybe do a cop just for the fun of it.

"Investigators are still trying to decide the relevance of the letters "tio" scribbled on the wall in the victim's own blood.

"More breaking news as it happens."

Billy, engrossed in the perversion he had committed against a helpless older lady, had completely forgotten about Becky, and she used the moment to go quietly to her room.

She did what she always did in times of crisis. She packed. When she was a girl, she would pack every day. She had resumed the fetish shortly after Billy came to live with them. Every day she would pack. Everyday Veronica would put her things away- just like her mother used to do for her. Veronica never asked Becky why she had resumed her old habit of packing. Her mother had never needed to ask. Every day, her father would open a new bottle. Every day, Becky would pack.

Several minutes later, Veronica came to her room stumbling from the alcohol. "Isn't he something, Becky? He went to college. He's smart. He's smarter than the police and the reporters. He says he loves me, and he wants to take care of me!"

Becky answered from under the pillow. "Oh, yeah. He's real smart, Vicky. He's so smart that he will get us both killed." It was so frustrating for Becky. She was unable to make it clear to Veronica the danger in which they found themselves. Veronica could not grasp it and shook her head at her poor booby-headed sister, Becky. Becky knew the situation with Billy was bad; it was far worse than anything Veronica could guess or be made aware. She knew Billy wasn't just dangerous. He was insane.

Chapter Four

Rob was on his way to the hospital under police guard, but he was oblivious to much that went on around him; for he spent most of the ride unconscious or just on the fringe of consciousness. His dreams were of his father under water or of his mother coming to his room and talking to him, telling him who had killed May and what to do about it.

Spark was taken to an animal veterinarian by Buck Jensen. Spark's dreams were of May.

The girl in the blue blouse made her way to her trailer and all her shattered dreams.

Mayfield Commers lay on the sand. Dead men have no dreams.

That left Peggy all alone to fend for herself and find her own way out of the grief of May's death. On the sand, seemingly between two worlds, she felt helpless, hopeless, and deserted. Her knees went out from under her and she found herself sobbing in near hysterics.

But for Mel, she would not have had a friend in the world.

Mel watched the ambulance bounce out of the lot onto the smooth pavement and speed away. Then he turned back to the beach and slowly scanned its entire width from the river's mouth on the south to the base of the cliff on the north. "Must be dozens of couples and families out here, right now. Many of them have a youngish woman with a blue blouse. Where to start? Where to start?"

Then he caught a glimpse of Peggy, on her knees, in the sand, and he knew where to begin. He didn't care about following the ambulance. He lost his desire to search the beach for a young woman in blue. He lost interest in interviewing possible witnesses to a crime that was most probably an accident. He only had eyes for the beautiful red-headed girl on her knees sobbing her heart out.

"Peggy," he said softly as he lifted her to her feet. "Peggy! I'm sorry."

She had few words. She was lost in a sea of emotions. For her, time had not only slowed to a crawl. It had exploded. It was like a nightmare... on a stick. She tried to cry out, but the enormity of the situation tore her breath away. She felt as if she was falling. Then Mel was there pulling her to the shore. "Oh, Mel! May is not dead!"

Mel, for his part, cared not for appearances. Uniform or not, he laid her head on his shoulder and hugged the girl to him. His entire life flashed before his eyes. His shirt quickly became tear-stained a dark brown to match its epaulets. The two of them stood like that for several slow minutes- she crying on his shoulder and Mel in absolute heaven.

"Oh, Mel?" she finally managed while pulling her head away from his shoulder. "What shall we do?"

Mel hated to see the moment end, for even though he felt like a heel taking advantage of the situation, he did not feel *that* bad about it. He had, for years, been one of the hangers on, one of the losers to May's charms with the girl. Hesitatingly, he relinquished his tight hold on her. He felt an emptiness as her bosom pulled away from his chest... for the first and last time. "I don't know," he replied, "but first we get off this beach, and I drive you home."

He drove slowly, and Peggy talked and cried and talked and cried. At her door, she more than politely declined his entrance, and he was unable to position himself for another hug. They agreed to meet in the morning at the hospital.

After the veterinarian's, Buck returned to the beach in search of a girl in a blue blouse with the saddest eyes he had ever seen.

Peggy Richards had difficulty even beginning the evening news. With due reason, she had no idea how she would get the strength to get through the entire broadcast. She was worried that it might be too obvious, to the television audience, just how extremely upset she really was. But she *was* upset, and the station manger had misgivings about allowing her to continue to work during her time of grief and stress at the loss of Mayfield Commers. Peggy, however, took her position as the anchor-reporter on the 6 O'clock News very seriously. It was the only similarity, to which she would admit, to that of an actress; the show must go on. She wanted to prove to herself that she could work through tough times; that she was a true professional, that she could do her job even if she were torn up inside, and her whole world had fallen apart.

No one at the station knew of Rob Smith. Her inward struggle with her emotions and attraction to Rob remained her secret trial and dilemma. May had only been dead a few hours. Rob was, so far, her burden, alone. But they soon would know all about Rob. It was, she told herself, the definition of double trouble. She had worked through her feelings for Rob Smith and was no longer confused, at all, about her feelings for him. She remained greatly saddened by the death of her lover, Mayfield Commers, but she had to admit that a lover was all that May had ever been. She had never before understood her feelings for Rob; for the first time in her life, she understood the term, love at first sight. There was a great difference, she told herself, between being someone's lover and being in love. Never again would she settle for the former. Her first sight of Rob, at the barbecue, he had sent her heart all aglow, or agitated, or nervous- something nearly indescribable.

Tonight at the station, she had honest misgivings about her ability to be impartial with the newscast, and she was struggling with those misgivings. She was adamantly supportive of Rob Smith, and she knew in her heart that he was not guilty of murder. But, could she be totally impartial and report the facts as they fell? She hoped she could. She reminded herself that she knew so little about Rob Smith? She had hugged him once and kissed him once, and that one kiss had been enough for Rob to run away and return to Seattle. His sudden departure had stirred suspicion in May. But she hadn't tried to contact Rob, and she hadn't tried to discuss the situation with May. Nonetheless, the attraction was there in all its raw power and could not be denied. She wasn't sure if she had believed in love at first sight before meeting Rob, but whatever it was that she had felt last summer at the barbecue- it trumped her feelings for May.

She gave the news director what she hoped was a steady look. "I can do this, Ernie. I am a professional broadcaster. You can't kick me off the news just because I happen to know someone in the story."

"Someone in the story! Ah, kid. You look like hell!"

"Thanks!"

He put a hand on each of her shoulders and gave Peggy what he hoped was a steady look. "Listen, love. Everyone in town knows you and Mayfield Commers were together. Everyone! They are going to be watching this broadcast with a fine-tooth comb."

"Watching with a fine-tooth comb?"

"You know what I mean, Peggy. People all over town will sympathize with you, and rightly so, but this station is committed to giving first rate news reporting- without bias. Our license depends on that. My job depends on that. You mess up this broadcast, and the boss gets hell, I get hell, and you get hell. It's a vicious ball of circle!"

"A vicious what?"

The director rubbed his forehead with the palm of his hand. "You know what I mean. Everything goes down hill. I get it, you get it, and, boy-o-boy, do I not want to get it!"

"You've been trying to get it, for years."

"Peggy!" he blurted.

The director walked away. When he crossed the room, he quieted himself, stood with his back to Peggy for a moment, and then turned and looked back at her. He took a slow breath and smiled. "Thanks, I needed that. OK. If you can joke about it, maybe you can do this job, tonight. But do it professionally, or don't do it at all."

Peggy turned to the mirror for one last hair check. Her eyes were steel-green.., just like her stomach.

As the director pointed to her, at her queue to begin the broadcast, as the red light came on the camera, she steeled herself to the task at hand; Peggy Richards took a long, deep breath and opened the broadcast. As always, all eyes in the studio were turned to her, but this time all eyes were waiting for something special- a slip, a falter, or a tear. Anticipation filled the studio. It was like a group of witnesses to an accident. The station's personnel couldn't look, and they couldn't look away.

"Good evening. I am Peggy Richards, and this is the Channel 22, 6 O'clock News!"

"There is a disturbing story out of Pacific City. The popular and beloved local artist, Mayfield Commers, has been found dead at the bottom of Cape Kiwanda cliff. His body was recovered by the captain and crew of one of the dory boats he was so fond of painting.

"For thirty years, Mayfield Commers cherished and loved the Oregon Coast. His love was returned by one and all. He was found this afternoon, with his loyal Irish Setter which had jumped into the Pacific Ocean in a vain attempt to save his master.

Spark was rescued by the dory boat, the Viking, and is recovering at a local veterinarian hospital.

"Commers' nephew, Rob Smith of Seattle, a children's book author of books such as *Zippity Zappity Land*, has been wrongfully arrested for his murder." Her face blanched as she read the name of the suspect. In the background, the viewers could hear a low muttered complaint and exclamation from the TV station's director. Of course, she wasn't supposed to have said the word "wrongfully". It was a departure from impartiality, and it was not in the script. In truth, she hadn't meant to verbalize the word, but she just could not bring herself to accuse Rob Smith of murder. She heard herself make the foopah, she heard the word come out of her mouth; and she knew her career was at least temporarily derailed. She knew she was off the air as soon as the news item ended, but she kept at the story reading her script as professionally as possible. She felt an errant tear begin to well up in her left eye and had no idea how to stop it.

Ernie had been correct. Peggy's relationship with the deceased artist was no secret in the small coastal community. May and her had often attended gatherings and camera events together. It was quite obvious to viewers, on the announcement of Mayfield's death, that Peggy Richards was having difficulty continuing with the story. "An autopsy is planned for…" her voice faltered and broke. The tear streaked down her cheek… "There will be a full obituary during tomorrow's newscast."

As the camera broke away to the weather report, evening listeners could hear Peggy's muffled complaint to Ernie. "Autopsy? Who wrote this? I'm supposed to read the word "autopsy" and not get upset?… Autopsy? On that poor man?"

Her worst professional fear was true. A story had become personal to her. It was the last time she would anchor the 6 O'clock News.

The next morning, Spark, the red dog, lay in the animal control hospital curled up on a soft cushion. His mind was fuzzy, but he was struggling against it. At first, he had no idea where he was but knew instinctively that the people around him were trying to help. Small cuts had been treated with alcohol, and he had received vitamins intravenously. Good, warm food helped. Mostly he was just resting and trying to recover from the ordeal of losing his beloved master of many years.

"You know," said the veterinarian to his assistant, "this is the most intelligent of dogs. He is extremely tired out, but he is also unexpectedly alert and attentive to everything around him. I have seen him before. I think I treated him, once, last year. Great dog!"

The assistant rubbed behind Spark's ear. "Wish he could talk. I remember him from the parade last summer. I have seen him on the beach with his owner. He was such a nice guy, too. Everybody loved him and his dog."

Spark listened to the soft, comfortable voices and drifted off to sleep again.

The next morning, Rob Smith lay in the hospital. His mind was fuzzy, but he was struggling against it. At first, he had no idea where he was but knew instinctively that the people around him were trying to help. Small cuts had been treated with alcohol, and he had received vitamins and a pain sedative intravenously. He knew he wasn't in bed in his lonely apartment, in Seattle. But where? His eyes felt glued shut, and there was a dull roar in his ears. He could hear a dong dong dong. His head hurt, and failed to move on his first attempt, and on the second attempt, he thought his head might fall off. Pain shot down his neck, and his back spasmed. His chest lifted off the bed, in pain, and he barely stifled a scream. His breath came raggedly. The donging kept up relentlessly. His distant and fuzzy mind, finally shocked into clarity by the pain, recognized the dongs as those often heard in a... hospital? Either that, or the French fries are done? Dong! Where was he? Dong. He had been visiting his uncle at the beach? He was on vacation? Dong! Then he began to remember. When his eyes started to open, he quickly slammed them shut in response to a searing, purple pain and the intrusion of a bright, white ceiling light. His stomach flipped.

Squinting against the bright light of his hospital room, all the tragic details began to slowly come back into focus, even if his eyes wouldn't. He remembered that he had found his uncle fallen off a cliff. Only his uncle hadn't fallen. He had been pushed, and he, himself, was a suspect in his uncle's murder. Rob remembered that there were only three people who knew that he was innocent of his uncle's murder. The mysterious young woman in a blue blouse knew the truth. Perhaps, she had even witnessed the murder? The murderer, who had actually fought with uncle May and pushed him over the side of the sandstone cliff into the cold and cruel Pacific Ocean, knew the truth. And, of course, Spark. Spark knew the truth, but he wasn't talking. Dong! These things Rob pondered, in his mind, as he lay in the hospital bed with his eyes shut tight against the reality of bright lights, obnoxious noises, and a lost and dead uncle. Dong!

Then he remembered other witnesses. There were two eye-witnesses in a dory boat who would swear, in contrast to the truth, that Rob Smith was the murderer, that they saw him push his uncle off the cliff and onto the rocks below. In a court of law, Rob knew that eye-witnesses would trump his pleas of innocence. From his years of police work, he knew that two eye-witnesses would make a fool out of him and his story. A jury would believe two eye-witnesses. With only one eye witness, it might be possible to convince a jury of the truth. But two? He was in trouble, and he knew it. But he didn't care. He might be in trouble, but his uncle was dead; and, for that murder, someone would pay.

All this his mind mulled over, as his body fought to control the pain. He tried moving different parts of his body. His arms refused to lift, his fingers hurt, his right knee felt ablaze when he moved it. And his head! His head felt like it was the size of a basketball…in flames. What really alarmed him was that, try as he might, he could not move his left hand and arm.

Through the fuzz and haze, he lay there trying to clear his mind. As from far away, he began to hear a persistent voice calling to him, a woman's voice, a voice he knew he should recognize. "Rob? Rob, are you awake? Oh, Rob? Please wake up."

He waited. Perhaps the voice would just go away. But it didn't. "If I were awake," he said, "my eyes would be open."

Slowly his left eye opened. To Rob's surprise, his open eye revealed a beautiful lady with flaming red hair and behind her a uniformed sheriff's deputy. He remembered the deputy from the beach, after the dory boat brought him in with May's body half floating in the seawater and blood in the bottom of the boat. The lady, he remembered, was May's girlfriend. Except that May didn't have a girl friend any longer. Dead men don't have the pleasure. Rob grimaced. His lips cracked.

Carefully, he opened his other eye and spoke past his uncle's girlfriend to the deputy. His raspy voice was just barley audible. "You, there? Do you know the difference, yet?"

Peggy looked puzzled. She started to speak but stopped.

The deputy answered. "An epiphany is a life changing revelation... sometimes people are convinced the revelation comes from a higher power... It's a lot more than just a good idea."

"No. There's more... somehow, but I can't remember..."

Peggy looked from one to the other but decided it must be a private joke, and she decided to ignore it.

"I... can't... move... my left arm," Rob whispered.

It was then that Rob noticed that his hand was being held. To his relief when he glanced down, it was Peggy holding his left hand and not the deputy. She was squeezing his hand rather tightly.

"Rob. Oh, Rob!" she blurted. "We were so frightened for you! Do you remember anything, Rob?"

"I remember that my uncle was killed and that I was arrested.

"I remember having a discussion with my father- it seemed as if he was trying to give me a really good idea about God and forgiveness and being rescued... or something. It's all a little fuzzy." As he went on, his voice cleared and talking became somewhat easier. "But I know this. I was dying, and I just gave up. My father told me to ask someone for help, so I just said… 'God, help me'. That's funny, in itself, because I'd pretty much given up on the God Thing. Instantly, I washed up next to May's body, and I pulled myself up out of the water. And there was something about a government check being all scrunched up?"

"You asked God for help, and he did help you?" she asked. She shot a worried look at the deputy.

"Don't look so worried," Rob replied. "You never met a cop, yet, who was being shot at, or beat up, or in some other dire circumstance, that he didn't ask God for help. Ask your friend, there."

The deputy simply shot his eyes to the ceiling lights. Then he shrugged his shoulders and replied to Peggy's swift look. "Cops aren't supposed to be human, but we are. Some things just get to us." He looked at Peggy from the neck down.

Peggy, again, shot a glance from one man to the other. She had a complex look on her face as if she wondered that Rob might have lost his mind, and the deputy sheriff wasn't far behind. In the past, in times of confusion, she had grasped at comedy to spread oil on the waters and knew that it had often helped, so she tried it again. "Well..," she said slowly, "I was in desperation once, and I asked a… a cop for help! I couldn't find a god."

They all three chuckled.

In the ensuing silence, she tried again. "Don't all cops think they are gods?"

Nobody laughed.

Rob looked quizzically at Peggy as if for the first time noticing her. Then, he spoke again to the man in the uniform. "Deputy, did you check the crime scene on the cliff?

The deputy stepped around Peggy and nearer to the head of the bed. It gave him a clear shot, eye to eye, with Rob. "We aren't sure of much, yet." Then he hesitated looking from Rob to Peggy and back again as if he was expecting trouble.

"It's… like this, we don't think there was a crime. The sheriff's department is thinking that May probably just slipped and fell off the cliff. We lose half a dozen people up on that cliff every year. Most of them are kids, but sometimes an adult who should know better will get too close to the edge. Then too, sometimes people are just blown off the cliff by a gust of wind, and they end up in the ocean. Once you are in the water, you are not supposed to be able to survive. You, Rob, are the first one who has ever been pulled alive out of the water at the base of Cape Kiwanda."

"But the dory boat captain and his nephew?" weakly interjected Rob, "swear that they saw me fighting with Uncle May, and that they saw me push him to his death?"

"Sure, but we didn't find any evidence of anything other than an accident. So, you are not under arrest.., yet. And the captain of that dory boat had been drinking."

"It's a crime. I just know it is," insisted Rob.

"No," replied Mel. "Many of the dory boat captains drink on the job."

Peggy slapped Mel on his arm, in disgust.

Rob waved off the humor. "It's a cop-to-cop tradition, Peggy. It's called gallows humor," whispered Rob. "You used it, Peggy. Besides, nothing is sacred to cop humor. Thanks for the compliment, Mel. I'm not really a cop any more, you know.

"My uncle was murdered. I know he was."

Mel looked at his feet rather apologetically and then raised his head. With a level stare, Mel answered with finality. "We don't see it that way."

Rob tried to sit up but found that he could barely move. To help him, Peggy stuffed a pillow under his head and neck. Her breast accidentally brushed his face. Rob definitely noticed. Her nearness aroused him somewhat… and reminded him of the barbecue. He dismissed the arousal as a positive sign that he was not hurt all that badly. He thought of the barbecue, last summer, and dismissed his current feelings as just natural animal instincts with such a lovely girl… with the greenest eyes he had ever…

"How do you like that?" she asked about the pillow.

"Oh, I liked it just fine!" But he didn't verbalize the thought. "Umph," was all he could murmur.

"Why can't *I* ever be hurt?" asked Mel with a wishy and sympathetic look.

Rob wanted to shake his head to clear his mind, but he was afraid. He was afraid the headache might return, or something vital might fall out a recently created opening, or his head would simply fall off and roll into the corner.

"It's a crime scene," Rob said as emphatically as he could to the deputy, but he found himself looking into Peggy's eyes instead of the deputy's. His throat was sore and raw, and speaking was becoming difficult. His voice was harsh, but he tried anyway. He tried to raise his voice for emphasis, but his shout came out a whisper. "Did you check the area on the cliff for blood?"

They looked at each other, the deputy and the girl, with a sadness in their eyes as if they were not sure how to tell Rob that he was being silly.

The two of them looked, to Rob, as if he was about to be patronized. He didn't want that. He wanted understanding and agreement, but if he had to work alone to prove his uncle was killed, he would. He would find the killer himself. Rob desired allies, but he was used to being alone, used to going his own way.

"You two must know that I have a great motive for murder."

"You mean alibi," said Peggy squeezing Rob's hand again.

"No, he means motive," said the deputy very slowly and carefully. Peggy thought his words carried unusual emphasis even though quietly spoken. The deputy continued. "While Rob was asleep, I looked into the matter. He stands to inherit quite a bit. He is the only living heir to May's fortune. There is life insurance, real estate, paintings. Is that what you mean, Rob? Is that your motive?"

Rob took an offered sip of water from Peggy and found it eased his speaking. "By default, I inherit. May was my mother's brother. I am the only one left. May was very fond of me. Because I am the only one left in the family, I am a prime suspect. I had motive and opportunity. If I killed him, I inherit. I could have been up on that cliff with him before he died. I could have pushed him off. Even the dory boat captain and crew say that they saw me push him off!"

The deputy shook his head. "Nah. That doesn't fit. Then why would you jump into the ocean?

"Just to make it look good," answered Rob.

"Look good? You damn well killed yourself jumping like that! Nobody, and I mean nobody would jump off that cliff and into the Pacific Ocean and expect to live. No one who had half a nut for a brain!"

"Spark did."

"Well, yeah!" replied the deputy. "But Spark loved that man."

Rob sighed deeply. "So did I."

The room was quiet for a full minute while all three tried to get a grip on all that had happened.

Finally, Rob asked the deputy, "What did you find up on the cliff, Deputy.., what's-your-name?"

"Mel. Mel Engel. We found the paints all scattered, and we found the easel knocked over. We found no evidence of a crime, and I haven't been able to locate a young woman in a blue blouse nor to convince anyone else to look for her. There were a dozen women on the beach fitting your description."

"Would you check the area for blood?"

Mel shook his head. "There were so many people up there, before and after, that it is impossible to find much of anything definitive. You know, that is one of the most popular areas around? There have been dogs, and people, and birds. Half the vacationers on the beach ran up to see where all the action had taken place. They tromped the area, destroyed any…"

"Yet, with all the summertime vacationers," interrupted Rob, "someone found the opportunity to approach May, fight with him, and push him off the cliff- all without being seen? I would consider it a special favor, to Uncle May, if you would check the area for more evidence."

"Of what? How?"

"I don't know," Rob answered. "I don't know. But there must be something up there. Check it for blood."

"How would I do that?" Mel plead.

"With a presumptive blood-splatter test kit and a black light… You'll have to go back up there at night."

Peggy interrupted. "What are you two going on about? Rob has just awoken from death's door, and you two are going on about crime scenes like this was some police science class, or something. What is a… a blood-splatter test kit?"

The deputy played with his hat in his hands. Then he lifted his eyes. "You're right, Peggy. I'm sorry, Rob. There is plenty of time for this later… when you are feeling better."

Rob made a gallant attempt at an exploding temper, but, under the conditions, he could barely lift his head and chest off the pillow. His voice was getting weaker, again, and raspy. "No, it's not OK for now! And I am never going to feel better about this! You need to get your butt back up on that cliff, and check the area for blood and any additional evidence you can find. Uncle May was murdered! I am sure of it! And I'm mad as hell about it!"

The deputy shrugged and looked at Peg.

"Or do I have to get up and do it for you?"

Peggy leaned closer to Rob. "Rob, you know what that will mean, do you? I mean, if we do find any evidence that leads the police to suspect murder?"

He relaxed his body onto the bed mattress. He was so tired. "Yes, I know," he replied. "Once again, I will be the suspect in a murder."

Peggy was confused. She asked a question, but Rob was so exhausted he fell back on his pillow and was out as if someone had turned off the switch: not exactly off, just fading fast like a dimmer switch. He heard the question but had not enough energy to open his eyes, let alone answer her. He knew it would take a long and complicated answer, and that answer would just have to wait.

"Once again? You mean you have been a murder suspect before?" she asked.

Mel looked at Rob, and his jaw tightened. "Yes. I think he has."

It was midnight and a starless night. The only light was the lone parking lot light next to the Pelican Pub. All the tourists were wrapped tightly in their beds. No one stirred on the beach, except Mel and Peggy. Weirdly, the phosphorescence of the waves crashing against the shore reflected off the low hanging clouds and cast a glow that lit the beach. Even away from the sole parking lot light, there was enough light from the phosphorescence that Mel and Peggy could see without the use of a flashlight.

The deputy and Peggy unloaded the spectrographic equipment and set the boxes in the sand next to Mel's old Buick. "You know, Peg, it's real good of you to help me with this. It's quite a ways to lug all this equipment, and I can sure use the company. It gets pretty lonely out on the beach at night."

"That's why I came along, Mel. To hold your hand and make you all strong and brave. Can I hold your Glock?"

He laughed. "No, but you can hold the spectrographic box."

Quietly she shouldered a large black box the size of an antique video recorder. "How does all this fancy stuff work, Mel?"

He picked up two other boxes, containing a heavy battery pak and additional equipment needed for testing and analyzing, and began to explain as they started out across the loose and shifting sand. "Know how a black light lights up colors?"

"Yes."

"Well..," said Mel very quietly, perhaps too quiet for Peggy to hear, "that's how I feel about you."

"What?" Peggy answered innocently.

"The black light is not quite the same principle, but the effect is similar," replied Mel as innocently as he could. "The results anyway. When you turn on this black light in the dark, just the tiniest amount of blood makes this unit light up like the Fourth of July. Then the light-gun automatically takes a photo of the blood. This is really a nifty machine! If there is any blood, up there on the cliff, we stand the best chance of finding it with this new equipment. It's like a metal detector for blood."

"Sooo," replied Peggy. "Ve are loooking for blood! In ze night on yonder, lonely hill?'

To both it seemed incredible, for off in the distance there really did come the howl of a wolf... or at least a Rottweiler.

"Don't do that again, Peggy!"

"I won't."

It was a steep climb up the sand dune, and for both of them, the boxes seemed to get heavier the further up the hill they trudged. Half way up, they were both panting and gasping for breath. It was the same climb that Mayfield Commers had made lugging all his paints and his heavy art easel. It was the same climb the murderer had made just before killing May. It was the same climb that Rob had made to find Uncle May and Spark in the water.

During one of the stops to rest, Peggy carefully lowered her box to the sand and asked Mel a question that had been nagging her, something she kept hearing but did not understand. "What's all this talk about an epiphany?"

Mel turned, all out of breath, to look squarely at her.

He tried not to pant. He always tried not to pant around Peggy. "Yeah, I guess we can sit and rest for a minute.

"I guess, from being battered and beaten against the rocks, Rob had just about given up, when he had what he says was an epiphany. He thinks that when he was being tossed to and fro under the water he was visited by his long dead father, and this father-vision gave him a good idea, a way to survive. The good idea involved asking God for help. I think it's kind of a joke with Rob. I've seen people like him before. When things are serious, they joke about them. It's nothing new for a cop to call out to God for help. It's like a soldier in a foxhole. Once the bombs start coming in, you can't find an atheist."

Peggy looked down the expanse of beach laid out before her, the purple-black sky, and the lights of the city, far below.

"What's with all the talk about sins and seeing God, and all? I didn't think he was religious… especially, not after the barbecue."

Mel laughed and slapped his knee. "That barbecue! That was something, wasn't it?

"But to answer your question?" Mel continued, "No. I don't think he is particularly religious. I know how most macho guys think. We cops see an awful lot of what is good and bad: mostly the bad. The bad kind of sticks out at us at every turn. But mostly, we are like all men everywhere. There is nothing like a near-death experience to bring out the religion in a man. I've met plenty of men like Rob. The question is, did his father give him a really really good idea, or was it something larger, bolder. Was it an epiphany? Or, is a really good life-changing idea the same thing as an epiphany? Or, is it just a good idea to have an epiphany when you need one? See, it's kind of a joke. Get it?"

"No."

"I've met a lot of guys like Rob, before, Peggy. He'll be all right. He'll come around."

She contented herself to watch the phosphorescent

white of the waves crashing below and was mildly disappointed when Mel picked up his load and, once again, started up the hill. She was thinking about what he had said about meeting people like Rob before. She mumbled out loud but not so that Mel could hear, it was more like a personal affirmation, or like a door opening, it was like a really really good idea that might… change her life.

"I've never met anyone like Rob before!"

The trouble was that Mel heard her… loud and clear.

After spraying a liquid out of a bottle and then shining the black light all around, they did find blood in the sand where May's oil paint tubes had been thrown. The light gun clicked away taking photos where the spray turned bright blue. The blood-trail trickled nearly up to the edge of the cliff but did not lead over the edge. Surprisingly, the blood seemed to turn and trail off down the sand dune, all right, but not towards town. The trail led around the back of the dune to the north: instead of south towards town. Mel and Peggy tried to follow the blood-trail to the north, but it faded out, lost in the myriad of footprints, and animal tracks, and small sand avalanches on the north side of the dune.

After following the blood-trail as well as they could, they went back to the cliff where Mel picked up some bloody sand and placed it carefully in a small plastic testing device.

Peggy was in awe of the whole process. "OK, Mel. How does this work? I'm getting tired of this feeling of woodoo voodoo, mumbo jumbo!"

"It's quite simple," he said. "It is a presumptive test."

"Oh! That explains it."

"This sample receptor tests for hemoglobin. If this blood reacts with a reagent consisting of blue colored particles…" He looked up at Peggy. Her eyes were crossed.

"Wellll, if this little thing turns blue, then we have found blood. We will still need to determine if it is human blood and not that of an animal. But, if it's blue it's blood.

"Step one: we found blood.

"Step two: determines if it is human blood or animal blood.

"Step three…"

Peggy held the flashlight for Mel as he placed a blotch of blood on a test strip and then immersed the strip in a plastic tube. They both watched with anticipation. Time slowed to a crawl. After a few seconds, the indicator turned red. "Red. It's human blood," he said.

"Now we go on to step three."

"Three? Ze suspense es killing me."

"Step three is up to the lab to test it for DNA."

"DNA?"

"Right. Years ago, we couldn't go much further with this evidence. Today, we can tell if this blood belonged to Rob or May."

"Or someone else," put in Peggy.

When they turned to go, Mel's light fell on one of the metal fence posts near the very spot where May had fallen to his death. On the top of the post, someone had scrolled the letters, "tio". Mel wasn't sure what the inscription meant or whether it was pertinent to the case, or not, so he took a photo of it.

The blood was sent to the state crime lab for DNA testing, the photo he put in the evidence locker.

Mel knew that based on May's death and the evidence Peggy and he had gathered, a Lincoln County Grand Jury would convene to consider the evidence against Rob Smith… for the charge of murder.

The next morning, Rob carefully walked out the front door of the hospital and stood in the bright sunshine- glad to be alive and on dry land. But even as glad as he was, the suddenness of the bright sunlight nearly bowled him over. The loss of his uncle came back in earnest. Rob might be alive in bright sunshine and on dry land, but his uncle was dead and on a dark, cold slab. The thought sickened him, and it made him angry.

"You know, Peggy, jumping into the water, like I did, was the worst decision of my life… it, nearly, cost my life. It did not do one single thing for my uncle or for Spark." He limped on his game leg more than usual but was helped, somewhat, by the cane supplied by the hospital. "I tried to help, but I just made it worse for everyone."

Peggy put her arm around Rob's elbow to help him walk, and hugged his body close, a little too close. "How so?" she asked.

"I risked the life of the dory crew, did not save my uncle, and nearly killed myself."

"You did what only a brave man could do, what May's nephew would do," she replied coldly. "Your heroism would not have surprised May. I wish he knew what you did, and how hard you tried for him?"

Rob fixed his eyes on the horizon. He was lost in remorse. He realized that he had not told Peggy about May opening his eyes for a second before death took his life. Rob took a deep breath trying to think of the right way to break the news to her, when suddenly his knee buckled out from under him.

He would have fallen if Peggy had not been there to help. "You should not have argued with the nursing staff. There is a reason they have a rule about taking patients to their cars in wheel chairs?"

Rob merely shrugged his best John Wayne imitation, regained his stance, and started for the car. Peggy tried to help him and to have him lean on her as they walked to her car, but he shook off the help- not maliciously- but with his familiar crooked little smile. It was what he had always done: tried to make it through life's difficulties alone and without help.

He was trying to make sense of Peggy being around, so much, and her being so helpful. He was trying to rationalize that she was just acting like Uncle May's friend would be expected, but he was having difficulty believing that. Every muscle in his body was sore. His mind was fuzzy, and his emotions were running rampant. Every time Peggy brushed up next to him, or stood just a little closer than he thought necessary, the air got thick, and he had a more difficult time thinking clearly in his muddled mind. He wanted to cry over his uncle's death, but, then, every time she brushed against him, he wanted something else. He shook his head in an effort to clear his thoughts, but those thoughts kept going back to the barbecue. Rob remembered how he had jumped into his truck and raced back to Seattle without even saying goodbye. He remembered he had left in such a hurry because he was afraid his urges were uncontrollable around Peggy Richards- like being afraid of a height because you might jump. Last summer he did not trust himself around Peggy. Now, after six months, he still did not trust himself around Peggy.

In spite of his objections, Peggy put her arm around Rob's waist to help him into her car. When her body pressed up against his, he thought he would pass out, and both knees again threatened to buckle.

"Are you all right?" she asked.

"No more so than Mel when you get so close," he answered.

She pretended to be mildly shocked. "What?"

"Nothing."

"Huh?" she asked again.

They stood with the car door open. "Mel's got a thing for you."

"No." she replied. "Mel's merely a nice guy. I don't have a thing about him. He's like a little brother to me."

Rob just growled. "Let's go get a drink." It wasn't what he wanted to say. He had no idea what he wanted to say? Her face was so close to his, her hand tight on his waist, her breast hard up against his right shoulder. Would he faint from pain? Swoon like a little girl? Finally, he just crumpled into the front seat of her Honda and muttered his perpetual one word answer to the troubles of his life. There was no reason to believe anything had changed. "Rum."

Peggy drove him to a bar away from the water where the sight of the ocean would not be a distraction. "I thought," she said, as they sat at a table, in back, away from the highway, "that you might be more comfortable where you can't see the ocean."

"Got that one right on. I've had enough water for a while. Still, I don't know how one avoids it in a beach town? I'm not mad at the ocean. It just scared me for a minute… or two. I like the ocean. I love it. But there are some pretty hard rocks underneath all that beautiful, blue water." He put his hand to his head and winced a bit. "In fact, all there is down under the water are rocks and more rocks. When you are down there bumping around, it's a little difficult to keep your head. No pun intended."

The waitress handed them both a menu, but Rob tossed his aside.

"Rum."

"Don't you want to eat something, Rob? You've had nothing but hospital food."

He politely ignored Peggy's question. He just smiled that crooked little-boy smile of his and looked up at the waitress. "Rum. Then food."

"Hey! I know you!" blurted the waitress pointing with her pencil. "You're the guy that killed that artist fella! I saw your picture on the news!"

Peggy started to get up, started to object, but Rob reached out and held Peg's arm to stop her. Somehow, he noted, Peggy's green eyes had turned to a kind of cold sea-green or cold blue-steel.

Rob looked at the waitress and quietly and simply said, "Please. You get me rum, now. I will settle up with the TV reporters later. You know how reporters are."

After the drinks arrived, and the waitress dutifully spilled some in Rob's lap, he explained to Peggy why he was not in jail. "My freedom is only temporary. I might end up in jail after all this. I don't know. Mel's boss, the Sheriff, let me off on my own recognizance, as they call it, partly because of my status as Uncle May's nephew and partly because of my being a retired cop. I know that sounds weird, but there is also another reason or two.

"How so?" asked Peggy.

"Mel put a rush on the blood-type analysis in the lab. He called early this morning with the results. Neither my blood type, nor my uncle's, match the blood that you and Mel found at the scene. I don't have type-A blood. The blood they found on the cliff was a solid type-A. None of May's blood was up on the top of that cliff."

"How do you know that?"

"Only the bad guy's blood was on the cliff. Both May and I have type O."

Rob gulped the last of the rum and waved at the waitress. "I'd like to wear another rum, please?

"Besides, Peg, it won't matter much in a couple days. The Grand Jury will return a True Bill, blood type or not. Blood-type can be explained away. Then the Sheriff will be forced to lock me up. So, I figure I have two days, at the most three, to solve this case. After that, I go straight to jail. I don't pass go. Then it won't matter if the Sheriff and I did work a patrol district, together, in Seattle ten years ago."

"I'm in on the hunt, Rob," stated Peggy. "I'd like to help."

"Why?"

"I figure you can use the help. You can use a good friend, and I believe in you.., and I have A-type blood. The last time I heard, the girlfriend was always a good suspect.

"And, I think that I am in love with you."

Across town, a young man in a red jeep was sitting on a residential street watching an old man packing up a motor home in obvious preparation for an extended trip. The old man made several trips inside, and then an older woman came into view carrying bags of food on one trip and blankets on another. Billy watched and decided that the house looked good for his purposes, and since the two homeowners were advertising their upcoming trip so openly, he might, as well, return, at night, to see what they left behind. It looked like an easy setup: a house on the beach, again, so access to the back of the house was no problem.

As long as Billy's fence in Pacific City was trump with ready cash to buy stolen property, Billy would continue robbing the rich to give to the poor. If the old couple was as rich as they looked, Billy was poor enough to receive. For, like a politician in heat, he felt that it was his god-given destiny to redistribute the wealth to all mankind. As long as it wasn't Billy's wealth that was being spread around. He would scroll "tio" on the old couple's wall just before midnight.

When Billy returned to the double wide, Veronica came to the door with all smiles and a kiss. Becky didn't show. Billy and Veronica made plans for the job and waited for late evening when Billy was sure the change of shift would allow for fewer police cars on the street. Becky remained in her room and prayed that just this once they would forget her and not ask her to drive the getaway car. She wanted nothing more to do with the crimes Billy and Veronica planned, but she knew of no way out. There was another reason Becky stayed in her room laying low- she was suspicious that Billy was planning her murder just as she was planning his.

When the time came for the job that evening, Billy did remember her, and Becky drove without saying a word. At first, everything went as planned. Becky drove the jeep, and Veronica went into the house with Billy. To help make the police presence scarce, in the neighborhood in which they were pulling the job, Billy phoned in a disturbance call across town. At ten minutes to midnight, Billy and Veronica casually walked up the driveway and around the house and into the back yard. Becky parked the car several blocks away in the parking lot of a nearby Indian casino where her red jeep became lost in a myriad of cars coming and going. She thought about just driving off and leaving Billy and Veronica to their own devices, but she could not bring herself to abandon her sister. Then too, what would she do with her life if she left Billy and Veronica? She had no other life, no where to run. All Becky had, in the world, was a troubled sister and a highly sharpened shim.

The burglary was too simple. Billy found the side door unlocked, and he and Veronica simply walked into the kitchen of the old couple's home. All was quiet, and the home was neat as a pin. The carpet was spotless and had even recently been vacuumed as if the lady of the house had backed out the door with the vacuum. On the walls were amateur paintings of the beach and a dozen grandchildren's photos.

"This is too good to be true," he said. "You wait here, Veronica. Rut around in the cabinets, and see if they have any booze. I'll case the joint, and we'll have a couple drinks when I'm done." He took her in his arms and pulled her close. "Then.., you know."

"Girls don't rut."

Veronica heard the sounds of Billy rutting around, though, and in just a few short minutes, he returned to the kitchen with his pockets stuffed. "Jewelry," he said, "and cash hidden in the dresser drawer beneath the socks. How unique."

He placed his loot on the kitchen counter and took a long pull off a bottle of Peron that Veronica had discovered. Then he took Veronica into his arms. "Too easy," he told her. "Way too easy." With wanton passion, he kissed her and crushed her tight against his body. "Way, way too easy!"

Then he slapped her.

Veronica was so shocked, at the slap, that she fell over backwards onto the kitchen floor barely catching herself by an elbow. She didn't understand? But, then, how could she? By definition, if Billy's conduct could be understood it would not be insanity. She watched, from the floor, afraid to rise as he gulped more of the tequila spilling some down his chest like a pirate in an old black and white movie.

"It was too easy!"

"Huh?" she whined. She held the side of her face where he had hit her. "All I said, was that girls don't rut!"

In a heartbeat, before she could move to get up, Billy was on her. He straddled her like a cowboy cinching a calf in a rodeo. She was pressed onto the hard, cold tiles. He pinned her arms to her sides with his knees and took another shot from the tequila bottle. Then, he casually slapped her… Then, he slapped her again. "It's not… exciting! Make… it… exciting!" He threw the bottle, and his hands went about her neck. Slowly, he began to choke her with slight pressure at first… then more… and more.

Her eyes were large in terror. Then they grew a lot larger.

Later, the two of them walked outside as Becky drove up in response to Billy's cell phone call. As always, Veronica and Billy got into the back seat. Billy was fairly jumping with excitement. His eyes were blurry from the tequila, and his smell was something special. Becky noticed that for the first time after a burglary Veronica was not jubilant and excited but was silently crying.

As Becky drove them away from the house, Billy reached into his bag and brought out a stunning multi-studded diamond necklace and proudly put it around Veronica's neck. At first, she made a move to pull away from him, as if she were afraid, but when her eyes made out the sparkling of the diamonds, and as she realized that Billy was putting it around her neck, she acquiesced. Her eyes lit up, and her fingers caressed the necklace where it hung around the front of her neck and dropped onto her chest. "Oh, it is so lovely!" She sat up tall in the back seat, so Becky could see the necklace in the rear-view mirror. "See what he gave me! See what he gave me!" She was like a little girl showing off that daddy liked her better.

Becky was suspicious. After the tears, she thought Veronica was doing a little bit too good a job of trying to sound excited.

As she drove the jeep back towards Pacific City, Becky watched in the rear-view mirror. She watched very carefully. After a few minutes, Veronica ceased jumping up and down with excitement and bouncing on the car seat. Becky saw Billy's hands all over her sister, and Becky saw a tear roll down Veronica's cheek.

Becky decided, for the last time; she would kill him. She didn't know how. She didn't know when. But even though he threw a large wad of money over the front seat to her, she swore under her breath. She would kill him…. Soon.

Chapter Five

The next morning while Billy was sleeping in, the two girls finally had time for a talk. Veronica explained to Becky what happened on the kitchen floor during the burglary the night before. "I don't quite understand. He slapped me, and then he started choking me. First he loved me. Then he hated me. Then he loved me? When he began choking me, I..,"

"Choking you!"

"I don't mind telling you that I was pretty scared."

"I'm going to kill him." It was a simple statement for Becky. A statement of fact. She said it quietly and calmly, as if she were telling Veronica that she was going to the store after bread. "Soon."

Veronica shot a quick and fearful glance over her shoulder to the bedroom where Billy was asleep. "Oh, don't even think it! I don't want him killed, Becky. I just want him to be a nicer man."

Becky looked at her sister with pity and whispered "It's the only way. He will never be a nice man."

Becky took out her shim and waved it into the air as if cutting someone's throat in a pirate movie. "On the other hand, maybe it's the same thing. That man will only be a nice guy when he is dead! Maybe the only nice man *is* a dead man!"

Veronica burst into tears and Becky halted her theatrics. She let Veronica cry for a few minutes and then guided her back to the story about the night before.

Veronica's voice began a dull monotonous drone as if she were recounting a dream. "His eyes were weird. They started out small and beady and then seemed to grow. He hated me. He wanted to kill me. Then he loved me. I think hate, and love, and lust get all confused in his head."

"Well.., yeah! But not in yours, huh, sis?" shouted Becky.

The two girls sneaked outside and sat on an ancient bench as far away from the home as they could. Just out of their sight over a sand dune was the ocean. They could hear the pounding of the surf as it broke against Cape Kiwnada cliff, the same cliff where Mel and Peggy Richards had spent the night away with the black light gathering evidence, the same cliff where Becky had seen Mayfield Commers murdered.

"I am confused by all this, Becky," confessed Veronica. "When we first met Billy, he was just a nice guy. Then we found out he was a thief and a bank robber. He makes money at it, and we both know it has been a long time since any man took care of us; so we let it slide. I don't know what I did wrong the other night at the robbery to ruin it for him? I have no idea what I did to make him hit me?"

Becky was dumfounded. She just looked at her sister long and hard. Becky thought she might be hearing Veronica's life breaking on the shoals of Billy's insanity. To not recognize evil for evil but to try to make some sense of it, to find a rationalization for it, to misunderstand it as normal, and then to project the cause of the evil as one's own personal down falling was.., well.., crazy. Becky lacked the words, lacked a sufficient vocabulary. She lacked the ability to communicate with her sister, to explain about Billy's insanity. Veronica could not face reality; but her sister, Becky, could, and she possessed the ability to make a decision. Other than the shim, it was just about all that Becky did have. In the end, it was that decision that saved everybody.

Becky was too nervous to sit in one place. She stood up and casually plucked a blackberry from a nearby bush. Her knee kept bouncing up and down when she tried to sit still, and she thought that standing and picking a berry, while trying to look nonchalant, might be a smart idea, especially if Billy was watching; the two of them in the garden might just look, to Billy, like two girls having a harmless sister-to-sister chat, instead of a plot to commit murder.

"Tell me more about what happened last night? When you got in the car your face was all red, and you were crying. You tried to put on a good face. But I knew he scared you."

"Scares me? He frightens me! But he turns me on like nobody has ever turned me on!"

"Last night the back door to that house was open, and there was plenty of cash, and jewelry, and booze. It was too easy for him. He likes to break glass or figure a smart way in. He loves the challenge of it all. We always make love inside the houses we rob. He might have a head problem about that?"

"You think!" Becky blurted out. She wanted to cry but found herself with a wry little smile, instead. She turned from Veronica back to the berry bushes, so her sister would not see. She smiled because she knew the answer. She had found the solution that her sister would never understand. She knew what she would do. She just didn't know where or when.

"So, he slapped me around a little.., you know, just to get his excitement going."

"You said that, Veronica!"

Becky reached around to her back pocket and again pulled out her small knife. The handle grips had broken partially off sometime before she found it, so the knife was thin and easy to conceal under her shirt. She held it up to the sun and looked at the blade.

"What are you, really, going to do with that?" asked Veronica.

"Kill him!"

Becky looked at the blade for a few seconds admiring the light as it reflected off the razor-like edge. Then she placed the knife back into its thin sheath in her pocket and pulled her shirt down over the handle. Then she remembered Billy and was afraid that he might be watching from the house. She regretted having pulled out the knife to show Veronica. But showing it to Veronica made no difference at all, she told herself; it was a forgone conclusion what she would do with the knife. Becky doubted, however, that Veronica would ever understand. Becky knew that she would kill Billy no matter what her sister thought.

"What else happened in the house we robbed last night?" Becky asked.

"That's just it, Sis," Veronica whispered. "I don't mind getting knocked around a little bit. But he choked me, and I thought he was going to really kill me. I was really scared."

The two girls talked and cried and cried and talked the way some girls will. In the end, Veronica decided on nothing, only to let things ride for a while. It would be a day or two before Billy would plan another robbery. By then, maybe something would turn up.

It would.

Just before Veronica went back inside, Becky told her about meeting Buck on the beach. She told Veronica some of the highlights and left out the parts that might send Billy right over the edge. "You would have really liked that guy who took the dog."

Veronica shot a quick eye towards the house where Billy was sleeping and then turned back towards Becky. "You did what?"

"Yeah, I know," Becky answered. "I know. Billy said not to go to the beach. Billy said not to meet anyone. Billy said! Billy said!"

"Yeah, well.., you know, Becky, that he gets a little bit excited when you do things he warns against."

"It wasn't like that, Veronica."

"Tell me, sis? How was it not like that?"

"He was a nice man."

Veronica rolled her eyes. "Oh yeah! Like you or I would know a nice man when we meet one? He wasn't dead, was he?"

Becky looked into Veronica's eyes and waited for her to calm down and realize that she was being serious. "He was different." She raised her hand to stop her sister's objections.

"He wasn't like dad! He was like dad was supposed to be.., like all the dads in the old black and white movies. He looked like a kind man. He helped a wounded dog."

"I see," was all Veronica said. She was remembering their father. And their uncles. And their brothers.

"Do you think, Veronica," asked Becky, "if there really are kind and honest men; I mean.., honest even with women?"

"No," replied Veronica.

Becky tossed a berry away and began slapping angrily at the bushes with a stick. "I want to see him again… I am not sure what he is."

They both walked back towards the mobile home. Veronica stopped her sister just out of earshot of the home. "Watch his hands, sis."

"No. It's not like that," Becky replied. "It's not like a boy friend. He's just a nice guy who was kind and… and… wise. I think he's married."

"Married?"

"Pretty sure."

"Stay away from married men," warned Veronica.

"Veronica!" Becky answered. "When did *you* ever stay away from married men?"

Rob and Peggy pulled up in front of Uncle May's beach front house on Shore Drive, in Pacific City. It was a two-story shake house on a dead-end street only two houses away from the back door to the Pelican Pub and was painted the nearly obligatory gray with white trim to match the beach scene.

Rob reminisced. It was the perfect house for a gregarious man like Mayfield Commers. Inside the house, or on the beach, May would spend his days painting on canvas never minding the constant and frequent interruptions from a surfer, beach comber, or neighbor. May never kept track of time, or days. He would just as soon set his brush down and talk, if the conversation was pleasant and interesting. Life was long, he was fond of saying, and there was always time to create. He was wrong about that, of course, for his time to create was cut short. His home was, arguably, the beach center of Pacific City and the comings and goings were many. The coffee was always on, and the beer was always cold.

In actuality, the Pub was probably city central, but May's home, only being two doors down, was adopted as part and parcel. It helped when May put in a solar-paneled outdoor shower with hot and cold water. It was May's way of giving something back to the community. The surfers became instant friends with May… and his shower.

Arriving in town in a rush and running toward the waves, the surfers never had a moment to chat. They would hurriedly nod with excitement and run down the sand carrying their heavy boards. After a long time in the water, however, they were content to dawdle in the hot water of the outdoor shower or sit in May's kitchen shivering over a hot cup of coffee. If they wanted to talk he would oblige. Sometimes several surfers would be warming themselves over coffee and May would just sit and sketch, listening all the while to the conversation but joining in sparingly. He knew not to intrude into the conversation too much; he was aware that there are two types of people in life, and May was not a surfer. The surfers appreciated him and admired him, but he would never be one of them. He had made peace with that fact. They could not paint.

Rob sat for a few minutes in Peggy's car hesitant to go into the house for the first time after May's death. Never again would he find May inside with a smile and a wave. Always, he had smelled faintly of oil paint, and as Rob remembered it now, he doubted if May had one single shirt or pair of pants without a splotch of paint. "Hazards of warfare, my friend," May would say. "Hazards of warfare."

That was how May always spoke of his work, as if the painting was a struggle. His paintings, for the most part, exuded peace and tranquility, but belied the struggle and the fight to pull out of each canvas, and a few ounces of paint, the scene locked up inside. It was a labor of love, but a labor, nonetheless, to finally discover in each canvas a tranquil scene to make a person sigh or remark that the painting brought back that feeling of the sea, of salt in the air, of gulls on the wing, of... a vacation at the ocean. To capture that feeling was the center of May's life. It was for what he had lived.

As difficult a loss as it was for Rob, it was doubly so for Peggy, for she had been May's confidant and lover. For two years, she had looked at his house as sanctuary from the storms of life, and she looked at May as her best friend. She had wanted more than the deep friendship they shared, but somehow it never developed. Now, suddenly, her chance was gone, ripped from her and cut off with no way to get it back. If she thought, even for a moment, that Rob was responsible for May's death there would not be a chance for their relationship, but she was utterly convinced that Rob had nothing to do with the murder of Mayfield Commers. And she dearly wanted her chance at a relationship with Rob.

Finally, Rob broke the trance that had captured the two of them. "I am a little surprised that the house has not been sealed off by the police. I'm surprised that we can just go in."

"Why do you find that strange?" asked Peggy. "It is your house now."

"I suspect that it is the beach, Peggy? Everything (including the police department) is a little behind the times, or slow, or maybe just what you would call laid back. If this was Seattle, they would have yellow police tape all around the house and an officer guarding the door. Since there was a murder, this house would be cordoned off to preserve any possible evidence inside." He waved his hand at Peggy's objections. "I know. I know. The murder happened way up on the cliff, so what does the house have to do with it? Plenty. Maybe? Maybe nothing at all? That is just the problem; nobody is sure if this house might be connected or have vital evidence concerning May's murder even if the murder happened elsewhere. Nobody knows! That is the problem. In a big-city department the house would be sealed until the case was further developed. For in truth, this house and the secrets inside, could be vital to the investigation."

"But the police are confused about that," Peggy replied. "Half the cops I have spoken to think there was no crime. The other half think you are a murderer."

Rob opened the car door. "I guess the reason the house is not sealed off doesn't matter right this minute. So, let's go in and get started. Now, how to get in?"

Peggy's emotions finally broke down as they approached the front door, and the tears welled up. "I don't have a key. For two years I loved that man, and I don't even have a key to his house!"

"I didn't know you loved him, Peggy," said Rob as tenderly as he knew, but he was out of practice. Way out. "I knew you were close, but I didn't think you were really in love." She turned her head and without a fair warning looked deep into Rob's eyes. He held her gaze, but just. "That's just it. I wanted to be in love with him. I think he wanted to be in love with me. It just… never happened. You hear about people being committed to each other. Is commitment what is left over when the love is gone? Or is that what happens when love never arrives in the first place?"

Rob dropped his gaze and pretended to be busy looking for a key. He didn't know the answers to questions like that. Ask him about the working parts of an M16 assault rifle, or, for that matter, the working parts of a sentence, but don't ask him about love and commitment. He had tried them both and had been found wanting. Still, here he was in a strange town flirting with both. He wasn't sure if one could commit without loving. He knew, for a fact, that you could not love without committing.

Admitting her failure with May seemed to make things worse for Peggy, and her chest began lifting and falling in huge sobs. "Oh, Rob! May is dead!" She turned away and walked down the street towards the pub.

Rob watched Peggy walk away and liked it too much. His feelings towards Peggy bothered him; it was if he was taking advantage of his uncle's death. Well.., maybe bother was too big a word, he admitted. Peggy was an extremely attractive woman. His uncle was dead, after all, and Peggy had been his uncle's friend, and Peggy was his friend, and he had been his uncle's friend, and.., well, friends should take care of friends, and… Rob decided that he could sure use a nice cold beer and wondered if there were any in the fridge. He went back to looking for a key.

When Peggy returned, her sobs had subsided, and Rob put a tentative arm around her shoulder with about as much tenderness as putting an arm around a telephone pole. He was afraid to actually hold her. The last time he had done that he'd had to leave town.

After a while, she quieted enough to talk again. "We were committed to each other. I lived in my apartment in Lincoln City, and he lived here, but we both spent a lot of time at each other's place. I don't think either of us would have been with another lover. We were committed but not in love. Does that make sense?"

Rob's eyes were looking all around trying to stay busy intentionally trying to keep distracted without her knowing. He tried the multiplication tables. It was duplicity, he knew, but it was also self-preservation; he was supposed to be looking for clues to his uncle's death not putting the make on his uncles touch.

"Does it make sense, Rob?"

He tried thinking about her question, and then realized he didn't really know what Peggy's question was. "I dunno. In a way… Yeah. Pretty much."

Peggy twisted her body so that he was forced to hold her tightly against his chest. "Huh..? What.., Rob? That makes sense to you?"

Her question and sudden closeness demanded that he be more attentive and responsive, but he just hadn't heard her question. Nonetheless, he took another stab. "I don't know, Peggy. It's… quite a bit beyond Cop 101, you know. I have met couples that.., well, like.., have that problem."

Peggy pulled her head away from Rob's shoulder to again look deep into his eyes.

"And..," he continued- diving in even deeper, "you know.., they can lead very happy and fulfilling lives.., nonetheless.., like."

She continued to stare into his eyes, but it was like trying to read a freeway sign with no lettering. As she looked into his eyes her head craned up exposing the soft whiteness of her neck.

That did not help Rob. "But I, of course, would not want to live like that," he tried. He had not a clue.

She turned away and wiped a sniffling nose. "Well, we were happy when we were together, but I was certainly not fulfilled. Perhaps May was. That kind of thing was easier for him. He had his paintings, and his collections, and he was always musing about this and that." She looked up and down the street. "Perhaps there was never a man more involved with his neighbors and community. He loved people, and he was always caught up in anyone with a problem. "I don't know, Rob." she added. "Do you think May was more like a father than a lover?"

"*They put people in jail for that,*" he thought, but he sure didn't even think of verbalizing that… not for a second. "Well…"

They tried the house doors only to find them locked. Finally, the only option left to them was an open second story window, so lugging a heavy ladder from the carport, he made the climb. Luckily for him the window did not have a screen. He crawled right in the open window, but the rough sill on the vinyl window chaffed the palm of his left hand.

"May always left that window open," Peggy called up to the window. She could no longer see Rob. "He loved the fresh air, and with the tree so close no one from the street could see that the window was open. He always left the window just wide open. Every time I closed it, he opened it."

Rob popped his head out the window and leaned his right hand on the sill for balance. Again, the vinyl sill tore at his flesh. He looked at his hands, plucked quickly at a wood sliver, and mumbled something about getting old and tearing both his hands just climbing in a window.

He looked down at Peggy and smiled. "What did you say? What about the screen?"

"You don't need a screen here at the beach," she replied. "There are few bugs, and people come to the beach to get as much fresh air as possible."

"Not the guy next door," Rob said, rubbing his hands where they had chaffed on the window sill. "The people next door have their window shut." He thumbed directly across at the next house and Peggy's gaze followed.

Rob looked at the distance from May's to the neighbor's house and estimated it at no more than five feet. "I wouldn't want to live that close to someone else."

"Why?" she called up. She felt foolish calling to a man in an upstairs window.

"You could hear everything that happened."

"Nothing happens, there," she replied in a loud whisper. "He's single."

"Well, he could hear everything that happened, here," Rob answered. As soon as Rob verbalized that foopah, he was glad that she hadn't heard it.

Peggy knew her way around the kitchen and started coffee while Rob explained where they should start their investigation. "The first thing we have to do is try to figure out *why* May was killed. If we can figure out a motive, then all we have to do is start eliminating everyone who could not profit from his killing or whoever has a great alibi. Whoever is left is the killer. It's basic police science, academy stuff. She appeared impressed, so he went on. "That's not where we should start, here, though. Well, maybe it is, but there is something else that probably fits in the scheme of things, so we don't have to begin so blindly."

"Yes?" she answered. "What else do you have that fits into the scheme of things?" It was the way she drew out the word, "Yess", that made him turn away from her to face the picture window to the beach.

"We don't really have to start out cold. That's our edge. It's the reason I came to Pacific City, yesterday."

Peggy opened the frig door for the coffee and water. "I am still not sure why you *left* Pacific City so quickly last summer? You left pretty fast after the barbecue. And you stayed away six months!"

Rob came back from the window and sat down on one of the bar stools at the counter. He watched her pour the water into the coffee maker. How she could manage to make pouring water into a coffee pot something suggestive, was beyond him. She stopped without putting the water jug down and turned to look at him. She didn't say a word, she just looked at him and held that jug.

"Back to the point," added Rob. May called last week and said that he had something special to show me. He said it was very important."

Peggy slammed the jug onto the counter. "He wanted to show *you* something important! How about *me*?"

"Well, actually Peggy, he said he had something to show us both."

"Sure!" She said wiping at spilled water. "I know he didn't say that. But thanks."

"Peggy," Rob said very quietly, "I know how hard all this is on you… well, maybe I know. I've never been a woman. But, look here, you are going to have trouble separating your emotional side from this investigation? This will be very difficult. Are you sure you want to go on with it?"

Peggy started scooping coffee very quietly. The lid dropped with a plop, and she flipped the switch. They both watched the light turn red as if it was something to behold. Neither of them spoke for a few minutes as the coffee started boiling and then filling the carafe, below.

"I hope I can do that, Rob. I will try. But how, in the world, do I not take this personally?"

After a few moments, she sighed with resignation. "OK. What about this special thing May wanted to show you? Maybe that is the motive, like you said?"

"Sure. Good place to start. Wish I'd thought of it. Any ideas? He wouldn't tell me what the special thing was, but he was sure excited about it."

"Nope. He didn't tell me, either," answered Peggy. "But then, everything was so exciting for him! He would get excited about the view, excited about the ocean, excited about his most recent project or new painting. He got excited a lot."

Peggy's eyes gleamed a little, and she shot Rob a little teasing look and then looked away. "He could control his excitement a little better than you." She whispered it just loud enough for Rob to hear but not so loud that her words were distinct.

"Huh?" He gulped at his coffee.

Peggy turned to face him full on. She took a deep breath, a very deep breath. "Where would you like to start?"

Rob rubbed his palms together but was afraid that if he said anything his voice might crack.

"What would you *like* to do?" she repeated.

Rob rubbed his palms together, slower.

"Then," Rob stammered, "we begin by just looking around the house."

"What do we look for?" She breathed again. Very deeply.

"Now, cut that out, Peggy!"

"What?"

Rob stood, and then he changed his mind and sat down again on a bar stool. "We have a lot of very difficult work to do, and we must concentrate. Solving a murder is not an easy job. If we can't work together.., really work together.., then we will have to work separately."

Peggy gave Rob such an innocent look. Then she turned sideways, took a deep breath and held it.

"Can we work together, Peggy?"

She gave up… and exhaled. "OK. We solve a murder. We solve us later. Where do we begin on the murder?"

"You would be the best judge of that, Peggy," answered Rob quite relieved. "We are looking for anything different, anything out of place, anything unusual."

Peggy pulled up a lower stool in front of Rob's taller bar stool, and took his hands in hers. "What's wrong with your hands?"

The sight of her in front of him, like that, did odd things to Rob's sense of chivalry. "Huh? Oh, nothing. I just rubbed them climbing in the window."

"Sure, big strong man." She turned them over towards the light. "See, here is a wood sliver."

Before he could do much objecting she had tweezers out of her purse and was performing surgery. He winced a little, and she teased him relentlessly. "Big boy! Big strong policeman! See, here is a big bad sliver… Ooh! That must be a quarter of an inch long! How awful! Ohhh. It's as big as a tree! Sliver me timbers!"

Rob sucked on the palm of his hand. "It's shiver me timbers."

"OK," she answered, "But be careful for what you ask."

They searched the entire house, and the two of them shared an eerie feeling going from room to room through May's things. They felt like they were prying- that at any moment, May might come through a doorway and demand their business with his private things. Obviously, May had not figured on dying the day he climbed the cliff, so things were just casually left lying around. He had expected to simply come home from painting and take his nephew to dinner at the Pelican. But May never came home. He never would. The thought of that reality hit Rob like an echo lingering in the shadows and behind every door.

"You know, Peggy," yelled Rob to her from the next room, "he was awfully excited about his big surprise. To ask me down from Seattle whatever it was had to be something more than his usual excitement at finishing a painting. But I just can't figure it?"

She didn't answer. She hadn't spoken much since they climbed the stairs to May's bedroom and his art studio in the next room. Rob began humming to try to alleviate the heavy mood that had fallen, but he could hear Peggy throwing things and banging around in the bedroom. The only tune he could think of was, "*My Boyfriend's Back*". But he sure couldn't hum that one.

After a while, they gave up their search of the upstairs and walked downstairs, again, to the living room where Rob walked over and stood staring at the fireplace. "I don't know? This fireplace mantel may be a little weird? It is the only thing remotely different that I can see. Last time I was here, it was just crammed full of photos, and it had a large painting right in the middle of the mantel shelf. But now, the mantle is empty and doesn't have a single thing on it. It looks like it was cleaned off for something?" He turned to smile at Peggy. "Something special? It has been cleaned off for something special.., something special that is missing!"

Peggy walked up and stood next to him, very much next to him. "Usually, Sherlock, there are a couple small mementos, or May's most recent painting on this mantle. He liked to look at new paintings for a week, or so, before sending them out. Your picture, Rob, was always here on the right, and sometimes he would put a picture up of May and me next to yours. The mantle changed often. He might have just cleaned it off in preparation for a new painting he had completed."

Rob had a feeling they were on to something, but what? "Yes, but there is no newly-completed painting. There is nothing new in this living room or in his studio; there is nothing that we can find that seems to be destined for this mantle. If this mantel was his showplace for special works, then where is that special work?"

Peggy flopped down on the couch across from the fireplace. "I don't know, Rob. Maybe it was here, but it was stolen?"

Rob went to the kitchen for a couple coffee warm ups and returned to sit next to Peggy. As he handed Peggy her cup, their fingers accidentally touched, and neither pulled back very quickly. Their eyes met.

"So, why *did* you run back to Seattle?"

"Let's go with that thought about something stolen," he answered. "If someone stole a painting, or something else special off the mantel, why kill Uncle May? Why not just take it and be gone?"

"Good point," replied Peggy. It was growing increasingly difficult for Peggy to concentrate on their mission. She realized that she was sitting too close to Rob, but she did not move, and neither did Rob. There was electric static in the air, and Peggy contemplated Rob and her together, alone, on the couch…and realized she was there already. They were, both of them, on the couch.., and except for the ghost of Mayfield Commers they were alone. She shook her head to try to clear her thoughts and was relieved when there was a knock on the front door. The knock was followed by a loud bark.

That bark was like music to Peggy's ears! She knew who was at the door and ran screaming with glee. "It's Spark. He's come home!! It's Spark. He's back!"

Mel was standing at the door in his civilian clothes doing his best to hold Spark's leash, but he was loosing the battle. Finally, he just let go when Peggy fell to her knees and wrapped her arms around the faithful Irish Setter. But she could not hold the dog. Spark broke away and scurried quickly through the kitchen barking with pleasure. Then he bounded up the stairs and searched every room in the house letting the leash bounce on each step going up and each step going down.

Mel finally caught up to Spark and freed him from his tether. "He's looking for May," he said.

Then he spoke to the dog. "You won't find him here, boy." But Mel's words failed to stop the dog. The three of them watched as Spark went dashing, again, from room to room until he finally exhausted himself of the search and snuggled into his bed in the corner of the living room by the front picture window. Spark gave a slight whimper and hung his head over the side of the whicker basket. His head would jerk, and his eyes would dash about every few seconds when he heard a noise in the room.

"I guess this is your house, now, Rob," said Mel. "You are the only heir."

"It's a good house," admitted Rob.

"I like it. It's comfy," said Peggy. She snuggled her back into the couch, tipped her head back and closed her eyes. Mel gave her a slow look.

"Waterfront property is at a premium, so these houses scrunch together to save space," put in Mel. "Setbacks are only two and a half feet, so that makes a total of five feet between the houses. On the positive side, it's only two doors from the Pelican. Your neighbors may be close, but you will never be out of cold beer."

"Two doors from the Pelican. You are right, Mel. That clinches it!" He laughed. "I'm going to live here," Rob announced. "I like this house. I wish I had moved here earlier when Uncle May was still alive. I'll vacate my apartment on Lake Washington and move in here."

"That's a good idea," said Mel, "because you also inherited a dog, and he likes it in Pacific City."

Mel looked at Peggy. She had her head back with her eyes closed. One eye opened and turned to Mel. "Don't call me a dog, Mel."

They all had coffee with a little rum to warm themselves against the coolness of the room. They talked of the house, the beach, Uncle May, and his unfailing sense of humor and his practical jokes. There were long periods of silence when no one spoke.

"Remember the time May changed the signs outside of town and the tourists just kept driving around and around in circles following the detour signs?" Peggy just laughed and laughed to tears. "It must have taken him an hour to change the signs, but he thought the joke was worth it. The city council, however, was livid!"

Mel looked at the floor until Peggy quit laughing. "The door was my favorite."

"The door?" asked Rob. "I don't know about the door."

"He painted the bathroom door to look like it was open, so that when someone went to walk into the bathroom they would bump into the door. It looked open, but it was closed. Then, when they were finished in the bathroom and turned to leave the room, they were startled by the other side of the door; he had painted a full-sized portrait of himself looking over the top of his glasses as if he had been watching the whole time they were in the bathroom! It was hilarious!"

Peggy's eyes wandered towards the head of the stairs. "Oh, he was funny.., sometimes."

Rob decided to just blurt out his secret. "He was still alive when I climbed out of the water and up next to him on the ledge!" The abrupt news was like a hammer on a steel hull. No one moved. No one spoke. It was as if Rob's voice echoed against a brick wall.., and the wall cracked. "For just a second, he opened his eyes, and I think he smiled in recognition. He didn't say anything. Then his eyes just clouded over, and he was gone. I… didn't know how to tell you."

For a long while they sat and stared out the window at the blue sky and surf trying to comprehend Rob's revelation. Peggy's eyes were tearing up when finally Spark whined, and, as one, they turned to gaze at the dog.

"Spark!" growled Mel imitating Uncle May's voice. "Remember how May used to just go off when anyone would call that dog Sparky?" They all laughed. "It would bring tears to your eyes!"

"No. No. No. Let me do it?" begged Rob. He made his voice raspy and harsh. "Sparky would be the name of a firefighter's dog. This dog hates firefighters! Chews 'em up! My nephew, THE COP, gave me this dog when it was just a little puppy. His name is Spark! He's a cop's dog!"

"Oh, yeah!" chimed in Peggy laughing a little giggle and wiping an errant tear. "I will never forget! He used to frighten children with that. But, it didn't make any difference at all; when they made Spark the Grand Marshall of the Pacific City Children's Day Parade, the banners all read Sparky. May just could not win."

Spark whined pitifully and trotted up the stairs. They watched the dog until it was beyond the top stair and out of sight. Then Rob spoke into his coffee. "It'll take a couple days, and then Spark will quit looking for May. He'll just become resigned to his loss. I have seen dogs go through this before. They adjust, but it often takes a few days. It'll take longer for me...us. When my younger brother died, his dog sat on the stairs by the front door waiting for him to return. For three days, the dog remained at his post and then, finally, just got up and walked off.

"Spark will be OK, but it might take a while."

Rob cleared his throat. "So, back to the task at hand. Where do we start to solve this murder? Any suggestions, Mel? You are the reigning expert police officer, here."

"Well, let's see," Mel replied, "there is a quarter million in life insurance. We did an A search, and you are the only benefactor, Rob."

"I make a good suspect."

"Then..,"

Rob interrupted him. "But did you check into my current assets, Mel?"

"No...What do you have other than that old Toyota truck you drive?"

Rob stood up and went to the picture window. For a few seconds, he stood with his back to Peggy and Mel. Then he turned to face them both. He wore his most sober expression. "I shouldn't be a suspect because of the inheritance. One of the things May appreciated was that he was absolutely sure I was not after his money, that I did not care a wit about his fortune, that my affection for him was genuine."

Peggy just looked at him. "Huh? What's this about?" She looked at Mel, but he just shrugged.

"It's not my first inheritance," answered Rob. "I'm pretty well off. I sure don't need May's fortune."

Mel did not look convinced. "Yes, but..."

"Mel, I'm a millionaire... couple times over, actually."

Peggy's second, "Huh?", was louder than her first. "You are a what?"

"And it's mostly liquid, not just paper money. Peg," he said, "I've a couple million. It's hard to say just how much. Not that there has never been a millionaire murderer, before, but it's just that I have too much money already. I don't want any more money. If the District Attorney examines my lifestyle, he will see that I don't spend. I don't have the need or the desire for more. I am not a gambler, and my vices are few. I'm kind of boring, actually. I write novels. And.., I write novels."

Peggy tried to take a sip of her coffee but spilled it onto her white blouse. The spill turned her blouse nearly transparent, but she did not seem to notice.

Mel noticed.

"Your truck is five years old, and... and... and you

wear the cheapest shoes!" she nearly shouted.

"That's it, exactly," emphasized Rob. "My truck is five years old, and it runs perfectly. So why should I buy a new one? When it does break, I will have it repaired and then drive it another hundred thousand miles, or give it away to someone who needs a truck. Then, I will purchase a newer truck for myself."

Peggy just looked at Rob until Rob, finally, felt self-conscious enough to sit back down. But he sat across the room in a single chair in order to face both of them. "It's like this," he said, "I know a couple in Seattle who have a decent sized family house in the Queen Ann neighborhood. They told me, recently, that they are planning to buy a larger home just up the street.

The room was quiet for a few seconds as Mel and Peggy tried to understand where Rob was going with his illustration. "Yes?" said Peggy sopping at her spilled coffee. "Do they need a truck?"

Rob smirked at her. "I advised them not to buy another home. All they do, now, is watch TV all evening and then go to bed."

"Huh?" mused Mel with a small sideways smile at Rob. He didn't take his eyes off Peggy rubbing the coffee deeper into her blouse.

"I told them to purchase a big-screen TV."

"Huh?" mused Peggy trying to figure it out. She stopped rubbing the coffee stain and returned Mel's stare.

"Well, it's the television they watch all evening. What difference does it make what kind of house you live in if all you do is sit and watch TV? Television looks the same in a small house or a large one."

Mel continued to stare.

"I see," said Peggy. She made big bug eyes at Mel and then looked back to Rob. "So, the District Attorney will see that you don't have huge gambling debts, a Leer Jet, or a harem of beautiful women and will conclude that money would not be your motive for murder?" She was staring at Rob with something akin to wonder- or confusion. She, pretty much, had the same look on her face that Mel had on his. "Is that right, Rob?" she asked.

"What's wrong with my shoes?"

Peggy didn't answer Rob, but she looked, again, at Mel. His fascination with the spilled coffee was becoming annoying. Mel offered her another paper towel, and a leer. She took neither.

"Yeah. That's about right, Peggy," said Mel, answering for Rob. "But still, it is a sizable amount of money in May's estate."

Peggy continued to allow Mel to hold the offered paper towel in the air.

"He did not leave anything to anyone else. Did he, Mel?" she asked. "Nothing, to anyone else? Right?"

Mel dropped the paper towel and just let it float away. "Nope. Everything goes to his only living relative, Rob Smith."

"Yep," said Rob. "I am the only benefactor. I make a great suspect?"

"May had savings," added Mel. "May had many assets."

"I am still the suspect. You are doing real good by me, Mel!"

"His painting inventory…" Mel's eyes scanned the living room walls. "There must be twenty paintings in this room, alone, and they are all worth over a thousand dollars each. You are quite an outstanding suspect, Rob. You are the only one who stood to gain from May's death. You were on the cliff when he was killed. You have a motive, and you had opportunity. Without motive who else would kill him? Without opportunity who else could? Who else would be motivated to kill May? You should have stayed in Seattle."

Peggy stuck her tongue out at Mel.

Rob looked down at his shoes, up to Peggy, and then

to Mel. "That's the key… I know it is. Motivation," replied Rob. "Someone else profited. But how? Who? Let's start by taking an inventory of all of May's paintings. We should do that anyway."

"That's the easy part," put in Peggy. "He kept a book of each and every painting he ever made. Each painting has a color copy, the date it was painted, and the date it was sold. If it did not sell, he has the gallery in which it is currently hanging. About some things May was very careful."

"Great! Let's find that book," said Rob.

"First, there's something you don't know?" said Mel. "Last night there was another home invasion. Nobody was hurt. The owners were away on vacation. The house was looted. The suspects are a young man and woman seen in the driveway. They were seen getting into a red jeep."

"I have an alibi!" dead panned Rob. "I was in the hospital all beat up from my brush with the rocks at the bottom of that cliff."

Mel went on. "They wrote on the walls again."

"What was it?" Rob asked. "Go on!" he said quickly to Mel's slowness of speech.

"Well, they wrote, 'tio', again."

With a little searching, they found May's record book easy enough and went around the house matching paintings to the book. It turned into a tour of love as they relived memories of paintings and discovering new works they had never before seen, or had forgotten. They were surprised to find that Mayfield had a little known span of time when he painted only flowers, followed by a western period. For the last ten years, most all the paintings were scenes of the local beaches.

"I didn't know he was so diverse," mused Peggy.

"I grew up to him painting cowboy scenes," said Rob. "I guess, now, looking back on his paintings, he wasn't all that great an artist back then. But life and art are like that, both are a growing and changing process. After flowers, May painted cowboys. I have some of his earlier florals in Seattle. He was very talented with floral scenes, but he couldn't sell them."

"I didn't know," she said again in wonder. "I just thought he was always here in Pacific City painting landscapes?"

"Nope. His flower paintings didn't sell in Seattle, and many people thought that he must have been gay because of his subject matter. He finally gave up on the Seattle scene and ran away to the beach. Here, he found himself. Here, he became the May we all loved."

"He definitely was not gay!" put in Peggy. She let out a little giggle. Mel's head shot up.

Rob was surprised to find that one room held paintings by other artists, some framed, some not. The room was a collage of another artist's works. "What is this room, Peggy? Got any ideas?"

"It's his Matisse room," she answered. "He loved Matisse. He idolized his work." She looked around and, once again, accidentally brushed against Rob. "There are some Picassos and others, but most of these are Matisse. All of these are copies. Some of these paintings are rather poor copies, snippets out of magazines, cheap prints, copies found in galleries from all over the northwest. His one big desire was to possess a genuine Matisse."

"It is a pretty amazing room, isn't it," said Rob. "I have always been in awe of the weird working of the artist mind. It looks more like a fetish, this Matisse thing."

"How so?" asked Mel.

Rob pawed thru a pile of paintings. "Well, look around. I guess May loved the work of this guy, Matisse. But May never incorporated the Matisse style into his own beach scenes? A lot of these are of the same painting over and over again. It's like a guy's garage with naked girls on the walls. Only May's naked girls are Matisse paintings? Go figure."

Peggy lifted one particular print. "This painting was

his obsession. He desired it more than he desired... me... or any other woman. It's *The Blue Nude,* by of course, Henri Matisse."

Rob looked at the print, rotated it and looked at it upside down. "I don't get it! Why didn't he try to purchase one? I don't know, maybe there is a Matisse out there a guy could buy... if he had enough money?"

"That's the problem," said Peg. "May was well off. Well off people don't own one of these paintings: rich people do. Unless you've got a loose million, you can forget it. Besides, he didn't want just any Matisse. He wanted *The Blue Nude.* Nobody, but nobody, can afford *The Blue Nude.*"

"Well," interjected Mel, "I agree with Rob. These copies are all kind of weird, anyway."

Peggy teased. "Oh, yeah, smart guy? You should really be the one to recognize a fetish, Mel. How many guns do you own, Mr. Hot Shot Policeman?"

To Peggy, it looked as if Mel's eyes threatened to cross. He dropped his head a little and seemed to be lost in thought. "I... I don't know. Twelve, maybe thirteen."

"You don't really know, do you, Mel? You ran out of fingers and toes, didn't you?" She threw a convenient eraser from the desk at him. "Yeah. You're not weird? You don't have a fetish? But, you are right. May was an artist," Peggy added. "And artists are weird by definition."

Peggy changed the subject. "Let's go look at the local gallery in town. It's just up the street a little, and it has five or six of May's paintings. It will be good for you, Rob, to meet the gallery owners that currently hang May's work. The paintings belong to you, Rob, but to make less trouble in the future you should meet the gallery owners as soon as possible and establish your claim. Besides, the gallery owner in town, here, is your next-door neighbor. Nice guy, too. May and he were good friends."

Mel had other plans and left for Lincoln City, so just the two of them took Spark and started out the door.

The day was typical for August. The weather was unbeatable. The sand was warm. The gulls were calling.

Then everything that could go wrong- went wrong, of course. All of a sudden, and without warning, Spark shot down the street toward the pub and attacked a heavy-set man who had been trying to force his car door closed against his sleeping bags and beach paraphernalia. The attack caught Rob and Peggy so much off guard that it took them a second or two to realize what was happening and more than a few seconds to race over and stop the attack. By that time, the man had been chewed up and was on the ground bleeding.

Nearly at once, Rob had sprung into action and attempted to run down the street to, once again, save the red dog. Running was difficult for Rob since just about everything on his body still hurt, and his game leg made running difficult, in the best of times. As always, his injured leg continually made everything difficult. As always, he tried to ignore the pain. Whenever necessary, he just ran on the leg, anyway, just like he continued doing everything else in his life, with or without pain from his bad leg. It is a choice a disabled person makes, Rob groused to himself as he ran along. The choice is to surrender to the pain or to run. Sometimes, he wished he *could* surrender, for if he could surrender, he never would have jumped off the cliff. He could, given the time, recall a dozen things in his life that would have been easier if he would have just surrendered to the pain, enfolded himself in drugs, and adapted a sedentary life style. The running after Spark emphasized his limp, made him imagine he looked like Chester running after Mr. Dillon. Nontheless, Rob ran. And limped.

Peggy got there first.

It was a horrible few seconds for Rob and Peggy, who were naturally yelling at the dog to come back, don't do that, and leave the man alone. But Spark ignored their pleading.

To Rob and Peggy's horror, as they ran they helplessly watched as Spark jumped up and tried to bite the man on the back of the neck! Thankfully, Spark's leap was blocked when the car door sprang open and deflected the dog's attack. Spark turned, and, faster than Rob could believe possible, grasped the back of the man's ankle.

The man never saw the dog coming, never expected an attack. At Spark's first lunge, the man turned sensing something wrong. When Spark bit his leg, he cried out in alarm and somehow spun loose of the dog's grasp. The man turned to face Spark. Surprisingly, Spark stopped immediately when the man turned to face him. By the time Peggy reached Spark, the dog was already docile and whimpering. So quickly had the attack started- it had ceased.

Free of the dog and realizing that the attack had stopped, the fat man dropped onto his backside beside his car. His leg was bleeding, and his breath was labored from the shock of the moment and the exertion of the fight.

"Wha…wha…?" was all he could say.

Spark just went limp and continued whining pitifully. All the fight went out of him, and the old and peaceful Spark magically returned. Whimpering pitifully, he tried to crawl up next to the fat man, but Rob held him off.

Seemingly from out of nowhere, appeared another large man (larger even than the man Spark had attacked). He was carrying a towel and a first-aid kit. "I saw the attack from my office window."

Rob turned and looked where the large man had indicated. Less than a hundred feet away a small trailer had a large red banner that read, "Shoreline Properties Homes For Sale!"

Peggy yelled, and fell to her knees at the feet of the man Spark had attacked. "Buck! Thank you, Buck!" she said. Tears came to her eyes.

Buck smiled at Peggy, glanced quickly at Rob, and without another word knelt next to Peggy in front of the bitten man. "Let me look at that leg, pardner. I'm kinda good at cuts and things."

"Sure, buddy. I'll take any help I can get, here. What the hell happened?"

"We don't know," Peggy said over Buck's shoulder to the man. "This dog has never been violent at any time in his life. This is the most docile dog you have ever met!"

"Lady, I love dogs," he replied. His breath was coming in short sobbing gasps. "If you say he is peaceful, then he is peaceful. But not today, huh?"

Rob put his belt through Spark's collar and led him back to the house where he locked Spark securely in the garage and then limped back to Peggy and the fat man. Rob's leg was burning from the abuse, and he was sure that it showed. More and more, he felt like Chester and less and less, he felt like a marine or a police officer.

On Rob's return, Buck was just wrapping the man's leg in a gauze bandage.

"How is he?" Rob asked Buck, but the injured man answered for himself. "Oh, I'm all right, mister. He's just a dog, and sometimes dogs do funny things."

Buck stood up with a grunt and held out his hand to Rob. "Hi, ya. The bleeding stopped almost right away. He'll be all right."

Rob shook the large man's hand and smiled back. "Who are you?"

Peggy interrupted. "Oh, Rob! This is Buck Jensen. He's been a good friend for a long time!"

"Like I said," repeated Buck, "I saw the attack from my office. I couldn't believe it when I saw Spark jump this guy! I know Spark, and he's not that kind of animal."

"Oh. That's OK," said the bitten man, again.

"That's OK?" blurted out the surprised Peggy.

Rob was just amazed at the fat man's agreeable attitude and began explaining as best as he could. "Really, he is a very peaceful dog, but he has had a couple extremely stressful days. Please don't report this to the…"

Peggy lifted her head to the sound of a distant siren. "Oh, no! I guess somebody already called the police."

Buck pointed to the coming patrol car and picked up his things and walked off.

"Who was that masked man?" asked Rob.

Buck turned, in his retreat, and smiled, but he kept on walking.

"Listen, fella," Rob said, kneeling down and helping the fat man to his feet. "This is the dog you probably heard about on the news; the one that witnessed his master, my uncle, murdered. This dog jumped into the ocean to be with my uncle. This dog has never bitten anyone, before. It must just be the stress. Must be the stress!"

A sheriff's car pulled down the street and stopped a few yards away. Slowly a deputy opened the door and got out of the car. The deputy cautiously placed himself behind the car door and scrutinized the situation. At a quizzical look from the deputy, a tourist family pointed in unison at the fat man.

Seeing the approach of the police officer, the fat man spoke quietly to Rob. "Be careful what you say if you love that dog as much as I love mine. I'd hate for this to happen to me."

Peggy hugged him and then kissed the man on his cheek. "This *is* happening to you."

Rob and Peggy were flabbergasted when the man stood and just returned to the sorting and packing of his vacation belongings. He actually started humming a little tune.

The deputy walked up, hooked his thumbs in his duty belt, and asked what the problem was? He said that he had received a call about a dog attacking a man.

Peggy took note of the deputy. He was not a young man, past his prime, short and unkempt. She thought he looked.., well.., kind of married.

"I received a call about a mean and vicious dog attacking a man near a green car," began the deputy. "You folks know anything about that?"

Rob just shoved his hands deep into his pockets and said, "I dunno? You see a dog?" He fixed his eyes on the weathervane on top of the roof on the Pelican Pub. It was obvious, to the deputy, that he was lying, but Rob wanted it that way. He wanted the deputy to know there had been a problem, but that it was resolved, and he hoped that the deputy had a sense of humor and was a dog lover, himself. Rob wanted it obvious that he was lying, not out of spite, but because whatever had happened, here, happened among friends and was all settled; no one was challenging the deputy's authority, but that there was just no need for police intervention. It was a delicate balance between that and the deputy thinking they were uncooperative and hiding something.

The deputy looked hard at Rob for a full minute. Then he rocked on his heels. He tilted his head. "This, here's, a green car." He thought himself a funny man and added, "We are trained in such things."

"Deputy?" asked Peggy. She started to speak and then stopped. She was not sure what to say.

The deputy turned his head to look at her. His face had a quizzical look. He stared for a few seconds. "Miss Richards? From the 6 O'clock News? What about this dog attack, Miss Richards?"

Peggy, also, decided that the weathervane looked pretty impressive. "I dunno." She hooked her thumps in her waistband and rocked on her heels. As she did so, she shot Rob a quick glance and a smirk. Then she broke her gaze from Rob and smiled at the deputy. She tried to smile the way Mel would like a smile.

"What's goin' on, here?" asked the deputy. "Somebody get bit, or not?" He pointed to the fat man's ankle. "You've got a little blood on your leg, there, mister?"

The fat man looked down in mock surprise. "Oh! This? I've had this for.., oh.., for a while. It is absolutely nothing to be concerned about." He emphasized his nonchalance by turning back to his car again. The door easily swung shut with a resounding click. "There! Nothing at all to worry about, around here. If someone had been attacked by a mean, vicious dog I would have seen it."

Once again, the deputy started to object, but the fat man interrupted him, placed his thumbs in his belt, and simply said, "I dunno. And I would consider it a favor if that would be all right with you, deputy."

Rob's and Peggy's heads snapped around to the fat man. They both smiled.

The deputy started to argue and then stopped. Carefully he looked at Peggy and then Rob. "Yeah, I know… you dunno. They dunno. Everybody dunno." The deputy turned towards the family that called in the dog bite to the dispatch center, but they had moved on to more important vacation matters. "You dunno. This bitten guy dunno. Nobody is around that knows… anything. Who bit whom?"

"You see a dog, deputy?" asked Peggy.

The deputy pulled his thumbs out of his belt and started to speak. Rob could tell that it was not going to be nice, so he quickly interrupted. "Look, deputy," explained Rob, "you don't see a dog. You don't see a bite victim. You don't have any reason to take time out of your busy day and write a report. You look like a nice guy. I know that I look like a nice guy. This call looks unfounded, 10-26."

"10-26?" responded the deputy.

"He's a retired police officer," Peggy explained.

Peggy's declaration seemed to take the edge off the deputy's anger. They talked with the deputy for a few minutes and then he left for other business. He was aware of the death of Mayfield Commers, and after the first few minutes had recognized both Rob and Peggy. When he realized that his dog bite call might be part of an ongoing investigation, and when he finally became frustrated with Rob, Peggy, and the fat man giving him the, "I dunno", treatment, he threw up his hands in surrender and drove off. Obviously, he could have done more, but he was afraid to do anything that might interfere with the ongoing homicide investigation.

As the sheriff's car disappeared around the bend of the highway, Peggy turned to Rob. "Since when do you look like a nice guy?"

The fat man they took for a few cold ones at the Pelican. He was a true animal lover, and he had heard the story about Mayfield Commer's death on the news. He understood, and he was not interested in making any trouble from his end. Rob figured he had made a friend for life and gave the man his cell number in case he changed his mind or there were complications.

"Next time you come to Pacific City, don't bother to bring a sleeping bag," Rob told the fat man. "There is a room for you in my uncle's house, here. If I see you sleeping on the beach, I will be insulted. The beer is always cold, and dinner is at six. Bring a friend."

Just before the fat man stood to leave, Buck walked into the pub. The bench shook as he sat down. He nodded to the bitten man. "So, what? About three hundred pounds?"

"About," replied the bitten man. "You?"

"I'm not really tellin'," replied Buck. "I shouldn't have asked you. But, just like you, I'm a big guy, and I own up to it."

Peggy gave a shot for Buck. "Fact is," she put in, "Buck is a real big guy. Everybody knows that. But everybody loves him, anyway. And the ladies? They love this guy! You should see the women this guy gets. Why it is positively cra…"

"Peggy!" blurted Rob.

Peggy spoke at him with a laugh. "Size really matters, Rob?"

Everyone laughed. The bitten man and Buck laughed most of all.

"Well, it's like this," began Buck, "we both know we are big guys. It's no secret, and I'm kinda teasin' this guy to get on his good side." Buck smiled his best Burt Lancaster imitation. He tilted his head and bared his teeth like he was cruising for bugs at sixty without a windshield.

"That is a frightful imitation," teased Peggy.

The bitten man made his apologies, slid off the bench and stood to leave. "Folks, I'm rightfully sorry about the whole thing. I don't figure on making a big fuss over this. As far as I'm concerned, nothing much happened here. I'll stop by in a couple months and say, hi."

Not quite believing their good fortune with the big man, Peggy, Rob, and Buck watched the man leave. "Now, there, goes a genuine nice guy," said Buck.

"That's what they are going to say about you, Bucko," put in Peggy. "They are going to say that you were a nice guy, and that Rob, here, *looked* like a nice guy… in cheap shoes."

Her tease caught Rob in the middle of a sip of his beer. He spilled a little and hurriedly wiped it off his shirt front. "Hey! And.., and.., what's wrong with my shoes? Buck do you like my shoes?"

At that, Buck just looked from Rob to Peggy and back again. He didn't look at Rob's shoes. "I wouldn't know. Of course, you look like a nice guy. But you need to put on some weight."

Peggy turned to face Rob. "Buck, here, has spent many many hours at May's kitchen table."

Buck nodded. "Many's the time, May bored me to tears attacking me with tale after tale about his nephew, the cop, up in Seattleland."

Scott, the bartender, walked over to the table with another huge pint of beer… for Buck, even though he hadn't ordered it.

"Scott waits on you personally without you even ordering?" asked Rob. There was a bit of unbelief in his voice. He watched Scott walk away, and he shook his head in wonder. "He won't, usually, even talk to me. He nods, but that's about all."

Buck took about a half gallon of liquid in one long and very full pull and wiped the back of his hand across his mouth. "Yeah. He's kinda quiet. He's got one of those dry senses of humor. Quite a funny guy, though, actually."

"He just won't open up to a tourist, Rob," put in Peggy. "Many of the locals are like that. It's kind of a small-town snobbery, I guess. But really, for the locals it is more of a matter of survival."

"You'll have to forgive him, Rob," added Buck. "I will put in a word for you. I'll tell him you are a local, now. But it will take about five years for him to accept you. The locals, here, make money off tourism, but you wouldn't believe what tourists do to the locals? They get drunk, skip out on bills, forget to tip, or leave a big mess behind that the locals have to clean up. Tourists come here, party, and go home. Locals get kind of hardened to tourist's stupidity, rudeness, and big-city snobbery- so they just naturally return kind fer kind."

"You don't seem to be like that," answered Rob. "What's with you?"

"I'm a salesman. I'm a salesman through an' through. I like people. I like to make deals with people. After the sale, I'm still their best friend, or it wasn't the kind of deal in which I get involved. Besides, I am originally from Portland. I remember how difficult it was to become one of the locals." He laughed. "I had to buy half the town to become an insider."

Peggy looked at Buck with stark admiration and affection. She looked at Buck, but she spoke to Rob. "You know, Rob, there are rumors that Buck owns part of this pub."

Buck started to speak, but she was too quick for him.

"Oh, he will deny it, but it is just difficult to believe that there is something this profitable in town in which Buck doesn't own an interest."

"Whal," drawled Buck. "she's nice isn't she. She should put on some weight, though. Truth is, if it has got anything to do with houses or buildings in this town I own it, a part of it, or am making plans on it." He laughed and shook the table. "Real estate is my passion."

"The truth, is," added Peggy, "that Buck would be the mayor of Pacific City if we had one. He knows everything that happens in this town. You can't buy, rent, or sell without him knowing about it."

"Where were you when my uncle was killed?" asked Rob.

Peggy exploded onto her feet.

Buck just sat quietly and looked into Rob's eyes. After a few moments, he spoke quietly. "No. No. It's OK, Peggy.

"I was in my office collecting a monthly rent check on a mobile home I rent out. When I saw the commotion on the beach I hurried down. I got there just as they were hauling you out of the boat, Rob. I am more than sorry about your uncle, and I am not upset because you asked me about my whereabouts. I might have asked, myself, if I was in your place."

"He *looks* like a nice guy," murmured Peggy.

"Rob," continued Buck, "I am the one who picked Spark up and took him to the vet."

Peggy was surprised that Rob did not react with contrition. He just held Buck's gaze. "Thank you."

"Oh, it was not a problem, at all," replied Buck. "I was your uncle's friend. That means something to me. Spark had his head in the lap of a young woman in a blue blouse with worried eyes. She was being very kind to Spark and was relieved when I said I would take the dog to a veterinarian."

It was Rob's turn to explode! The blue blouse! He had finally found someone who saw the girl? "Blue blouse! What did she look like? What did you talk about? Where did she go? Do you know her?"

Buck knew he had touched something sensitive to Rob, but until Rob explained it all Buck had no idea that he held a possible key in clearing Rob. "Well, I had no idea. It could be she was the same woman you saw on the cliff, but how can we tell?"

"We have to phone Mel about this!" insisted Rob. "It might be the same girl! At least it's a chance!"

The three talked and schemed over the beers and finally called it quits. Rob was sure he would be seeing a lot more of Buck, that he might help replace Uncle May in some way or give Rob someone to talk to, someone with whom to be a friend. To Buck, Rob could be someone Buck could still visit in uncle May's house, for Buck had also lost a loved one and good friend.

After all the beer, Buck still walked out sober as a judge. Rob felt a little whoosey, and after leaving a hefty tip for Scott, he helped Peggy make the walk to May's house.

They found Spark just his normal self, but Rob thought he looked a little guilty and shamefaced. Rob knew the look.

Suffering from the beer, Peggy laid on the couch and tried to close her eyes to the spinning room and the spinning events of the last few days.

Rob went to the picture window and sat in May's favorite chair with an over-view of the beach. The corner window faced north where Rob had a clear view of the surfers and the smooth white beach all the way up to the base of Cape Kiwanda, itself. The view sent a shudder through him.

Slowly Rob began, once again, to summarize what evidence there was concerning May's death. There wasn't much. There was some blood, but one might find blood anywhere in small quantities, and with no suspect to whom to tie the blood it just wasn't anything of import. DNA is only valuable if one finds a match. Buck meeting the girl in the blue blouse was a stupendous revelation, and, at the same time, nothing at all; she might be an entirely different girl. Even if she was the girl Rob had sent for help, her whereabouts were still unknown. Of course, there was still the fact that two eyewitnesses were willing to testify that they had seen Rob kill his uncle.

"We've got nothing!" he murmured out loud. "We've got nothing but a clean mantle, something special May wanted to tell me.., and two guys who say I committed murder!"

He pushed his head back into the cushion of the chair and closed his eyes. Deep in thought he pondered the situation. Deep into sleep he fell.

An hour later, Rob was startled awake by Spark's weight on his feet. The dog had lain down on top of Rob's toes the way the dog was so fond of with May. At first, Rob jerked awake and then, realizing what happened, leaned back into the cushion and smiled.

"I'll do it, Uncle May," he whispered. "I'll take care of them all." He waved his right arm in a grand gesture. "I'll live in your house. I'll love your woman. I'll keep your dog." Then his voice accidentally rose to an audible pitch. "But first, I will find your murderer!"

Peggy woke to the last words. "Rob. What is it?" She crossed the room to kneel at his side. "What is it?"

Rob looked at the sincerity and care in her face, and it shocked him. He rubbed his face with his hand to awaken fully. "I… I… think I was dreaming. You know, that place between dreams and reality?"

"Yes," she whispered. "It's always twilight, there."

Rob shook his head. Then he smiled. "Don't be too concerned about it. I was just dreaming. It is where I get a lot of material for the books I write."

"What are you writing now, Rob? Or are you between books?

He was glad for the diversion. "I'm four chapters into a novel about my dad's tour of duty in the Philippians in World War Two. It's a book about dad trying to get home to mom and us kids before Christmas. I think I'll call it, *Come Home for Christmas*."

Peggy laid her head on Rob's arm. "A Christmas war story. Humm? I like it."

They both looked down at Spark nestled at Rob's feet.

"I think I will write an Irish Setter into the story."

They were afraid to leave Spark alone, so they put him in Peggy's car and drove off with every intention of visiting several art galleries.

At the Pacific Crest Gallery, they left Spark in the car with the windows down and went inside. Rob was surprised to find that he was actually excited about seeing his uncles' work hanging in a gallery.

They found the front door of the gallery open and no one in sight, so they walked around the gallery, for a minute, noting that May's paintings were prominently displayed in the very front of the gallery where great works deserved to be hung. Peggy reminded Rob how laid back the beach businesses could be, that it was not unusual to find a business open, the door unlocked, and even the cash register unattended. It was the beach, and a slower and laid back beach mentality prevailed.

As they wandered the gallery, they found the door to the back room standing open, and they could hear voices coming from within. It sounded like the gallery owner was involved in some business deal or other, for they could hear loud voices in disagreement. Just as they were giving up and about to leave, they saw a young man in his early twenties rush out the back door. It looked to Rob and Peggy like the young man was stuffing a wad of cash into the front pocket of his blue jeans.

"Must be a local artist, Rob," Peggy said. "It's his lucky day. He sold a painting, so he can pay his bar tab, or rent. Wonder who it was?"

After the young man ran out the back door, Rob and Peggy started towards the office just as an Asian man burst from the back room nearly knocking both of them down. He was not a tall man, at least a foot shorter than Rob's six foot height, but he was nearly as hefty as the man Spark had attacked. At first, he looked fat, but, on a second glance, Rob decided that he was extra-powerfully built and gave the impression of incredible strength. He also gave the impression of being overly startled as if Rob and Peggy had interrupted some private discussion in the back room. The man was sweating profusely.

He recognized Peggy right off. "Oh! Peggy! I'm sorry... about May. I was coming over this evening to give my condolences."

That caused Peggy to start tearing up all over again, and she had to introduce Rob to Wi through her tears.

Wi shook Rob's hand vigorously. "You have just to ask, Mr. Smith. I loved your uncle." Wi started to tear up in sympathy with Peggy, but he stopped himself. "Your uncle and I were friends, Mr. Smith. If you get a lead on his killer, I am your man to help. Call me Jan."

"Thank you. Call me Rob. If you and May were friends then you and I are friends, already."

"Who was the guy that just ran out the back door?" asked Rob.

"That young man that just left? He can paint...quite talented, actually, but what a problem! If you see him in town, don't even address him. He is as antisocial as they get. He's some kind of weirdo from Portland."

"Perhaps we could see his work, Mr. Wi... Jan?" asked Rob.

"Gone. It's already been picked up by a buyer from Portland. It's funny, almost. Some nearly dysfunctional soul comes from Portland, paints a dark and ugly political painting, and someone from Portland comes down to the beach and buys the work to take back to Portland."

After a few minutes of discussion about May's work, Wi showed Peg and Rob a couple of Commers' paintings, and he was forthcoming about all the works May had placed in the gallery on consignment. Wi held nothing back, and Peggy and Rob were sure that he had truly accounted for all of May's paintings. The gallery's paintings fit May's tally book exactly.

With their business concluded, Peggy and Rob decided to visit the only other local gallery carrying Uncle May's work and made their goodbyes to Jan Wi.

Then the strangest thing happened- again? When the three walked to the front door of the gallery to say their goodbyes, the nearly always (up until today) docile Spark exploded once again. He jumped out through the car window, dashed through the open front door of the gallery, and attacked Jan Wi. The dog made one upper body lunge and missed for the second time in the same day. Then he spun back and began biting and tearing at Jan Wi's leg. Once again, so fast and unexpected was the attack, that Rob could only follow frantically around Jan Wi while trying, unsuccessfully, to grab Spark. The fat man spun in mad terror with Spark chewing on his leg. Unlike the earlier attack, Rob and Peggy had great difficulty pulling Spark off Jan Wi's leg where Spark had taken a firm hold. When they finally separated the two, there was blood on Wi's pants leg and on Spark's muzzle, and Spark continued to bark and pull against Rob's hold even after Rob separated the two. Spark was foaming in hatred.

Although the attack only lasted a matter of moments, it seemed longer to all involved. Rob returned Spark to the car and tightly rolled up the car windows. Spark continued barking. He was livid with rage and terror and just kept barking and barking. He crashed repeatedly against the windows of the car trying to get out in an effort to resume the attack.

After the attack, and while awaiting (once again) the arrival of the police whom Wi had phoned, Rob attempted to explain to Jan Wi that dogs experience stress just like humans; and that Spark must be just a little crazy over May's death, that dogs experience joy, grief, hunger, and pain just like humans.

However, right then it was Jan Wi experiencing the pain and grief, and he was not in a forgiving mood. He demanded that they wait for the police to arrive.

Peggy used the time to, once again, try to explain to Jan Wi that it really wasn't Spark's fault, that Spark had just recently experienced the very painful tragedy of the death of his long time master and was undoubtedly suffering from what humans would call situation psychosis. She reasoned, untruthfully, that Wi was the first person Spark had encountered since being returned from the veterinary office, that Spark was not a danger to anyone, normally, and that if he would not press the issue everyone would be eternally grateful.

Wi, however, was determined to be eternally vengeful. He would have no part of the explanation that Rob and Peggy were begging on him.

"I just don't understand?" admitted Peggy to Rob while they were alone outside the gallery waiting for the sheriff. "This man was supposed to have been a friend of May, and Spark knows him. Spark has spent many hours in the same room with Wi? I just don't understand?"

The canine unit placed Spark in a cage to be transported to the impound in Lincoln City. They had no choice, really, for even with the delay time it took for the deputies to arrive, Spark was still just livid with rage and resisted the canine deputy's attempts to quiet him.

One of the deputies, a young woman in her late twenties, approached Rob and Peggy after interviewing Jan Wi. She listened patiently to Rob's explanation of the dog's recent stress.

"Folks, I want you to know how sorry I am about all this, but that dog is vicious!" She held up her hand to stifle Peggy's disagreement. "No, no. I heard your explanation. It doesn't matter why the dog is crazy. He just is."

"Mr. Wi is in need of medical attention. As far as vicious goes, Mr. Wi is also a little upset about all this. He's refused an ambulance, although he is bleeding all over the place. He says he will take himself to County General, and has stated that he wants the dog destroyed. He is adamant about pressing charges. He appears nearly as vicious as the dog."

The deputy continued. "That Irish Setter is foaming at the mouth with rage, trying to bite everyone who comes close, and he doesn't have much of a chance in the system."

"What does that mean, deputy?" asked Rob.

"Unless a miracle happens, that dog will be put down."

During the eighteen mile trip to the dog pound, Spark again became his docile self and simply curled up in a pile in the far corner of the cage where he had been incarcerated. On arrival at the pound, he was led into a noisy and smelly room full of cages where the constant din of barking and whining dogs would keep anyone awake- anyone except a dog who had lost his owner, been tossed to and fro by the Pacific Ocean, and was recovering from the trauma of the last few days. Spark, nearly exhausted from his trauma, pain, and exertions curled up and slept around the clock.

Chapter Six

A few blocks from the Pelican Pub the Nestucca River winds its way through the town of Pacific City to spill into the Pacific Ocean. The joining of the river to the ocean kicks up a violent area called a "bar" where the churned-up sand turns the river water a sandy brown before it mixes with the blue and green of the ocean. It is a violence of the sea, a turbulence, a resisting and struggling where sea meets the river, as if both are hesitant to take the leap. The word chaos could have been coined where a large river meets the sea. To watch the churning waters of the bar can be intriguing, is often frightening, and is always dangerous if one gets too close.

Rob and Peggy sat at the base of a small dune and stared at the river's crinolines, where its outward flow competed against thousands of miles of ocean and a relentless incoming tide.

The word chaos could have been coined where a man's stubborn will meets the bar of choices between a world of what is known and comfortable, and the mixing with something attractive but unknown. It is a violence of emotions, a turbulence, a resisting and struggling. It can be intriguing, is often frightening, and is always dangerous if one gets too close. Rob was afraid that the further he climbed up the tree the more of his crinolines would show.

After the deputies had driven off with Spark, Peggy and Rob retreated to the solitude of the mouth of the Nestucca River. They felt largely helpless for Spark's cause, and both felt the need to get away to somewhere quiet.

For that matter, they both felt helpless for their own cause, but certainly not hopeless.

They packed a quick bite to eat and just started

walking. They ended up sitting on a large piece of driftwood in the sand facing the river bar, fascinated with the churning and forever mixing of two, heretofore, separate and powerful entities. Neither of them spoke very much at first.

Peggy stared at the churning water.

Rob stared at Peggy. He found that, for some strange reason, he could not keep from looking at her, as if seeing something new in her, something that wasn't there before; a change had taken place and he wondered, to himself, if the change was in Peggy or himself? He wanted to remark on that change but did not quite know how or where to start. In the end, it was Peggy who broached the subject.

Rob turned to the water and contemplated his crinolines.

Peggy was sitting very close and holding his arm at the elbow, holding his elbow close up to her chest as they both gazed at the turbulence. Neither was innocent: the embrace nor the turbulent flow of water. There were dangers in both, and as close as he was to both, Rob felt the dangers acutely. He was used to the imminent threat of danger, but he was resisting jumping in again, for he knew that relationships can be intriguing, are often frightening, and are always dangerous if one gets too close.

"Rob, it is no secret what is happening, here," Peggy said, hoping to finally approach the subject and get it out into the open to get things started one way or another. "We are attracted to each other."

Time slowed to a crawl. Rob's entire life flashed before his eyes.

"Oh, well." He didn't say anything else. He decided to be content to just let Peggy stumble through it, to let her form her thoughts in her own time. He was afraid that, given the chance, he might stumble and phrase his thoughts incorrectly. "Well.., uh..," he repeated.

She was mildly irritated by his two syllable answer but was not about to let the matter go that easily. "I don't know anything about you? Who is Rob Smith?"

He stood to his feet and moved to sit facing her. At first, he thought moving to face her would help him to think clearly and speak precisely, but right off he regretted his move. Instead of seeming debonair and sophisticated, the move made him feel distant and aloof.

"I'm nobody. Nobody but what I seem: a half used up old cop in a lot of trouble... again. But I feel the attraction between the two of us. Why do you think I left so fast and ran back to Seattle after the barbecue?"

"I know why you went back to Seattle. I just didn't *want* you to go. You kept me awake nights for a week. Then, finally, I just went back to May as if nothing had happened."

She was undaunted by Rob's move away from her. She simply relocated next to him and started all over. Her move, she thought, was symbolic of what she wanted out of the rest of her life with Rob.

"Rob, I think you are more than you put on. There are lots of retired police officers out there. They're not all special. They don't all write children's books. If nothing else, that is a little different, a little special; wouldn't you say?"

"I write a lot more than just children's books," answered Rob. "In fact, although I am known best for *Zippity Zappity Land*, I have written many other books and short stories. It's just that *Zippity Zappity Land* is the best known... Actually, it is about the *only* thing for which I am really known. Not that I haven't tried with other things. I've written several novels. But if you ask anyone, I am the *Zippity Zappity Land* author."

Peggy got a little impish look to her eye. "I read *The Dream Book*, she said. "That is one strange book!"

Robed faked a dagger through his chest. "Hey! Those aren't my dreams! I interviewed dozens of people for that book. I spent months researching the weirdest people who had the wildest dreams and bi-polar experiences!"

"Sure. But a bi-polar cop? Who would have thought?"

Rob went on. "But even if they were my dreams or experiences, a writer bares his soul… to stir another's. He writes to… awaken the heart of humanity. He tells intimate secrets of his inner-self to… challenge and uplift his fellow man! My soul is… all on fire!"

"Shut up."

"OK."

"Want another beer?"

"Yeah."

Peggy leaned over to the cooler. "I'll open two more beers, and you start talking for real. I want to know Robert Smith. I want to know things about you. Why aren't you married? Why do you have that little limp? Why aren't you a police officer any longer? Where did you go to school?

She did not get any more out of Rob for a few minutes. He just took a sandwich and a beer from her, set both down and did what he had been wanting to do all day, what he hadn't done since the barbecue. And it felt good! It was also what she had really been needing and wanting; and both of them knew it. She lingered in his arms and then snuggled deeper.

After a long time, and leaving her head firmly on his shoulder, she asked, "So are you just replacing May with his house, his dog, and his girlfriend? Or would you like more out this relationship?"

He was too far up the tree, and he no longer cared who saw. But he still needed humor to help him through. "More.., I think," he replied. "I'm going to send that dog to obedience school."

"Rob! That's not funny! Oh, I get it. That's more of that cop gallows humor? If the situation is really really dangerous, you resort to gallows humor. How bad is the situation, Rob?"

"It's terrible!" he replied. "I don't think I'm going to get out of this one alive!" Rob put on his best little-boy smirk, and then his serious look, then his court-testimony blank stare.

Finally, he became serious. "I want much more out of this relationship than mere fun. Much more. I have been alone for much too long. Until today, I thought I wanted to be alone. But I'm through with that.

"What about you, Peggy. I mean, I know that you have not been alone, and I know that your relationship with my uncle was less than desired, but do you want more than just a casual relationship? Wouldn't it be more satisfying to share a life?"

"Well..," she replied. It was his turn to talk. "You tell me about your family and growing up."

"Oh, that's the easy part," he said trying to figure a way to make it sound simple. "I grew up near Seattle. Bremerton is a naval town, and on weekends, dad was the civilian commandant of the Navy Base. He didn't start out as the commander. Most of our life we were dirt poor, and then dad started earning promotions and ended up in charge of everything.

"My mother was a saint, sort of a saint: at least to this little boy.

I had four brothers. One died young. The oldest died of cancer a couple years ago, and Tommy suffered with excruciating pain from some unknown illness."

"This is beginning to sound sad!" said Peggy. Her eyes were large and full of compassion. She snuggled into Rob's arm for comfort.

"It is sad. But reality is like that. If one lives long enough," he replied, "More and more acquaintances die or go away. It's either them or you. Personally, until recently I'd rather that I had gone first. Not anymore."

"Tom was also a writer. *The Jesus Mystery?* Perhaps you read it?"

"No. It sounds religious."

"Yeah, I guess it does. But Tom would have said that one object of the book was to take the religion out and replace it with the humanity of Christ."

Peggy thought about that. "You mean that Christ was just a regular Joe... who just happened to be divine?"

"Well, I don't think Tommy would have put it that way. Tom's life was a struggle to get the average guy on the street to think of religion as normal. I think Tommy would say that Jesus was Divinity who decided to become a regular Joe; that Jesus did not want to be some sanctimonious religious fanatic, that Jesus... oh, I don't know...that Jesus was God who actually *liked* people."

"Is that where you get all the ideas about forgiveness of sins and epiphanies from God?"

Rob looked at her with a worried look in his eyes. "You mean when I was under water? After I jumped off the cliff?"

She just nodded. She was afraid of the subject. She was afraid that it might drive a wedge between Rob and her. Religion could do that, and she feared anything that might break the spell.

"I need you to know, Peggy, that what I saw under water, what I heard and the people I saw? That whole experience was very real to me!"

"Oh, Rob!"

He waved his hand in a manner that looked dismissive, but he didn't really mean it that way at all. "Oh, I know. It all sounds weird, but I was probably more dead than alive when I saw my father and mother. I had been under water for a long time. I am sure I was dying and that I was right on the verge of death when I finally had.., well.., when I finally received the idea to ask God for help?"

Peggy remained serious and skeptical. "That really was just coincidental, wasn't it, Rob?

"Coincidental!! Let me tell you something, Peggy Richards!" He pushed her out to arms length, held her by her shoulders, and peered deep into Peggy's eyes. "The fact that I asked for God to help me, and then Uncle May was right there, immediately? That felt like more than just coincidental!

Providential is more like it! You would have a different idea if you were the one under water, out of breath, and out of choices."

They turned away from the river, and began to walk up the beach. They strolled slowly along both of them trying to understand what had happened.

"You know?" Rob finally answered, "at one point I thought about telling God that if he would give me another chance, I'd be a better person, that I would not do the things that I have done, that I would... oh, I don't know... feed the hungry and help the poor? But I knew it would be a lie. Why would I be different with a second chance?"

"So.., you..?" led Peggy.

"So, I didn't make any promises. I just asked God to help me, and he did. Or was it just coincidence that in all that time under water I never came near to getting to safety, but the second I asked God for help I was there next to May?"

"I don't know?" she answered.

"That makes two of us," he said very quietly.

"So..?" she said trying to change the subject. "You said you had four brothers, and you only told me about three?"

"Oh, yeah. Wesley. I have a brother named Wesley."

"What happened to him?"

"Nobody knows. He was the smartest and brightest of all of us all. But... nobody knows."

"Nobody knows?"

"Yep," he answered. "He's like aether in space."

"Huh?"

He gave another wave of his hand and arm. "Nobody is sure. He hasn't been seen for years. He is just.., out there. One day, he borrowed my truck and just drove off."

"Tell me about your leg?" she asked.

It was shortly after Rob's first wife had died, but he did not mention his wife to Peggy; he thought he would leave that part out for now and bring his wife up later. For good reason.

He was sitting in a Seattle bar trying to get drunk, but it wasn't working. It was late in the evening just an hour before closing. It was a usual slow Tuesday night with no one else in the bar except Jess, the bartender.

Rob had been telling Jess all about his troubles, when he heard the squeaking of the front door open behind him. Rob figured it was about time for the district uniform to stop in, but the newcomer was not a police officer. He did have a gun, but he sure wasn't a lawman.

Jess looked up and somehow sensed trouble. "Oh, oh," he said quietly under his breath. "I've got a bad feeling about this guy."

Before Rob could turn fully around to look, while he was still trying to focus his rummy vision, the young man approached the bar and stuck a gun out past the right side of Rob's face and pointed the revolver directly at Jess.

"Give me all your money, sucker!"

How could the young man know that it was not the best of times to try a robbery? It should have been the perfect opportunity, but it wasn't. Only one half-drunk customer and one, lone bartender on a Tuesday night occupied the bar. It should have been simple; however, in the bar that night there was a dangerous combination of forces aligning themselves against the young man. Rob was armed, as always even though off duty, and he was not all that interested in living. He had tried living and found it less enjoyable than expected. He just no longer cared. His life was crashing headlong into a resisting and turbulent world. The word chaos could have been coined where a destroyed life hits the crinolines of an arbitrary and unrelenting blue world turning brown.

For the last two hours, Rob had been boring Jess, telling him how he just did not care, if his wife was gone, Rob's life might as well go right along with her, and if he wasn't such a coward, he would have ended his life long ago.

Perhaps, Rob often wondered, if lovers really do meet in the after life? Or if that's all a cheat, too?

Slowly Rob turned his head and found his face mere inches from a revolver. A big revolver. He tried to focus his rummy eyes. The revolver was a chrome snub-nose Colt .357, a very dangerous weapon, easily concealable; and easily capable of blowing a very big hole… in anything. "Sure glad that's not pointed at me," Rob said. "I really hate it when guns are pointed at me."

"No," replied Jess very calmly in answer to the gunman's demand. "No money."

Rob turned and looked at Jess. "No? Jess?" Rob slurred his words a little less and was sobering quickly. "That is a very big gun, Jess! Well, the gun isn't all that big. But it fires a very very big bullet. I think it can hurt you. My brother, Harold," Rob went on, "said that a .357 bullet will go clean through the block of a V-8 Chevrolet engine."

"No."

"Yes it is true. That's what Harold said!"

Jess looked from the young man's eyes to the gun barrel and back again. Then he looked at Rob and smirked at his attempt at humor.

"No. No money," repeated Jess.

At that, Rob looked at Jess with a new appreciation. "At-a-boy, Jess. Give it to him!"

Rob looked at the young man. "Your move!"

Scared was the young man. Scared, desperate, and confused. His arm was shaking so violently it was a wonder he held onto the handgun. Perspiration beaded on his forehead. "What do you mean, 'No?' Listen, Sucker!" he yelled. "Give me the cash out of the till, or I will shoot you!"

At Jess's irrational and steadfast refusal, the young man began casting furtive glances back and forth- from Jess, to the window facing the parking lot, back to Jess. Outside, Rob could hear the getaway car's engine revving. Clearly the young man was upset by Jess's refusal, confused by the rantings of the drunk at the bar, and frightened by the turn of events. His mentors had told him it would be easy, this first test for initiation into their gang; stick the gun in the bartender's face and demand money. How tough could it be?

"Go away," said Jess calmly. "We don't like to be robbed here. I don't care about the bar's money, but the tips for all the waitresses and waiters, from earlier in the evening, are mixed in with the house money. I'd hate to disappoint those kids after they've worked so hard all day. Try robbing the store on the corner."

"Oh, that's good, Jess." Rob could feel himself losing his drunk and becoming more sober by the second. Guns will do that.

The young man was nearly dancing with fright and unexpended energy. His leg was bouncing up and down, and he kept glancing back out the window. "Give me the money, or I'll kill you! I'll shoot you, man!"

Rob analyzed the situation as best as he could under the circumstances and the rum. Time for action was getting short, and he was sobering rapidly with the need of the moment. He wasn't quite there, yet, when the need for action finally arrived, but he figured sober to be just a state of mind, anyway, and Jess was pleading for some kind of help- drunk help or sober help- Jess did not care.

Jess' eyes stayed hard on the young man. "*Rob?*" Jess could sense that the young man, with the gun, was teetering on the edge of a decision, and he knew that there were only two decisions to be made with a gun in your hand and pointed at a target. He figured it was a fifty-fifty situation he was in, and he had heard Rob being very adamant that the bad fifty always had a sixty percent lead. It might not be mathematical, but it sure had a way of turning out that way.

Since the gun was so close, and the drinks not doing that much to stop Rob's pain, and since the young man with the gun was in such dire stress, and because Rob was worried about Jess doing something foolish, Rob decided that if anyone was going to do anything foolish it might as well be him. So.., he volunteered again. He hated that. He was afraid Jess was just about to attempt some heroic role, and he couldn't have that while he, himself an off duty police officer, just sat on the barstool? Besides, Rob was beginning to feel left out of all the fun. He did not really formulate a plan, and he sure did not think his actions quite through. He just casually reached across his body and closed his left hand over the revolver making sure the web of his thumb was jammed down in between the hammer and the firing pin. Then he tightened his grip around the fingers of the young man's hand locking the hand firmly to the gun.

The young man could not fire, and he could not let go of the gun.

Up to that point, so intent was the young man on Jess, that he had never even really noticed Rob. The young man's eyes got even bigger than they already were when he tried to pull his arm back, for Rob's grip was strong and held the gun and the man's arm frozen in place. True, the gun was still pointing towards Jess, but it was absolutely harmless. As Rob's grip tightened, the young man's desperation grew- so much so that his fear was nearly a palpable thing in the room. The young man winced in pain as Rob's grip tightened up a notch. The young man's knees threatened to buckle…

"Thank you, Rob," delivered Jess very quietly.

Rob spoke steadily as if he was simply giving advice over a quiet drink. "Never done this before, have you, son?"

The young man again tried to pull his hand away, but Rob held it frozen in place. With no other alternative, the young man pulled the trigger, but the hammer fell harmlessly against the webbing of Rob's hand. At the fall of the hammer, Rob began to slowly twist. "I've always had a good grip, son. It's something you should, maybe.., work on developing. You'll have little else to do for a few years."

"Don't hurt him, Rob," said Jess. "You just hold him, there, and I'll call it in."

But Rob did not just hold him, there, as Jess suggested. Rob pulled the young man's gun up against his own chest. "Jess's the wrong guy to shoot, anyway. Always- now pay attention young man- always assess the situation before you act. Before you ever do this again, work on assessing the path of the most likely looking threat."

The young man had been nervous and shaking all over *before* Rob grabbed his gun hand. Now, Rob was just plain scaring him. His plans foiled, the young man wanted nothing so much as to be out of that bar, except that he would have to deal with his waiting accomplices in the car. Failure was a little recognized gang option.

"Shoot *me*. Why don't you just shoot me?" Rob repeated with the gun pointed at his own chest.

In desperation, the young man tried to punch Rob with his free hand, but he was off balance, and his punch lacked power. Rob just took it without a flinch and squeezed his grip a little tighter on the gun hand.

Jess shook his head at the young man. "Uh.., you probably shouldn't hit Rob. That has a way of backfiring on you."

It did. "Was that what that was?" asked Rob. "I knew he did something to me, Jess. But I've been punched before, and I don't think that was a punch." Rob looked at the squirming young man and twisted his gun hand mercilessly. "Was that what it was, punk? Did you hit me?"

With Rob's left hand still clutching the gun, he used his right hand to grab the young man's belt in the small of his back, hoist him over the bar, and let him fall at Jess's feet. Rob tore the revolver from his grip as the young man fell and then handed the revolver to Jess. "Can you handle that, Jess? I'm going outside to speak with his friends. Don't be too rough on that poor guy. I think I might have accidentally broken a few of his fingers. And don't forget to finish calling it in, huh?"

Rob went out the side door unobserved by those waiting nervously in the car. He approached the car, unseen, from the right rear just like it was a training exercise in the police academy, drew his off-duty .45 calibre Glock from inside his jacket and pushed it through the open window up against the temple of the back-seat passenger's head… Then Rob cocked the hammer. The click of the hammer cocking was distinctive and left little doubt, at all, as to what the sound was. All three occupants of the car froze in place.

"Now, you fellas just stay real still," Rob said. "I'm a police officer, and you are all three under arrest. Your friend, inside, did not do the bang-up job you had hoped. He won't be coming out. But ya'all will be meeting him, again, real soon."

"Fool!" The driver swiveled his head to look back at Rob.

"Don't even move a muscle, stupid!" yelled Rob back at him. "If this car moves an inch I will shoot you, the driver, first. This is a Glock forty-five caliber semi-automatic handgun. It's a great gun to get into a shootout with, and it goes through things real good. I figure if anyone moves I will shoot you right through this guy's head!" Just for effect he pushed the barrel into the back-seat passenger's ear.

Rob went on. The moment exhilarated him and frightened him at the same time. There was no need for him to have gone outside to meet this danger. He could have remained in the bar and called 911, but being a police officer means desiring to meet danger, wanting to meet and destroy evil. It was a certifiable flaw in his mental make up, but it was Rob's choice, and he made it. Once made, it could not be retracted. He had known the ball would roll when he walked out the door towards the getaway car. At his first words to the bad guys in the car, he knew he must roll that ball through to the end- that there would absolutely be no way to back out of it, once started. He would honestly try to arrest the suspects in the car, but he knew that if shooting started it would be kill or be killed. He was in the state of mind that either option seemed acceptable to him.

"If I see a shoulder turn, if a hand moves, or if I just

get scared, I am going to shoot whoever moves or scares me. And I get scared easy. Real easy."

"Fool" again yelled the driver.

Rob started a continuous verbal rampage figuring that a steady stream of talking could, perhaps, dissuade the three young men from any action. He hoped that they might wait for a lull to do anything foolish. If he could just get them to keep thinking about what he was saying, they might be too busy to act. He was counting on simple words confusing simple minds. He railed on them about police work in general, about the robbery statutes, about what their mothers thought of them. He told them how he did not care about living, but that they should, being so young and with so much of life ahead of them, be more careful whom they robbed. He talked, and talked, and hoped to hear an approaching siren.

"Your friend, in there, he won't be coming out."

"That don't make no difference! We're gonna kill you!" came the driver's voice interrupting Rob's tirade. "He comes out or not, we're gonna kill you!"

It got real quiet for a moment. Rob was running out of words. "I know. But just before you try killing me," he replied to the driver, "I want you to know that if you so much as move a muscle it won't just be talk. I will kill you. Or you will kill me. Doesn't matter that much to me. Does it matter to you?"

When it came to it, though, Rob did not shoot the driver at his first movement, and it was too bad... for Rob. In fact, it was almost fatal for him. For all his tough, macho talk, Rob was not the self-described cold and calculating killer. If he had been, he wouldn't have limped all the rest of his life.

It always seemed amazing to Rob, when he thought back on it, how much happened in a very small span of time. Later, speaking to other veteran officers about shootings, they all said the same thing; time slows down to a crawl; nanoseconds crawl by like hours.

To Rob's disappointment and fear, the driver dropped his right shoulder, and Rob could see an Uzzi barrel swinging around in the driver's left hand. At the very same moment, the front-seat passenger's door flew open, and the passenger exploded out his door and attempted to roll onto the pavement to get a shot off at Rob. The mistake that Rob made was not shooting the driver immediately. Rob should have fired immediately, but he hesitated; and that hesitation gave the front-seat passenger time for his roll. That made it necessary to shoot both the driver and the front-seat passenger at the same time instead of one at a time, as the threats developed. And bravado aside, you just can not shoot two moving targets at the same time. You can shoot them rapidly, but separately. Then too, shootouts rarely go like in the movies.

Rob knew the front passenger was hampered with his long shotgun barrel, so while the passenger was rolling in an attempt to get enough room to bring the long barrel around, Rob shot the driver- twice- once in the back of the neck and once in the middle of his back. The second shot was so reactive that Rob wasn't aware, until later, that he had shot the driver twice. The first bullet pushed the driver into the steering wheel; the second bullet thudded into a corpse. At the death of the driver, the clutch came out, the car lurched forward three feet, and the car's engine died with a jerk and shut itself down.

The jerking of the car as the clutch came out turned out to Rob's advantage, since the back-seat passenger was thrown back against his seat making it impossible for him to get a ready sight picture on Rob.

After firing on the driver of the car, Rob dodged instinctively to the right to change his location, so the man with the shotgun would be forced to take an additional fraction of a second to relocate Rob; and, once again, the passenger would be hampered by the long barrel of the shotgun. Perhaps, just that additional fraction of a second delay, in bringing the long barrel onto target, might make all the difference in the world. Rob's teachers at the police academy had been good. They had drilled into him how targets on shooting ranges stand still, but if a shooter in a real-life shootout wants to live, he moves after each shot to improve his position and confuse his opponents. The suspects did not have the advantage of police training.

Rob shot the front-seat passenger just as the bad guy's roll on the pavement ended, and the man was lifting his shotgun; the barrel of the shotgun came up, loomed ominously large and dreadful, and then fell harmlessly, as Rob's bullet took the shooter chest right. The impact of the bullet spun the shooter 360 degrees in some weird ballet. His body thudded to the pavement and skidded backwards up against a yellow parking curb.

Rob meant to quickly spin his attention back to the rear-seat passenger who was still armed; he meant to quickly focus the Glock barrel back on the last of the three; he tried to do it in lightening speed. But he could not manage the recoil of his automatic and his turn fast enough; his turn was a millisecond too slow.

In the middle of his turn, Rob felt a horrendous shock and was thrown to the right by a mysterious force. For some unknown reason, the blacktop was rushing up to meet him? Funny he thought, as the blacktop quickly grew closer and more definite, how the blacktop surface looks vaguely porous when you are standing. Time slowed to a crawl. As the blacktop came closer and closer to his face, he could see that the surface was actually comprised of huge cavernous valleys and mountains of large, oily rocks? Finally, and to his great surprise, the blacktop just rudely jumped up and hit him in the side of his face with a terrific wallop that nearly knocked him unconscious. He landed hard on his cheek bone and right shoulder, and Rob's Glock was knocked out of his grasp by the impact with the pavement. His automatic slid away and settled under a nearby Porsche.

He realized then, as he saw his automatic sliding away, that he must have fallen; no, he must have been shot; and the slam of the bullet knocked his feet out from under him. It hadn't been the blacktop rushing up to him- he was knocked off his feet by the impact of the bullet, and it had been his face that was rushing to the blacktop. Vaguely, he thought he should look over his body and check for a bullet hole; that if he was shot, he must be injured. How injured he was he had no idea? He tried to roll onto his back, but his body seemed to be responding in slow motion.

Then he remembered the back-seat passenger. Rob's vision caught a movement to his left, and he slowly turned his face to meet it.

"Fool!" yelled the back-seat passenger as he climbed out of the car. He walked casually to stand over Rob and pointed his handgun down at Rob's head. "That's right! I shot you! Now, I'm going to kill you!"

Surprisingly, Rob found that he just did not care. He hadn't really cared about anything since Wanda died, and he felt strangely relieved in some odd way. "OK, punk!" he replied. "What are you standing there yelling about? You've got the gun. Do it. I'm not going to beg, if that's what's keeping you." Rob was more tired than he could ever remember.

Rob calculated, without looking, that he was five feet from his Glock.

"I'm going to kill you!"

Slowly, Rob managed to roll onto his side. "You said that. But if you give up, right now, and lay that gun down on the pavement, I promise not to kill you."

"I'm going to kill *you*, man!"

As the passenger continued to scream, Rob turned away from him and started edging over toward the Porsche; Rob simply turned his back on the man and began pushing himself with his good leg and wondered if he would feel the bullet or hear the bullet first. He left a wide trail of blood on the blacktop.

The man yelled again.

Rob was three feet from his gun and counting. "You better shut up, and do it then. 'Cause when I get my gun back,

I'm sure enough going to kill *you*! Just like I killed your punk friends." Time slowed to a crawl… and left a trail of blood.

He was two feet from the Porsche when it all ended. The bad guy uttered two more words, and then it was all over; as fast as it had started, the robbery was over, the shooting was finished, and there was nothing to do but wait for the on-duty officers and the ambulance.

While the passenger had been busy yelling and jacking up his courage to shoot Rob again, Jess came out the front door of the bar. He watched in horror as the backseat passenger shot Rob in the leg. Jess ran the fifty feet to where the bad guy was yelling at Rob and threatening to shoot him-and then Jess merely lifted the .357 Colt and shot the bad guy in the back of his head. It was nearly point blank and impossible to miss even for a man not experienced with firearms.

Jess had no police training, had no experience with guns, had no idea what to do in an actual emergency of this sort. He simply was very much afraid that the man would kill Rob before he could save him. In Jess's mind, he yelled several profanities and orders at the man with the gun. In reality, he simply ran up behind him, leveled the gun, and fired. They would argue about it in the future, Rob and Jess, and each was sure of his point of view. One thing was sure. Jess had saved Rob's life.

Rob would never find out if a .357 bullet could penetrate all the way through a Chevy engine block, but he saw, first hand, that it would go through a man's head and just keep on traveling. They never found that bullet that Jess fired. It just cleared the man's head and traveled to unknown parts in search of Wesley and space aether. It ended up, in Rob's words, "Just out there somewhere."

Rob reached under the front wheel of the Porsche and grabbed his automatic, carefully let down the hammer, and slipped the safety to the "on" position. Then he slid the gun back into its holster in his belt.

Jess hadn't moved. With his arm still raised where it had been when the bullet went out the barrel, Jess stared mutely at the dead man.

"Great shot…What took you so long?" asked Rob.

Jess attempted a smile, but his lips started shaking and then his teeth began chattering.

Lifting himself up to a sitting position, Rob leaned his back onto the Porsche's chrome wheel. "Thanks, Jess."

Jess applied a much needed tourniquet to Rob's leg to staunch the rapid flow of blood and explained about the young man inside the restaurant. "I cuffed one arm of the guy you threw over the bar to the beer taps with some handcuffs left over from something a long time ago. I figure that by now he's downing some free beer."

"Let him have it," rasped Rob. "It's likely to be the last drink he'll get in a long time.

"That tourniquet is tight enough. Fetch my gun from under the car, will ya?" asked Rob.

Jess just looked at him. "You already did that."

"Oh.., yeah… I know that."

They were both surprised when the man who had the shotgun regained consciousness and began talking. The shotgun had spun away from him, so there was no further danger from that quarter. Rob and Jess turned to him with quiet surprise. Rob met the fear in the man's eyes and held it there. After a few seconds, the man looked down in shock at the bullet wound in his chest.

"You killed me, man! You killed me!"

Rob looked down at his own leg with the tourniquet and then back at the dying man. "Try not to take it too personal."

At the sound of the sirens, Rob and Jess turned to look at a skidding police car pulling into the lot.

"Slide that .357 away from you, Jess. I wouldn't want the uniforms seeing you with a gun and getting confused. Be careful what you say. Tell only exactly what happened, and don't be surprised if you are treated like a suspect for a few minutes. It's just their job. They won't mean anything personal by it."

At the use of the word "personal" again from Rob, Jess turned back to the man with the shotgun. The man's eyes were rolled back and to the sky; he had taken it about as personal as he could.

A uniform officer ran up and crouched into a shooting stance. "Nobody move, I'm a…"

"You're a little late, Mark. Everybody has already been shot. "Except Jess, here. He saved the day."

"Rob Smith? How the…."

"So you see, Peg," I wasn't really the hero. I tried to be, I guess. But Jess really did the job!"

Peggy just shook her head and then tried to look deep into Rob's eyes, but he was staring out over the ocean, once again, lost in the horror. The telling of the story had pulled him away, somehow, and he felt distant and alone. Distance wasn't what he really wanted. It was just that recounting the gun fight made it difficult to get back into the moment with Peggy.

"Looks to me, Rob, like you are definitely the hero of that story! You got three out of four. What did you expect with those odds?"

After a few moments, he risked a quick glance into Peggy's waiting eyes and then finally settled there. "I didn't care, right then. I didn't care about much of anything. It just made me mad when that first punk stuck a gun in Jess's face with me sitting right there. He ignored me!

"When I was shot in the parking lot, the bullet struck a nerve in my leg the wrong way, and the doctors say I will always limp a little, that I've gotten about as much improvement as I'm going to get."

Peggy reached up and playfully slapped Rob's forehead with her open palm. It made a flat and comically splatting sound. "You dumb, worn out cop!" she said smiling. "There's no *right* way to shoot the nerve in your leg!"

They both laughed.

They walked away from lunch and kicked sand. It was then that Rob first noticed they were holding hands. When she had taken his hand, he did not know. They walked along, that way, for a while, taking in the sand and sun. Twice they stopped, and she kissed him not caring at all that the beach held the occasional tourist.

"So, when did you write *Zippity Zappity Land*? How did a killer cop get to writing children's books?"

"It was during my convalescence that I started writing," he replied. "When I learned I would never work again, I had to examine my life and figure out who I was and who I wanted to be for the rest of my life. A friend came in and said that he wished he could just clap his hands over his head and make the hospital and my mutilated leg just go away, and life would be just like it was before the shooting.

"That sparked something weird in my head. My imagination started going wild like it never had before. I found myself fantasizing about clapping myself into a better land. The idea just would not go away, so I put it down on paper. I had no idea that people would adore that little story or identify with it. And it was fantastic when May agreed to illustrate it.

"Weird is going into a store and seeing something I wrote on the shelf with my name on it or have mothers point at me and tell their little children, 'Look, darling, it's the Zippity Zappity man!'"

"I read Zippity again last night, Rob." No wonder it's such a winner! People love it. It helps them teach their children about kindness and gentleness, and May's illustrations on each page are wonderful!"

Rob sighed deeply. "Yeah, I shoot people, and I write children's stories."

After a few moments, Peggy again broached the subject of the two of them. "Rob, what's going to happen to us and all this mess we are in?"

"I don't know, honey. Tomorrow is the first hearing for Spark. Then there is my grand jury. I guess we will take it one day at a time. I've been thinking real hard about why Uncle May asked me to come down here, and I think I have an idea what his surprise might have been.

"Yet, I don't know if anyone can help Spark. I'm afraid he might be killed!"

They made a turn and started back towards their lunch when Rob asked Peggy about herself. It wasn't a question he really wanted to ask, right then, but he thought it might take their minds off Spark, and he felt obligated after her inquiry into his life.

Peggy told Rob how she had been raised in a Tibetan orphanage until the age of fifteen when the monks performed a sex change on him/her, and how she had been married thirty-two times before she was nineteen.

Rob walked along without saying anything much, lost in pondering the evidence in his uncle's death.

As they neared their lunch basket, Peggy wrapped up her tale of escaping to America where she ran a brothel in Missoula, Montana.

As he reached for the lunch basket, Rob simply said, "Oh... Good. That's nice."

Peggy laughed so hard she nearly fell over.

Chapter Seven

The next morning, Rob and Peggy went upstairs in Uncle May's house to what Rob began calling the Matisse room. "I don't know for sure, Peggy, but, like I was telling you yesterday on the beach, it seems to me there is a lead, here, somewhere. Somewhere, in this room there is a clue. He pronounced the word *clue* like Inspector Cluso. Peggy laughed, and Rob decided that he liked the sound.

"Look, here, Peg." He was studying many copies that uncle May had painted of the same painting, a quiet nude laying in front of the typical swirled Matisse background. "Was May trying to paint a copy? Forge a painting? Could be, he was killed for his forgery? Perhaps, it turned out so good that it was mistaken for the original?"

Peg didn't think so. "No, that doesn't make sense. Anyone who would think May's painting was an original Matisse would not know Matisse very well. Only those people who are very knowledgeable would ever consider buying one, or killing for one. Anyway," she continued, "May wasn't the type to steal something or forge anything."

She leafed through a stack of loose papers. "He just had to always be studying something unusual or working on something new." She set one stack of paintings down and picked up another. "You know how he was. There is, like, a Matisse club back east with which he was always corresponding. A man with all his talents and potential, yet he was never satisfied with what he was doing. He was always looking at new things. He was always studying and learning. He was the consummate renaissance man."

"Well," mused Rob while rifling through another stack of May's paintings and loose papers, "I know the *clue* is here. I just know it is."

But it wasn't. Well, it was, but they didn't recognize it.

Mid morning found them both at the Lincoln County Humane Society in Lincoln City. The hearing was in a small court room too near the dog pens for Peggy's nose. They had expected the hearing to be a small meeting with just Rob, Peggy, and the animal control officers who had originally taken Spark into custody. Surprisingly, the room was jammed with people who had driven the nineteen miles from Pacific City, and the courtroom was abuzz with excitement. People arrived in two's and three's and families full of children. There were children of all ages, business men, and housewives; It was more like a country fair than a court room.

Rob and Peggy, full of amazement at the diverse crowd, sat down at the defendant's table. They were doubly surprised when, just before the meeting began, Mel showed up and sat with them.

"What is going on, Mel?" Rob asked. "This looks more like a circus than a hearing?"

"Well, Rob, you may own Spark, but the people of Pacific City love him. Remember, he was last year's Children's Parade Grand Marshal, and he has been in art shows and fair events alongside May for years. He plays on the beach with everyone he sees. He fetches, runs, barks playfully, and has been to nearly every picnic there has ever been on the beach. He is just one popular dog!"

"Well, yeah," Peggy said. "But it nearly sounds like a description of *my* last two years with May."

Mel choked, and Rob wasn't sure whether to laugh or cry, so he tried the gallows humor approach again. "You don't bark… much… for a cute girl."

Mel choked again.

But Peggy laughed. "This is one human interest story the station is missing. Look at all these people," Peggy said. "People love that dog. Even the Pelican Pub lets Spark just curl up on the floor at the end of the bar. Spark is an integral part of Pacific City, and the people love him. They loved May, and they love Spark. It was difficult to separate them. When May and I would go to a special occasion or just down to the store, people would always ask, 'Where's Spark?' It made me kind of wonder if anyone ever asked where I was?"

The court was called to session as the hearings officer came in and took his seat at the raised dais. He explained to the throng his shock and surprise at the participation of the community. He then explained the applicable rules and laws concerning dogs convicted of biting. "Hmmm? So, to sum it all up, I am not a real judge; I am just a hearings officer. Testimony and evidence will be admitted, but admitting rules for both testimony and evidence are looser and more relaxed than in a real court of law like a criminal court, that is. Hmmm? If a dog bites once, the county is prone to forgive and monitor the situation. If he bites a second time, he is put to sleep. The law is pretty cut and dry, and I hope (no, I am confident) that we won't find that situation here, today…Hmmm?"

His gavel hit the table with a resounding and official sounding wooden clump. "Deputies, please bring in the dog and state your case."

Spark was led in to cheers from the bystanders. If it had been a real court of law the hearings officer would not have allowed such a disturbance in court, but this particular outburst was excused. The hearings officer did ask the people to try to hold down their excitement in order not to arouse the dog too much and, therefore, hurt the dog's case.

When Spark was led over and given to Rob, Spark acted as if he had once, again, found a long lost friend. But he quieted right down as if aware that something important was happening. He just sat on his haunches, looked at the judge as if he really did understand English, and panted away.

Mel leaned over Peggy and whispered to Spark. "Try not to lick your… I mean, try not to do what dogs sometimes do. This is a court, you know." Mel thought that was funny, but he was sitting too close to Peggy. Mel's ribs ached for an hour.

"You try to control yourself, too, Mel," she growled. "Hmmm?" Her elbow hurt for an hour.

The court listened to the dog control deputy summarizing the case. She told how they had been summoned to the art gallery and found Spark restrained, and that there was evidence that an attack had been committed. "So, Your Honor, to sum it up. Spark, here, was the dog which attacked the victim, Jan Wi. It was Spark, here, which we took into custody without further incident."

The court listened to Jan Wi's account and examined photos of the bite marks. Rightly so, Jan Wi stated that he was in his art gallery talking to Rob and Peggy when Spark just ran in through the front door and started biting him. It was an unprovoked and surprise attack. No one could figure a reason for the dog's actions.

"You did not go to the hospital. Hmmm?" asked the judge.

"No, Your Honor, I just took these photos and bathed the wounds in alcohol."

The photos were placed in evidence, and Rob was called to the stand.

"You say," asked the deputy, "that this is your dog by inheritance?"

"That is correct," answered Rob. "The dog's owner, Mayfield Commers, died shortly before this attack. He took a fall off Cape Kiwnada. The dog was in the water, with Mayfield Commers, off the Cape Kiwanda cliff but was eventually rescued. He suffered extreme stress. The attack on Mr. Wi was completely out of character. The dog had just seen his master murdered and jumped into the water in a valiant attempt to save Mayfield Commers. The dog was battered by surf and the rough rocks below the Cape, sustained minor physical injuries, and spent the night in a veterinarian's care.

Prior to the attack on Mr. Wi, Spark suffered great lose and physical trauma. Spark was undoubtedly experiencing stress-induced trauma on the day he attacked Mr. Wi. He was hardly himself. Normally, this dog is intelligent, gentle, and caring. He never hurt anyone before the day he bit Mr. Wi."

The deputy began to ask Rob another question, but the hearings officer broke in. "Hmmm? Excuse, me deputy. I think I get the point of this. We all know what happened to Mayfield Commers- or at least we all know that the dog was severely taxed during that unfortunate event."

The hearings officer turned from the deputy to Rob and Peggy seated at the defendant's table with Spark. "You understand I am sure, Mr. Smith, that one more incident of biting, however, and the county will have no recourse. The law is very simple but also very rigid. One bite can be considered an accident and out of character. Two bites and we have a vicious dog that needs to be exterminated. Dogs go crazy just like people. Hmmm?"

There was something about the way Rob lowered his eyes to the table in front of him that disturbed the hearings officer.

"Mr. Smith," continued the hearings officer, "this *is* the first biting offense? Is it not? Hmmm? Hmmm?"

"Of course, it is!" yelled a young boy from the crowd.

"He's the paperboy!" whispered Peggy.

The boy delivered May a newspaper every day and often took a moment or two to play with Spark, and Spark loved to follow the boy for some blocks on his paper route barking and chasing the newspapers as the boy would throw them up onto porches. "Let Spark go! He's a good dog!" the boy yelled.

Rob started to speak, but for a few seconds, the murmur of the crowd was nearly too loud for his words to be clearly heard. When the room quieted, the hearings officer waved his gavel at Rob. "Well?"

"No, Your Honor."

The hearings officer again called for quiet in the room and then spoke regarding Rob's testimony. "Hmmm? You should be advised, Mr. Smith, that the court has been made aware that you are an officer of the court, sort of. You are not fully retired from the Seattle Police Department, so technically you remain a police officer. True, your status is a police officer from another state, but you are still a police officer. As such, you are defined by statute as an officer of this court; as such, your testimony is given a little more weight than that from other witnesses. Because of that, there is also a higher expectancy for your accuracy and honesty. While it is true that you are a police officer only in Washington State, there is a reciprocal agreement that police officers in both Oregon and Washington are officers of the courts in either state while testifying, therein.

"Do you understand that, Officer Smith? Hmmm?"

"Yes, sir. I do." Replied Rob quietly but firmly.

The hearings officer restated his question. "Is this the first time Spark has ever bitten anyone?"

Peggy put her hand over Rob's arm. "Oh, Rob? Don't!"

From the first row behind the defendant's table, Rob heard a familiar voice; Buck spoke up just loud enough for Rob to hear. "You'll have to tell, him, boy. It's the right thing to do."

Peggy shot her head around with tears in her eyes and looked long and hard at Buck, but Buck just glued his eyes steadfastly on the back of Rob's head. "Son?"

"Yes, sir. I mean, no sir, Your Honor," answered Rob. "Spark bit a man about an hour earlier."

"Hmmm? Do you mean to say that your testimony of a few minutes ago was not truthful?" asked the hearings officer. His scowl could be seen in the back row. "Hmmm?"

"No, sir." replied Rob. "I said that Spark had never bitten anyone before the day of the attack on Mr. Wi. But Spark attacked a man a couple hours before attacking Mr. Wi."

There were howls in the hearings room as the room nearly erupted with pent-up emotion and surprise. It took a few minutes before calm and order could be restored. The newspaper boy was standing on his seat yelling at the judge. Someone called Rob a murderer.

The officer's gavel hit the dais with a sharp whack! "Hmmm? So, your testimony of a few minutes ago was the truth, but it was a lie?"

"Yes, sir. Sort of. It was a version of the truth. Fer.., sure."

"I am sorry, Mr. Smith. I am forced by Oregon State Statutes to sentence Spark, the dog, to be put down. Sentence to be carried out at the earliest convenience of the animal control officers. Does anyone have anything to add before I terminate this hearing?"

Adults were standing and booing. Children were crying. A few wads of paper were thrown in the air towards the hearings officer. In the middle of the melee, Rob stood up quietly and signaled for silence from the crowd.

"There is the matter of the injuries to Mr. Jan Wi, Your Honor."

"How so? Hmmm?"

"Well," put in Rob, "I never actually saw the injuries, and I am not sure if the canine officers saw the injuries? I know it may be just grabbing at straws, Your Honor, but all we have are photographs taken by Mr. Wi, himself. It seems like a very important legal point."

"Hmmm?" asked the hearings officer.

"Well, Your Honor.., it seems.., Your Honor.., that it is just possible that Mr. Wi's trousers were torn. But if he wasn't actually bitten, then Spark has only bitten one person. If that is the case, he may be pardoned from death, if you are so inclined."

Mr. Wi jumped to his feet. "Are you calling me a liar, why I... I..."

"Rob, what are you doing?" whispered Peggy low

enough for only him to hear. "I like it, but..."

Rob sat down next to her, and both Mel and Peggy leaned their heads toward him for a quiet mini-conference. "I don't know, Peg, but I have a hunch. Always follow your hunches. There is something here? I don't know what? Have a little patience with me."

Buck was smiling.

Rob stood and turned to face Jan Wi. "Liar? No, sir. Not at all. However, this is a court of law, sort of, or about as much a one as Spark is liable to ever get. We should rely on evidence properly submitted. We all saw the photos, but we need to see your leg, in person, up front, and personal. It is the Rule of Best Evidence. Since you are present, Mr. Wi, your leg is the best evidence, not a photo of your leg."

"Mr. Wi?" asked the hearings officer. "Do you mind? He is right. It does seem trifle to sentence such a fine animal to death if we haven't seen the best evidence. The best evidence, in this case, is your leg. Please step up to the bench. Hmmm?"

A white haired man in the back of the room stood and begged the hearing officer's attention. "Sir, I am a doctor, a psychiatrist, really. Since this is an animal hearing, perhaps my credentials will suffice. I am also a fully qualified medical doctor, but I don't practice except for psychiatry. My name is Dr. Edward Rhapp. I would be glad to examine the gentleman's leg. True, I am prejudiced in this case toward mercy for Spark, for I was May's friend, but I am certainly capable of rendering a small examination for such a worthy cause."

Mr. Wi did not like it. Not one bit. He voiced his opinion that baring his chewed and bloody leg in a public setting, like this, was beyond his sense of propriety. But he relented when the hearings officer pointed out that it was just possible that the case would be set aside without an examination. It would not be necessary for him to hold up his leg for all to see; the doctor could examine the wound and stipulate that the photos factually represent the injuries.

Jan Wi walked up front to stand in front of the hearings officer's tall desk.

Spark growled as Wi walked past.

So did Peggy.

Doctor Rhapp simply walked up and suddenly knelt at Jan Wi's leg. Neither Rob, nor the hearings officer, nor anyone else in the room, could see Mr. Wi below his knees; their views were cut off either by the defendant's table or the small wall separating the visitors from the front of the courtroom. So quick was the doctor's kneeling, that it caught Mr. Wi off guard. He had expected they would go into another room behind the witness stand for privacy. But the doctor just unexpectedly dropped to his knees and suddenly pulled up Mr. Wi's pant leg. So sudden was the doctor's kneeling, that Wi actually jumped and attempted to pull away from the doctor, but it was too late.

With a troubled look on his face, the doctor stood to his feet and stared into Wi's eyes without saying anything- just stood there looking at him. "May I see the photos, please?" he asked the hearings officer. He carefully examined the photos, looked darkly at Mr. Wi, and knelt again. Then the doctor stood and silently compared the injuries with the photos in evidence. "Yes.., Your Honor.., the injuries in the photo match... perfectly."

The room exploded once again with yells of protest. Children cried. Peggy knelt and wrapped her arms around Spark's neck.

Rob stood once again. "Your Honor. In the interest of justice and mercy, I petition the court to allow a stay of execution for seventy two hours."

The hearings officer slammed his gavel onto the table top. "In all my years as a hearing officer I have never had to quiet the room with my gavel. Now, tonight, I have done it three times! You people must maintain order!" Even with the gavel, and his plea for quiet, the hearings officer had to raise his voice to make it heard.

"Officer Smith? What is your petition based on?"

"Perhaps, Your Honor, somethin' will come up."

"Well, that's not much, Officer Smith," replied the hearings officer. "But the petition is granted. Hope it does. Hope it does. Hearing dismissed. Hmmm?"

Rob could not sleep, so just before closing time he walked from his house to the Pelican and sat in Uncle May's customary seat at the bar. There weren't too many people in the bar at that time of night, mostly just a few locals wrapping up their day and a couple men, from out of town, putting the last touches on their attempts to get lucky with local beauties.

The bartender was an older red headed man Rob had seen several times at the bar. He spoke to Rob in a quiet and reassuring tone- not at all cold and aloof like Scott. "You've had a tough time of it. You can have one on me. I'll not be thinking you had anything to do with your uncle's death."

"Thanks, uh… Irish?"

"Name's Pat: Pat Miners. It's a good old Irish name, I'll grant you. My family might have all been in the local jail a time or two, but we were in Ireland, just the same! And, well, being in an English jail in Ireland is not the same as being in jail in this fair land."

Rob smiled to be polite, but he was barely listening. His mind was elsewhere.

"Awh.., and the dog, then," Pat went on. "I heard about the dog. The news is all over town, it is." He shook his head as he wiped the bar with a towel. "Sad, it is! I think we should break in and steal that dog. It would be kind of a jailbreak. The Irish know all about jail breaks."

Rob took the beer, sipped, and then set it down. He rubbed his eyes. "Oh, yeah. Add a charge of burglary to the homicide charge looming over my head? But even if we broke

Spark out of jail, what would we do with the dog, then, Pat?"

"Make a run for the border."

Rob smiled and started to put a fiver on the bar, but Pat pushed it back. Rob nodded his thanks, rubbed his eyes again and murmured. "Yeah. Spark was sentenced to death by a shrink named Rhapp. Huh!" Rob slapped his leg. "Dr. Shrinkwrap!"

The bartender laughed at that, and then to mourn Spark's troubles, he poured himself a beer. He took a long and slow pull. "This town must be changing. First a fine man like your uncle dies. And now Spark is to be killed? Then we have a stabbing in the parking lot earlier tonight! A sad day it is."

"A stabbing?"

"Aye, and the bar's been a hothouse all night. It just quieted down before you came in. We've never had a stabbing, here, you know. It's a quiet town."

Rob listened. He wasn't sure if he was much interested in bar gossip, but Irish just went right on with his story.

"About ten tonight, this new guy starts getting into an argument with a few of the locals. He was spouting some Marxist crapola about the state taking care of the average working person. How did he say it? Oh, yeah! The state should be a benevolent uncle instead of the tyrant it is now. We should all be friendly cousins and share the wealth. He was all upset about a bumper sticker on a car in the parking lot- my car as it turned out."

Rob laughed. What's it say?"

Pat rubbed a sticky spot on the bar. Nothin' much. Just, "God Bless America!"

"Yeah?" asked Rob. "And the other sticker? What does the other sticker on your car read?"

"Oh, well… 'Socialism's Great Until You Run Out of Other People's Money!'"

"He didn't like that, huh?" asked Rob.

"Nah. And then somebody else stuck up for the marines and the navy.

"We don't normally care what people talk about, here, in the bar," Pat continued, "but this guy was so radical that people were yelling at him. He was getting real red in the face and yelling something about redistributing the wealth of society."

Rob just looked at Pat Miners over his bear and took another slow sip.

"Then one of the locals got in his face when he started dissing the president, and apple pie, and mom back home. Finally, I just kicked the guy out."

"You said something about a stabbing?" asked Rob.

"Oh, yeah, so this local guy who stuck up for the marines, mom, and apple pie? The same guy got stabbed and robbed when he went out to his car."

"Anybody see the bad guy?"

"Nope," answered the bartender. "The victim just got stabbed and lost all his money."

"Any ideas?" asked Rob.

"I didn't see it," answered Irish. "But I think it was a little redistributing of the wealth of society, I do."

Rob swiveled on his bar stool and looked out the window into the night as if he were trying to see back into time when the stabbing occurred. "Huh?" he said over his shoulder to Irish.

The bartender wiped the bar again with a towel. "Yeah, you know. The great uncle wanted to take some of the wealth and redistribute it to the poor downtrodden nephew."

Rob nodded, and Irish went down the bar to serve another customer.

Just as Rob was thinking of leaving, Buck walked in with about a 9.5 on his elbow.

"Hey, Buck! Sit down next to me and let Irish, here, recount to you the trouble in the parking lot."

Buck and the beautiful lady sat obediently at the bar although Rob could tell that she would rather be alone with Buck.

"I've heard a little bit of it, already," put in Buck. "But come back, Irish, and tell me all about it. I would like to hear it all in detail from an eye witness."

Irish repeated the story for the fifth time that night. It gave him a feeling of importance. He was an eye witness... nearly.

When the story was finished Rob turned to Buck. "You know, Buck, that is pretty unusual for Pacific City."

Buck's eyes had been glued to Irish during the story. It was if he hung on every word. "I want to tell, you! This is just one sleepy little coastal town. We don't have stabbings and robberies. Something has changed. And you know what? There is something to this story... something nagging... as if we are missing something?"

Rob couldn't help notice how Buck's beautiful Hispanic girlfriend listened just as intently as Buck. After hearing the story and thinking for a few moments, she spoke to Irish with a mild and attractive accent. "So, this man weeth the knife? He keep talking about how the government should be some kind and caring parent, or something, like a grandparent? He sounds like a socialist. I fled my country because I could not stand the socialism."

Irish leaned his elbows on the bar to get a better view... and to make his point. "No. Not like some grandparent. This man, with the knife, he said that we should be nephews to a great and caring welfare state."

"Oooh, a nephew?" she said slowly. "A tio... er, how you say, uncle?"

Rob and Buck's heads shot around in unison. "Huh? Tio?!"

Rob dialed Mel's number on his cell phone. He recounted to Mel, the entire story and then hit him with the finish. "It's like this," he spoke into the phone, "according to Buck's beautiful friend, here, tio is Spanish for uncle."

The next morning, Billy was standing in the back yard of the double wide hideout looking up to the top of the roof. His neck was sore from the strain. "Vicky, what do you think she's doing up there?"

Veronica handed him another beer and joined him in staring up at her sister.

The sun was shinning. It had warmed after a little fog in the very early morning hours. A lovely cool breeze was blowing in from the ocean. Becky was up on the roof. It seemed natural to her, and she liked it up on the roof in the cool air and sunshine.

"Well, Billy, I think she is just sitting on the roof." Veronica pulled up a lawn chair and sat down. "You've been yelling at her for half an hour, now. Haven't you ever seen a girl on the roof?"

He rubbed the back of his neck. "No."

Becky would not come down from the roof. For the longest time, she wouldn't even acknowledge that Veronica and Billy were yelling up to her. From the roof, she could see just a patch of the surf rolling in, and she could see all the way down the beach to the front of the Pelican Pub. She was trying to pray for help. She had no idea how, but felt a lot closer to God up on the roof than in the double wide- with the bed in the next room rocking and making noises. Desperately, she was searching for a way out of this triangle of crime she had been drawn into, and she was trying to pray for help. She was praying for her sister and for the people they robbed. She did not want to see any more people hurt, except for Billy, of course. Most of all, she was praying that Buck would come and rescue her. Desperately she prayed for a hero.

"How did she get up there? There's no ladder?" he asked.

Veronica answered for her sister. "She pulled the ladder up after her. It's an old trick. I swear, I think she spent half of her childhood years up on the roof of our old house. She always pulled the ladder up after her so dad couldn't get up there and beat her more… or whatever he wanted to do to her."

Becky could hear them talking. Finally, she turned her head to look at Veronica, and after a moment's pause stuck out her tongue. "It wasn't his beatings I was hiding from up on the roof, and you know it, Veronica!"

Billy pulled up a lawn chair of his own and popped a top. "Becky!" he said with a slurp and a burp, "what are you doing up there?" He burped again.

Becky stared down at him from the edge of the roof. "Nice sound effects, Defect! You can be charming... Kill any old ladies today?"

Billy jumped to his feet and threw the can at her, beer and all, but she didn't move a muscle. The can missed her by a foot. She knew it would.

"I'm going to kill you," she said just loud enough to be heard over the sound of the distant surf.

Billy sat back down. He looked over at Veronica and sighed with a deep and exaggerated exhalation. Veronica had a very frightened look on her face and with good cause. Billy watched Veronica for a few moments, and then he looked back up to the roof and shrugged his shoulders. "I know."

Spark tested the cage with his nose. Then he tried to pull the wire fence towards him with his teeth, but the wire mesh was tight, too tight to pull loose. For just a few seconds, he pawed at the floor, but it was concrete, and he gave up almost immediately. Involuntarily, he let out a little whimper.

Out in the office, the night clerk was watching TV. From the pens, Spark could hear the laughter and the voices on the television and could see the lights from the screen bounce off the walls. The sounds and the lights reminded him of home and his warm bed near the fireplace. The sounds from the television were both comforting and distressing at the same time.

In desperation, Spark ran full bore and hit the wire mesh of his cage with the full weight of his body, but he was thrown back, lost his balance, and fell over. Quick as a wink, though, he was on his feet and facing the wire. The other dogs in the kennel cages were confused and excited by Spark's actions and began howling and barking.

Spark remembered his warm bed and thought of May, his owner and friend. He circled twice, gave up to the wire, whimpered once more, and settled down to his fate.

Chapter Eight

Silently, and with heavy hearts, Rob and Peggy walked into the Grand Jury waiting room and took two seats in the far corner. The tension in the room was nearly palpable in the small and stuffy waiting room. A dozen wooden chairs crowded along two walls. A single closed door stood ominously in the corner and led into the actual Grand Jury room where fates were dealt out by three men and three women jurists, where questions were asked and answered, where crimes were examined, where lives were changed forever.

Grand Jury is always a shocker for first timers. Rob knew what to expect from his years as a patrol officer in Seattle, but Peggy, on the other hand, was shocked to see the dory boat skipper and deck hand waiting in the same small room with Rob and her. The detectives who had done the original on-scene work on May's body, while it was still on the beach were also there wearing bored expressions and holding rolled up police reports. They nodded in reply to Rob's hello.

This particular Grand Jury waiting area was a room full of mixed emotions. Rob would always have a warm place in his heart for the skipper and mate. After all, they had saved his life in a daring and dangerous rescue at great personal risk. However, the skipper just glowered at Rob whom he still considered the murder suspect. The younger man, with the dory captain, kept turning from Rob to the captain and back again as if trying to figure a puzzle. The detectives watched this silent interplay but after a few minutes felt uncomfortable and got up to converse in hushed tones in the hallway.

All in a whirl, Mel rushed in and sat down out of breath. "Didn't think they would call me. I don't really know anything about this case. I was just the responding officer on the beach. Yet, here I am."

Rob started to say something, but Mel raised his hand to stop him. "Nope. We aren't supposed to talk together about this case. It's the Grand Jury rules, and all. They are pretty one way about that."

"That's kind of stupid," Peggy whispered to Rob. "He's been working with us from day one. He's been there every time either of us has needed anything. He has spent more time at May's house since the murder than I have!"

Rob looked over his nose at her.

"Well," she admitted, "perhaps not that much., but he's sure discussed this case with us. What gives with his attitude, now?"

Rob knew all that she said was true and wondered about Mel's indiscretion in associating with a suspect, wondered how he was getting away with it with the sheriff's office. It certainly would not be accepted on a large city police department. He thought about Mel's unusual friendship, and cooperation, and wondered silently to himself? There seemed to be only one explanation for a police officer to be so actively involved with a suspect in a murder?

Mel heard Peggy whispering and answered under his breath trying to keep the dory captain and mate from hearing. "Trouble is- I am your friend. I have broken department policies left and right, on this. I think I might be in just a little trouble over it, but I will cross that bridge when I come to it."

Half an hour later, the district attorney opened the single ominous looking door leading to the impaneled Grand Jury and called the dory boat deck hand. The captain grabbed the boy's arm. "You just tell them like I told you, Jimmy." But Jimmy didn't. He told them the truth, instead; the cliff had been too far away for him to see clearly who was fighting with whom. He trusted the captain completely, but just couldn't lie for him. He would die for him, but not lie.

Next they called the captain.

You could cut the tension in the small waiting room with a knife.

When the dory boat captain went in to testify, Peggy took the moment to ask Rob if he was all right, if he was handling the suspense and strain?

"Well, sure. I've done this a time or two. But, there is something I should tell you two, something about my first wife."

Peggy put her hand on Rob's bicep and sweetly squeezed it just a bit. "Is it real important, Rob? Do you need to tell us now?"

"Yes. It is very important. This isn't the first time I have…"

Before he could say any more the captain walked out, and Mel was called to testify.

They watched Mel walk into the small room and they waited without speaking. Peggy and Rob just sat there looking at that ominous door as if it was the doorway to heaven or hell, hope or disaster? It truly was. It was fate's door, for sure. A trickle of sweat rolled down Rob's back.

To the surprise of both Rob and Peggy, Mel was with the Grand Jury for just a brief few minutes when the door opened, and he walked out.

"Mr. Mayfield Robert Smith, please?" the District Attorney announced.

"Mayfield?" Peggy blurted out. She grabbed Rob's arm. "I didn't know your first name was Mayfield?"

Rob turned to Peggy and Mel. "There is something else. Something that the District Attorney will use against me. You must trust me. I…"

"Mr. Smith!"

As Rob walked through the doorway, and the door closed quietly behind him, Peggy turned to Mel. "Did you know Rob's first name was Mayfield?"

"Sure."

"What do you mean, 'Sure'? It's that simple? Just, 'Sure'? How did you know?"

"It was on the printout."

"Printout? What printout?"

"I'm a cop. I check on things. It's my job. I have read all the reports."

"He's your friend. We are both your friends. Reports?"

"Friends, girlfriends, lovers, mom; they are all the same to cops; we check them out. We have to do that. If you want to be near and dear to a cop, you have to understand. Cops check things out. It's a matter of personal survival."

Peggy sat back in her chair with a hrumph. "Rob hasn't checked me out," she said.

Mel simply lifted one eyebrow.

When Rob walked into the Grand Jury room, he was amused at how similar it was to all the jury rooms in which he had been before. There were six responsible looking citizens sitting around a table. The District Attorney motioned Rob to the witness chair and then walked to a desk of her own that was set apart from the table of jurists. She turned towards Rob and administered his Miranda Rights.

The District Attorney, to Rob's surprise, summed up the case and the testimony received, so far. "Officer Smith, you have been summoned, here, to answer questions to this Grand Jury. This is a very serious inquiry. You are a person of interest in a murder. If this Grand Jury renders a True Bill, the case will be remanded to court for a trial. If it renders a Not True Bill, it will mean that you are exonerated. Do you understand all this?"

"Yes, I do," answered Rob. "I have no trouble with this proceeding, at all."

"Thank you, officer. You are a Seattle Police Officer, are you not?"

"Yes, but I have been fully disabled since I was shot during a holdup attempt. Now I am a writer. I have written several novels, one of which is *Zippity Zappity Land*."

A younger woman juror, surprised at meeting one of

her favorite authors in such a setting, blurted out, "Uncle Neddy!" Hastily, she put her hand over her mouth as if to call back her words.

The other jurors looked at her in surprise.

The District Attorney gave the young juror a stern look and then turned back to Rob. She hesitated. It looked as if the outburst confused the D.A.'s line of questioning. She looked again at the juror and then, with obvious resignation, asked Rob, "Who is Uncle Neddy?"

Rob cast a friendly smile at the young woman and then at the other jurors. "Her reference to Uncle Neddy was a literary comment. Uncle Neddy was a children's writer in an old black and white movie. Perhaps you have seen *The Ghost and Mrs. Muir*?"

"Just what does that have to do with this proceeding?" asked the District Attorney.

"Nothing, really. I imagine it is an accidental reference to a character in the novel. You see, in *The Ghost and Mrs. Muir*, the heroine of the novel discovers that a person in her everyday life is Uncle Neddy, a famous children's book writer. People are sometimes shocked to discover that I am the author of *Zippity Zappity Land*. I have been called Uncle Neddy, before this."

Rob turned to the embarrassed juror. "Thank you for the compliment."

The D.A. coldly resumed her questioning. "You are still a police officer, are you not?"

"Yes, I am," answered Rob. It was then that he decided on his specific line of defense. Rob had been in court many times (but seldom as a defendant) and decided that his defense needed a direct and bold offense. "Yes, I am a police officer, but I was not acting in my official capacity when I leaped off that cliff in a vain effort to save my uncle… and his dog."

He could tell that the members of the grand jury were a little shocked at his directness. Nevertheless, he continued undaunted.

"You can call me officer or mister; either one of those titles is okay with me. I am permanently disabled from police work and expect to never return to it, so mister seems more apropos."

The District Attorney's lips pouted together. It was clear that she was miffed at his extended reply and interpreted it as an attempt to take control of the hearing. She was annoyed, and she was not going to have any of it. "Officer Smith, please contain your answers to my questions. Do you understand?"

"No, ma'am."

"What?" she replied.

"No ma'm. I am under suspicion of murder. It would not serve justice, or the court, for me to simply answer with the correct grammar and with short sentences. You are suspicious of my having committed murder, and in a direct attempt to allow this Grand Jury to come to the *correct* decision I will answer the questions in a way that will carefully tell the truth, and the whole truth, so that the Grand Jury, here, will be allowed to come to a correct and honest decision."

"Mr. Smith! I must ask you to keep your answers brief and to the point!"

Rob did not answer. He looked slowly at all six members of the jury. It was a blue-ribbon panel called to visit only important cases such as this one. The panel members appeared, by their clothes and deportment, to be of the upper business class. He kept his gaze honest and true and looked each member directly in the eye. Then, he turned and looked out the window as if he was on a holiday. In the distance, he could see just a glimpse of white sand and blue sea.

Rob kept looking out the window for nearly a minute- a long time when a room is full of people waiting for an answer and watching you. Then, he turned again to cast an even and steady gaze at the District Attorney.

"Mr. Smith! Did you hear me? You will keep your

answers brief and to the point!"

Rob looked again directly into the D.A.'s eyes until she lowered hers to her yellow legal pad. But he did not mutter even a single word.

"Mr. Smith! Will you please answer my question?"

It was an important moment; it was a pivotal point in his life, and he knew it. If his answer came off haughty and proud, or if it looked like he was anxious or duplicitous, he could get into deep trouble. He took his time. "No ma'am. I already answered that question." Then he turned to the Jury, itself. "I have been to many a Grand Jury in my time. I have always given sworn testimony as a police officer. I have never been the suspect in a murder. My answers will be full and truthful and accurate. But I will not simply say yes or no when a full and more complete answer is necessary."

He could tell that his timing had been just perfect and his tonal expression exact. It had needed to be. The District Attorney, however, was turning red in the face and had the look of someone who exasperated quickly. He made a mental note not to take advantage of that and embarrass her. If the Grand Jury members saw him as manipulative or pushy, he could fail in this stuffy, small room. And that would be disastrous. He knew that nothing could turn a jury as fast as a witness making a woman look bad. He had seen that happen before.

The questioning went on, not with his personal history (as he had expected), but with his arrival on the cliff. When Rob related finding his uncle's paints scattered about, the District Attorney began a direct attack on his credibility. "Isn't it true, Officer Smith, that the sheriff's department has not been able to locate any young lady matching the description you gave, the young lady you said was kneeling in the sand and looking over the cliff at Mayfield Commers in the water below? Isn't it true, Officer Smith, that no young lady exists?"

"Not exactly."

"How is that?"

"It is simple. They can find, anyone can find, many young women in Pacific City who match that description. Trouble is that not one of the young girls the police have found, so far, is that specific individual who was actually on that cliff when my uncle was killed. Only one woman in the whole world was on that cliff, only one woman saw my uncle murdered *prior* to my arrival. The sheriff's office has not found that specific woman.., yet."

The D.A. waved her hand in exasperation. "Mr. Smith. Please!"

"No ma'am. This is important." He turned again to the jury. "The sheriff's office has been unable to locate a very important witness to this murder. Don't be misled into believing that you must, therefore, convict an innocent man to get the sheriff's department off the hook. I arrived on the cliff *after* the murder. Therefore, I could not have committed the murder. I am not guilty just because a witness could not be located."

The D.A. let the room quiet down and then began another line of attack in a different direction. Her face quieted, and a look of smugness neatly crossed her features before she checked it. "Mr. Smith, what is your marital status?"

At that question, Rob visibly flinched. He had not meant to, but it was involuntary. The flinch and the cold look on his face had an immediate and visible effect on the jury. Several of them leaned forward in their chairs.

He answered quietly. "I am... widowed."

"I am sorry, Mr. Smith," lied the D.A. "Does that mean that your wife died?" She kept her face still and bereft of emotions. The Grand Jury members turned, as one, to give her a surprised and pitiful look.

"Of course," Rob answered. "She died." He sat back in his chair. He wanted to look out the window again, but he was afraid that he might look distracted or guilty if he did.

"So, then, Mr. Smith," continued the D.A., "back to when you jumped off the cliff to save your uncle and his dog.

Was that the first time you ever jumped off a cliff to save someone?"

"Well, I.., well…"

"Mr. Smith? Officer Smith?"

No," answered Rob. "It was not."

"Is it true, Mr. Smith, that you are the sole heir to the late Mayfield Commers estate?"

"Of course it is. But you see…"

"Is it true, Mr. Smith, that Mayfield Commers left you, his only heir, a small fortune in life insurance, bank savings, deposits, and paintings? Why, the paintings alone must have a retail value of nearly a quarter of a million dollars?"

"Yes, but…"

"Now, Mr. Smith," she continued, "about jumping off cliffs and people dying from great falls from cliffs whenever you are around..? Please, tell this Grand Jury how your wife died?"

The room was quiet. It was still. It was as still and stuffy as a tomb. Rob knew he had failed. "She… fell off a cliff… into the water."

Several of the jury members slumped in their chairs. The young woman, who had called him Uncle Neddy, broke her pencil.

"Did you," went on the glorious District Attorney, "also jump into the water to save her?"

"Yes, I did."

"Were you, Officer Smith, acquitted of any criminal charges in her death?"

"No. I was never charged."

"Of course. It was in Seattle. Mr. Smith, did you inherit a small fortune upon your wife's untimely death?"

Rob should have known that this line of questioning had been inevitable. He should have planned for it, but even if he had there was no way he could get through it calmly and innocent appearing. He was visibly shaken. "Why, yes. Of course. But.., no. I did not inherit the money. It was mine when

I married. We weren't like that with our money. We shared everything. It was mine as well as my wife's *before* she died! After… she died, it remained mine. It was mine before she died!"

"A million dollars from your wife's father because he died one year before your wife?"

"Well..,"

"I grieve with you on your loss, Mr. Smith.

"But one other thing. Mr. Smith. Is it true that the medical examiner found your wife with child.

"Well…"

"You don't like children, do you, Mr. Smith?"

"Of course. I…"

"One more question, Officer Smith."

"Yes?

"Wasn't Uncle Neddy, actually, a married man who was having an affair with a young woman?"

Game. Set. Match.

"Well..?"

"That is all, Mr. Smith. You are dismissed."

Rob, Peggy, and Mel walked out of the court house together to the small park across the street, where Rob slumped onto a bench in the shade of a cottonwood. The others followed suit. Rob's skin was pale. It was clear to Peggy and Mel that he had been shaken by the hearing. Nobody spoke for a few moments.

Rob didn't seem willing to talk, so Mel finally broke the silence. "I've been suspended." It was a quiet statement made in a conversational tone.

The news hit Peggy pretty hard. She turned to Mel in alarm.

"I received a telephone call while you were in with the Grand Jury, Rob."

"I would have been surprised if you hadn't, Mel," answered Rob. "You have been rather friendly with a suspect in a murder."

"I never considered you a suspect, Rob."

Rob waved his hand in a dismissive gesture and bent to pick up a pine cone fallen from one of the nearby trees. "Yeah. You didn't. But your department sure does, and that Grand Jury is going to return a True Bill on me."

"Oh, you mustn't say that!" replied Peggy. "They won't do that!"

"Look, you two," insisted Rob, "that Grand Jury didn't go too well. I'm in dire trouble. Of course, I didn't kill May. I loved him. But that Grand Jury was shocked by the things they heard today!"

Mel picked up his own pine cone and tried for a nearby squirrel. "I'm not a witness. Neither is Peggy. We won't be called to testify if there is a trial. So, why don't you just share with us what happened in there?"

Rob related how the District Attorney had him tell the jury about his writing career after becoming disabled. "The D.A. accused me of writing pornography… and junk."

"You don't write junk!" interrupted Peggy. "Do you? I mean, lots of people buy your books."

Mel put his arm around Peggy's shoulder. "He does not write *junky* pornography!"

"Knock it off, will you, Mel?" plead Rob. "Honestly, your dark humor is going to get to me."

"That was humor?" chimed in Peggy. A cute little giggle broke from her that nearly put Mel over the edge. Slowly he removed his arm from her shoulder.

Rob looked from one to the other. Neither one of them understood the seriousness of the news Rob needed to share. Their humor was relentless. It was like a disease the both of them shared.

"Well," kept up Mel, "you don't write pornography… or junk. Do you, Rob? I mean, really… I know pornography when I see it, but junk? I mean.., isn't pornography junk by definition?"

"You look at pornography, Mel?" asked Peggy. "You know it when you see it? Did you really say that?"

There was no answer from Mel. He just adopted a look of innocence and stared into the distance.

"Now," continued the smiling Peggy- on a role, "if you did write *junky* pornography, I could understand the condemnation."

"Well put, Peggy," added Mel.

"Do you write pornography, Rob?" she asked. "Maybe Mel has looked at some of your porn?"

"Of course not… I mean… stop it, you two! I don't write pornography. But the District Attorney put the thought into the jury's mind. She asked about *The Maltese Fulcrum.* That's…"

Mel broke in. "In all seriousness, Rob, that is a pretty funny piece of detective comedy!"

"Thank you," said Rob, "But the D.A. read just a couple lines from it. You know, about the woman who thought that the man she married might be her grandmother."

"Oh, yeah!" interjected Peggy. "That's funny! But that's just humor. There is nothing dirty in that book."

"You know that I write clean stories and books. There is nothing in any of my books that my mother could not read!"

"Well, yeah..," put in Peggy. "But your mother was no virgin!"

"Hey, that was good!" added Mel.

"You two! Well, I guess it's how it's presented," answered Rob. "Then the D.A. alluded to *The Dream Book.*"

Peggy laughed out loud. It was a deep gut-wrenching laugh, a real head-back-and-roaring laugh to bring the house down. It was completely out of place in such a quiet park setting. They had been discussing Rob's future, his possible trial for murder. He could be tried, convicted, sentenced, and executed. But Peggy laughed. How she laughed! She looked at

Rob, and then at Mel's startled expression, and slapped her knee. "I'm sorry, guys. But that *Dream Book* is a real killer! I mean, it is funny! It reached up and bit you on the butt, didn't it, Rob? Maybe the jury will read the book? That will really confuse the hell out of them… Your soul's all afire!"

Peggy's laughter was too contagious for all three of them. They all laughed, and then Rob got back to his retelling of his testimony.

"But, look, both of you, there is something you don't know. I should have told you before; I should have warned you.., only it sounds awfully incriminating."

Finally, they stopped laughing, and Mel said quietly, "We are your friends, Rob. You can tell us anything."

Peggy giggled. "We will probably laugh at it. But we are your friends!"

"You know that I was married before?"

"Yes, we know," answered Peggy.

She turned to Mel. "Did you know, Mel, that Rob and I are going to marry?"

Mel's head spun around at that. It took a few seconds, then he shrugged, turned, and smiled at Rob.

"Only this, Peg," continued Rob, "my wife died."

"I knew that. You told me."

"Well, did you know… that she fell off a cliff? Did you know that I jumped in to try to save her? Did you know that I inherited a lot of money as the surviving spouse?"

Peggy jumped to her feet. Her mouth was open, but no sound came out. The humor was gone.

Mel spun off the bench and walked away.

Peggy was on his six.

The Maltese Fulcrum
By Rob Smith

She walked into my office unannounced. She was tall, beautiful and blond. She wore a mink stole that must have put some poor schlump back a thousand bucks and a low-cut blouse that paid the schlump back but kept few secrets. Well.., to be precise, it kept two secrets. Barely.

When she came thru the door, I had my feet up on the desk lighting a Lucky Strike in my cupped hand like I had seen Bogey do a dozen times in old black and whites. My good eye looked over my cupped hand at her. The Lucky Strike started to wilt.

Without saying a word, she walked up to my desk, leaned over and placed a small, mysterious looking item on the ink blotter in front of me. She paused before straitening up. Her eyes lifted to meet mine to see if I was pondering her secrets.

Then she looked at my Lucky Strike. Her voice was sultry and low. "You have to puff on those things to make them work."

It was too late. The match had cowered out. I flipped the unlit cigarette toward the waste basket near the window.

She crossed the small office and sat down in the only other chair in the room. With a flourish, she negligently crossed her legs.

"What do you think of it?"

"I think about it all the time," I said.

"There used to be two of them."

"Two!"

Her eyes were speaking dollar amounts that had bankrupted the shlump and that I knew *my* soul couldn't cash. In life, the revelation of well held secrets comes costly. I was well acquainted with that truth. I had gone bankrupt a time or two trying to pay that particular price. A quick calculation, however, reminded me that I had… nothing left to lose.

"My husband," she said with her voice as smooth as silk, "who I suspect is really my grandmother, took the other one. I'll give you $1,000 a day to find the other one."

I dropped my feet to the floor. "I imagine, then, that you are referring to this small mysterious looking item you placed, here, on my desk."

"For now, yes. It is solid gold, you know."

I lifted the item. "This… small… hmm. Solid gold, you say?"

We finished the business haggling, and she walked out the office door.

Five seconds later I was on my knees trying to locate my cigarette that had rolled under a table next to the waste basket. Like I said, it was my last Lucky Strike.

Just as I found the cigarette, a lady screamed in the hallway outside my office door. The scream was followed by three quick shots from a small-caliber firearm.

I listened.

There was a heavy thump of a body falling onto the hardwood floor.

A few second later, a shadow crossed the smoky windows of my hallway office. The shadow approached my office door. I did not move.

"Perhaps," thought I, "that person will just go away."

To my relief, it was the blond who walked back into my office.., but she was holding a smoking revolver in her left hand. Women with guns always frighten me.

"You always hide under tables at the first sign of shooting?"

"Mostly.., always. Yeah. Uh, huh."

"I'm not married anymore… I found my husband."

"That's nice," I said. That sounded dumb, even to me, but for the life of me I just could not think of one other thing to say, or a reason to come out from under the table. It was nice down there.

"I still want you to find the other missing item," she said calmly.

She placed the small revolver in her handbag and turned to go. But before walking out the door, she turned back to face me, once again. "One more thing," she cooed. "I'm tall. I'm blond, and I own a liquor store. When this is all over do you think a swell looking chump like you would be interested in a dame like me?"

"I don't know," I replied, "I've kind of been waiting for one that lights up and kills bugs."

"You are a real funny guy," she said. "One more... thing before I go."

"Yes."

"I lied to you."

"They all do. It comes with the license."

"There aren't two of those."

"Huh."

"There are three. The dwarf has the third one. He's in... Istanbul."

Chapter Two

A few minutes after the blond left my office, I

recognized Rachel's quiet, even footsteps climbing the stairs. At the head of the stairs, where the body lay, her evenly timed steps did not miss a beat.

Rachel opened the office door and nonchalantly walked over to the coat rack. I was afraid to look up at her. With practiced deliberation, she took off her hat and heavy woolen coat and hung them on a hook just like she had done every day for three years.

"You know, boss, that there is a dead body in the stairway… again?"

"Uh, huh," I answered. "Wanta call the police and report it that way? I don't know anything about it. I never heard a thing. I came in the back way. I have an alibi."

"Boss, we don't have a back way."

"Oh, yeah. Well, forget about it, then. Maybe the body will just go away."

"Private detectives," she muttered under her breath as she dialed the police precinct, "are supposed to be a little quicker on the uptake."

I listened to her haggling with the desk sergeant, arguing with him that she knew what a dead body was and that there sure was one too many of 'em in the hallway. "We don't know who it is. There is just a body on the stairs." She looked up at me over the phone receiver as she continued to talk to the Sergeant. "No. We both met this morning at the bottom of the stairs, by chance, and came up together…. No… We won't touch anything. No, I don't think Wes shot anybody… again!"

She hung up the phone and shot me a look that could fry bacon on the sidewalk. In December.

"Thank you, Rachel," I said.

"I *guess* you should thank me! Who is that dead guy in the hallway, anyway?"

I tipped my hat back on my head like I had seen Bogey do when he was deep in thought. How could I explain that body to Rachel? "He's either our client's husband or our client's grandmother. I don't know which. And I'm afraid to go look."

Rachel did not look up. She just began working on the papers at her desk. "Sounds like the case we had last week."

Buck walked up to the bench in the park and sat down uninvited but definitely welcomed.

Rob was completely surprised. "Buck! How did you know about this?"

"Well, Rob, I figured you might need a friend. The Grand Jury is a matter of public record, so I knew when and where." He took a long and deep breath. "It's nice, here, in the park."

"Yeah, but…" began Rob.

"I was your uncle's friend, remember? My friendship with May meant quite a lot to me."

"Yeah. Well, *I'm* a little short of friends, this morning. Mel and Peggy just found out that my first wife died falling off a cliff and that I inherited her fortune."

"I knew about that, Rob."

"You knew about that?"

"I figured you might need a friend this morning. I know all about your marriage and your wife's death. May told me everything."

"Everything?"

"Nearly," replied Buck. "I tried to get to the Grand Jury, but I was late. I saw the three of you, here, while walking back to my car. Nice and quiet park, this?"

"Peggy and Mel didn't like it much."

"Rob," he said, "they will be back. Me? I learned a long time ago that people are what is important. Real estate is my job. People are my passion. I figured that Peggy and Mel might have a difficult time with the information about your wife's death, so I thought I would stop by and see if I could help."

"You knew the information about my wife's death

would come out today?"

"No. I didn't *know*. But I figured. The D.A.'s investigators have been snooping around and asking questions. They got to me yesterday. They were hinting around about your life up in Seattle, so I led them on a little and kind of turned the interview on them."

"Huh?"

Rob and Buck sat for a few minutes watching the squirrels.

"You're a smart guy," said Rob. "Who killed my uncle. Why kill my uncle?"

Buck looked at Rob rather impatiently. "You are too close to this to think straight. Part of it is easy. Part of it is difficult. Who killed your uncle? I'm working on that. Why? That is the easy part."

"Huh?"

For a minute, Buck watched a couple girls walking through the park. Then he sighed and continued his line or reasoning. "Like I said, part of it is easy, part of it is difficult. May had something, something extremely valuable, valuable enough to kill. So, what could it be? What did he have?"

"Well, I've already got plenty of questions. What I don't have is answers," was all Rob could manage.

Buck continued. "It couldn't have been one of his paintings. He would have given any one of his paintings away to anyone that loved one that much. You knew him. He would have considered it a compliment. May was weird that way. No. It was something else, something very, very valuable."

"So," put in Rob, "we are no further along than before."

"Sure. Sure we are," answered Buck. "It was something May had just recently come by, and it was extremely valuable."

"Huh?"

"The only thing of value to May was people and art."

Rob's mouth was hanging open.

"So," Buck continued, "May recently came by a very valuable painting, and someone in the art world found out about it and killed him for it."

Rob looked at Buck in wonder. Finally, he spoke up. "One of those Matisse paintings, I guess?"

"We are on the same track, Rob. Weird paintings, though."

"He particularly liked a naked blue woman," replied Rob.

"Don't we all."

Buck paused and looked at the sky. He sighed deeply, again. "Weird painting. I don't... remember... naked women being blue?"

Rob sat at the bar late that night in the Pelican. It had been early when he arrived, but the hours had ticked away. Time to time, as business allowed, Irish came over and leaned his big arms on the bar. "It's trouble you are in, my boy. Sure it's an Irishman, you're not? You've trouble 'nough even for one of us blokes."

"'Nother beer," Rob said. It was about all he had been saying all night. He had been filling Irish in on the Grand Jury, his memories of Wanda, his uncle's death, his nagging leg, Mel's and Peggy's anger- it was all too much.

Sensing his bad Karma, the other patrons in the bar had pretty much left Rob alone all evening. Some of the locals recognized him, wanted nothing to do with him and avoided him. One local passed close by and called him a killer. But for the most part, no one knew what to say or do, so they whispered and pointed but left him to his own devices.

"'Nother beer won't help you, lad. But I'll pour it. Not like you're getting drunk off 'em, though. But why don't you just go home? There's notin' for it tinaight."

So, he did. It was one hundred and seventy five paces from the back door of the Pelican to the front door of May's house, and it was a good thing it was no further, for Rob was exhausted. But even drained of nearly all his energy, he instinctively pressed the flashing red light on the answering machine as he passed through the kitchen and staggered towards the stairs. A frightened voice was speaking as he rounded the landing half way up.

"Call me, immediately, on my cell. Your life is in danger!"

"Oh, I hope so!" he said stumbling up the stairs. "That would just top off my day."

He went upstairs and fell onto the bed.

Meanwhile, Spark was trying to get adjusted to his new surroundings, but it wasn't easy. He was used to being treated like a king. In the pound, he was in a wire cage with a concrete floor. Twenty other dogs continually barked or whined. There was hardly a quiet second among the many dogs crowded together. A huge Rottweiler barked or howled constantly.

The night officer knelt beside Spark's cage and eased his fingers through the mesh. Spark quietly turned his head and licked the fingers. Spark was especially grateful for kindness, here, where he felt so lonely and forsaken.

"There, boy," the officer said quietly. You have the best temperament of any animal I have ever seen." He looked at the other sleeping dogs quartered immediately to Spark's left and right. "Why, you even have a quieting influence on those around you." He handed Spark a little treat from his coat pocket. "You're a natural born leader, you are. I think I will take you out of this cage for a little while. Would you like that?"

When he walked into the front office with a dog on leash, Larry took exception. "Ralph," asked the other officer on duty, "what, exactly, are you doing? We don't bring animals into the office, here. You know that?"

"Larry, this is no usual runaway or stray dog. Don't you know who this is?" Ralph dropped to his knees and gave Spark another big hug and a rub. "This is the Irish Setter from Pacific City."

Larry didn't know. He just kept that lazy expression in his eyes that told Ralph all he needed to know about Larry's level of concern.

"You know? The artist's dog? Haven't you ever been to Pacific City for Dory Days or the kids parade?"

"Not exactly."

"Well, this dog, exactly, was the guest of honor last year at the parade."

"No!"

"Larry," continued Ralph, "this dog belonged to that artist, what's-his-name. You've seen him on the news. I know you have."

"No."

"In the news? The artist who was killed? The guy who was shoved off Cape Kiwanda?"

A slight flicker of light appeared in Larry's eyes before he checked it. "Oh, yeah. So? So what?"

"So, this is the guy's dog!" replied Ralph.

Larry looked through the records and came up with the file on Spark. "Oh, yeah. Hey, so that's where the dog got so beat up? He looks a little ragged. It says, here, that the dog is to be put down. They are going to kill this dog, snuff him out."

"Larry," replied Ralph sarcastically. "You have always been the epitome of caring and involvement. But I know you've seen this dog before."

Larry had seen the dog, but he just didn't care enough to get involved. His job was to keep the cages clean and maintain reasonable order throughout the long nights. He could not understand Ralph's interest or concern. "The pay is the same whether I recognize this dog or not." He threw the file back on top of the metal cabinet and turned back to Ralph. "Man, it's fifteen dollars an hour whether I like dogs or not.

No matter what, it's fifteen dollars an hour. And I have to clean all the cages. Fifteen dollars an hour!"

Ralph walked Spark to the door. He didn't care, much, if Larry liked it or not. "We are going for a walk." He held up his hand to stave off Larry's protestations. "No. No. We are going for a walk. This dog and I! A bright and beautiful animal, like this, will go crazy in a cage all day and all night with nobody but you for companionship. I nearly go crazy, myself, but I'm only here for eight hours at a time."

"Ralph," spoke Larry to his back, "you have never taken a dog for a walk, before. Not once. Not, exactly, one time!"

"Exactly."

The night air was cool, and there was no traffic on the deserted road. Ralph held the leash tightly and Spark was excited and relieved at being outside, but he stayed close and tried not to pull away from the officer. He was nearly breathless at the opportunity to leave the cages and be out in the cool breeze coming in from the Pacific Ocean. He danced in appreciation, but he did not tug or strain the leash.

They walked up one side of the street and then down the other. At the dog's good behavior, Ralph relaxed and held the leash a little looser. Spark responded by being more subservient and obedient. He had been trained how to walk on a leash, and, somehow he sensed that this walk was important, that it might be a test of some kind.

"Hey, boy, you are a really good dog!" spoke Ralph to him in the darkness. "Most dogs just pull and tug and make walking on a leash more trouble than it's worth. You have had obedience training. I can tell. And I have an idea."

When they returned to the station Ralph placed Spark in a cage next to the nosiest of dogs. Larry came to the door to watch and see if he could add a nay-say. "What, exactly, are you doing, now?" he asked. "That's the wrong cage for that animal."

"I'm putting Spark next to this trouble maker. You

know if we could get this Rottweiler to quiet down you might get some peace and quiet, around here. That way, you wouldn't miss your usual nap on city time."

The two dogs met on either side of the mesh. Spark casually placed his nose to the wire. The Rottweiler huffed and puffed and ran back and forth. Then he began howling anew.

"Didn't work, exactly," said Larry.

"Well," replied Ralph, "I think we will let them get used to each other. Let's go back into the office and just see what happens, exactly."

Back at his desk, Larry sat down and leaned back in his chair. "Only thing is, Mr. Dog Whisperer, that Irish Setter is scheduled."

Ralph was not amused by Larry's behavior. He had never really warmed to lazy people. "You know, Larry, I think I will transfer to another shift... away from you."

"Yeah?"

"Yeah. Exactly," replied Ralph. "When I see a mess around here, I look at it and try to figure a way to clean it up and make what ever caused it a little better."

"Yeah?"

"When you find a mess, Larry, you ask if the mess can be blamed on someone else."

"Yeah. OK, Ralph. But that dog is still scheduled."

"You told me, already."

"To be exterminated. In twenty four hours."

Ralph dropped the file he had been looking through. "They won't do it. We won't do it! Not that dog!"

"Scheduled," said Larry. "Exactly."

Chapter Nine

As tired as Rob was, he could not sleep. His mind kept going back to Wanda, and how good life had been with her. Those had been the good old days.

If ever you are lucky enough to sail into the lovely, blue and jade-green waters of Puget Sound and the San Juan Islands, relax and reminisce on life. Ponder on how sweet and pleasant living can be, how wholesome the air smells, how very vivid life can feel. The picturesque waters of Puget Sound twist and turn for hundreds of miles amongst pine covered islands and turquoise peninsulas. The waters and islands are truly beautiful to behold.

Fortunate souls own homes along the many granite pebbled beaches dotting the shorelines. There is so much water, that while actual water-front property might be at a premium, property with a view is commonplace. Picturesque views are shared by the common and the privileged alike. Low-income rental properties overlook breathtaking nautical vistas. Gas stations have views of bays and inlets of which dreamers only dream. It is, quite literally, a paradise.

Not quite in the San Juan Islands, but their nearby adopted capital, Seattle, is a lovely cacophony of modern skyscrapers and quaint shops along an aging waterfront. It is a huge, thriving metropolis, by any standard, but one may still drive down to the waterfront, and launch a small boat, and leave all the world behind. From Pier 54, in the midst of the small shops and tourist attractions, Rob and Wanda Smith launched their day cruiser. Rob was a content man; he was taking his world with him.

As the pier shrunk in size behind the Marlin, Rob was teasing Wanda about her name and his inability to come up with a suitable nickname. "Wan? Would you hand me a beer?"

he would say. Then, "Da? How about some chips?" She just called him Rob, or Vanilla. As they crossed the expanse of Elliott Bay, she wished for an auto pilot, so they could both go below. They had been married only a year, and she was still in love, and she had a wonderful surprise to spring on Rob at just the right time.

It had been a wonderful year, that first year with Rob, the first of married life, the first year setting up their home.

Her father had died in that first year, that was true, but his death was almost a god-send. He had been in such pain for so many years, and although his death had been a blight on their first year's bliss, she knew that her new life with Rob was just beginning.

Her father's life of pain had ended, but she was so proud of her father. He had known that his life was nearly over and just leaned into it. She admired her father for his attitude and acceptance of something he could not control. For her father, time had slowed to a crawl. Finally, out of desperation he had simply said, "Oh, God. Help me." And He did.

Rob had been so understanding and supportive during that time. In spite of her father's death, Rob and Wanda were happy, and their relationship was stronger for the testing.

Today in the Marlin, Rob and Wanda were heading for Illahee State Park across from the west shore of Bainbridge Island. Wanda knew, as she watched the trailing phosphorescence behind the motor, that they might just as easily end up in Port Orchard walking among shops full of antiques, or they could anchor at the Boat Shed for a beer and some oysters. That's what was so special about their outings together. Once away from the regiment of police work, Rob was fond of saying, with an expansive wave of his arm and his huge and homey little-boy smile, that they were simply going, "Thataway, just… thataway."

This time they docked at Illahee, as planned, and went ashore with their picnic basket. "I would like to take the trail to Sundown Beach," said Rob. "We used to go there as a family when I was a boy. I haven't been on that trail for fifteen or twenty years. You can't pull a boat up to Sundown Beach because of the shoals. It's a bit of a walk, but we are both strong and the sun is shining!"

It was a glorious day. The breeze was cool off the water, bees hummed in the pine trees and among the wild flowers. Rob was happy. Wanda loved that special day as she had loved few times before. She had a sense that life was special. Rob was special. His job was special. And now that she had a secret to share with Rob, she was also special. She hadn't told him about the baby. She was waiting for a special time, a special place to tell him that she was special… too. To tell Rob that he had given her something to make her special. It was spring-time on Puget Sound, and she thought that she could feel life, itself, in the air. But it wasn't life in the air that she felt. It was eternity on the threshold.

It was then that she fell.

It was then that it all ended. All.

It wasn't much- just a twist of an ankle and an upturned tree root where the trail took a clumsy turn, and Wanda was in mid air as her feet flew out from under her. She grabbed her stomach as she somersaulted. Her last thought was of her baby. She wondered how the baby would ever survive such a fall?

Rob was carrying the basket and whistling gaily on the trail ahead. He turned, with his ever-present little crooked smile, and saw his entire life flash before his eyes. He saw his life, as he knew it, perish. Even with Rob's trained reflexes it took him a second before springing into action. The heel of Wanda's left foot was awkwardly upside down and in the air… off the path? It was difficult for his mind to process the sight, and that confusion slowed his reactions. But a second, or a year, mattered little. Wanda was gone.

So quickly he ran back down the path, that he actually saw Wanda hit the water far below.

He jumped immediately with his arms all akimbo

without a thought for his own safety or chance of survival. The wind tore his sunglasses from his face. He heard someone yelling Wanda's name. His entire life with Wanda flashed before his eyes. That life had been good, wonderful, blissful. It had been a paradise.

As he hit the water, he thought he heard someone crying.

He knew, immediately, on surfacing with Wanda in his arms, that his wife of only one year was no longer his. She had hit the water wrong, and her neck broke on impact.

The sea along the shore was calm and between tides, at the moment; it was something the fishermen call a slack tide, a short period of time when the waters calm, a time between two opposing forces, a time of change. The water was like glass. It was like a glass door you could just step through… to eternity. And she did. And she took along her unborn baby.

Rob simply pulled her over into shallow water and walked out of the water with her snugly in his arms, carried her up to the pebbly beach and laid her body carefully on the sand and small granite stones. Behind Rob, the water remained completely still… like the ice of his heart. Carefully, and with great tenderness, he straightened Wanda's dress and then her hair. She had lost a shoe.

He had no idea that Wanda had been pregnant. The news from the medical examiner hit him like the proverbial ton of bricks. On that news, he lost his breath. Then he lost his lunch. He had nothing else to lose.

He awoke in his lonely bed glad to put his recurring nightmare behind him. Rob lay there in bed, in Pacific City, thinking and re-thinking what he had to go on concerning May's murder. It was still not much. May had been pushed off a cliff and intentionally killed. Why? Pushed off by whom? Killed for a painting he had just purchased? He laid there considering all the possible solutions. Did May's paintings, really, have anything to do with it all? Was Buck correct about May purchasing a valuable Matisse? Tio bothered him. Right this moment tio might be invading someone's home, hurting or murdering. From the pub, he had called Mel's cell and left a message about the stabbing in the parking lot, and hoped that Mel had relayed the information about tio and his stereotypical socialistic ideas about redistributing wealth. It was, perhaps, the first real lead the Lincoln County Sheriff's office received in the case.

What of Peggy? Was he truly in love with Peggy so soon? Did she think he killed Uncle May? Did she really think he could have killed his first wife, Wanda? He had worshiped Wanda.

In those early morning hours, while he was slipping in and out of a deep but troubled sleep, the intruder quietly opened the front door. Rob put away too much alcohol the night before to hear the break-in.

He awoke to the early morning light but did not know why? He was still tired. Had something awakened him? For a long, few minutes, he laid awake listening. Had he been startled, or was the sound in his dream? Then he heard it again.

Silently he slipped into his trousers, grabbed his Glock by the bed, and made for the top of the stairs. Slowly and carefully he avoided the creaky board on the top stair and started down. Three steps down he shifted the Glock to his left hand for a better angle around the corner at the bottom of the stairs. Five steps down and he clicked off the safety. In answer, he heard a small click from below. Was it also the safety being thumbed off a semi-automatic hand gun? On the eighth step, he stopped to listen. His heart was in his throat.

Humming? He could hear humming? How pleasantly surprised he was that Peggy hummed when she made coffee in the mornings. Peggy clicked on the coffee pot and turned to Rob's light steps on the stairs.

He put the Glock down on the stair tread and walked casually down to meet her. She was standing there, in the kitchen, with an open red flannel shirt. The tail of the shirt was tied around the waist of her blue jeans.

"I thought you were going to sleep all morning. You left the front door unlocked."

"I didn't think I had much to wake up to this morning."

"Huh?"

"Well, I've been in this town a very few days, and already I have been in the hospital, and I've been arrested for murder. I don't think there is a part of my body that is not still sore from the jump from the cliff. I've made two friends, and they both left in a huff yesterday thinking I had killed my first wife."

Peggy pushed the toast down and buttered the first piece. "You didn't have anything to do with your wife's death." She took a bite of the toast, a gulp of juice, and poured Rob some juice. "I know you didn't… Did you?" She knew that she shouldn't have even asked, but she wanted to hear it from Rob's lips. She wanted to look deep into his eyes when he answered. Somehow she would know the truth if she could just see deep enough.

Rob slumped into a chair. "I loved her. We were walking along a cliff by the water, and she simply fell off. I was not even close to her when she fell. I was utterly devastated by her death."

Peggy sat down next to him and leaned her head on his bare shoulder. "You jumped in, didn't you."

"Yeah. I'm real good at jumpin'… Not too good at saving."

There was a tear in her eye for him, or for Wanda, or for May. "I'm sorry, Rob. I'm real sorry."

"I know."

"You lived in Seattle, then?"

"Yeah. But I couldn't stand to be in our house without her. I rented it out and took an apartment on Lake Washington. Lake Washington is fresh water. I only jump into salt water."

She looked up at him. "Rob, I'm in love with you. I want only you.., forever. Take me upstairs to the bedroom? It is a lovely summer morning at the beach.., and I want you."

The toast popped up.

Arm in arm, they walked slowly up the stairs, but Peggy drew up when she saw the Glock on the step. "You're not too used to women breaking into your house in the morning, are you?"

"Out of practice. I could catch on again.., with some practice."

They embraced at the head of the stairs. She squeezed up as close to him as possible. "You're not too sore all over your whole body for a little… practice?"

Arm in arm, and with great expectations, they turned and were about to walk past the Matisse room when they noticed it all amuck.

Peggy broke from Rob and ran inside the room. "Someone's been in here, Rob!" Stacks of paintings that had been leaning on the walls were tipped over and spread out on the floor. The contents of all the shelves had been thrown onto the floor.

Rob remained in the hallway. "So.., uh.., practice is over?"

Peggy was already on her knees searching through the paintings for… what.., she had no clear idea. "Oh, Rob! Look at this room! Who did this?"

"I don't know who, but I can figure *when* they did this?" said Rob. "Probably, during the Grand Jury. They could pretty well count on me not being home for several hours. What they were searching for, I haven't a clue. Whatever the special thing is that May was going to show us must still not be in the thief's possession. Or they wouldn't keep looking for it. Perhaps, Buck was right."

On one wall, there was a three-letter word scribbled with crayon that gave Rob a chill. It simply read, "tio". Peggy shivered noticeably. She felt as if she, herself, had been violated in some way even though it wasn't her house.

Rob dialed Mel's cell phone. He promised to come right over.

Peggy stooped to lift a painting, just one of several of the nude lady on a blue background. "You've thought all along that there was something to this room. I guess you were right about that. Wish we could figure it out."

Rob slapped his forehead. "The message!" He ran from the room.

She followed him downstairs, and he punched the red button on the telephone recorder. "I recognize the voice," she said. "It's May's friend and co-conspirator in their fetish with Matisse. He's a doctor, or professor, or something in Baltimore."

"Any idea what he is talking about?" Rob asked, "about my life being in danger?"

"No, I don't, Rob. But maybe we should take it seriously. I think we might be able to find his number around somewhere."

They were looking for his number when the phone rang again, and a man asked, after a long pause, to speak with Mayfield Commers.

Rob put the machine on speaker-phone. "I am sorry," Rob answered, "I am his nephew from Seattle. Uncle May has had a tragic accident." Silence was the only answer, so Rob spoke hastily, before the caller could hang up. "Are you his friend from Baltimore?"

Still there was no answer for a very long time, and then finally the caller spoke. His voice sounded worried and frightened. "There… was a young woman there with whom I spoke a time or two. I think I would recognize her voice. Is she there?"

Peggy spoke up quickly. "Hello, professor."

"Please, do not use my name. It is not safe to discuss this over the phone. You have no idea how much money and international intrigue is involved here. You are in great danger!"

"Well, yeah!" Rob answered. "Uncle May was killed!"

Once more, the professor did not respond for several seconds. "I must go. I am reviewing Le Cygne at the port. I must do it right away; next... even. Pity you can not meet me there." With that, the mysterious caller hung up.

Rob just stood dumbfounded, staring at the phone as if it could reveal more if he looked at it hard enough. "International intrigue? Did he really say intrigue? As in an old black and white movie intrigue?"

"Yep. Get dressed."

"Huh?"

Peggy turned and ran back upstairs yelling over her shoulder. "Get dressed." She disappeared into the Matisse room. "Never mind about a shower. Just get dressed. We don't have much time."

A few minutes later, when they met on the stairs, she was holding a large oversized book of Matisse paintings. Rob started to ask her about it, but she shushed him with a soft finger to his lips. "We don't have much time," she whispered. "We are in danger! Get dressed! Bring a gun! Bring two guns!"

Peggy was driving north out of town on Highway101 passing through Tierra Del Mar before she said anything or would answer any of Rob's repeated questions. She could tell that he was getting a little hot under the collar, but she was concentrating on driving and watching for any signs of being followed. It did feel to her like she was in some cheap who-done-it detective book, but she also knew that what was happening was real. And it was dangerous. May was dead. May's home had been burglarized, and now the weird phone call from the professor in Baltimore.

Finally, on the open road with few adjoining roads or turnouts to worry about, Peggy turned to Rob. "Turn to the index in the front of that Matisse book."

Rob just growled in acknowledgment. It was morning. He was hungry. He hadn't showered or shaved, and he couldn't stop thinking about the practice session that was put off. He was also all on edge from not knowing why they had left in such a hurry- or where they were going.

"Look," he groused, "if someone wants to hurt you, or me, let him come on. I didn't spend all those years as a police officer, and before that a *U*nited States Marine, to take easily to this running away! I am tired of not meeting whoever it is face to face. I don't *like* running away. Whatever this is, I don't like it!"

She power shifted around a tight corner near the Whiskey River Salmon Hatchery and hit the gas as the road straightened.

"We aren't running away from anything. How did you get that idea?

"Turn to the index in the front of the book."

"How did I get that idea? 'Rob, hurry up and get dressed. Don't shower. Rob, bring a gun.' It was mostly the gun part."

She just smiled. "Open the book. I know what I am doing… I think."

When he ran his finger down the list of Matisse paintings, Peggy stopped him at one painting simply titled, *Le Cygne*. He turned to the page directed and opened the book to a painting that turned out to be a simple drawing of a swan. "A bird. A great big bird. Is this a clue? We are going to the bird sanctuary. A great big swan, or eagle, or something has swallowed a microchip with the secret plans for the construction of the Death Star. Right? I know I'm right. I'm good at these things."

Peggy ignored his humor. "That bird? Rob, that swan is a clue gigantic! I hope!"

Rob rotated the book to look at the page upside down.

"Stop that," she said to him. "Try to keep on track, and

be serious for just one moment, will you?"

"OK. But just what do we have here, Princess Leia? First, you ask me to take you upstairs. I kind of think that was a great idea! Then, all of a sudden, we are in your car driving along, ataboutwarpfour, trolling for a state trooper with a laser gun. We are looking at some dumb picture of a bird. Not even a good picture of a bird."

She took a hand off the gearshift and tapped the page with the large swan. "That's it," she said speeding east from Netarts Bay. "It's a bird. *Le Cygne* means swan. The professor is flying into Portland on the next flight. 'I must go. I am reviewing *Le Cygne* at the port. I must do it right away: next... even.' He's flying to Portland on the next flight...'Wish you could meet me there,' he said."

Rob slammed the book shut, but he wasn't mad- just confused. His disposition suddenly got better now that he knew what they were doing, but he still felt in the dark. "OK. But why the mystery? If someone was listening on the phone, they could look up the *Le Cygne* up just like we did? I'm sure that some international spy ring killed Uncle May to find the secret to cold fusion, or something!"

Peggy continued east approaching Tillammok. "Wiretapping. The professor was worried about somebody listening in."

"Wiretapping?" declared Rob. "Come on! Wiretapping a phone conversation is extremely time consuming and costly. The professor might think that some league of world-wide killers is after him, but I happen to know how difficult it is to tap a phone conversation."

"Dinner and a chance," was all she said as she pulled across the Wilson River bridge at sixty in a thirty-five.

Rob craned his neck around following the thirty-five-mile-an hour sign as it disappeared behind them. He looked over at the speedometer. "You better slow down if you hope to ever get to wherever we are going, or Tillamook PD will be depositing your little backside in the county jail. Not me, though. I'll just tell the police that I was kidnapped."

"And… what's a dinner and a chance got to do with wiretapping?" he asked.

"That's all it costs to listen into a phone conversation."

Rob just slunk down into his seat. "OK. OK. What do you mean, now, Princess-on-her-way-to-rescue-us-from-the-Death Star?"

"One time I needed to listen in to a phone conversation for a story I was working on for the news station. I knew it was illegal, but there was just no other way."

"Yes?"

"This guy at the phone company just pushed a couple buttons, and the conversation came out the speaker in his office! What that taught me was that while the government might find it difficult to listen into a phone conversation, a man in heat can do miraculous things when he is properly motivated."

"I don't think I like where this conversation is headed," said Rob.

"No. I don't either," she agreed. "But I just wanted to explain to you that if there is an international ring of murderers, spies, or whatever, and they wanted to listen in on May's telephone line, they sure could. And if they were listening, that hint about that large bird, as you call it, was very good."

Rob was not convinced. "Ohhh. Sure! If there was an international terrorist organization or an organized band of killers listening, the professor was justified in being careful. However, anyone could look up this painting and come to the same conclusion you did."

"I don't think so," Peggy continued. "That swan drawing is rare even in lists of Matisse work. May and I did an awful lot of research on Matisse, together, and I learned quite a bit along the way. That book you are holding is one of the only books that include that swan drawing. Whoever the professor is worried about, it might take them quite a while to find *Le*

Cygne. It might even be a while before they realize that it is a Matisse painting. And even if they simply Google it, they would still have to figure out its significance. The lag time might just be enough. It might just be enough time. Especially if they are already in Pacific City, and we know they are, because they burglarized your house yesterday. If they were in Pacific City, they are behind us on the road. We are out ahead, and we can get to the airport first."

"Wish I had a police mind," Rob answered with that funny little quirk of a smile. But, your reasoning about *Le Cygne* not being in art books falls a little short."

"How so?"

"It's probably French, or something, right?"

"Oh, oh!"

"You said it," added Rob. "If this crazy speedboat ride we have been on for a few days contains international thieves, there is a good chance that a common French word won't fool them very much."

"Rob, call the airlines and find out when the next flight leaving Baltimore arrives in Portland? It's not a very long flight."

A few minutes later she was driving through Tillamook and heading east approaching the coast range towards Portland. Rob got the call through just before they ran into the mountains and out of service.

"If he got on the very next flight, if he just happened to hit it lucky, he will be in Portland at 12:30, just after lunch," he reported. "There is no hurry for us, because we will arrive in Portland way before the plane lands. So you can slow down some… Please."

"What do you think this is all about, Peggy? I mean, Why? Do you have any better ideas now that we talked to the professor?"

"Rob, forget about *Le Cygne*. That was just a convenient code that the professor is hoping we picked up on. May's murder has something to do with a Matisse painting called *The Blue Nude*. I know it does. That's the painting that May and this mysterious professor were always researching. It's the painting in May's room. *The Blue Nude*. You remember? He had several copies of the same painting. Remember?"

Rob whistled. "What do you mean, 'something to do with a Matisse'? Like, a real Matisse painting? Like, perhaps, we are talking about a Matisse painting actually being in Pacific City? In May's house? Whew! No kidding! That's the same thing Buck figured!"

"Buck?" she yelled.

"That Buck!" affirmed Rob. "He had it figured before either one of us!" Rob was amazed.., again. "International intrigue? I guess! We must be talking about a million dollar painting! We actually *could* be in a lot of trouble."

Peggy glanced over at Rob as she sped past Fox Creek and the old burned out Wilson River Restaurant. She kept her voice very steady and quiet. "Or, we could be in the morgue if we make a mistake, Rob. It's more like a twenty million dollar painting!"

Rob thought about that. If she was correct, they could both be in a lot of trouble. They could very easily end up in the morgue over twenty million dollars.

Using his police connections, Rob pulled a couple of strings that allowed Peggy and him to meet the professor on the ramp. As soon as the professor exited the plane's passenger door, they were immediately whisked through a side door and down a flight of stairs to the ground level where the three of them were scooted off to a private runway exit. Peggy's car was waiting. Two airport police cars were stationed nearby.

The professor sat very quietly in the back seat not saying anything until just before Peggy started the car. Then he demanded identification from both Peggy and Rob. He did not write down their names but just looked at the ID cards carefully. "Mayfield often mentioned you both." He spoke evenly and carefully. "You, Mr. Policeman? You gave May a dog named Sparky, I believe?"

Rob turned to face the professor. "Spark... Sparky would be the name of a firefighter's dog."

"Please, drive me downtown if you do not mind?" the professor said. "To someplace where I can rent a car. I don't want to rent one, here, at the airport. I am not going to the coast with you." He waved a dismissive hand to Rob's objection. "There is no need for me to go to the beach. I can tell you all you need to know in just a few minutes. What you do with the information is up to you. Besides, Mayfield's home is quite a dangerous place, right now. I would not advise anyone to spend time there.

"Tell me," the professor asked, "about my friend's death?"

"That is just it," said Peggy. "We don't know much about it. His body was found in the ocean at the foot of a cliff. We don't know who killed him? We don't even know why he was killed?"

The professor waited a long, few minutes before speaking. "The two of you... the three of us... are embroiled in a case of almost unparalleled intrigue."

Rob shot Peggy a quick look and slowly raised an eyebrow. The action was observed by the professor.

"No? You doubt that, Mr. Policeman? Let me tell you.

"Mayfield and I were co-conspirators in an extremely interesting hobby. He thought it a hobby. We began studying Matisse, and then, eventually, our study centered on one particular painting, *The Blue Nude*. We both loved it. We both cherished it. It was a very enjoyable hobby, too. Only, Mayfield's interest turned into an obsession. The only logical conclusion to his obsession was to find the original and view it in person. Then, he wanted to purchase it. I tried to dissuade him as much as possible, but he would not listen to my advice.

"When I informed him that I had located the original but that it would cost several million dollars, he became despondent. It was then that we came upon the idea of copies of *The Blue Nude*."

"Copies!" Rob blurted. "People are not murdered over copies of paintings!"

The professor turned his head and watched Lloyd's Center pass the car window. "Well... maybe not, routinely. But it has happened. It does happen. It will happen, again, in the future. A good copy of a Matisse, a really authentic copy, might sell from fifteen to fifty thousand dollars."

"Oh, professor," blurted Peggy. Rob could hear the astonishment in her voice. "Do you mean that May was killed for a fake painting, just a copy?"

"No, I don't," he answered. "Not quite."

Rob drove down Second Avenue and pulled directly into the basement of the Portland Police Headquarters. "We should be safe, here, for a while. You tell us about all this, professor?"

The professor looked around carefully, and then, apparently satisfied, he slouched lower into the back seat and began his incredible story.

"This all started in 1913, in Chicago."

Rob shot a quick look at Peggy. They both silently mouthed the date.

The professor began. "Matisse painted *The Blue Nude* in 1907. It was not readily accepted by the art world; none of his early impressionist works were initially received well. Matisse was one of a loose group of new impressionists and cubists. He was a friend of Picasso. At least, at first they were friends. Their style was too new for the art world to accept, and problems developed. Change comes very slowly, does it not?

"In 1913, the Baltimore Art Institute loaned three Matisse works, *The Blue Nude*, *Luxury*, and *Gold Fish* to the Chicago Art Institute chaired by one Newton Carter. Mr. Carter believed in the work of Matisse and the new and daring artists of the time. He was a visionary. Unfortunately, he was also a bit of an opportunist.

The students at the institute rebelled against such flagrant use of colors and patterns and the unusual compositions of Matisse and Picasso. Most everyone found the new Matisse style very shocking, indeed. Even a small handful of diehard Matisse defenders were uncertain about the new paintings. Matisse detractors thought them barbaric. In short, Matisse work was new, and the students felt a need to protect the older tried-and-true styles. In short, Mister Policeman, they wanted a tree to look like a tree. Impressionism does not so render.

"The Art Student League began a series of demonstrations that finally ended in the burning, in effigy, copies of all three paintings."

"But not the originals? Is that right?" asked Rob.

"Well?" replied the professor. "The official record states that the students made copies of the works and burned the copies. Later, the originals were returned to Baltimore. But what really happened was more... how shall I say, complicated than that."

"Well, don't let that stop you, professor!" sneered Rob. "We're getting pretty good at complicated around here. I've been in town less than a week, and I've been nearly complicated to death!"

Peggy slapped him on the leg.

The professor went on undaunted. "Mayfield and I uncovered what we believe is the truth about those borrowed paintings; and recent, disturbing news in the art community bears our theory out. Certainly Mayfield's death proves our theory beyond a shadow of a doubt."

Peggy found that she was glued to the professor's story! She had heard parts of it from Mayfield and had overheard other parts from telephone conversations between May and the professor, but she had never been able to put it all together.

"There was," the professor said, as he went on,

"larceny in the Art Director's heart. Newton Carter realized the value of the paintings; for he realized that out of such controversy and opportunity diamonds are formed. He knew the work of Matisse, and he believed in it. Time has certainly vindicated his opinion of such painting technique and style.

"In the beginning of the student uprising, it appeared as if the original paintings were in great danger. The students carried on a general student strike that included a series of protests and demonstrations. The student demonstrations became more and more threatening, so Mr. Carter removed the paintings from the institute and secreted them away. He then engaged the students in negotiations. The result of the negotiations was that the students agreed that their important point was to make it absolutely clear to the art world that the new art styles were not acceptable. Therefore, at Mr. Carter's direction, the students created copies of all three paintings, so the *copies* could be burned in effigy. It must have been at this point, in time, that Mr. Carter received his inspiration. It seems that Newton Carter, the Art Institute Director, was quite an artist, himself, and he had unlimited custody of the original paintings. Since, for safety sake, he had moved the paintings from the school to his home, he took the time to paint an excellent copy of *The Blue Nude*. Of course, he created an extremely good replica, what we would, today, call a certified copy."

The professor laughed at his own telling. "It really is a very interesting story, isn't it?"

"Yes, it is," answered Rob. "Go on?"

"Oh, yes… yes. Well, the students held their final demonstration and burned their own copies. The three originals were shipped back to Baltimore."

Rob and Peggy both responded in unison, "Huh?"

"Well, that's just it," said the professor. "That is just it indeed! Newton Carter told the world that the three returned paintings were the originals. In reality, he kept the original *The Blue Nude* and mailed back to Baltimore his homemade replica! Two of the paintings he returned were authentic, no doubt about that. But *The Blue Nude* was a forgery!"

They sat in silence while Rob and Peggy let the professor's fantastic story settle in.

Finally, Rob broke the silence. "That doesn't make sense. Surely Matisse would have recognized the copy from his original!"

"Oh, yes. Oh, yes!" giggled the professor again. "That is just the, ugh… ugh… rub, as you might put it. Matisse never saw the originals again, and Matisse paintings were all too new to be known, that well, by the art critics and curators of his time. It was a very good copy that Mr. Carter painted, and nobody recognized it for a forgery."

"How's that all possible?" asked Peggy. "Rob is right. Matisse would have known a fake. Why didn't he ever see the painting again?"

"You see," the professor went on, "the Baltimore Art Institute was owned and operated by two extremely beautiful young ladies. They had inherited the Art Institute on the death of their father." He giggled yet again. "They were both in love with Henri Matisse! They were in the habit of visiting him in his home in France, or wherever he was living. He was quite transient in his living arrangements, during those years. They purchased many of his paintings directly from him. They were very fond of both the artist and his work.

"Well, you know how love is, perhaps? Huh'?'" asked the professor.

Rob was suddenly afraid to look at Peggy.

"Well," went on the professor, "they fell out of love with Henri Matisse and into love with another artist named Pablo Picasso! Henri was never, again, invited to the Baltimore Art Institute to see his three paintings after the paintings were returned from Chicago."

Peggy became aware that her mouth was hanging open in astonishment. "Wow! What a story! So, where does that leave us? Why was May killed? I still don't get it.., quite."

"Quite simple, my dear. Quite simple. Recently, the last of the two ladies passed on, and an audit was performed on all the paintings at the Institute. Rumors abound in the small elite circles of those in the know that, as a result of that audit, *The Blue Nude* is suspect; that *The Blue Nude*, that the Baltimore Art Institute owns, is a fake!"

Chapter Ten

The professor was very serious about the imminent danger. Rob remained less than convinced, and he told him so. "Professor? We are in the basement of a police station. What can happen, here."

"You, yourself, drove right in without being questioned," answered the professor. "Please, drive out of town on the freeway. It must be, infinitely, safer moving about than being parked in one place."

Rob remained unconvinced. "We could step upstairs to the precinct, or even detectives. We will be safe in the police station."

"No, Mr. Policeman. I mean, yes, for a short while. Sooner or later, however, we would be forced to leave the building. What a target we would make on the sidewalk in the sunshine!"

Rob acquiesced. He decided to have Peggy drive just in case there really was trouble. Free of the driving, he could do much more to quell any attempt on the three of them from unknown sources. He felt foolish, but he took the passenger seat and placed his Glock on the seat between his legs.

"You are armed, I see, Mr. Smith?" the professor asked from the back seat.

"Yes, sir. I have a Glock .45 caliber, at the ready."

"He can shoot two people at one time," chimed in Peggy.

Rob ignored both Peggy's remark and the professor's quizzical expression.

"Professor, let me recap this to see if I have it all straight? While the painting was on loan, a very good copy of the painting was switched with the original. The original was then hidden away and the *copy* returned to the museum. The switch was never discovered because the work of Matisse was not that well known at the time? Now, it has been discovered that what was thought to be the original is, in fact, a copy? It makes my head spin. Where, then, is the original?"

As Peggy drove over the Hawthorn Bridge, the professor leaned forward in the back seat and replied to Rob's summation. "You have it exactly correct. Head spinning is a very good description. Head rolling might be more exact. There have been a number of suspicious deaths over this. The two sisters never had a clue that, for all those years, they were displaying a forgery. For years, they thought they had the original Matisse. The forgery was a very good copy."

"How would they know?" asked Rob. "How would anyone know? How could anyone tell the difference from the original and the copy… and especially after all these years?"

"That, my friend," replied the professor, "is a very good question. Your best question, so far, Mister Policeman."

Peggy interrupted. "Wait a minute. If May was killed for the painting, then where is it? None of the paintings we saw in his house were good enough to be confused with the original."

"That," replied the professor, "is *your* best question, yet."

"If May was killed for the painting," put in Rob, "why would they still be looking through his house for it? Just yesterday, professor, someone broke in and searched May's house for the painting. If May was killed for it three days ago, why break in yesterday? Who is still looking for the painting?"

They rode in silence.

"There is a man," said the professor. "I believe I may have met him once. I am not sure. It is wild conjecture on my part, but I think he could be the one who broke into your house. He is very dangerous. He has a very great and ruthless reputation."

"Do you know who he is, professor?" asked Peggy, as she pulled onto the freeway.

"Who he is? Yes. He speaks very clearly and

concisely, but with a slight European accent. His is not known. No one knows his name. Probably not even his employer. Men like him seldom have names."

"His employer?" Rob blurted.

"Mister Policeman! Please forgive me. I am sure that you know everything there is to know about police work in a large city. No, no, I do not mean to rile you... but there is an enormous world of intrigue centered around art work, like this. *The Blue Nude* is of inestimable value. There are clubs, there are societies, there are organizations, and there are individuals who track, plot, destroy, and seize what they may. It has always been so. It always will be so.

"Recently, a lone man walked into an art show in Brussels and simply removed, from the wall, an original Picasso! Do you really think that the theft was a simple, how do you say in police work, snatch and grab? Bah! It was rehearsed for weeks, perhaps longer. Probably, most certainly, there were a minimum of five to ten confederates. The theft was accomplished so easily and swiftly because it was so carefully and thoroughly orchestrated!

"Your life is in danger, Mr. Policeman. My life is in danger. Not tomorrow, or next week, but now, right now, this very minute! There are very dangerous people who are looking for all of us. We know that they do not have the painting because they are still searching. Once they have it, they will disappear. You and I will not be in danger, then. Anyone who gets in their way, before they have the painting, will be eliminated. They are utterly ruthless.

"But someone has the painting.., right now. Who, I wonder?"

Peggy could not help herself and started to tear up. "We don't have the painting! May didn't have the painting! We don't know where it is."

"May *had* the painting." It was not a question. It was a statement of finality from the professor. "May had it for a week or more. He was killed for it!"

Rob put his left hand on Peggy's leg for a moment. "That, my love, is what Uncle May wanted to show us! That was his big surprise! He had an original Matisse, and he wanted to share it with his only living relative and his best friend! He wanted to share it with both you and me."

"Oh, Rob!" was all she could get out. The tears were flowing as she left Portland and made her way over the Willamette River and then south through Wilsonville.

The professor waited a few minutes and then he continued. "Back to your question. How to tell the original from the copy? There are differences in paint from oil paints in America and Europe. But the differences are very subtle. There was an overabundance of lead in European oil paint in the early 20th century, and the canvasses also had small differences. But the thing nobody realized at the time was Henri's initials."

"His initials?" Rob asked.

"I have been for years, and continue to be, the world's most thorough expert on Henri Matisse! I never met him, of course, but I have met and talked with many who did know him. I have visited his homes, talked with his widow, and have viewed, personally, every single Matisse that is available. I have even examined a few Matisse paintings that are not readily available, paintings that few reputable experts know.

"And I am responsible for your uncle's death, young lady!"

Peggy's head shot around. "You, what?"

The professor held her gaze for a second, but as Peggy turned back to traffic, the professor turned to the view from his side window. "I… I… I took advantage of your uncle. I found *The Blue Nude* at a time when the holder of the painting needed cash much more than he needed a painting that must be always secreted away, always hidden, always protected from those who would stoop at nothing to remove it from his grasp. I should never have told your uncle. But I, too, am an opportunist. I knew that if your uncle had the painting, I could see it, hold it, touch it. Who knows? Perhaps, one day I might have even possessed it, myself!"

"Back to your question. Henri Matisse always put his initials on the canvas, under the flap, on the back of his painting. Most, so called, experts did not realize that until recently. Undoubtedly, you are aware that a few years ago the Barnes Foundation was sued over its plans for restoration of several Matisse works? While repairing a small bit of damage in one painting in order to send it on tour, a restorer found a small red HM under the flap of canvas.

"Well," the professor went on, "the technician noticed the small "HM" on the curled under-edge of the canvas, and that discovery led to more investigating. As it turned out, all authentic Matisse paintings have that small red "HM". It is not well known. It is a closely guarded secret in the art world. If it was not a closely guarded secret, forged paintings would begin showing up with small red initials."

"If it is a closely guarded secret, how then, did you come to know of this, professor?" asked Peggy.

"As I explained when we first met, today; I am the ruling expert on Henri Matisse. And, of course, I have visited with Violette de Marzia!"

Rob shook his head in the affirmative again. "Uhg, huh! The Violette de Marzia! Of course! Why didn't I think of her!"

Peggy slapped his leg, but the professor did not see, or at least he pretended. Almost without pausing, he went on with the story. "Violette de Marzia was the artist's mistress and nurse at the time of his death. She, herself, amassed a noteworthy collection of Matisse paintings. She was the subject of many of his drawings. You know, or course, that she went on to become the Vice President of the Board of Directors at the… Barnes Foundation. Remarkable, that!"

Rob spoke up. "Professor, of course, we did not know all that. But tell me, is it really relevant, or is it simply very interesting background information?"

"Relevant? Relevant? It is relevant! I visited with Vioette de Marzia prior to her death, when I was still a young man. She was very… cooperative. I spent a month in France. She was, let me say, impressed, well.., with my credentials and knowledge of Matisse works."

"Oh, you are a player!" blurted out Rob. He turned around to look at the professor. The professor was smiling in return. "You *were* a young man once!"

The professor beamed. "She shared with me that little secret of the initials. Because of her, I knew of the initials before all the self-important art experts of the world!"

Rob was incredulous. "You knew about the initials years before the rest of the entire world?"

"You must understand, Mr. Smith. I am not overstating the intrigue and danger. When one delves under the scene, one finds dirt. Art is a peaceful and tranquil world on the surface, but once one begins a quest for priceless paintings and sculptures that are not quite the kind sold in shops.., well, it is rather like the search for the Holy Grail. It is most deceptive and dangerous. I have been doing art research for years!"

Peggy stopped at the rest area near Chautauqua but pulled into the truck area where there was more open space. She parked in the back where they could still keep a lookout all around the car.

She turned and looked over the seat at the professor. "Professor, we do not have the painting."

"My dear. Make no mistake about it. I was Mayfield's friend. I have already told you more about this matter than I have told anyone for years. But Mayfield was my friend, and I owe him something. If he had not been my friend, and if I knew the location of *The Blue Nude,* it would not be safe from me, anymore than the others."

Rob looked at the professor for a long time. "Where do you think the painting might be, Indy?"

The professor did not hesitate. "If you are very sure

that it is not in May's house, then someone else removed it before my mysterious friend arrived on the scene. Be very careful of him. I do not think he has orders to harm anyone; that is not the way of most of his employers. But if need be, I am sure he would not hesitate to complete his mission successfully in any way necessary. The others? They might kill in an instant with little provocation. They have killed before. The others are very unscrupulous."

"Others?" asked Rob.

"Oh, there are others, many others. How many is difficult to tell. I am not sure if my European friend really knows all his competition. They know him, and his team, and steer clear. Any one of the others would risk his life to gain the millions the painting is worth. They are cutthroats, pirates."

"Are you sure there are others?"

The professor was glancing all around. It seemed he never stopped his surveillance, and spoke to Rob and Peggy while looking over his shoulder. "There were others on the plane with me from Baltimore. I have been followed for days, now."

Rob looked at Peggy, and it was clear that she was growing more agitated and nervous by the minute. "Please, try to relax, Peggy," Rob encouraged her gently. "We might not be in control, but we are going to pull through this. We will be okay."

"What do we do, Rob?"

"The first thing you are going to do, if you, please?" interrupted the professor, "is to drop me off in the next town. I don't care where. A spontaneous corner is best. I will manage. Then you two go back to Pacific City and find that painting. If you find it, you must publicize it immediately. That will bring it all into the light, and the would-be thieves will scatter like roaches. They all want *The Blue Nude,* but they cannot risk the attention from the local authorities or Interpol."

They dropped the professor on Lancaster Boulevard and turned Peggy's car toward the beach. It was still early afternoon, and Pacific City was only an hour away. They drove for miles with neither one saying much at all.

Passing through Grand Ronde, Peggy finally broke the silence. "What will we do, first, Rob?"

"Find Mel."

"Mel?"

"Yep. I am going to need some backup. By now, Mel has had a chance to get his head straight about all this. And I need his help."

When they arrived back at May's house, there was a note on the door. Mel was waiting for them in the Pelican. He was at the bar when they walked in. The restaurant was beginning to fill with the late afternoon dinner rush. Mel stood as the two walked in, and they all sat in a booth for more privacy.

"Where have you two been, Rob?"

"Portland."

Mel looked from Peggy to Rob expecting one of them to smile and tell him where they had really been all day. "You have been in Portland? Why?"

Rob was looking all around as he spoke, taking stock of immediate neighbors. He reminded himself of the professor and his never-ending surveillance. He was seeing spies, and thieves, and international gangsters in every corner.

"You first. Where have you been, Mel?"

"Seattle. What a whirlwind trip that was! I flew to Seattle, then drove over to Bremerton, and finally flew all the way back here in a little bush plane that would make a grown man scared. I was scared; and I'm fearless! I am exhausted, but the trip was worth while."

"It figures you would go to Seattle," replied Rob.

"I had to find out a few things.., you know, about your wife's death, and all."

"I figured."

Peggy interrupted them. She wore that little smirk of a smile of Rob's that was beginning to rub off onto her. "You have to be careful with Mel, Rob. He checks computer records on his mother, even."

Rob just looked at Peggy as if to say that he already knew that, of course. "Yeah?"

"I flew up to Seattle," began Mel. "If I'm going to put my career on line for you, I had to get some first-hand information. Seattle PD wasn't very helpful. I don't think they felt free giving out information on one of their own."

"I hope not. I could have given you a name, though?"

"What good would that have done? He, or she, would have been selected by you. I needed some unbiased information."

"What did you get?"

"Nothing much in Seattle. They did say you were top notch, and they were very concerned that you had been arrested. A couple guys volunteered to come and bust you out of jail... you know, tie the jail bars to their saddles and then ride off with you into the sunset. Kind of weird people, up there."

"I expect," answered Rob. "It is Seattle. Perhaps they are upset that a Seattle Police Officer could innocently drive down to Pacific City and be arrested for murder? Funny thing, that?"

"So, I went over to Bremerton where Illahee Park is located. I spoke with a retiring Officer Johnson."

"Johnson? I could have given you his phone number. He was our neighbor growing up. His dad was a local police hero. The Johnson you spoke to, the son, has been a longtime Bremerton cop in his dad's footsteps. Both Johnsons were great cops. When I was a Boy Scout, Johnson Sr. gave me classes for my fingerprinting merit badge."

"Weird!" blurted out Peggy. "But it figures. You were taking fingerprints when you were still a Boy Scout. And Rob checks out his mother on the police computer!"

"Yeah," went on Rob. "Well.., when I was a Scout, Johnson Sr. showed me how he sewed a handcuff key into the right cuff of his uniform shirts."

Mel was shocked. "What? I have never heard of that one. He must have been a little off, huh?"

"Well, I don't know, Mel," added Rob. "I read an article, some years back, about a Bremerton Police Sergeant who was overpowered by a bunch of kids down at the park and was handcuffed to a tree using his own handcuffs."

"Yeah?" chimed both Mel and Peggy.

They left the Sergeant handcuffed to the tree, but using the key he had sewn into his shirt, he opened up the cuffs!"

Peggy just laughed again. "Straight on! That guy had it all together!"

"But, you don't know the half!" said Rob. "One lonely night, he stopped three men pushing a stolen Chevy on a back street."

"Yeah?" Mel asked.

"It turned out that they had just stolen the car and were pushing it home to one of the guy's garage, so the three of them could strip the stolen car. Sergeant Johnson doesn't remember much after getting out of his patrol car, and they never found out who two of the men were."

Peggy looked at both Rob and Mel. Mel was looking down at his napkin quietly waiting for the conclusion of the story. She thought she had it all figured out. "They found out who one of the men was? Why didn't they ask him? Couldn't crack him, huh?" she asked. "They could have used bright lights, a water board, maybe bamboo under his fingernails!"

Rob smirked at her. Other than the smirk, he did not react to her sarcasm. Rob continued. "Sergeant Johnson remembers stopping his patrol car, turning on the overhead lights and walking up to confront the men. Next thing he knows, he is waking up in the hospital. It seems a passing motorist found the police car with the lights flashing and the stolen Chevy parked, there, in the middle of the road."

"Yeah?" she asked.

"Johnson was shot in the neck and unconscious. The bad guy was lying in a pool of his own blood with two in the heart!"

Peggy was incredulous. "You guys that do that job! What is wrong with you? You must be nuts to take chances like that!"

Mel glanced slowly over his beer mug. "Well, yeah.., but that is the reason we do the job. We want to stop people from stealing cars… and killing little, old ladies in burglaries."

"Yesss," agreed Rob. "That shooting was before he was handcuffed to the tree, years later. What a hero Johnson was!"

"Yesss. Well, Johnson Jr. set me straight, when I went up to Bremerton," added Mel. "He cleared you completely in Wanda's death. He said there was a witness to your wife falling off the cliff. You didn't tell that in the Grand Jury."

"They didn't ask. Besides, I wanted you and Peggy to believe me for belief's sake. I wanted you to trust me, and I wanted to save something for the Grand Jury, when it goes to trial. I figured that I would save the witness revelation for my court trial. I would kind of slam the prosecuting attorney with it after she implies to the court that I killed Wanda!"

Out the window, they watched as surfers lined up a hundred yards off the beach waiting for the perfect wave. Once in a while, a rider would try a desultory wave without much success. The lowering sun was starting to reflect off the water casting the rock into a golden haze.

Mel and Peggy, both, were feeling a little guilty about not trusting Rob's account of his wife's death. After a few moments, Mel finally spoke up. "I trust you now, Rob. One hundred percent!" he said it evenly and deliberately.

"That's good, because Peggy and I need you," answered Rob. "Let us fill you in. We had a pretty interesting day in Portland."

They ate while Peggy and Rob recounted, to Mel, the meeting with the professor. For much of the account, Mel's eyes were big with wonder, or his mouth was open in awe.

"No kidding?" he asked when they had finished the story. "You guys just left him on the street to fend for himself?"

Peggy continued with the story. "Yes. He thought it was very spontaneous, that way, and difficult for someone to track. He said that his life was in danger, too, since his visit might look as if he was the mule to accept the painting and transport it back east. He said that he could take care of himself, and I hope so. He was a rather likable, old, grandpa type who had taken on this battle for an old friend."

They talked, whispered, and conspired for over an hour while they ate dinner.

Somewhere during the story, Mel had begun seeing spies, and thieves, and international gangsters in every corner... just like Rob and Peggy were.

After dinner, Mel rented room 304 in the Inn at Cape Kiwanda, across the street from the Pelican. The room afforded him a lofty view of both the Pelican Pub, and May's house, as well as a spectacular vista of the beach; He could see for a mile to the south; to the north he could see up the cliff almost as far as where May was killed, but not quite. He took along a pair of high-powered binoculars and a high-powered sniper's rifle that he habitually carried for swat duty. He couldn't imagine firing from up high and across the roadway, and it would have to be a very important emergency to do so, but if he found it necessary he sure wanted the sniper rifle with him. To shoot across a roadway would break many of the local laws, and he was interested in maintaining his career with the Lincoln County Sheriff's Office.

At Rob's insistence, Peggy went home to her apartment in Lincoln City.

Rob returned to May's house. He thought he would lie down for a minute but then decided, instead, to walk outside to watch the beach and the surf. He plopped onto a log that casually separated May's yard from the beach.

Mel was sitting out on the balcony of the motel when he noticed, over the roof of May's house, Rob standing on a log to get a better view of one of the surfers.

"What the deuce!" exclaimed Mel to himself. *"You are supposed to be inside sleeping. I'm guarding the house, but you are supposed to be inside- and I cannot see the beach side of the house!"*

Then, to Mel's consternation, Rob sat down on the log and was completely blocked from view. Mel understood the danger they were all in but was not as convinced of the immediacy of that danger as he should have been. If he had been convinced, he would have run out of the hotel and across the street to cover Rob. It turned out to be a very lucky thing that he was not convinced. Instead of taking immediate action, Mel pondered the situation for a few minutes and, finally, decided to dial Rob's cell phone.

As he watched the beach scene, Rob was re-thinking the dilemma of the missing painting, and May's murder, and all that the professor had revealed to them. He grabbed a handful of sand and threw it down wind. Musing to himself, he watched some of the sand blow lazily away. The sand was warm even late in the day, and the air held a strong odor of salt in the on-shore breeze over Haystack Rock. It was like a… like a holiday, Rob mused. But it surely was not a holiday. A young girl, about ten years old, walked past in a blue bikini with a matching blue bucket. She smiled at Rob as she passed. She was missing her two front teeth. Rob wondered if the bucket contained a hidden microphone- or a bomb- he wondered if the little girl was an international terrorist in disguise? He kicked at the sand and laughed.

Then his cell phone rang. He was just about to pick it up when he was stopped by a commanding voice behind him. "Don't pick that up! Please, don't turn around! I won't hurt you if you don't turn around!"

Rob froze. The second he heard the voice he realized that, by sitting on the log, he had probably put himself right out of position for Mel to cover him from the balcony. What good is cover if you don't utilize it, he asked himself? He was supposed to have phoned Mel if he left the house. Even walking a few feet outside and sitting on the log was a breach of etiquette in an operation like this one. He should have phoned Mel or stayed inside May's house. He realized that his log sitting might prove a fatal mistake.

Rob spoke very carefully. "I'm real in to people not hurting me." He kept his head towards the surfers but wasn't really seeing them. His mind was racing. He allowed his eyes to wander towards the bikini-clad girl to assure that she was out of danger. The least he could do, he decided, was to try to put the man behind him off his game a little bit, try to get him off balance. "I won't move. I imagine it would be best for me not to know any more about you... than I already do."

The voice was surprisingly close, no more than three to five feet away. Rob marveled at the speed and dexterity of the man to get so close behind him unheard and unknown. How could the man do that without being heard or seen?

"You know about me?" asked the mystery voice.

"Six feet. Two hundred pounds. Brown graying hair. Sunglasses. You walk with a slight limp. Right leg, just like mine. The professor calls you his mysterious, European friend."

"Amazing!"

"You are covered, you know?" Rob said without turning.

"No. Not if you mean by the man on the balcony across the street. We are just out of his line of vision, I imagine. It is true, however, that we are covered. *My* operatives are covering us."

"Amazing! How do you know about the man on the balcony already?" replied Rob. "He's only been there a few minutes? Five, or ten, maybe."

"Mr. Smith?" the voice said with an even and precise, European accent. "You do not appreciate the danger of the situation. The danger is not just from me and mine. There are other forces at work, here, other teams that I do not control. They can be ruthless."

"Well, let me see, my mysterious friend?" Rob countered. He picked up more sand with his left hand. "I've taken a fall off a cliff, suffered a concussion, been arrested, and there is a man at my back with a gun. I assume you have a gun? All this in a matter of a few days, and you think that I don't appreciate the danger?"

Rob shifted his weight ever so slightly. On his right side, near his front pocket, he carried his Glock tucked tightly into his belt. There was just the slightest chance that he might be able to draw it out of its holster and spin off the log. The log, itself, might turn out to be good cover from which to fire at the mysterious European.

The unmistakable click of a hammer being pulled back seemed to echo all around Rob. It filled his being. Time slowed to a crawl.

"Mr. Smith, please, do not move. I know about the Glock in your belt."

Rob sighed audibly, dropped the sand, and put both hands on his knees. "OK. I give up. What next? Is there anything you don't know?"

"Is the gentleman in the motel your friend? Do you care about him?"

"Yes."

"Please call him, and tell your friend that you are all right, and that he should not leave the room under any circumstances."

"Huh?"

"Mr. Smith? Please. There is not much time. If he should think you in danger and leave the room to come down here, where we are, my confederates would certainly protect me and have very little compassion on your friend."

Quickly Rob dialed Mel's number just as Mel was reaching for the door to leave the motel room. Normally, Mel would not have answered, but he recognized Rob's number. "Yeah?"

"Mel! Do not leave the room! Stay there!"

"Ohhhkayyy..?"

"Just do it. Do not leave the room! I will call you back." Rob flipped the phone shut and set it on the log.

"Thank you, Mr. Smith. I have a proposal for you, Mr. Smith."

"Yes?"

"You have many questions, do you not? I have many questions. For the next three minutes, or so, we will both answer each other's questions completely and truthfully? Deal?"

"You saw that in a Humphrey Bogart movie."

The mysterious European shrugged. "It is fun, nonetheless. It has a certain charm, and it is a helpful method for us both to understand the situation a little better."

"OK. Sounds good," answered Rob looking directly into the sun and sea. "But me first."

"By all means," answered the mysterious voice.

"Who killed my uncle?"

"I do not know. It is only my concern, peripherally."

"What is my life expectancy?"

There was a silence… and then, "Several hours, I should think…Perhaps more…It… depends."

"What can I do to prolong my life expectancy to say.., oh, thirty years?"

"Give me the painting."

"I don't have the painting."

"Unfortunate. Then I should think that we are back to several hours.., perhaps. If things go well."

"Who do you *think* killed Uncle May?" Rob asked.

"That is elementary. Whoever has the painting, killed him."

"Who is that?" asked Rob. But only silence answered him, and he knew that his had been a silly question. It was the solution to the puzzle, he knew. Rob realized that if the man with the gun on his back knew the answer to that one question they would not be having the conversation.

"Mr. Smith, let me tell you a story. It is about a lost painting."

"I know the story, friend," Rob answered. "What I don't know is where the painting is, who has it, and who killed my uncle."

"Ah, the professor! He, how do you say, filled you in… on the history of the painting? We lost the professor when he got off the plane here in Portland. I did not think it that important, at the time. I knew he would end up, here, at the heart of the matter. But I am glad that he disappeared. The others are dangerous for him. I hope he is safe. He is, basically, a harmless old man in a tweed suit… who knows absolutely everything about Henri Matisse."

"He spoke highly of you!" chimed Rob, but his voice was not sincere.

"We are both, sometimes, in the same business, he and I," replied the voice. "From time to time, his hobby is searching for lost items of art. He is very talented. But he does tend to become rather excited."

"You don't?"

"I am a professional. I cannot afford to become excited. The professor has no resources; but for all that, he has accomplished some phenomenal feats. He really is legend in his field. He has nothing to fear from me, Mr. Smith. The others, though, these young fortune hunters, do not care for the past, for history, or for innocent people. They respect only profit. I have learned there is more to life than profit."

"You sound… tired."

"Ahh… Mr. Smith, the time is short. Let me get to the heart of the matter. My employers want the painting. My employers believe that they are supposed to posses the painting, that it rightfully is their property; and my employers have recently become embarrassed over the.., uh.., entire matter."

That, Rob told himself, settles who the employer is. The Art Institute needs the original painting returned.

"Mr. Smith, if you can arrange to give me the original of *The Blue Nude*, I think we can settle this whole matter; you will live to a ripe old age, the killer will be punished, and I will fulfill my contract."

"If I don't give you the painting, you will kill me?"

There was a shuffling of feet behind Rob. Surprisingly, the man came forward and sat down on the log next to Rob. "Please, for your sake as well as mine do not look at me, directly. We will, both of us, content ourselves to look at the sea while we speak? You see, it is my leg, like yours.., it nags."

Rob grunted and kept his eyes on the little girl with the bucket.

The mysterious man began speaking to someone else, and Rob realized he was speaking into a headset. "I know!" he said very forcefully. "Who is in charge, here? Procedures are mine to establish or alter."

The mysterious man's voice changed in tone. "They are upset that I have sat down with you, Mr. Smith. Rightly so. I have never done it before. They are very angry."

"I guess!" answered an excited Rob.

"Well, this is my last job, my last employment. I am growing too old, and everything… hurts. I am not as strong as I used to be. Listen, Mr. Smith, I am just an old policeman, like you. Let us talk.., policeman to policeman, as they say?"

Rob kicked the sand with his foot but still kept his hands rigidly on his knees.

"So, let's get on with the Humphrey Bogart movie. Shall we?" prodded the European.

Rob shot his eyes towards Haystack Rock. "Please, spare me. Should I sit calmly on this log and banter movie details with a killer?"

"Mr. Smith. I'm not going to kill you. I don't kill people.., not usually. But the other people involved.., the interlopers who are trying to profit over my employer's loss? They will certainly stop at nothing to achieve their goals! I am not a treasure hunter. But rest assured, the others, they are very dangerous and will stop at nothing!"

"Oh, but you won't?" accused Rob. He tried to speak calmly, but he was angry and found it difficult not to raise his voice. "Just what is the difference between you and those… interlopers?"

"Mr. Smith. Mr. Smith. The difference is that the others are seeking treasure for themselves. They are opportunistic, gold-hungry pirates."

"You?"

"I am a business man."

"A what?!"

"I recover lost or stolen items. I am presently employed to find *The Blue Nude* painting."

"If you find it?"

"Then, I return it to its rightful owners."

"It's worth millions!"

"It is a matter of ethics, Mr. Smith."

"Ethics?"

"Certainly. Mr. Smith, I do not steal the property of others. I am not an opportunist. I am employed by reputable people and powers to provide services not quite available in the field of civil service. I provide a necessary service for a fee. Admittedly, I charge a very large fee but certainly not more than a tenth of the value of the recovered property… after expenses."

"A guy has to work," replied Rob.

"Mr. Smith. Please. I have put my revolver away. I have sat down on the log with you to show my goodwill. The gun? It was only a matter of show, anyway, something to get your attention. You are still covered… from more than one direction. We… both are covered.

"You seem astonished that a man in my position could have ethics? But you, really, should not be astonished at that. For many years, now, I have provided my services to employers all over the globe. It is a matter of pride for me. An employer needs a service, and I provide it."

"I don't have the painting!" Rob's teeth nearly grated together.

"I did not say that you did. But if I were you, I would certainly find it. I would find it quickly. Time is of the essence. These others, these interlopers, have limited budgets and lack patience. I would expect that one, or quite possibly more than one, are planning something rash very soon, now."

"If I do find the painting?"

"Then you could sell it to me, of course."

"Sell it!"

"Of course. I am not a thief, Mr. Smith. Call it a finder's fee, if you like."

"Huh?"

"Please, Mr. Smith. I am like you, an ex-soldier and an old police officer trying to make do with what I know. If you, and your friend in the motel, were not law enforcement officers I can assure you that this entire matter would have been handled quite differently."

Rob was becoming frazzled by the entire series of events since coming to Pacific City, and he was finding it increasingly difficult to maintain a civil composure. "Just cut to the chase, here! Are you trying to make me a deal, or what? What is it that you want me to do?"

"Why, I want you to solve a crime. Isn't that what police officers do? It is quite simple, really. Find the painting and deliver it to me... to me only. I will pay you one million dollars. You get the money, I get the painting. The man who killed your uncle? Well, I assume you will take care of him. Or if you like, I can take care of him for you. It is quite a simple thing, actually."

"I thought you didn't kill people?"

"Well.., not as a matter of course. But I have killed before. Have you not? You have never killed anyone in the line of duty?"

Rob threw up his arms in desperation. "Two things!" he blurted out. "You and your cohorts guard Peggy. I want a certified copy of *The Blue Nude*. I don't really know why I want that, but I think I would like to give it to a professor I know."

"Deal."

Rob repeated himself. "So.., it's a million dollars, I get a certified copy of *The Blue Nude*, and you protect Peggy from… whomever?"

"Deal."

"One thing more," Rob said.

"It often grows... Yes?"

"You, or me.., someone gets the guy that killed Uncle May."

"Deal."

"Even if I am killed? If I am killed, Peggy gets the million. Even if I am killed, you get the man who killed my uncle? You will take care of him for me?"

The mysterious European stood and stepped backwards towards May's house. Never, for an instant, did he take his eyes of Rob. His voice faded. "Deal. Even if you are killed. It is a matter of honor between you and me. I will take care of the murderer, and I will keep Peggy safe until all this is concluded."

After a few moments, Rob sensed a change. But he waited, nonetheless. Then he waited some more. He stood and very very slowly walked towards the breaking waves. With each step, he knew not what would await him. He walked to where he was sure that Mel could see him. When he had walked fifty feet, he slowly turned- keeping his arms well away from his clothing. There was no sign of the mysterious man with the gun and the limp. He gave Mel a wave and then a thumbs up.

Rob phoned and directed Mel to meet him in the Pelican but that he should (just in case) wait another five minutes before opening his door.., and then to be very careful since he was being watched.

Mel shouted into the phone. "I'm being watched! I'm supposed to be watching you!"

"Yeah, well," said Rob, "if I was you, I would figure there is a sharpshooter on the ridge behind the motel with a very high-powered rifle and scope. You are probably covered by someone over by the new condo construction, also; so, don't try to go down the balconies in front, either. Wait five minutes just to make sure that communication among those people is adequate."

They met in the bar, sat in the back corner, and Rob once again brought Mel up to speed.

Hannah, the waitress, came over with a couple beers. "You boys keep meeting in the corner, like this, and whispering back and forth, and people are going to think you like each other, or something."

Rob just shot her an irritated look, but Mel limped a wrist. "Sure, Hannah. I need one more problem in my life."

She spoke to Mel. "Well," she replied, "I never see you in here with a girl, Mel. Just this killer."

"Well, Hannah. *You* are a girl."

"I've been hoping you would notice, Mel."

It was four in the afternoon when Ralph walked back into the animal control office ready for his first night on the early shift. It felt good to be away from Larry. Working the early shift would allow him to go home and sleep from midnight until the morning, like a normal person.

The receptionist, a cute girl named Lucille, greeted

him when he came into the lobby. "Hey, didn't you just leave when I came in this morning, Ralph?" Lucille was a late twenties young woman full of office efficiency and spunk. Ralph liked her. His eyes liked her all over.

"Yep, but it's good to work a different shift once in a while. I took a nap, so I should adjust to the sleep change."

She continued talking to him instead of just letting him go to work. "So, you can sleep at night like other people... like I do."

It's funny how your luck can change. Ralph smiled and decided that he might be a few minutes late getting into his first roll call on the early shift.

A few hours later, he decided that it was fun to work the different shift, to actually go on patrol while it was still daylight, to drive through town and cruise neighborhoods while the sun was still up. After dinner, he returned to the station on an errand, but to his disappointment Lucille was off shift. Unconsciously, he touched a piece of paper in his shirt pocket... a folded message with a home phone number. Ralph smiled.

When Ralph walked into the office to fetch his errand.., out of one of the cages, the night clerk noticed that Ralph had forgotten his uniform badge. Ralph remarked that he was so used to working the midnight shift, where it was very laid back, that it might take him some time to get back into the swing of things on a normal shift where citizens expect the animal control officers to look more like police. He expected trouble from the desk officer about the badge but didn't get it. "Who's to notice on the midnight shift? There is just nobody around?" Ralph offered.

Ralph took his errand out the back door on a leash, opened the truck door and breathed a sigh of relief. Step one, in his plan, had gone off without a hitch. To his delight, Spark just jumped right in and took his place on the floor in front of the passenger seat. "Hoe! That was easy, boy!" He patted the passenger seat with his hand. "You can set up here, though. I don't figure anyone will mind." Behind the visor, Ralph found a pair of sunglasses with Larry's name scrawled on one of the bows. Spark voiced no objections when he put the sunglasses on the dog. Passing motorists didn't mind, either; the sight of a large Irish Setter in the passenger seat looking out the side window wearing sunglasses was hilarious… for one and all.

After the last couple days in a cage, Spark thought he was in heaven. For a peaceful, intelligent dog used to human companionship, the dog pound had become tedious and confusing to him. He was used to riding in a car with May or Peggy, and enjoyed the sights and sounds of the city. He recognized some of the streets; especially those on Logan Road, when they neared Peggy's house tight up against Road's End Park.

Coincidentally, and to Spark's delight, Ralph pulled over at Roads End Park and walked Spark on a leash. They patrolled the park together, and as they walked, Ralph decided that he liked the dog, more and more. Spark was attentive and enthusiastic but not demanding.

Out on the grass with families all around, they were greeted by three children who ran across the park to introduce themselves to the Irish Setter and animal control officer. The children loved the dog, and Spark acted thrilled. Ralph kept him on the leash, however, not really trusting that Spark would not run.

"Why don't you let him go, officer?" asked one young girl.

"Well, I can't," he replied. "He's under arrest.., sort of."

The girl knelt and patted Spark softly like he might break.

The girl never took her eyes off Spark, never quit stroking his neck. "Badges. We don't need no stinking badges!"

"What?" exclaimed Ralph.

Her brother answered for her. "She's weird."

"I forgot my badge. I didn't think anyone would notice. Especially not a little girl in the park? What did you say?" he asked the little girl again.

The girl continued stroking Spark as if the dog was made of porcelain. She answered in a sing-song voice. "Humphrey Bogart."

The girl's brother looked up at Ralph. "I have tried to explain to her that people are not going to like her."

The little girl warmed up to Spark and knelt even closer. Then she hugged the dog but spoke again to Ralph. "I had an aunt. Her name was Archy."

Ralph laughed out loud. "Hey, that is good. Anarchy!"

The girl looked calmly up to him with a deadpan expression.. "Yes. But she was wild."

The boy shot his eyes to the clouds. "My sister's name is Twisted."

After laughing, Ralph asked the girl. "What does your daddy call you?"

"Precocious."

"I give up. But I think I might be in love," Ralph said.

The little girl laughed softly and smiled at Ralph out of the corner of an eye. She kept petting Spark. "I like you, too."

Ralph explained to the children the story of Spark, The Red Dog, as Ralph called him. He built Spark up as best as he could. Ralph told how Spark must have fought with his master's murderer, how he jumped off the cliff to save his master, and how he stayed by May's side on the shelf below the cliff.

The older boy had seen the news story. "Hey! Aren't they going to kill this dog?" he asked falling down beside Spark and crowding his sister. He wrapped his arms around the dog's neck. "I saw that on the TV! They are going to kill this dog?"

The boy's sister became alarmed and put a death grip around Spark's neck. Ralph thought she looked like a little blond angle when she leaned her head gently on Spark's shoulder. "Why are they going to kill him?" she asked.

"Oh, silly," her brother answered. "They always kill heroes."

It was then that Ralph made up his mind. He held no further indecision. He just loved dogs, some dogs more than others. He realized, right then, that this dog was special, that it would not be put down. Not on his watch. It was time for step two.

Late that night, Becky parked the jeep on the far side of a small airstrip that services Pacific City. She didn't like where Billy directed her to park the jeep- on the end of the dead-end service road. The fact that there was only one way in and one way out bothered her, and she was surprised that Billy had chosen such a parking spot. She pulled up, nonetheless, where he directed and did not say anything negative about the location. With Billy's temper, it was always better that way.

Veronica and Billy got out, and without saying a word they walked off into the dark of the night. Becky's eyes strained until she could no longer make out their dim forms, hoping they would get back without trouble but at the same time hoping they would never come back.

When Veronica and Billy got out of the Jeep, Veronica just smiled sweetly and then casually walked off into the darkness next to Billy. She took his arm like they were merely going for a leisurely stroll. They disappeared into the darkness across the great expanse of high grass bordering the air strip.

"Sure. You guys have the easy part," she whispered to no one. "You go break into places, but I have to sit in the car and sweat for half an hour." She opened the door and somehow felt better standing outside in the night air. "I'm not going to stay in the car and just wait," she whispered out loud. "It's bad enough having to wait and worry about a cop accidentally coming by. But I just can't sit in the car. Not tonight! Not on a dead-end street." Her right leg started bouncing. Becky had been forced to park a long way off from the gallery that Billy and Veronica were breaking into, but Billy said that there was no help for it. "No hope for it?" Becky whispered out loud. "Sounds like my life!"

Even though it was the darkest of nights, both Billy and Veronica felt exposed as they crossed the blacktop runway, itself. Billy was surprised when they had to manage two ditches laid parallel to the runway. The unseen ditches were to control water run-off and were treacherous in the dark, and although Billy had reconnoitered the path in the daylight, he hadn't seen the ditches. The lowest six inches of the ditches were full of cold and murky water, brambles that clung, and a horrible stench of garbage and decay. He was breathing hard when he finally pulled himself up onto the dike bordering the last ditch. He just managed to pull Veronica out. They were both breathing hard and loud.

"I don't believe this!" whispered Veronica. In the silence of the night, her whisper sounded like a shout. "What is that smell!"

"There was no help for it," answered Billy. "The front of the gallery is exposed along the highway, and both sides are covered by bright lights. The only way for us to get in is straight in from the airfield. There is a line of shadow straight out from the back door, and we can walk up to the door by just staying in the shadow."

"What *is* that smell."

The back door of the art gallery came open easy enough with just two twists with a pipe wrench; the door knob fell into Billy's hand and then a quick turn with a screw driver, and the door swung inward. It was a crude entry method but adequate and nearly noiseless.

Billy went directly to the small office and was not surprised when he found it locked. Inside the gallery, he was less concerned with noise, so he simply kicked the hollow-core door inwards. It flew completely off its hinges and crashed onto the floor of the small office.

Veronica was puzzled when Billy didn't rifle through the office desk. Instead of searching the office, he looked quickly in several large art cabinets and then went immediately through the small office into the gallery storage room beyond. She shrugged her shoulders and started rummaging through the office desk, herself.

She found a few rolled up bills and- to her immense surprise- a small-caliber handgun. Both of these she put in her pocket without telling Billy. She also found a ring that she thought she recognized from their last house burglary in Lincoln City? Sitting in the desk chair, she mused over the ring turning it over and over in her hand. What was the ring doing in an art gallery in Pacific City? Billy said that he had sold it to his fence…? She put the ring on her finger. "Twice stolen," she whispered. "Twice mine."

Meanwhile, in the storage room, Billy was throwing paintings right and left. He was getting hotter by the minute.

Amused and frightened at the same time at Billy's show temper, Veronica went into the back room to watch his tirade. Obviously he was not finding something specific for which he was searching. He looked on the top of shelves, under cabinets, behind desks. His search was becoming so frantic, and remained so fruitless, that Veronica's amusement was turning slowly towards fright. She had seen Billy disappointed before, and it was not a pretty sight. She knew that his temper always needed to vent but thought the situation would be all right as long as he kept throwing paintings. When he stopped throwing things, then she would begin to worry.

Finally, he stopped. Sweat was dripping down his forehead and into his eyes. He was panting for breath, his rage exhausted in the search. He took a few moments to catch his breath.

Becky started to back out of the room.
"What's that smell?"
"I think it's us, Billy."
"You find anything… in the office?"

"Eleven dollars."

"It's not here," was his short reply. "It's not here."

"What?" Veronica asked.

"Huh? Oh, nothing. Let's go."

Ten minutes later they climbed into the jeep.

To Becky, Veronica looked like she had swallowed the proverbial Cheshire, but Veronica gave her a stern look. "Don't ask," the look said. So she didn't.

"The two of you smell special. Did you roll in something wonderful?"

Chapter Eleven

About the same time that the gallery office door was being kicked in, Rob was ordering another beer in the Pub. He noticed Dr. Rhapp, the doctor from Spark's hearing, sitting at the other end of the bar. "Howdy, doc," he said taking the next seat.

The doctor tried to focus but was having great difficulty. He had obviously been taking a few drinks before Rob's arrival. His face was flushed, and his eyes were red. Rob decided that he should have been cut off by the bartender long ago, but... "*It's the beach*," Rob told himself one more time.

Even through the beer, though, the doctor seemed to recognize Rob right off. "Oh, hey! Rob Smith isn't it?"

"Yep. Uncle May's nephew from Seattle. Well, I guess I'm from here in Pacific City, now. I plan to just move into May's house. Maybe, I should paint instead of write."

"You might be better at it."

Rob laughed.

The good doctor leaned into his drink. "I haf read some of your works."

"Really, no kidding aside?"

"Yes. Many of your works. You should paint." He said, but he smiled broadly.

"Hey, come on!" smiled back Rob.

"OK. No kidding esside," said the doctor. He was trying to be sober but failing miserably. "You are myyy favorite author. May introduced me to your books. I p a r t icularly liked *Leonard, Arizona Ranger*. I have, I think, allll your books!"

"That's funny!" answered Rob. "Why did you pick *Leonard*?"

"*Leonard*?....It's a funny book! Whhhen the cowboys

got naked in front of all those Indians... I just about lost it... there! I mean fourr cowboys with nutttin on but gun belts ad cowboy boots! Whhat a riot!"

"Well, at the time, doc, it seemed like a good idea."

Rob spoke over his beer. "Hey, doc? Did you say you are a psychologist or a proctologist?"

"Proctologist! My arse!" blurted the doctor in response. "Oh... heyyy... I told a funny?"

They both laughed and then their mood quieted. They were thinking of Spark, and that thought put a damper on their conversation.

After a few moments, the doctor tried to change the direction of the conversation, but Spark and May were the reasons he was drinking, and he could not get those tragedies out of his mind. Nevertheless, he lifted his glass in congratulations. "I'm glad to finallly meet you, and it's good that you will live here, I think. Only think is, I hear they are going to put Spark down tommmorrow. I hate to seee that; Spark's a good dog!"

"They won't put him down if I can help it," replied Rob. "I plan to see the hearings officer first thing in the morning. Perhaps something will come up. We are all hoping and praying for it."

"A jail break. It's the only think, I can thing of," slurred the doctor.

"I hear that a lot," replied Rob.

"You have had a diffcult time of it since you came, here, to seee your uncle."

"You can say that again."

"What a sham."

"Doc, I want to thank you for volunteering to help at the hearing."

"It was leas I could do. Yep. They are going to put Spark down. Your uncle is gone. He was my friend, you know. That creep, Wi, had better see a doctor about hisss legs, or I am pretty sure they will get infected. Sometimess, it seems like everything is falling apart and we can't do anything about it!"

Rob didn't know what to say, so he didn't say anything. He just sat next to the doctor while they both finished their beers.

At a wave, Mel came over from where he had been covering Rob, and they decided the good doctor had better stay in May's place until he sobered up enough to drive, so they helped him over to the house and flopped him on the couch. Then the two of them made coffee and sat at the kitchen table.

"We don't have much to go on, do we?" asked Mel. "Your uncle is dead. The red dog is going to be killed. The painting is gone. We are being stalked by thieves and killers."

Rob put some rum in his coffee and offered a shot to Mel, but he refused. "Yeah, Mel, I thought it was bad yesterday. But, now to add to the situation there are thieves and killers! This is a lot more interesting place to live than Seattle. I was never stalked by thieves and killers, there. I was never the suspect in a murder, in Seattle... Oh, yeah, well.., hardly never.., almost never."

Mel put his hand over his coffee cup to stop Rob from splashing in the rum. "No thanks, Rob. No rum for me. I'm the designated shooter."

"Kind of fun isn't it. But you know, Mel, I am forgetting something. Something is gnawing at me. I have missed something. I have missed a clue or a lead, somewhere."

"Yeah, what is it?"

"Funny guy, Mel. But I do know what we should do right now. I have a plan: a foolproof plan."

"Yeah?"

"We need to do something rash like our European friend suggested. We need to do something that will stir things up. We should... start a beach fire, a rip roaring fire in the middle of the beach. A fire halfway down to the water where everyone can see us."

Mel just looked at him. "Got marshmallows?"

"No, but I have got a couple paintings that look very

much like the original painting for which all the world is searching!"

Mel leaned over and picked up the rum. "I will have some, after all. That will bring them out, you know. That will bring them all out... They will try to kill you."

"I don't care."

"Oh, you care, Rob. You really care. So does Peggy. Say, where is Peggy?"

"She's at her place tonight. I arranged for her to be kept out of this for a couple days, but I will see her in the morning when I appeal to the Animal Control Hearings Officer to stay Spark's execution for a couple more days. I am going to beg, cajole, barter, and plead. If that doesn't help, I'll have to revert to the jail break idea, but I am going to talk that hearings officer into setting the date back a couple more days. One way or the other. If nothing else, I will just tell the truth."

"Do you think he will go for it?"

Rob rubbed his forehead and then took a slow sip of coffee. "I don't know? I hope so. During the court hearing, he delayed Spark's execution in hopes that something would come up. Something has definitely come up."

That night, Becky had finally given up. She was at a loss what to do to glean anything good for Veronica and her out of their present situation? When Billy was gone, she simply left the front door of the double wide open and walked off into the darkness. She was never going back. She was not going back for her sister. She would not go back for anything. The branch had broken. She had decided. That door was closed.

However, Becky was only part way down the dirt driveway when a small red car surprised her. She stepped into the brush and thick bushes as the car approached. As luck would have it, the car stopped just a few feet away from Becky. She recognized Billy in the front seat. She did not recognize the blond. Billy sure did. His hands were recognizing her all over.

Becky was afraid to move for fear that Billy or the blond might notice the movement in the darkness, but when Billy opened the door and put a leg out she nearly jumped. She heard him speak to the woman. "I'm going to kill them. I have to. They know too much. I'm going to kill them tomorrow. Then I will pick you up, and we can blow this town."

There was more, much more, but Becky could not remember. It was all a blur. Her mind whirled around the words and the sights. She nearly fainted when Billy got out of the car mere feet from her and stormed towards the house.

After half an hour, she went back to the double wide and snuck into her bedroom.

When Mel and Rob awoke in the morning, they were both surprised to find the good doctor already gone.

"He slipped out during the night, and you didn't hear him?" Rob chided.

Mel didn't need chiding. He was nearly devastated. "Nearly everything has gone wrong on this case! I lose contact with the subject I am supposed to be guarding? People come and go from the house I am supposed to be securing? I forgot to load my gun?"

"You what?" Rob involuntarily spit his coffee.

But Mel only smiled. "Got yah."

The day dragged on as days do when something big is expected to happen later. The face of the clock was just about worn off by the two men's glances. Mid morning, Rob finally left to pick up Peggy and then to see the hearings officer. They would plead Spark's case and hope for the best.

While Rob was away, Mel didn't leave the house but kept tabs on the beach through the upstairs windows. All day long, nothing much happened on the beach except that there were more than the usual number of small pairs and groups of people who seemed to be just idling about. Mel took notes and compiled a lengthy page of descriptions.

On the way to Animal Control, Rob began to fill Peggy in on his conversation with the mysterious European, but he kept leaving things out and jumbling it all up. "Wait until we see the hearings officer, will you?" he plead. "I'm always like this before something big, but when it's my turn, it all straightens itself out."

"Really?"

"In the last minute, I'm always brilliant."

He wasn't brilliant, however, while pleading with the officer about Spark. His mind was still sorting out information and making plans as he talked. He knew he was missing much detail and not putting the facts together correctly, but he just could not get a handle on it. He told the hearings officer about the European and the stolen art, about the teams of international opportunists, and about the burglary, and finally about *The Blue Nude*. Rob told everything he could think of, but he wasn't convinced that the officer was believing it at all.

In reality, the hearings officer listened inattentively, at first, but then began warming to the story. When Rob was only about half way through, the officer's mouth was hanging open. He asked a few questions but mostly just sat in amazement and silence.

"Well. Hmmm?" he finally said when Rob was finished with the story, "that's the best I have heard! That is quite a development! Quite a development! But how much does it bear on the case with Spark? Hmmm? I am naturally inclined toward leniency, good judgment, and mercy. And I love dogs as much as the next guy, but let's not lose sight of the case, here. As I see it, the facts are simple; Spark has bitten two different people. It's a good story, but what bearing does the rest of this have on Spark? Hmmm?"

Peggy was confused. "What does it have to do with Spark? Are you listening?" She was on her feet leaning on the hearings officer's desk. "Are you deaf... or... or just stupid?"

She turned to rob. There were tears in her eyes. "He just doesn't *want* to listen, Rob."

The officer simply leaned back in his chair and put on his best look of patience. He had seen this before. People often begged him for an animal's life, and while he was not immune to emotional appeal, he had acquired a certain amount of necessary indifference. He knew he would sign the execution order in an hour, or so, and then Spark would be put down. People were always coming up with fantastic yarns. *"But this is a good one,"* he told himself. He made a mental note to smile about the story later when no one was watching. The officer looked calmly at Rob and Peggy and waited for more, but there was nothing more.

Finally, Rob stood and patiently pulled Peggy away from the officer's desk and back down to her chair. "Let me see if I can connect the dots for you," he said very quietly. "I did not come here, this morning, to beg for Spark's life simply because we love that dog."

"No? It happens all the time. Hmmm?"

"No. At the hearing, the basis for my plea was that something might come up. I know that wasn't much on which to base an appeal, but it was enough for you, at the time."

"Yes, but..."

"Well, something has definitely come up! You say that Spark has bitten two different people, but I cannot help but think that the murder, and the theft of the painting, and the biting are, somehow, related."

"Hmmm? Mr. Smith," began the officer again, "I am not making light of this fantastic story about a missing painting and gangs of thieves on the beach. But how is it related? On what basis can I say that this fantastic story mitigates this case?"

Rob thought about it for a full minute. "Well, let's go over what has happened and see if the three of us can come up with an idea. Will you spare us that much time? Please." With a nod and a shrug from the officer, Rob continued. "We know that Uncle May is dead, and that Spark ended up in the water with him. Now, I happen to believe that May was murdered and shoved off the cliff. We know, absolutely, that May was shoved off the cliff; we have witnesses to that. Perhaps Spark fought with the assailant. It would be difficult to believe that May could fight with someone without Spark getting involved. He is just a dog, but if he saw someone fighting with his master, it would be natural for him to attack. So.., back to Spark biting people. Perhaps Spark attacked the first man because he was having trouble closing the doors of his car, and perhaps Spark interpreted the man's difficulty as violence? The man was really having a tough time of it slamming and slamming the car door over and over again. The man was excited, heated up, and mussing under his breath."

"Well..Hmmm??" put in the officer. "I don't know if..?"

"No. No. Have patience with me, please," plead Rob. "The second person he attacked was Jan Wi, the gallery owner. Spark attacked when he saw the two of us shaking hands. Perhaps Spark misinterpreted shaking hands for the two of us fighting, and he thought that he had to get involved, again, to help Peggy and me? Perhaps Spark is just re-living the last few moments of May's struggle and death? Spark could just be high-strung and over-quick to lean toward violence because he still remembers May's death? It's not like a dog can talk it all out and get over it!"

The officer was quiet for a minute and then took a pipe out of his desk. Turning the pipe over and examining it from all angles he said nothing, at first, and then he placed the pipe carefully on his desktop. "Hmmm? Hmmm? I am sorry, but you condemn the dog on your own testimony."

"Oh, don't say that!" begged Peggy.

The officer held up his hand to stay Peggy's further appeals. "No. You must realize that an animal that has gone through as much as Spark has… well, one would not be surprised to find him upset over violent and questionable events. But if he is prone to attacking people seen in the simple act of shaking hands, he cannot be trusted to be in the general population. The State would be remiss to allow a dog to run free that sees violence in simple acts of greetings or compassion."

This time, it was Rob who jumped to his feet, but the officer waved him off with a humph. "No. I am sorry. Hmmm? I am not unmoved.., though, by the theory that this is all, somehow, tied together and related. I am not staying the execution. But I will give you a couple more days."

Tears flowed down Peggy's cheeks. "Oh, thank you. Thank you!"

"Not at all, Miss Richards. But only a couple days. After that, you might as well save yourselves the trip and energy. I will not stay this again without clear and convincing evidence that clears the dog."

"Then what?" asked Rob.

"Maybe somethin' will turn up," replied the hearings officer. "Maybe somethin' will turn up."

"Hmmm?" said Peggy. She smiled.

Rob had already decided not to tell Peggy about his plans for the fire. It would be the second time in history that *The Blue Nude* would be burned in effigy. "*It is like a cheap who-done-it-novel*," he thought. "*If it works once, do it again.*" He had bargained to have Peggy kept safe during the fire, but the fire was not planned for several hours, and he was, justifiably, excited about spending a few of those hours with his new found love, for he and Peggy were like lovers everywhere young or old. He parked in front of her house, and they walked the short, few blocks to Roads End Park in Lincoln City.

Although nearing noon, neither one of them felt like eating. What they felt like doing was not walking to Roads

End Park, either, but Rob was trying to keep his mind clear and not lose his grasp on the situation. Neither of them spoke for a few minutes. They just watched the surf roll in. Gulls were diving near them to catch bread crumbs thrown by a smiling and laughing little girl.

"What's your favorite movie?" he asked Peggy.

Her eyes brightened. She was glad to be talking about something else, glad to be getting to know each other better. She was in love, and she was delighted to be sitting in the sunshine with the man of her dreams.

"*Sabrina*," she answered.

"Oh, that is such a surprise."

Her lips pouted out just the cutest, little bit.

"No. No. It's OK. But I should have guessed that it had to be *Sabrina*. Seems like it had to be either *Sabrina* or *An Affair to Remember*."

She nestled into his shoulder. "Nope. *Sabrina*. I love that movie."

"The new one or the old one?"

"Old one, what?" she asked quite seriously.

"What?" he said with a smile. "The old black and white!"

She pinched his arm. "Never saw it. There is an old black and white movie of *Sabrina*?"

"What! You don't even know about the old one?"

"You keep saying that."

"William Holden, Humphrey Bogart. It is a really funny movie."

"It isn't supposed to be a funny movie," she said. "Who said *Sabrina* was supposed to be funny? It's a movie about a lovely girl and two men who love her. Or.., it's about a lovely girl and two men she loves. I don't know, but it is a lovely movie, and it ends well. From a girl's point of view. It touches my heart."

"Save me, Sabrina Fair."

"Stop that," she demanded and slapped him playfully

on the leg. She pretended to be angry, but how could she be angry?

"The old movie is better from a man's point of view," he began. "Well, on second thought, I don't think it really has a man's point of view. It was just entertaining, to me. Both the new movie and the old black and white are fun movies. They are both about a bad man who turns out to be the good guy."

"Don't ruin it for me, Rob. I like that movie."

"I don't want ruin it, but isn't the movie, *Sabrina*, about a man who makes up for lying and cheating by just saying that he is sorry? The world is supposed to roll over and play dead even after his deceit and trickery- just because he is remorseful? No, that is not correct, either," Rob added "It is a movie about a man who gets so caught up in his own lies that he begins to believe them. No, that's not correct, somehow. *Sabrina* is about a man who finally learns to recognize his lies for what they really are."

Peggy looked carefully at him as if, once again, sizing him up. Then she said, "It's about a man similar to May. He didn't realize, until too late, that he held the world in his hands and that he had not taken it seriously. Harrison Ford had the opportunity to correct his mistakes in *Sabrina*. May's chance, at that, was cut short."

Rob couldn't think of anything to say to that, and the moment had turned morbid. So, they walked, and then, further up the beach, they stopped and leaned on a tree trunk that had washed up on the sand.

An Affair to Remember?" Rob asked.

Peggy looked into his eyes. "That's about a woman who had to choose between a good man she was very fond of and his nephew whom she loved."

Rob threw himself away from the tree. "Cary Grant wasn't the good man's nephew."

"You know what I am saying, Rob. Don't act so dense. May held the world in his hands and never took advantage of it. I admired May. But I am in love with his nephew, however dense he may be. Hmmm?"

"This conversation surely got deep awfully quick.
Let's walk some more."

"Oh, no you don't," she said pulling him back against
her. "What is your favorite movie?"

"*The Time Machine*. No. *Soldier*."

"Huh? Why?"

"Cause in the end the hero gets the blond."

"Oh. You like blonds?"

"No. I like redheads."

"Hmmm?"

Shortly after Rob and Peggy left the park, Ralph
happened to drive to the same park with Spark. He had a plan.
He was free of Larry and his fifteen-dollars-an-hour theory, for
Ralph knew that life, itself, was more precious than Larry
would ever know, and the life of a beautiful and intelligent
animal, like Spark, was worth more than all the fifteen-dollars-
an-hour jobs in the world.

As he and Spark roamed the park, Ralph was amused
to find himself looking for the precocious seven year old girl
and her brother from the day before, but they were nowhere to
be seen. It made no difference, he reassured himself, but he
had to laugh when he realized that he wanted to have an
audience to witness his one great act of courage and kindness.

"Perhaps," he told himself, "it is better if no one does
see me do this. No witnesses, that way." Ralph dropped down
to look Spark in his eyes. He wasn't sure what he would see
there, he did not believe that dogs could speak or that they
could understand very much language, but he was absolutely
convinced that dogs (good dogs) could understand compassion
and kindness in humans. He looked into Spark's eyes and
unfastened Spark's chain.

Ralph watched as Spark walked a few steps away and
then stopped. The dog turned back to him as if to say, "Are

you sure you know what you are doing?"

"Go on, Lassie," he said. "I am not sure where you are going, but find your way in life. Don't get caught again. I don't think you can survive another time in the dog pound. If we catch you again, it's the gallows for sure."

Spark turned and trotted off.

Ralph whipped the chain tether against his leg. "Take that, Larry!"

Spark knew exactly where he was going. He was in his element, and in Peggy's neighborhood, and he knew the way. Many was the time he walked with Peggy and May in these blocks, and it wasn't long before he ran up to Peggy's door.

In response to a whine and scratch at the door that she just barely heard, Peggy opened the door to peek out. As it just so happened, entirely by chance and at that very moment, a uniform Lincoln City Police car was driving past Peggy's house as she opened the door and found Spark waiting with a smile and a pant. Mere routine patrol brought the officer to Peggy's neighborhood at that particular moment, but the shock of finding Spark on her porch and a police car in the street hit her hard like a one-two punch that fate is so fond of dealing. The officer actually turned and smiled at her just as he turned and routinely smiled at every pretty girl. He wasn't looking for a red dog. He was always looking for the other. He never even saw the dog.

So instantaneously did Peggy recognize Spark and incorrectly size up the situation with the police officer, that she hurried Spark inside, grabbed her purse, and pulled Spark out the back door- all in a matter of seconds. A minute later, they were both in the living room of the kind, elderly neighbor on the street behind her house. In seconds, again, Peggy's life changed. She was in the neighbor's house hiding out, as it were, from the police, whereas just a minute before she had been with Sabrina Fair and dreaming of Rob.

Of course, Peggy was completely wrong about the police. She was wrong about them coming to get Spark and take him back to the animal control center, but how would she know? In the end, it was a just lucky happenstance that brought that police car and Spark to her front door at the same time; for she not only evaded the police (who, of course, weren't even yet looking for Spark), but her rapid escape out the back door also evaded the lone team member sent by the professor's mysterious European friend. In five minutes, she was in the neighbor's van and driving out of the neighborhood.

She hadn't had time to devise a plan. She simply believed that if she was to save Spark's life she must remove him from Oregon; for Spark had been sentenced to die in Oregon, but not in the neighboring state of Washington. And Washington state was only one hundred and ten miles north on Highway 101.

Spark settled down next to her and looked contented as could be. As far as Spark was concerned, if he had found Peggy, he was halfway home.

Lincoln City has only one way out of town to the north, and as she left town she thought she might have been holding her breath. *"Remember to breath, Peggy,"* she told herself as she took the coast highway. *"Remember to breath, and remember what you are doing."*

Spark stirred at her words. She patted him on his head. "Making a run for the border, fella!"

Peggy tried phoning Rob as soon as she left the city. As the golf course whizzed by, she dialed his number. North bound, at sixty miles an hour, she pressed the re-dial button until her finger grew tired. How was she to know that Rob and Mel were testing the phones for use that evening? She knew nothing about their plans, about the beach fire, or about the teams of fortune hunters closing in.

At Neskowin, she passed a state trooper along the side of the road and her heart rose in her throat.

Crossing the Salmon River she was in a quandary. Soon she would be in Pacific City, but surely the police would be watching Rob's house for Spark? Rob's phone remained busy, so she could not get any advice from him. At the junction, she just could not bring herself to take the turnoff for Pacific City. She was minutes from Rob, she knew, but that might be minutes from capture? What was she to do? Now that she had Spark again, she would never give him up. With or without Rob, she passed the southern turn off for Pacific City and just put the pedal to the metal. It was a jail break, and they were making a run for the border.

When she came to the northern turnoff for Pacific City, however, she took it at the very last second. In a millisecond, a plan formed in her mind, and she knew what she would do. The border could wait. At the stop sign, north of town, she drove around the white barricade meant to stop motorists from the small gravel road that, in times past, lead down to the beach. Since caving in during a winter storm, the road ended half way down the hill, was deserted and lonely, was never patrolled, and seldom used. It was a dead-end road to a steep cliff. But for Peggy and Spark, it was a great find.

"We will stay here, fella," she told Spark. "We will just wait here for dark. Then, you and I can hike over the dune and down to the beach and into town. We can sneak up on the beach side of May's house, I mean Rob's house, and meet him there."

She tried her phone several more times, but there was no service. She looked at the sign at the end of the road. "Stupid sign, really," she said aloud. "Of course there is no beach access! It's straight down that way. No beach access. No phone service. No Rob. No food. No water. No coat, and it will be cold when the sun goes down. No nothing. But, somehow, I have gotten you again, and Rob and I are going to save you, boy!" She sat on the cliff and wrapped an arm around Spark's neck.

At about that same time, back in Lincoln City, Ralph was placing a white poodle in a cage in the animal shelter. The poodle wore an identifying chain with Spark's name and number. Ralph chuckled a little as he locked the cage. He knew the poodle was not in danger, since it would not match Spark's description. Chances were, he told himself, the switch would not be noticed for a day or two- perhaps not even until the execution time drew near. Then it would be curtains: but not for Spark; it would be curtains for Ralph's fifteen-dollars-an-hour job when his boss reviewed the video tapes of the cage area. He wore a wry smile as he walked away from the cages; and thought of Larry, of how Larry would be smug about Ralph loosing his job. "But I haven't lost anything," he said out loud, again. "It's Larry that lost something... a long time ago."

Chapter 12

When Rob returned to Pacific City, he found Mel going from window to window in May's house making notes and trying to categorize and list everyone in sight.

"I've identified several little groups of people that must be the interlopers your mysterious European friend mentioned… or perhaps they are the mysterious European's team members. How would we know his team from the pirate teams?"

"I don't know that it matters, right now?" answered Rob. "I think we will know soon enough, but probably anyone you can see is not associated with the European. He strikes me as being a little too efficient for his people to be confused with these others."

Rob hurried from window to window. "Show me what you have in your notes."

"Sure. It was easy, really," replied Mel. "These people, I noted, don't have little children or dogs. Ever see anyone here without little children or a dog?"

"Sure," replied Rob. "Lovers."

"These people aren't in love. Look at them." He pointed out two easily recognizable groups. "See those two people halfway to the water in front of your house? They are turning and looking this way more than they are watching the ocean. What about that guy in front of the Pelican leaning against that log? Ever seen anyone, there, before? He's not sun bathing, he's not watching the girls, he's not sleeping or reading. He's watching everything that happens at your house."

"It's like an old black and white movie," added Rob. "Have you noticed? The really interesting thing is that each, and every one, of the people we suspect has a pair of binoculars. Each and every person on your list has binoculars.

All of them?"

From upstairs, Rob and Mel counted seven people obviously out of sync with the sand and the beach scene. "There's more, too," said Mel. "There are more rented cars in the Pub parking lot than I have ever seen, and people are remaining in their cars instead of getting out. People often sit in their cars and eat lunch or drink a beer, but eventually everyone gets out of their car after the long drive to the beach. The object of going to the beach is to get out and walk on the sand. Not these people. They just sit there with their binoculars, watching."

"Some of them," pointed out Rob, "might be with my mysterious friend with the limp? There is just no way to tell."

"I don't think, so," replied Mel. "I agree with your earlier assessment. I figure his people for being a little more professional than the people we picked out. They will all try to blend in, of course, but the trouble with a beach operation is that it is extremely difficult to blend in. Cities lend themselves to undercover work. Beaches, and open spaces, make surveillance difficult."

"Yeah?"

"Yeah. Just the logistics of feeding and sheltering become difficult. Think about it logically," continued Mel. He was on a roll, and Rob let him talk. "How do all these people explain their business, here? Do they tell the hotel operator that they are here for the big heist? I don't think so. Here for the convention? No conventions, here. Big meetings, here at the beach, have ten people. What about lunch and dinner? All these people must be eating in the same restaurants at the same time! This makes for a very interesting situation."

They watched, for some time, as people came and went, and as they did, more loafers and suspicious people became obvious. Too many people had binoculars.

Mel laughed. "It's all so obvious after you catch on to the pattern!"

"We might need some help, Mel"

"We? Kemo Sabe. You are the one with the two and a half hour life span, not me.

"When do we build the fire, Rob?"

"After dinner. Just before sunset. If we can hold the fort that long."

Peggy decided to tether Spark; for intelligent dog, or no, Spark was just a dog. She was afraid that Spark might decide to run over the dune and head straight for May's house. "You won't run, now, will you fella? You need to stay with me. No dinner for either of us. You need to stay with me until just before sunset. Then we can both begin working our way over the dune towards May's house. If we can hold the fort that long."

Late that afternoon Mel snuck out of the house to get closer to the action, and, although it took some doing, he worked himself unseen down into a dune some hundred yards away from where Rob was starting a fire. The ghillie suit helped. Mel's place was well chosen; the dune grass was tall, and from only a few feet away, Mel figured that no one would be able to see him. From Rob's vantage point, even though he knew where Mel was, Rob could not pick him out. One second, Mel was there. The next second, he had vanished.

The sand formed around Mel's elbow where he planted it; the sand formed a good solid-feeling base for his elbow yet allowed him to smoothly sweep the beach through the rifle scope. Mel felt secure in his position, and he took comfort knowing how well he was healed. In addition to the M-16A1 sniper rifle, he carried a long barrel .357 backup in a belt holster, and for the backup to his backup he carried a mini-Glock securely strapped around his ankle. Rob suspected that Mel had another hidden gun somewhere on his body, but when he was asked, Mel simply smiled.

Cordless remotes, on their cell phones, allowed Rob and Mel to easily keep in contact, and reception was crystal clear. "Where did you go?" asked Rob on the phone. "I could see you as you settled into the dune grass, and then... poof!"

"Never mind, and quit looking at my location, will you?" ordered Mel. "I'm supposed to be covert. If you keep looking at me, it will draw the attention of those others."

Finally, the time arrived for the fire on the beach. First, Rob carried down enough wood to make a good blaze. That took two trips. He noticed several people concerned and took a mental note of each of them. No one is legitimately concerned about a fire in the sand at Pacific City.

He went back to the house for a chaise lounge. At least it would look, to observers, as if he carried only a chaise lounge. In reality, he had one of May's paintings of *The Blue Nude* hidden between the folding sections of the chair. He set down the lounge chair in the sand, still folded up, and kindled his fire. Then, facing the fire and with his back to the Pacific, he pulled a cold beer from the pocket of his jacket and took a long, deep pull.

"This might be my last beer?" he said out loud. "I'm glad it's in a bottle and not a can." He spoke into his phone pickup to Mel. "We must not be in a movie, Mel. If this was a movie, wouldn't someone have shot the bottle out of my hand when I took that last, long chug?"

There was no answer, but he knew Mel was, there, hidden in the dune grass... Like always.

It was getting on to dusk when Rob decided it was just about time to begin the fireworks. In half an hour, it would be dark, but he should be able, he told himself, to wrap it up by then. He knew that Uncle May's painting would not fool anyone close up, but he was counting on the glare of the setting sun to mask its features. Then too, he told himself, whoever was out there could not take the chance. They would be forced to show themselves.

"A half an hour of life left," he told Mel. Then he took another very long pull and finished the beer. He was counting on the look of him chugging beer, as if in a fit of a drunken rampage, the crazed drunk, Rob Smith, was going to burn an eighteen million dollar painting right here on the beach in front of everyone, as if the pressure was getting to him, and he couldn't take it any longer. It wasn't much of an act. He was hoping to fool everyone, but the truth was that the pressure really was getting to him, and he couldn't take it any longer.

North of town, on the closed beach access road, Peggy and Spark turned south and started climbing up the back side of the dune as dusk began its slow crawl across the hill. For Peggy, it was hard going, nearly straight up, and the shifting sand made any progress difficult. In contrast, Spark seemed to fly joyfully up the hill kicking sand in all directions. Peggy labored as she found the climbing much more difficult than she had expected. The hill, she found, was more of a cliff of sand than anything else. She kept calling Spark back, and the good natured, and ever obedient, dog obeyed.

Spark would run ahead barking joyously and then run back to Peggy when she called. He was happy. Peggy surely was not. Spark was free, and Peggy was sure that, somehow, he knew he was going home, but she, herself, was caught on a steeper and more perilous climb than she had expected, more perilous than she had ever attempted, more perilous than anyone without four-wheel drive, like Spark, should ever try.

In spite of Spark's exuberance, Peggy was filled with indecision. Perhaps she should have just kept driving north on the beach highway attempting to skirt Spark out of the state of Oregon. If they were caught now, Spark would be taken into custody, again, and almost certainly killed. But she wanted Rob around for the trip to Washington, wanted his advice, wanted his company. She wanted Rob. Rob would have all the answers. How serious would the police take the escape of an animal tagged for destruction? Would they even care? Would they scour the hills? Or was she over-reacting? Was this climb, and secret approach to May's house, the right thing to do?

A U.S. Coast Guard helicopter flew low over the dune without a thought about missing dogs and abetting women, but Peggy could not be sure. She halted her climb and prayed that the dog and she would not be spotted from the air. Of course, they weren't spotted. No one was looking. She was heartened when the chopper continued on its course. She continued to climb. Over and over, she tried phoning Rob and Mel, but still the reception was nonexistent.

She had no water and became parched quickly with the strain of the climb. Half way up the hill, she realized that she had miscalculated badly. She looked at the setting sun and feared that they would be making the worst, and most difficult part of the climb, in full darkness- that the best Spark and she could do was to crest the dune well after sunset. She frowned as she thought of the harrowing walk along the cliff's edge in full darkness. She would need to rely on Spark to get her through. What other option had she?

The usual tourists were lined up on the logs bordering the volleyball area in front of the Pelican. Actual tourists watched the sun setting low on the horizon, chased their dogs, or played with their children. Lovers held hands and cuddled together. Rob noticed that none of the cuddling vacationers, staring at the sun and sea, carried binoculars.

"I'll bet the binoculars are European made, too," he said out loud to no one but Mel.

As usual, two teams of young people were batting away at volleyball. It seemed to Rob as if a couple of the people sitting on the logs were paying too much attention to him and his fire, and he made note of their position to Mel. From where Rob was, the fire was in easy sight of the row of cars and vans parked next to the volleyball area. With all the potential teams of interlopers, he was counting on the fact that there were too many innocent bystanders for anything very violent to occur. He hoped he was correct. Then too, he reminded himself, many of the suspicious people were competitors, that they were actually working against each other. Really, he didn't know what he was hoping for; he was just shooting an arrow into the sky.

"Whew! he said to Mel on the phone. "Try to figure all the competing angles in this scene! Level on level of deception, greed, and wanton thievery! Amazing."

"We, Kemo Sabe?" he said to Mel. "Good point, that!"

He threw his beer absently into the sand and spoke into his speaker. "It was *Ice Station Zebra.*"

This time, Mel answered. "Huh?"

"Never mind, Mel. This guy, here in the cheap shoes, just remembered the name of the Ernest Borgnine movie where the spy and the good guy agree to tell the truth for three minutes."

"Hey!" put in Mel, "wasn't that about a bunch of spies and international intrigue?"

"Yes.., it was, Mel. You're quick."

"Maybe they will make a movie about this?" put in Mel. "My part could be played by somebody special and good looking, a real lady killer."

Rob looked around one more time trying to note all the competition. "I guess I will start the ball game, Mel. Here goes. If I live through the next ten minutes, I will live for thirty more years. Hope you've got a good sight picture on that M16?"

Without another word, Rob bent over and picked up, from its concealment in the chaise lounge, the copy of *The Blue Nude*. He held it towards the volley ball court, the Pelican Pub, the people sitting on the logs, and the cars in the parking lot. He held it there, in plain sight, for a full minute letting everyone have a good view.

Nearly in unison every pair of binoculars on the beach went up. Their lenses reflected the setting sun like so many scimitars being drawn for battle. Rob moved instinctively closer to the fire. He poised the painting directly next to and nearly above the flames, so that if anything happened to him the painting would fall into the flames and be destroyed. It was a threat, and he knew it. Even now, though, with this dramatic and crazy move, he was not sure what he wanted to happen? He just wanted *something* to happen, something that might start the ball rolling, something that might bring this crazy dream to an end. He didn't think this crazy stunt would solve May's murder, and he knew it would not reveal the whereabouts of the authentic painting, but he was tired of not knowing anything, of not being able to solve the murder or the theft. The only thing he knew for sure was that whoever had the painting was not on the beach, for whoever had the painting would not still be looking for it. He was just convinced that this might start bringing this awful situation to a climax; that it might force the, heretofore, unseen forces into the light of day. Eighteen million dollars is quite a bit of money to watch go up in flames, and he doubted too many people could just sit idly by and watch so much go up in smoke.

He was right.

A young couple in their mid twenties jumped to their feet and just stared openly at him. Their books, which they had not been reading, fell at their feet unheeded. While they did not move towards Rob, their eyes were glued to him. They stood like people might stand watching an accident happening, afraid to look, afraid to look away. The doors of a van opened, and from inside two men in dark clothes started toward Rob and then stopped in indecision. On the patio of the Pelican, a glass dropped and broke.

He was drawing them out, hoping to thin the competition, counting on the mysterious man who had earlier held a gun at his back. "Well, come on out, people!" Rob said out loud though no one was in ear shot. "Come on out!" He knew that the mysterious man, from earlier, was there, somewhere, and was also taking note of the competing groups. "If I only have a few hours of life left, let's spread the joy around."

Several of the small groups of people started toward him, stopped, and then looked at each other in alarm. Some of them looked around at their competition as if a light had suddenly been turned on. A car sped out of the parking lot. A car sped into the parking lot.

Rob was counting on the free market to whittle down the odds. "Some of you won't live as long as I," he said again… to no one in particular.

Then several things happened at once, as they often do in tragic and trying times. It may have been an epiphany, but it could have been simply that Rob just got a very good idea. It was as if a light bulb was turned on. In the house next to May's, Mr. Wi, the gallery owner whom Spark had bitten, came out the patio door. He was limping.

"Limping is in the air?" Rob mused. But… then… there was something in that limp?

Right then, for Rob, everything came into focus. What he had been trying to put his finger on, what had been nagging at him in the back of his mind; it all sprang into clarity. He again hit his forehead with his right hand with that familiar and flat splatting sound in the same way Peggy had slapped his forehead at the river bar. Unbeknownst to him, however, when his hand splatted against his forehead, his telephone headset fell from his ear. He did not realize it, but all communication with Mel had been severed.

He wouldn't have cared if he had known. The case was solved! Tunnel vision took over.

He simply dropped the painting into the fire. The sun simply dropped into the Pacific Ocean.

All these things, and more happening at once combined to make the next few minutes in Rob Smith's life just a little more complicated than he could believe.

Somewhere to the north, on the other side of the dune, Peggy was trapped on a steep part of the cliff. It was too steep to continue up and too steep and dangerous to descend. She wanted to climb higher but could not get a purchase. Every step slid her backwards towards the sandstone rocks far below. When she tried moving down, she began sliding out of control towards the cliff edge. She looked sideways and thought she might see a way, there. If Peggy could keep up her nerve.

Somewhere to the east, Becky was trying desperately to make Veronica see the animal that Billy had become. She tried reasoning with Veronica, but could not get a purchase; it was like climbing a sandy hill, one step up and two steps back. Nothing worked to enlighten the girl until Becky revealed what she saw Billy doing with his hands in the driveway- in the car the night before. That seemed to clinch the deal. They checked the revolver Veronica found in the art gallery burglary, and they decided on a plan, if Veronica could keep up her nerve.

Somewhere to the south, Rob knew who had the painting, who had killed his uncle, and what he was going to do about it. His time of inaction was ended, and he was relieved to be able to *do* something, if he could keep up his nerve.

As he dropped the painting into the fire, Rob knew that, for the next few moments, his life was in the most danger. No longer was there any safety net that the threat of burning the painting had provided, but he also knew that for most of those treasure hunters on the beach, any motive for killing him had just ended; their individual searches had terminated in failure and disappointment. Why shoot someone who *used* to be holding a treasure? He knew that if he lived through the next few minutes he would die an old man, but could he get through the next few minutes? He figured his chances at no better than fifty fifty.., and it seemed to him that the wrong fifty always had the house edge.

His mind was racing. He knew who killed uncle May, and he knew why, and he knew how. Pieces began fitting together, like pieces of a puzzle coming together. Seeing Wi limping was like receiving an unusually sudden realization. The essential meanings of the ragged pieces of the mystery, rattling around in his mind, had, finally, come together. Wi's limping was like a revealing scene in a movie. In a flash of insight, Rob solved the crime.

"Mel, I've got it! Do you know what an epiphany is?" he blurted out.

At that moment, Mel did not care what an epiphany was, and he did not know that Rob's phone pickup had fallen out of place, and even if he had heard Rob, he didn't have time to talk. He was trying desperately to keep all the moving and changing groups of interlopers and suspects in view and still guard Rob, who was his primary responsibility.

The couple who dropped their books split up and walked away.

Another man, who had been the closest to Rob, ran towards him with abandon and fell on his knees at the fire. He threw himself into the flames trying to rescue the painting, but the canvas was already burning furiously.

"Don't bother," Rob said to him but still looking at Wi's house. "That painting is a fake."

The man rolled from the fire and smoke. He came to his feet reaching for a handgun in his windbreaker pocket. From some sixth sense, Rob turned and saw the man's arm going for what could only be a firearm. Rob covered him with the Glock. The man froze.

"Throw it away. It's over. It's all over."

The young man, at Rob's persistence, dropped the revolver at his feet and whined pitifully. "Over? How can it be over? What is all over? How…" he begged.

"Your life, most probably. For what? Money?"

The man dropped to his knees in defeat. "You don't

understand what you have done!"

"Sure I do. I've identified you to a rival organization who is very good at eliminating their competition."

"The painting!" the man yelled. He still failed to grasp the situation, he was still holding onto his dreams of wealth and power. Greed kept his mind from working rationally.

Without another thought, Rob turned away from him. He was confident that even if the man took a dive for his tossed revolver Mel would get him. Rob walked away from the fire. His face was grimly set toward Wi's house. "All this time," he said, "and the solution's been next door!"

The young man pulled at his hair. There were tears in his eyes. "Where are you going?"

"I have to save a dog."

The young man dove for his discarded handgun, turned towards Rob with the revolver, and then the man's body spun away lifelessly like a rag doll being thrown aside at the end of a play. The revolver flew from his useless grip. An uninformed observer would have thought it a weird and confusing dance. His arms went all akimbo as his body fell to the sand. The impact with the sand tore the man's glasses from his face. He tried to scream, but couldn't. Time slowed to a crawl. His life flashed before his eyes… and faded.

It was Mel, of course, who had shot him. With the last vestige of sunlight, and using the short flair of light from the burning painting, Mel simply centered the crosshairs on the young man's chest and pulled the trigger. Later, however, when they recovered the body, the police would find two bullet holes in the young man's chest. One from Mel and a second one fired from the direction of the condos.

Again, things in real life do not always happen as a well choreographed opera. Actions jumble together. Dancer's feet tangle.

Veronica and Becky were hot into their plans. Their debate had ended with the revelation that Billy was planning to kill both of them in order that he might begin a new life of crime somewhere else with a new woman. The girls decided the best usage of the revolver which Veronica had found in the gallery would be for them to terminate Billy's partnership before he had a chance to terminate theirs. Becky remained amazed that Veronica had switched so easily. She had expected a much longer and more protracted fight, and she had held out little hope of convincing Veronica to her point of view. In the end, all it had taken, to Becky's relief, was for Veronica to hear of the conversation between Billy and the local beauty. One overhead conversation and Veronica was out of love and into hate. Big time hate. Veronica lusted to kill Billy, and Becky would take every advantage of that lust before it cooled.

In the quiet of the evening, the girls stole out of the house and decided on a walk out to the cliff to finalize their plans, to watch the sea roll in.., to plan a murder. Murder it was, and Becky knew it (although she was doubtful of Veronica's ability to understand completely), and Becky didn't care if society called it murder. She knew it was extermination of a vermin. For that sin, she told herself over and over, society should give her a reward. The realization that all of their troubles would be over if they simply killed Billy had come as an immediate leap of intuition. True, she had wanted to kill him for weeks, but to realize that the problem of Billy could be completely eliminated so quickly, that the two sisters could revert to their past, quiet lives together, that they could return to Portland and start over- that was a revelation. Becky was relieved that she had decided she would no longer let matters ride and just keep threatening to kill Billy; she could actually kill Billy tonight and get it done. Billy thought he had a date with a blond. He was partially correct. He definitely had a date.

As the girls talked on the cliff, as the sun was beginning to set, Becky sensed Veronica weakening.

"Do you remember, sis," she said very softly, "how Billy beats you up, sometimes, when he makes love to you?"

"Yes, I know, Becky, but that's only because I…"

"No, Veronica! It's not because of anything *you* do!"

Veronica had tears in her eyes when she turned from the ocean to look at her sister.

"It is because of him! Not you!" Becky shouted. "He slaps you because you are not the woman he really wants. He has some memory of another woman in his past that he really desires, and it is because of his anger that you are not that other woman- that is why he slaps you! He hits you and strangles you because the other woman left him- or he killed her- or something just as awful. Oh I don't know! But he is mad as hell at you, because you are not the other woman."

Veronica lowered her chin to her chest and thought it over. Then she wiped away her tears.

Becky rubbed the revolver between her hands. "So, we need to kill Billy. We need to kill Billy… tonight."

"Tonight?"

"Tonight! If I know Billy, he will start looking for us- if he hasn't already begun. He will start downtown because I am always arguing with him about going to that pub in the parking lot. Then, when he doesn't find us there, he will walk around the beach and end up climbing the dune to the top of this cliff to take the shortcut back to the double wide palace. If it works that way, we will kill him here. If he doesn't show up, here, we will simply go back to the trailer and shoot him as he walks in. We will gun him down before he has a second to talk us out of it!"

"Oh-h-h..?" said Veronica.

"Yes," interjected Becky before her crazy sister could soften again. "We will kill him like he killed that old lady in Lincoln City. We will kill him, so he can go to hell and live forever with that other woman he loves from his past. If we don't kill him, tonight, he will run off with that woman from last night! Do you want him running off with that blond? Do you want him slapping her and making love to her?"

Veronica's eyes turned very cold. She turned away from Becky and stared directly into the glow left from the setting sun without averting her gaze from the blinding light. "That other woman! That blond!"

Life is not a well orchestrated opera. Feet, do indeed, get tangled.

A few moments earlier, when the young man had first approached Rob at the fire, Mel heard a sound behind him; a sound that could only be footfalls in the sand. But the expediency of the moment would not allow Mel to take his eyes off Rob; he could not afford the luxury of losing his sight picture on the suspect at the fire. Rob's very life depended on Mel's full attention.

Instead of turning his head, Mel used the riflescope's eyepiece as a mirror. Drawing his eyes back merely an inch from the eyepiece on the riflescope, Mel saw, in the scope's reflection, a man approaching from behind. Using the scope eyepiece to look behind him was a difficult trick to master, but one which, thankfully, Mel had practiced and perfected. Mel spoke without turning. "If you drop your weapon, immediately, you will not be harmed." Then, without waiting for a response, Mel rested his eye back into position for a shot to protect Rob. The man behind him was out of his hands, now, and Mel knew it.

"Me harmed? You must be nuts," said the voice behind him. "We have won. You have lost. You're just another clumsy cop who let someone come up behind him. You are dead, my friend. The painting is ours. The money is ours."

As the man behind raised his revolver, one single shot rang out from somewhere in the houses lining the beach, and the man behind Mel was no longer searching for wealth and power. Mel knew that one of the other deputies in his swat team had taken out the man behind him. He had counted on that, and his faith in his fellow deputies had paid off. Like all the training drills, Mel just trusted his backup, and it worked.

Mel breathed easier and kept his scope on the young man at the fire. He knew he couldn't take his eyes from Rob at the fire- no matter what.

And, as it turned out, Rob just trusted his backup, and it worked. He turned his back on the fire and began walking toward Wi's house just as the young man, who had been trying to rescue the painting from the flames, landed face down in the sand.

At the shot, Mel rolled into a new position. "Two down!" he said and got up on one knee. The time for hiding was at an end. But no other shooters or targets were in sight. Instead, people were scurrying from the beach. All Mel could make out were people leaving- in a hurry. The sound of the first shot had alarmed everyone, but few could locate the shooter. The second sound of gunfire made things easier. As the young man's body spun, lurched weirdly and then collapsed in a very real picture of death, people scattered. European binoculars were in great supply… in the sand.

At the sounds of gunfire, people were scrambling all over the beach. Those who were earlier bent on finding *The Blue Nude* started hurrying away believing their long-sought treasure destroyed. The effect of seeing the young man killed, at the fire, had a positively chilling effect on the interlopers interest. Suddenly, eighteen million dollars seemed paltry when weighed against living through the next ten minutes. Priorities tend to straighten themselves out in the midst of gunfire and death.

Against his better instincts, Mel turned and looked over his shoulder at the dead man behind him. Only for a second Mel looked away from Rob, but that second was long enough; it was a breach of etiquette; turning away was something he knew that he should not do; for in that second

Mel lost sight of Rob. When Mel turned back towards the fire, Rob was out of sight and lost in the dimming light. In desperation, Mel screamed into his phone. Rob would have answered him, but the phone's remote had fallen into the sand, and all thought of Mel was lost to Rob- who had eyes only for Wi.

Behind the scenes, the mysterious European was directing his people in an effort to thin out the competition. He correctly guessed that Rob had not burned the authentic painting. He now had positively identified all the competition, and his people would soon get into positions to discourage any continued interest on the part of the interlopers. It was a ruthless world, this international crime and intrigue, but the rules had been clear all along. None could claim ignorance of the dangers.

Everyone, except the actual vacationers who were still in the dark and at a loss to understand what was going on, knew that it would only be minutes before a positive police presence would be established on the beach. Most of the interlopers were simply interested in leaving Pacific City as quickly as possible and lined their cars up on the highway like Iraqi tanks trying to get out of Kuwait. The State Police had a field day.

One would think that innocent beach vacationers would be scattering in response to gun play on the beach. In reality, very few vacationers realized that there had been two men killed and that the area was filled with suspicious people with guns. It is an innocent world- this going to the beach in the summertime. As a blood-red sun lit up a purple sky, the beach-goers began casually picking up their baskets, blankets, and beach paraphernalia and making for their vehicles. For the most part, vacationers and interlopers, alike, were simply interested in leaving Pacific City as quickly as possible.

Darkness fell.

Rob walked rapidly towards the house where he had just seen Wi in the doorway. He was oblivious to all the beach activity. When he found the sliding door was locked, glass flew as he simply threw a heavy landscaping beam through the glass door.

Wi was standing in the middle of the living room. "Get out!" he yelled.

Rob stepped in. He ignored Wi's protests and simply walked up to Wi and hit him as hard as he could. The shock of the blow threw Wi onto his back. "I always could hit!"

Rob waited for the big man to stir. With great difficulty, Wi climbed to his feet. His lip was mashed, and the side of his face was bloody. Without a word, Rob gave him another right, this time solidly to the chin. At the blow, Wi spun to his right and was thrown over a table and onto the floor. He lay there, on the floor again, unable to regain his feet and not sure he was that interested, not with a madman in the room bent on his destruction. Wi was very interested in leaving Pacific City as quickly as possible.

Finally, Rob broke his silence and spoke. "You killed my uncle!" he yelled. It was not a question.

With great difficulty, Wi finally staggered to his feet. There was no defense in Wi's posture, no defiance nor denial. He plead with his hands for Rob to stop, but there were no words he could say, no pleadings he could make. Rob smashed his nose with a left, and then, as Wi staggered back, Rob followed the left with yet another right. Blood flew everywhere... type A blood. Wi just laid there on his back on top of the sink. His legs bobbed in mid-air like Uncle May had lain on the shelf at the base of the cliff with his legs bobbing in the surf.

Wi's mind was reeling, trying to find a solution, trying to grasp what was happening, but his body felt folded, spindled and mutiltated.

"I finally figured it out, Wi," Rob said quietly. He laughed at himself. In his mind's eye, he saw himself standing in Wi's kitchen with blood on his knuckles and talking rationally to his uncle's killer.

Then he laughed aloud. "The doctor, at Spark's hearing, lifted the leg of your pants to look at your ankle where Spark had bitten you. Only he lifted the wrong pants leg! Remember the look the doctor gave you? Last night, I saw that same doctor in the Pelican. He said that he was worried about your legs becoming infected. Legs! Plural! Both your legs were torn up by Spark! One leg was bitten on the cliff when you killed Uncle May, and the other leg was bitten when Spark attacked you in the gallery!

"Just before Spark bit you in the art gallery, Spark attacked another fat man. I figure that from the back that other poor fella must have looked just like you- to a dog. As soon as that poor innocent guy turned around, and Spark saw that it wasn't you, he stopped immediately. It wasn't fat men that Spark hated. He hated you! I should have figured, then, that the suspect was a fat man. It would have helped me to narrow down the list of suspects. That's why Spark kept attacking you, why we couldn't pull him off you. Because you were the *correct* fat man. You were the fat man who killed Uncle May!"

Jan Wi stood and turned his back to Rob. Still, he did not reply.

"Spark must have been pleasantly surprised," Rob went on, "to see you in the gallery. Once he made positive ID on you, he might have killed you had Peggy and I not pulled him off. That's where you got the second ankle bite. Wasn't it! Spark bit your first ankle on top of the cliff when you killed May, didn't he? He tried to save his master- when you were fighting with May on the cliff. Then you killed May and threw Spark off the cliff, too."

Wi turned on the faucet and threw water over his face and then slowly mopped his swollen and bleeding face with a towel. The bleeding wasn't about to stop for some time, but the cool water allowed him to think, to try to formulate some plan of defense. Slowly, a possibility began taking shape.

He turned to Rob. "Are you through beating me up? I didn't mean to kill your uncle. It was an accident." With one hand behind his back, he picked up a large knife from the counter top. But when he brought it around Rob simply punched him in the stomach, and Wi dropped onto the tile floor like a rock. His wind was coming in great gasping breaths as the knife skittered away.

"No, I don't think I am through beating you, yet," said Rob.

"Let's go upstairs, Wi."

Wi's head jerked up. He spoke through the blood and the pain. "Upstairs?" he gasped.

"Yeah. I want to look at a window."

So keyed up was Rob that he half picked Wi up, half pushed him to his feet. Finally, the big man started reluctantly for the stairway. Wi stumbled at first and then slowly began climbing. His protestations landed on deaf ears."Why are we going upstairs? It was an accident!" At the top of the stairs, Rob pushed him through the bedroom door to the small room that faced May's upstairs window. Wi stood in the room with his back to Rob facing the accursed window.

Unexpectedly, Rob smashed a heavy punch to the back of Wi's head. He hit the floor and rolled up against the far wall. "It isn't fair for me to hit you in the back of the head is it?" Rob said quietly. "But I aint no paragon of virtue!"

Wi moaned and laid still. But no answer came.

"Was it fair for you to kill my uncle?"

Rob let Wi lie on the floor sobbing and went to the window. "I want to look at the window, here," he said, stepping around Wi's sobbing hulk. "Yeah. See, here, Winny! This window opens up directly opposite May's window. He never closed that window, and the window never had a screen on it, either. But your windows all have screens. All but this one… this one window that faces May's open window- has no screen."

Rob changed his voice to a crisp European mockery.

"Let us play a little game, here, you and I. For the next three minutes we will answer each other's questions honestly. Huh? I'll be Patrick McGoohan, and you can be Ernest Borgnine."

Wi didn't say anything.

"Well, OK! I will tell you what you did, how you killed my uncle, stole his painting, and did not lift one finger to help an innocent and helpless dog, and," his voice raised a notch, "did not care that I was arrested for murder! For the next few minutes, I will tell you what happened, what you did.., and you… you just lie there and whimper. You are good at whimpering.., whimpering and murdering."

"These two houses are only about five and a half feet apart. It must have been a simple thing to slide a ladder from your window to May's window. Is that why your windowsill is all torn up and damaged? May's is damaged identically."

Wi turned and gave Rob a smug look like he had missed something.

"Oh, pardon me," said Rob quietly. "It wasn't a ladder, was it? It was a heavy board, a heavy timber, one of those I saw in your yard used for your new landscaping. That's why I got a wood sliver in my hand on a vinyl window that day I climbed in May's window! Even a junior investigator should have figured it unusual to get a wooden sliver from a vinyl window."

Rob sat on the edge of the bed and kicked Wi in the ankle. It was only a light prod, really, but it just happened to land where Spark had bitten him. Wi yelped in pain. Rob knew he was being cruel, but he was past caring. He was drunk with victory after days of being suspect and being pushed around, strangers calling him a murderer, having guns pointed at him, and living in fear.

"It must have been a little frightening to crawl over the ladder to May's room, but it's less than six feet. The crawling wouldn't take long, and the chance of anyone seeing you was slight with that friendly tree obscuring the view. Besides, you probably told yourself, for eighteen or twenty million dollars, the risk was worth it. And you are in great shape even if you are fat. It wouldn't have been a problem for you. Just bring up a ten or twelve footer and slide it across from one window to the other."

When he received no answer, he nudged Wi's ankle again. "You knew about *The Blue Nude* didn't you? You are in the art world. Uncle May must have been delirious with joy over possessing that painting. I'm guessing he showed it to you, his friend, the gallery owner. He knew you would appreciate it. You are in the art business, after all. May just had to share the good news with someone. He phoned me and invited me down. But he couldn't wait. He showed the painting to you, didn't he?" It wasn't really a question, but Rob waited for a reply, nonetheless. When he didn't get it, he worried the ankle a little more with the toe of his shoe. Wi whimpered and tried to crawl away.

"So, you found the painting in May's house. Then you became frightened. You had the painting, but as soon as May returned he would know who took it. You were the only one who knew about the painting, and that kind of reduced the list of suspects. Didn't it? He would see the marks on his window sill, and then he would see the marks on your window sill. That's why, even though you had the painting, you still had to kill May."

"No. No," Wi whimpered. "I went up on the cliff to try to talk to him. To…"

"To what, Wi? Your story breaks down: doesn't it? There was no reason for you to go up on the cliff to where he was painting except to kill him. You went up there expressly to kill him. The courts will call that premeditated. The two of you argued. Then you fought. In the end, you overpowered him, and you pushed him off the cliff."

Wi wagged his head back and forth in protest. He opened his mouth to frame a reply, but the truth tore his appeal away.

"Oh, he fought with you, didn't he? But you pushed

him off and disappeared around the dune just as I was walking up. You almost got away with it."

Wi finally answered, and it gave Rob some comfort and, at the same time, some distress, yet he received some insight into Uncle May's last few moments. "He kept saying that you would kill me. May kept saying it over and over. 'Rob will kill you for this!' I didn't mean to kill May. I guess I was just crazy for the painting. Eighteen million dollars! Can you imagine eighteen million dollars?"

"No," answered Rob. "You should have just purchased a bigger TV!"

They both remained silent for over a minute, Rob setting on the bed and Wi whimpering on the floor up against the wall. Finally, Rob reached out with his foot and gave him one last, good, grind on his ankle. "Where is the painting, Wi? Where is *The Blue Nude*?"

"Under... the... bed."

"That was easy," Rob said. "Under the bed? Incredible! You hide an eighteen million dollar painting under a bed?"

Wi scooted himself into a sitting position. "I didn't know where to hide it! I just didn't know where?" That was true. At first he had hidden it in his gallery office. Then, afraid that Billy would look for it, there, he moved it. Once he possessed the painting, he found that he wanted always to be near it. He had become unsure if he possessed the painting, or if it possessed him. "I didn't know where to hide it? What to do with it?"

"Of course not," answered Rob. "So you hid it under the bed!"

He leaned down to look, and there under the bed he could make out the shape of a large black document carrier. It was all he saw before the lights went out. He reached out a hand for the black case. His fingers barely brushing the leather handle, when his head burst with pain and a red nausea coursed over his mind like the oncoming surf. Instantly, he was once again back under water being tossed to and fro by the surge of the sea, his head bouncing off underwater rocks.

All too anxiously, Rob had bent to look under the bed. In the excitement of the moment, he had thrown caution to the wind. But Wi wasn't as injured nor as helpless as Rob thought. Quick as could be and seizing the opportunity, Wi grabbed the bedside lamp and hit Rob in the back of the head. He was unconscious before his head hit the carpet.

"That was easy," said Jan Wi mimicking Rob. He kicked Rob in the ribs and mocked him more. "I'll tell you what? For the next three minutes let's tell each other the truth? The truth is that you are a loser, and I am the winner. Got any questions about that?" He put his shoe on Rob's ankle and ground his foot. "Not fair for me to kick you while you are down, is it, Rob? What is it you said, 'I aint no paragon of virtue!'"

His cruelty stopped him. For just a small portion of time, the green light of greed went out in Wi's eyes. "No. Not me!" He passed his open palm across his eyes. "What has happened?" He sat on the bed and looked down at his knees where drops of blood dripped from his split lip and battered face. "What have I done, Rob? You deserve an explanation. May deserves an explanation" He looked at the unconscious form of Rob Smith, soon to be deceased, on the floor and went on. "I have not always been like this. First, I began buying stolen things from thieves and vagabonds, then from Billy, that trash of the earth. Then, when your uncle, God rest his soul, showed me that painting, I realized that there was a path out of financial ruin and disaster. The *Blue Nude* and its opportunity haunted me. It just... haunted me." He nudged Rob's ribs with the toe of his shoe. "I don't know. I guess I went mad. I'm not a bad person. I... just became haunted." He let out a large sigh and continued his tale to no one. "I'm like the guy in the Bible who built his house on the sands of desire. When he molested the innocent, a stone was placed around his neck, and the stone was tossed over the side of Peter's boat. 'Peter, do you love me?' the Lord asked. Not if I have to give up this painting, I replied. It's mine!

"The women I can have with eighteen million dollars!"

Wi reached under the bed and extracted the painting for which he had killed, the treasure for which he had sacrificed his last thirty years, the treasure for which he had put his home and his entire life in jeopardy. For a few minutes, when Rob had burst in through his beach-side door, Wi had thought the painting lost, but now he had regained it all! All! He would take the painting to California to a friend of his who would ask no questions. Then he would travel. He would possess beautiful women that a fat man could never obtain without riches. He would live the good life. He would have it all! All!

In triumph, he stood and looked down at the unconscious form of Rob Smith. "I aint no paragon of virtue," he said again. He padded Rob down and found his Glock, looked down at the sleeping form at his feet, sighted along the barrel, and slowly began squeezing the trigger.

Rob was saved by a blue and red light flashing through the window. Leaving Rob on the floor, Wi ran to the window facing the street. There, in front of his house, was an ambulance and a deputy's patrol car, both with their lights blazing. Police and EMT personnel hurried here and there. Wi could hear Mel yelling for Rob, searching frantically, back and forth, between the houses. He hadn't, yet, spotted the broken out slider on the beach side of the house.

Wi looked down at Rob and worried his ribs with his foot. "You. You caused all this! It is all your fault. I had it all planned. Now, I will have to abandon everything. Everything, except the painting!"

Wi left Rob on the floor of his bedroom and ran downstairs. He wanted to open the garage door, get in his car, and make his getaway. He had hoped and planned for this, his final escape. His plans were for a slow and carefully orchestrated exit so as not to attract suspicion. Now, all must be abandoned except the painting. There was no hope for it, and Wi knew that. He placed the Glock in his back pocket, let Rob lay where he had fallen, and ran out the broken slider towards the beach with *The Blue Nude* in the large black carrying case. If he could just get to the Pelican Pub and the highway beyond, he reasoned, he might be able to get a ride out of town to… anywhere. Eighteen million dollars could finance a lifetime of luxury… even if in exile.

What Wi found, when he stumbled onto the beach, was that a safe route of escape would be nearly impossible. Immediately to his left, he saw several police officers with flashlights around the body of the man who had stalked Mel from behind. Directly between the house and the surf he saw more police tending to a body by a beach fire. He turned north and started walking, walking anywhere there were not sheriff's deputies. Escape from the crime scene was, now, of supreme importance.

Wi figured to cut along the north side of the Pelican Pub and cross the parking lot to the highway. But when he got near the Pelican his plans were again thwarted. For Billy (who was, of course, out looking for Becky and Veronica) caught his eye and started for the big man.

Billy saw Wi, with his particular fat-man waddle, walking hurriedly and carrying a large black document case? From across the parking lot from each other, both under street lights, both turned- one to hurry back into the darkness of the beach and the other to follow. Billy figured, correctly, what the contents of the black case must be. He had searched for the painting in Wi's art gallery. He had ransacked May's house.

Seeing Billy left only one direction for Wi's escape-up and over Cape Kiwanda cliff, the same cliff where he had killed May, the same cliff where Rob had jumped into the water to save Spark, the same cliff that Peggy was climbing from the opposite direction.

Wi started for the cliff half walking and half running

in the heavy sand.

Chapter Thirteen

The last place on earth Wi ever wanted to ever go again was up the cliff onto Cape Kiwanda. But he also knew that it was his only chance. If he could make it to the top it was a short, but steep, drop over to the other side. He had made that drop down the north side before- after he killed May. The trail over the north side was more like falling than anything else, but it was soft sand and he knew the way. Once over the top, he could make his was to Tierra Del Mar and buy a ride. He could buy millions of rides!

From Tierra Del Mar, the highway ran south back towards Pacific City or north towards Tillamook and eventually Portland or Seattle. Either would be a refuge until he could make it to California and finalize arrangements for the sale of *The Blue Nude*. He might be able to thumb a ride, or with Rob's Glock take a car from someone and make a run for the border. His mind raced. What was stealing a car after murder, he reasoned? Besides, it was his right. He was the sole remaining protector of a priceless art relic.

Even as he shuffled through the night, he was making plans. Thoughts of grandeur filled Wi's heart. He changed his mind about California. Surely, that road would be watched closely. He would try for Canada; of course, that route would also be watched, and the border agents would be alerted, but it was a shorter route; the danger would be over in a scant few hours one way or the other. He would make for a tourist destination and pretend to be a fisherman or a writer until he could make a deal for the painting.

He figured eighteen million dollars to cancel out a multitude of sins. He figured that if there was any justice at all, in this life, he should get a reward for acquiring *The Blue Nude*.

He trudged on into the darkness.

All his plans, however, hinged on one dark item. He never forgot that Billy was, behind him in the darkness. It seemed to Wi that Billy had been behind him in the darkness for weeks.

Back at May's, Mel was searching furiously for Rob. He had lost sight of him in the heat of the shooting, and then darkness masked Rob's movements. Frantically, Mel searched Rob's house, looked quickly behind the Pelican, and then ran back out onto the beach. But he could not locate Rob, and their phone connection had gone dead. In his haste and fear for Rob, he saw the shadow of a large man with a black valise heading for the surf… but, so troubled was he about Rob, that he didn't think much of it.

Then his eye caught the broken glass from Wi's sliding door, and he made for the opening all the time yelling at the top of his voice for Rob. To his great relief, just as he was about to step over the glass, he was nearly run over by a furious Rob Smith bleeding, once again, from a head wound.

"What the…" was all Mel got out as Rob stumbled into him.

The two men collided. "It's Wi," Rob yelled to Mel as if he was not right next to him face to face. "It was Wi all the time! He killed May for the painting. That's why Spark wanted to tear him apart, why Spark attacked the fat man! Wi hit me and took off with the painting!"

The blow with the lamp had knocked him unconscious, and when Rob finally awakend, he found it difficult to get to his feet, at first. He had stumbled down the stairs and had been greatly relieved to find Mel just coming in through the door.

Mel was incredulous. "Wi hit you? You let Wi hit you? Why didn't you just kill him?"

"I tried that."

"Don't' let him hit you, again, Rob. It's bad for your

reputation."

"I can't believe it, Mel! Wi, the gallery owner, killed Uncle May for the painting! He confessed to me and then hit me in the head with a lamp."

"I'll bet that put out your ligh.."

"You are a funny guy, Mel. I thought Peggy spoke to you about your humor." Rob reached up with his right hand, and it came away bloody... again.

"I saw a fat guy running, there," Mel said pointing. They both took off on the run, Rob stumbling more than running. "He's... got my gun, Mel."

"Great!"

Rob was wheezing for breath and having a difficult time running in the sand.

Mel spoke into his police radio and informed the rest of the swat team that they were in foot pursuit of an armed suspect.

Rob stopped Mel, with a hand on his arm. "You have a police radio?"

"Yeah. well... I was never really put on suspension. I've been working you, Rob. I'm sorry, but it's my job. My boss didn't want you to know. I've been on the case since the first day. I've been working May's murder."

As they ran, Rob's lungs were heaving, but his eyes kept searching the darkness ahead. "I figured it, though, Mel. I figured it, but you will have to explain it to Peggy, though. She might not understand."

Mel winced.

"Thanks for the help with the guy at the fire," Rob remarked as they both began to run again. "I should have shot him, myself, when he went for his gun. But I just hate shooting people."

"Sure."

As often happens at Pacific City, along with the early darkness a fog was closing in making it more difficult to see clearly. Up ahead of them, nearly half way to the cliff's base, they thought they could make out a man, or two, in the darkness and fog, but so far from the parking lot lights it was difficult to make things out in the distance. Perhaps there were more than two people ahead of them, perhaps only one? There was just no way to be sure.

Rob stopped again for a breath and put a restraining arm, once again, on Mel to hold him up. "How many swat-team deputies are on our side, Mel?"

"All of them."

"Funny guy, Mel. How many?"

"Seven on my team and a few deputies on patrol in the general area. Got some Staters too," replied Mel. "I tried to keep the State cops out, but you know how they like a good show. Besides, they were already on to all the teams of international bounty hunters."

Rob's breath would not come. "So, the FBI must be late with the helicopter, huh?"

"We could use a chopper, right about now," smirked Mel.

He looked anxiously at Rob then back over his shoulder to the cliff. In light of Rob's injuries, Mel figured that they could wait a few minutes, should wait a few days. "Look, Rob, we should wait here for our cover to arrive, anyway. It will take a few minutes for the rest of the team to catch up with us. You don't exactly look up to this."

Rob decided against the wait. He just wasn't willing to risk losing Wi in the darkness. They split up to insure that Wi couldn't turn back and slip past them in the darkness and fog. It made good tactical sense. Unfortunately, it also assured that neither one of them could cover the other in case something went wrong. In seconds, Rob found himself alone and stumbling in the dark of night and thickening fog. He wasn't sure, but he thought he might have seen a reflection of light up ahead on the trail- up the Cape where Uncle May had died. He winced at the thought of climbing that cliff in the dark but stumbled up the beach as fast as he could, nonetheless.

Up ahead, in the night and fog, the opera was unfolding its tangled feet. Things were coming to a head.

Vicky and Becky were there in the darkness. They were holding tightly to their plan to kill Billy. They knew that if they simply abandoned him and ran off they were sure he would try to follow and to track them down, for they were witnesses to much that could put Billy in prison. The two girls had decided that it would be better, for all, to end Billy's life of murder and mayhem, and Becky was sure that the mantle fell on her. As the two sisters had planned, she would shoot Billy with the small revolver Vicky had found in the gallery during the burglary. Vicky wanted to do the shooting in revenge for the blond in the car the other night, but Becky knew that she couldn't be trusted to go through with it.

Becky remembered how she was pleasantly surprised that she could bring her sister, Veronica, to the conclusion that it would be best this way. The bit about Billy being with other women had helped, and it was true. Left to his own devices, he was planning on killing both sisters and running off with the local beauty Becky had seen in the car. Becky knew that there was no way of telling how many times Billy had loved and murdered, how many people he had injured and robbed. But it had to stop here, now, tonight.

At first, Billy thought it would be easy to overtake Wi, but Wi had, somehow, disappeared into the darkness. Billy, in the dark and the fog behind Wi, was trying his best to catch up to him to examine that thin, black art case he carried; he was sure that it was the authentic Matisse in the case, and the painting needed to be recovered for the greater good of mankind.., and Billy, of course. Eighteen million dollars would be a huge redistribution of wealth. However, Wi was proving to be a worthy opponent in the chase. Every time Billy thought he was getting near to Wi, he found that Wi had changed his course. Minute changes and zig zags in the night and dense fog were enough to conceal even a large man like Wi. Billy cursed the tourists who had made so many tracks in the sand that it was, now, difficult to tell Wi's from in the churned up melee. It was not, as he had hoped, simply a matter of following the large man's tracks in the sand, but the cliff was a funnel, and Billy knew it, for while the cliff covered an expansive area at first, it narrowed down to a small chute. There was only one narrow defile at the top, and Billy made for it. His only concern was that he had to be careful that he not allow Wi to double back towards town.

Billy had plans. Pacific City had been good for him, but it was time for a change of both city and friends. He would leave tonight, as soon as he found Wi and recovered the painting. When he arrived back at the double wide, it would become Becky's and Veronica's tomb; a raging house fire would cover the double murder. He had done it before, and his new girlfriend would make up for the hassle. "Eighteen million dollars will cover over a lot of sins," he said out loud.

Wi was off the trail trying to conceal his whereabouts. He was no fool. A few yards up the trail ahead of Billy, he turned to catch his breath. The fog cleared for a mere second; for the shortest second the trail down to town cleared and he saw Billy. Some distance behind Billy, Wi spied a tall man with a limp he supposed to be Rob! Wi couldn't believe Rob could have recovered so quickly, but there Rob was- plodding along with that characteristic gimpy leg! Wi moved to his right into shadow, tight up against the edge of the dune, and resumed climbing. He hoped that his shift to the right had worked and that whoever was behind him might just pass him by. He tried not to wheeze for breath, but his wind was labored. He was glad for the fog, and he cursed the fog; the fog concealed his escape, but it also made climbing dangerous.

Rob almost stumbled when the level part of the trail started the climb up the cliff face. He sighed and then bowed his shoulders to the task. Wearily he started to climb. His leg nagged. His head hurt. He again put his hand to his scalp and felt blood, but it seemed less. His vision began to blur, but he wasn't about to stop. His uncle's murderer was somewhere up ahead, and he meant to return the favor.

To Rob's right, Mel hit the bottom of the cliff, also, and started climbing. Mel was not sure, at all, of his own exact location, but he knew that he had to gain elevation. He stopped and listened and thought that perhaps he heard a soft, scuffling sound to this left towards the sound of the surf, but he couldn't be sure. The fog thickened around him with his every gain in elevation. With less effort than the other climbers he gained height, but he unintentionally drifted off the trail and it took several minutes, stumbling in the darkness and fog, to retrace his steps and get back on the correct path. Even for Mel, the sand slipped away with each few feet gained in elevation. Each step had to be made twice to gain one. He wondered, and worried, that Rob might be having an impossible time of it. He knew Rob would not give up, but that he would drive himself regardless of his injuries.

Wi was also climbing in the dark, but he was higher up the cliff and found that he was climbing out of the fog. Admittedly, the trail was steep, but it was as true for Wi as for the others- two steps forward and one back all the way to the top. The difference was that the fat man was struggling for his life, and he knew it. Halfway up, he nearly came too close to the side of the cliff and only saw the night fall away, over the edge, in the nick of time; Wi stumbled, fell, and just caught himself. Rob's Glock fell to the rocks below. Wi pulled back in revulsion at the thought of falling into dark nothingness to the rocks below. He thought of May falling to his death and clenched tighter to the painting.

Rob, some twenty yards below and tiring too quickly, had stumbled onto what he thought might be Wi's tracks. At least he hoped they might be Wi's tracks, and he was making a little better time trying to walk where Wi had walked, where

Wi's heavy footsteps had packed down the sand. Like Wi, before him, though, it was only at the very last second that Rob threw himself to his right- barely avoiding a bad fall of seventy five feet to the rocks below. Rob figured that he had fallen or jumped off enough cliffs for one lifetime, but following blindly along in Wi's footsteps he had nearly walked right off into space, and the closeness of the fall frightened him and forced him to bring all his concentration to bear. He took a few steps to the right to put the cliff a few more feet away.., and resumed his climb. He was no longer in Wi's footsteps, so the climbing was more difficult, but he felt safer keeping some distance between his climb and the cliff edge.

He had nearly fallen, but locating the side of the cliff, and nearly falling, had been a type of blessing; it had shown him his location in the thick fog. No longer was he confused about his position on the dune. Soon, he told himself, he should see the wooden fence posts the authorities had placed on the cliff to keep tourists away from the edge. After that, he had to merely follow the wire fence. He knew where Wi was going, and he was not surprised when he again picked up Wi's footprints. Silently, he resumed tracking the large man. Rob was unarmed and injured, but he was determined. Revenge filled his thoughts, and he figured that gave him an edge.

Up on top of the cliff in front of Rob, events were coming together in a way no one could have predicted. It was all but an orchestrated opera. Science says that there is a way, with time, that flows and draws people and events together. Time, that evening, was determined to be a tragedy.

Vicky and Becky had not, of course, been following Wi, but as fate has that way of flowing things together, the two girls were sitting in the sand on top of the cliff near the exact spot where Uncle May had been pushed to his death. They were watching the fog come in, and they were making plans when they heard someone huffing and puffing and mumbling to himself. Both girls stood and backed up into the darkness.

They were, of course, expecting Billy.

A large man came into view appearing as a specter with the advancing fog. The man was carrying a thick black case. As he approached, they recognized him as the art dealer who would fence stolen items for Billy. The girls remained concealed by the shadows and watched as he kept turning and looking behind him. They had no idea that he was being followed. They were simply waiting for Billy and did not suspect that they were being caught up as fellow actors in the drama.

As the play would have it, however, out of the fog stalked Billy.

Wi spotted Billy and stopped dead in his tracks.

The younger man was not gasping for breath like Wi. Billy's eyes were gasping with desire and a hunger that Veronica and Becky had never seen.

"He's like a wild animal," Becky whispered.

"Oh, yeah. I've seen that look, before," agreed Veronica. "You better kill him, now."

Wi stood rooted in place by his fear and dread. Billy stopped ten feet from Wi and immediately on the edge of the steep precipice above the pounding surf below.

Billy's voice had a deadly ring. "I will take that!"

At the sound of Billy's voice, and hearing his demand, a wild look of desperation came into Wi's eyes. "You! You… have any idea what this is worth? What I have done for this?"

"Yes." Billy said, and he came closer. "Yes!"

Becky pulled the small revolver out of her pocket as Veronica silently fell to her knees.., and tried to pray but found that she had forgotten how or, somehow, had never learned.

Wi was frantic. "Eighteen or twenty million… dollars!" He pointed to the case in his right hand. "This is worth millions!"

Billy approached to within five feet of Wi and slowly pulled a knife from his pocket. With victory at hand, with nearly untold riches mere feet away, he started slowly forward.

"Not twenty million to you, Wi. No millions for you."

"Huh? What?"

"To you, the painting is just worth.., your life." Billy pushed a button, and a blade popped open with a metallic click that the fog swallowed and muffled like a wet blanket. It was the same knife with which he had killed the old lady in Lincoln City, the same knife he had used to stab the man outside the Pelican, the same knife he had used so many times before. He came closer and rested the sharp point against Wi's bulging and panting stomach.

Becky aimed the revolver at Billy, and the metallic click of the hammer being cocked back was swallowed up and muffled in the wet blanket of fog.

Wi took in a deep breath and held it against the sharp pricking of the knife blade. His wrongs engulfed him. He realized that his crime spree had all been for naught. He had killed his neighbor. He had schemed and plotted. He had beaten Rob Smith over the head with a lamp, and then he had run out into the dark of the night. His art gallery was gone. His house was forfeit. All his years of building his life were vanishing before his very eyes. He was afraid to let out a breath, afraid of Billy's knife. He had failed, and he knew it.

With the edge of the knife up against Wi's stomach, Billy slowly and deliberately removed the black art case from Wi's grasping fingers.

Slowly and deliberately Becky squeezed the trigger on the revolver.

The fateful bullet, as things will happen in such an opera, impacted Billy's brain just behind his right temple. It was a one in a million shot, like shooting a dragon with a bow and arrow while standing on one foot. The accuracy was beyond Becky, and it would have been a clean miss had not Wi's fingers refused to uncoil around his prize. Just that small resistance of Wi's fingers pulled Billy forward and off balance- and directly into the path of the .38 caliber bullet. A soft splat sound wafted off onto the breeze. Billy's facial expression did not change. He simply froze in place- already dead and yet still standing.

Wi realized immediately what had happened, saw Billy's head explode, knew that somehow he had been shot. He knew not from where the bullet came, but it was clear that his gloriously hard fought prize remained. For just a second, and then minutely longer, Billy's body remained standing in place, frozen in time.., and then he simply crumpled and fell onto the sand at Wi's feet. Slowly, and of its own volition, Billy's body started a slow slide over the edge of the cliff and slipped silently into the darkness. Wi thought he heard a splash but did not care one way or the other.

Wi was standing, there, facing the cliff and that awful drop into the blackest abyss when Rob approached. Unseen from behind, Rob reached down and grabbed the handle of the art case. Unexpected as it was, the case came easily into Rob's grasp and out of Wi's.

Wi spun around in alarm, and another struggle ensued. He beat on Rob's face with his fists. Of course, if Rob had not been already injured by the blow from the lamp, it might have been a more even match; but as it was, Rob was much weakened by the loss of blood. Close in and struggling together, Wi was the better man, and he dwarfed Rob in weight. Round and round they went always near the precipice. Round and round they went, both gasping for breath, both holding the valuable case as best as could be managed while hitting and being hit. It was a losing situation for Rob, and he knew it.

Finally, to Rob's alarm, Wi managed to keep one hand on the art case and begin pushing the struggling Rob backwards, ever backwards, towards the cliff edge. It was the same struggling and pushing that Mayfield Commers had experienced. There was a gleam in Wi's eyes. He had done this before.

Rob was hampered by the painting- how to hold onto the painting and fight Wi- at the same time? Suddenly, he heard a familiar sound in the darkness.

It was then that another of the opera players arrived to save Rob; from out of the darkness came a barking and snarling that could only be Spark! Rob wasn't sure what to think of it; the barking could be just a nightmare or a delusion brought on by the loss of blood, and the terrific struggle, and the very real fear of going over the edge of the cliff once again?

Wi was very sure. The very instant he heard the barking, the starkest fear took his heart and the gleam in his eyes turned to terror. How could it be the red dog? Was May with him come back for revenge?

Wi turned and lost his footing. It was as simple as that. With Spark still off in the distance and unseen, Wi turned in fright, and his foot slipped partially over the cliff's edge. Rob made a last, great and successful pull at the art case as Wi balanced, swayed, and waved his arms trying to fly his way back to safety. But it was too late.

Rob pulled the case to his chest and watched Wi struggle for his balance. Still, Wi waved his arms like a bird. For Wi, his gyrations seemed to go on and on. Time slowed to a crawl.

Rob held a firm grip on the case, and spoke to the doomed man. "Isn't this the same cliff you threw my uncle off, Wi?" Then, driven by some remote sense of decency, that Rob had been trying to repress, he reached to save the man, but it was not to be. Rob tried to reach for Wi's shirt- to pull him safety.

Wi's eyes were huge globes of absolute terror, but then he seemed, somehow, to steady himself... if just for a moment. Rob could not be sure, thinking of it in years to come, how Wi managed it, really; even though off balance, Wi bent rather weirdly at the waist and managed a terrifying hand hold on Rob's shirt. Then.., again, Wi's balance failed and Rob's weight was not enough to counter the big man. Wi teetered off balance for a few seconds, and then his huge bulk simply carried him over the edge never to be seen again. He fell, with his arms all akimbo, into the black void below, which would have been alright with Rob, except that he still held Rob's shirt in his grasp.

In Rob's worst nightmare, of which he had many, he had never thought to take a fall, again, off a cliff- especially not this same cliff where he had jumped before. But as Wi fell, his grasp on Rob's shirt pulled Rob forward, and he followed Wi into the darkness beyond.

As he fell, Rob's entire life flashed before his eyes, at least the last three days. He knew what the fall would be like, knew how breathtakingly cold was the water, hoped he would not survive the fall, hoped that he would hit a rock and end the nightmare quickly. Nowhere, this time, was there a rescuing boat. From nowhere would help come. He would die this time, he knew. He wondered if he would find his wife, Wanda, at the bottom of the ocean; if they would be re-united in their after life? He knew his father was there waiting. That thought made him smirk rather weirdly. He tried to scream.., and did. Very loudly.

As he screamed, Rob had that one great idea... again! Perhaps it was an epiphany, or whatever. He was nearly past caring *what* it was. He just knew that it had worked- twice before. Could it work again? He screamed aloud, "Oh, God! Help me!"

From up above, his yell sounded drawn out, more like, 'Hellllp meeeee!'

A hand grabbed his free arm.

His fall, which had just begun, was stopped short. Rob was slammed against the cliff wall, which was infinitely better than slamming against the rocks below. His fall was stopped from up above? His mind raced? He was impossibly held from falling by a grasp that felt like iron. He looked up. His emotions threatened to go into overload, but he managed to keep them in check- just.

To his surprise, it was not Mel, but the professor's

mysterious European friend who held his hand as firmly as if it were in a vise.

"We have an agreement, you and I," the man grunted. "You would not be trying to get away with my painting, would you?"

Rob could see the man's face clearly. He could count the beads of sweat forming on his brow. "You… are not as strong as you used to be."

"Please, my friend," the man said, "do try and get a foot hold, and I will help you up."

Rob did just that. He turned minutely and was successful in catching the toe of his shoe into an infinitesimal crack in the sandstone cliff.

They sat on the cliff edge dangling their legs over the side and listening to the surf and the donging of the warning buoy.

The European leaned over the edge into the night and peered down toward the sound of the crashing waves below. "Wi is gone, my friend," he said to Rob. His voice carried little emotion. "Gravity is such a harsh mistress."

Spark was there. From where he had come, and how he had managed it, Rob had not the slightest clue. He clutched at the dog's neck and held him tight. They sat on the cliff edge, for a minute, while both men got their breath.

"I believe, Mr. Smith..," said the European, "that the black case is for me."

"Oh. Of course," replied Rob. He handed the mysterious man the case without another thought to its value.

"Do you know the difference between an epiphany and a very good idea?" asked Rob to the mysterious man.

"I think so," replied the European. "Epiphanies are instantaneous leaps of intuition or realization, not slowly developed solutions. Newton was slowly trying to have a really good idea about gravity; but he wasn't getting it, so God dropped an apple on his head just to speed it up a little."

The mysterious man hugged the case to his chest and looked out into the fog. The two of them listened to the Haystack Rock bell in the darkness with its lonely and hollow toll.

"How the dog got here, I have not a clue?" said the mysterious European.

"You have kept Peggy safe?" asked Rob.

"I must confess that we failed you, there. Mr. Smith, I have protected kings and queens. My services are much in demand, and my reputation is much to be admired."

"Yes? Where is Peggy?"

"We don't know. She evaded us, somehow. Smart girl, that!"

Time flows. Operas come to an end. The curtain, eventually, begins to lower on all endeavors great and small.

Suddenly, and quite unexpectedly, Peggy came out of the darkness. "I am right here, boys. I see you found Spark."

Rob's mouth was open. "Sit down, here beside me, and I will tell you what just happened!"

A few minutes later, Mel rushed up with his Glock semi-automatic pistol held out in front of him pointed at the mysterious man. Casually, Rob, the European, and Peggy looked at Mel over their shoulders and smiled.

Rob simply said, "Put that gun away and have a seat, well you, Mel?"

"So?" said the mysterious man to Mel as he sat down on the far side of Peggy. "That was a good shot at the young man by the fire- into the glare of the sun and at a moving target. And with Rob, here, walking in front of your line of sight. Good shot."

Mel's mouth was open. He couldn't help it. Finally, he just shrugged his shoulders in resignation… but he still held the Glock at the ready.

"I will, on verification of authenticity," volunteered the mysterious man to Rob, "deposit the one million dollars in an account in your name, Mr. Smith. I believe that completes our contract."

"Where will you go from here," asked Rob quietly.

"Have you been to Stuttgart?" the European replied. "It is a quiet little town where a man could get lost and not found, easily, by those who might desire to disturb an old man's quiet retirement. Still… they will find me, of course.., eventually. And when they find me, well.., I was planning on dying, someday, anyway."

"This is a quiet little town where a man might become lost?" submitted Rob, "and if someone finds you, here, you will have friends to help."

Epilog

Pacific City is a small beach town in Oregon. On one end of town, the beach stretches out with the curvature of the earth until the beach finally disappears into a misty and far horizon. North of town, the surf batters up against a steep sandstone cliff and a high sand dune that is continually dotted with children. Pacific City is families, surfboarders, kites, beach-side fires and dory boats.

It was on the cliff above the dune that Rob solved the mystery of his Uncle May's murder.

If you ever visit Pacific City in the summertime you might find the town's favorite writer and emerging painter, Rob Smith, climbing Cape Kiwanda for a quiet afternoon of painting or writing.

At his heel, you will most likely find Spark, the red dog, pulling at a leash held by a smiling and laughing little boy with the funny name of Mayfield Robert Smith. They call him Bobby.

At home, two doors from the Pelican, you will most likely find Bobby's mom preparing dinner or perhaps brewing coffee for the drop-in visitors and surfers.

There is a new owner living in Wi's house next door to Rob and Peggy Smith. He is a tall man with a limp and a European accent. With him live two young women, both on probation.

About the Author

Leonard Collins was born in Bremerton, Washington.
He began writing novels and short stories in 1992 to help work through pain and suffering following a disability from the Portland Police Bureau.

Leonard is a US Marine veteran of the Vietnam war.

Leonard's novels include *Portland Police Stories, Homicide in Pacific City, Charley Scrimshaw and the Bird Sanctuary Killing, Homicide in Pacific City,* and *Come Home for Christmas.*

Leonard lives in Milwaukie, Oregon with his wife Elizabeth.